THE RACE

Eunice Walkup and Oscar Otis

SIMON AND SCHUSTER • NEW YORK

DAVIE'S PRIDE

Owner:
 Dennis Sullivan
Trainer:
 Dennis Sullivan
Jockey:
 Billy Hendricks

ARMADA

02/'24
STAND PRICE
$5.00

Owner:
 Lisa Cardigan
Trainer:
 Mack Herman
Jockey:
 Donnie Cheevers

MAGICIAN

FREEWAY

Co-owners:
 Mrs. Shelby Todhunter, Sr.,
 and Mrs. William Vance
Trainer:
 Shelby Todhunter, Jr.
Jockey:
 Rudy Maldonado

KENTUCKY DERBY

TO TICK AND DAVE
FOR PATIENCE "OVER AND BEYOND"

FRIDAY

ONE

Once there had been open fields here. From time immemorial, this had been a great, rolling, grassy plain on which, perhaps—long before the White Man had moved that far West—even the Indians had raced their horses, descendants of the runaways from the herds of the Conquistadores, to see which was the swiftest and therefore the most valuable. For then as always, competition was the crucible of a horse's courage, stamina, breeding, spirit.

Before men had tamed him to their own uses, the horse raced, galloping across vast meadows in an ecstasy of speed, glorying in his strength and freedom. Man had saddled him, bridled him, made him a part of *his* world, perhaps the most important part for over 2,000 years, during which the horse was king and a man marked his rank by calling himself a cavalier, proclaiming his nobility by the symbol of the spur, measuring the world by the powerful strides of his steed's legs, thrilling to the thunder of his hooves. Man lived to the horse's rhythm.

Here, in the limitless grasslands from which the Indians had only recently been driven, men set themselves to raise

9

heroic horses, imported famous sires to improve the stock, raced them to determine their quality and to discover whether they possessed that intangible attribute of heart that carries the great horse past the edge of physical exhaustion to that last spurt of effort which is the price of victory.

Here men raced horses, loved them for their grace, their beauty, the effortless ease of their movement, valued them for their victories, mourned their defeats, bought and sold them for their enormous profits, bet on them to the brink of ruin or riches. In the brilliant spectacle of horses racing against each other, men idealized their own struggles and ambitions. Long before The Race was formalized, men had staked their wealth, their names on the sinews and muscles and the will-to-win of a horse. And so it was natural that here The Race should become an institution, the verdant fields giving way to hard-packed· earth, the rolling hills to huge stands, the friendly camaraderie of personal bets in which a man's word was his bond to the impersonal mechanism of the pari-mutuel system and the electronic tote board.

But behind the money, the glamour, the profits, the publicity, The Race was still a simple thing, founded in the ancient knowledge of the bluegrass country, a test of a horse's natural desire to outrun his fellows, no different in its essentials from races in which naked Indians had whipped their ponies across the plains. Yet different, too: for The Race was an event, the place and the moment when the hopes and dreams of thousands of people, trainers, owners, jockeys, grooms, bettors, spectators, came together once a year at the climactic moment when the field of three-year-olds burst from the confines of the starting gate to run the longest, hardest, most famous mile and a quarter in the history of racing: The Kentucky Derby.

Lee Ames slumped wearily in the quiet office, his eyes only half-focused on the framed document which stood out against the dark paneling opposite his desk.

Its elaborate lettering read:

To All To Whom These Presents Shall Come, Greeting:

Know Ye, that   LEE AMES
Is Commissioned A

KENTUCKY COLONEL

. . . all the rights, privileges and
responsibilities thereof . . . in testimony whereof . . .

The rank of colonel went with Lee's position as President
of Churchill Downs. Such commissions were dispensed with
increasing rarity nowadays but there had been almost 90,000
of them since the first gubernatorial mark of favor was issued
back in 1812 and Churchill Downs had always shared in that
pleasant abundance.

Established by a Colonel, M. Lewis Clark, who inaugu-
rated the Kentucky Derby on May 17, 1875, it was another
Colonel, Matt J. Winn, who had built a failing facility and a
feature with only lukewarm regional interest into the most
exciting thoroughbred racing in the world. Now—after the
notable succession of devoted administrators who followed
Winn—Churchill Downs' representative Colonel was its
Chairman of the Board, Underwood Forbisher. Tall, distinguished, with snowy hair and a sunny disposition, The Colonel had become as much a part of the Derby as the playing
of "My Old Kentucky Home."

It was a boon to Lee Ames that The Colonel relished his
role, for never had a man more perfectly exemplified a beloved tradition. Lee himself, despite the framed testament on
his wall, did not fit with the standard image of a Kentucky
Colonel at all. Still in his thirties, he was too young, too dark-
haired and ordinarily too dynamic. But it was he, as president,
who actually produced the show.

His glance drifted to the early edition of the evening pa-

11

per which had been placed on his desk. The headline on the sports page reported:

CHURCHILL DOWNS TO OPEN TOMORROW

Automatically he began to check off the thousands of details which went into such an opening. Repair and renovation. Maintenance. Stabling arrangements. Personnel, public relations, tickets, reservations. Licensing, safety precautions, equipment rentals, crowd handling.

He stopped himself with a sigh. No use reviewing the list again. He had gone over every item a hundred times in the last year, made evaluations with department heads, implemented his decisions. If Churchill Downs wasn't ready for its Spring Meeting by now, it never would be.

There would still be unexpected crises. There always were, particularly during that first full week which led to Derby Day. But no point in worrying in advance. He would face the problems when they arose. He always had.

The only thing he was going to do now, he told himself, was get up and start for home. And then, go straight to bed. He had been at the track since before six that morning and here it was, long past dinner time.

Not that he cared about dinner. He had eaten far too much over at the Exposition Grounds during the "They're Off" luncheon which was Louisville's official opening of the Derby celebrations.

The Colonel, bless his smiling and indefatigable spirit, would represent Churchill Downs at this evening's highly social Derby Festival Coronation Ball in the Convention Hall. His magnificent figure would grace the front page tomorrow, crowning the lovely new Festival Queen.

Still Lee sat.

His gaze went down the paper's boxed listing of next week's probable Derby starters, arranged according to their likely odds:

12

Lucky Jim	7-5	Armada	15-1
Magician	9-5	Double Seven	30-1
Freeway	3-1	Davie's Pride	80-1
Dashing Lad	6-1	Sweepstakes	100-1

A short field, too short for comfort, he thought. Only eight horses. *If* they all ran. This was something you did not dare to count on with thoroughbreds when it was more than a week before the race. But a pretty good lineup at that, barring scratches, with four, maybe five really close contenders. Even the sixth choice couldn't be entirely ignored.

Somebody had been complaining about those last two colts recently, saying they were out of their class and shouldn't be allowed to run. You heard that every year about at least one horse. But he had replied, as he always did, "It's the natural-born right of any three year old to take a shot at the Derby, if it can, like every kid having a chance to be president." And this was true.

Yes, a good field. A broad one, too. Canada was pulling solidly for Armada, that country's impressive two-year-old champion of last year, though he had been raced very lightly since reaching the age of three.

Florida's sentimentalists were behind Davie's Pride, the homegrown "Cinderella horse," but Kentucky-bred Lucky Jim had won Gulfstream Park's important Florida Derby, which often pointed to the eventual victor at Louisville, and the more realistic rated him as the strongest contender.

Lucky Jim was Kentucky's overwhelming favorite, as well, though Double Seven and Sweepstakes were also products of that state. As a matter of fact, Freeway, the red-hot darling of the West Coast, had been bred in the Blue Grass, too, but despite this fact and his unbeaten record, the eastern turf writers tended to discount him on the basis that his competition in California hadn't been much.

In Maryland interest fluctuated between a pair of colts which had been foaled at that state's leading farm. Dashing

Lad, still owned by his breeder, had lost by only a nose in the Florida Derby and had beaten Lucky Jim in an equally prestigious race at Hialeah. Magician had been sold to a Chicagoan but he was still Maryland-bred and he had been a decisive stakes winner in New York and New Orleans.

Well, Lee concluded, getting to his feet at last, time and the race would tell.

He went out through the deserted general office and walked toward his car. The Derby wasn't different in itself from any other horse race. They all had the same basic elements, always had, always would: the matching of splendid animal against splendid animal and by that proxy the exhilarating contest of man against man. But if the Derby were only one more race, it had somehow over the years become a symbol as well. It drew its special significance from all races, he thought. And gave it back to each of them in turn. He was proud to be its Custodian.

When he reached his car, the two manila envelopes he had dropped on the seat earlier reminded him to leave by way of the stable area. He drove through one of the tunnels which burrowed under track and infield and pulled up at the stable gate.

"Evening, Mr. Ames," said the guard on duty there.

"Good evening, Earl." Lee held out the envelopes. "Listen, Freeway will arrive sometime before morning, his people called from L.A., and Mister Mack'll be in from Maryland with Armada, so you'd better hold their credentials." He laughed as Earl took them. "I might not have thought of these if Mrs. Nickel hadn't called to raise Cain when she wasn't allowed in the Derby Barn to see Sweepstakes without hers."

Earl grinned. "She's something else, ain't she?"

"She sure is." Lee sighed remembering. She'd been madder than hell. He supposed he should have offered to produce her credentials on the spot, but her outburst had made him dig in his heels.

Now, driving on toward home, Lee forgot about Gladys Nickel. His mind reverted with satisfaction to the lineup he had been reading in his newspaper.

If that paper carried any reference to the gruesome discovery of a headless, handless corpse which had been dumped down the Jersey Palisades, Lee had not noticed. Assuredly there was no mention in it of the FBI's involvement in a Baltimore kidnapping or the careful investigations being ordered by an Atlanta-based insurance company.

But even if he had known of these stories, only the wildest flight of his imagination could have suggested any connection with the Kentucky Derby.

That there might not *be* a Kentucky Derby would simply never have occurred to him at all.

TWO

THE UNSEASONAL FURY of the late-April storm had disturbed Gabe Hilliard. He had been dreaming, the same old dream, with the terrible heat and the dust in his mouth, but it was the telephone in his Beverly Hills apartment which finally roused him.

Without opening his eyes, he pushed back his sandy hair and then fumbled for the receiver with a thin freckled hand.

"Gabe! You awake?"

The excitement in the voice made Gabe sit up on the rumpled bed, his lids narrowing over a cold green glare. "I am now," he said, "but you're not my agent anymore, Nick, remember? You're fired."

"The hell I am," Nick Chambley said. "I quit and you

15

know it. I quit when you didn't show up to exercise that horse yesterday morning after I gave my word we would."

"Well, you should have known better. I'm not some punk kid around the backstretch that has to get up and work horses at the crack of dawn."

"Not horses, Gabe. That horse."

"I wouldn't care if he was made out of solid gold," Gabe said. "I'm not exercising any horse on the bare possibility of locking up the mount. If I were set to ride him in a race, okay. But just on the bare chance? Forget it."

"Oh, sure, forget it." Nick's notable temper was rising. "You think horses like that grow on trees, Gabe? Or that every other jock's agent in the place isn't trying to get on it? Or that you're the easiest goddamn rider in the business to find mounts for? Well, let me tell you something, Gabe, I never had to work harder in my life. And it don't matter how great you used to be!"

"All right, you've told me," Gabe said furiously. "And I told you you're fired!"

Nick didn't even hear. Maybe because he was so mad he had started to wheeze. "You're still great, you could be on top again, where you belong. But you got such a miserable disposition that half the owners in the country and three-quarters of the trainers wouldn't put you on a horse of theirs if I got down on my hands and knees and begged."

"You know what they can do with their horses," Gabe said. "And you, too." He hung up and lay back on his pillow, fuming.

Nick Chambley had grown bald and acquired his spectacular obesity in a profession which demanded a shrewd grasp of psychology as well as a capacity for infinite detail and a granite core of sheer, dogged persistence. He decided to give Gabe exactly five minutes to cool off and begin wondering why Nick had called so excitedly after yesterday's battle.

The two had fought so often that they had achieved a ritual of reconciliation which involved "chance" meetings in

16

the stable area of whatever track they were working, allowing each to save face. For Nick to phone this way was a distinct departure from pattern and Gabe would be quick to realize it.

On his part, Nick thought with a sigh, he probably ought to spend the wait in figuring out why he had ever accepted Gabe's book at all or stayed with him when the woods were full of good young kids who only needed a top agent to steer them toward success. Kids who still had wrinkles in their bellies, kids who would do exactly what he told them to do when he told them to do it.

But why try to fool himself? Nick knew the answer to that one backwards and forwards: It was because none of them was Gabe Hilliard. With all his faults, there just wasn't a better jockey in the business. The mold got thrown away after that little son of a bitch was made.

For once, Nick's vaunted psychological genius had failed. Gabe wasn't wondering about the unusual call. Gabe had become aware that he was alone in the king-sized bed.

He shouldn't have been. When liquor and satiation had hit him at about the same moment, somewhere around dawn, he had had a big-breasted naked blonde next to him. She had been as immovable as a dead cow on the bunched sheet he had tried to pull out from under her before he decided to hell with it and went to sleep on the exposed ticking of the mattress.

Christina, Christina Swanson, that was what she called herself, though the name was undoubtedly as phony as her bleached mane. She had made him think of a cow even when she was awake, not so much because of the spectacular udders she bared to his hands and mouth but for her passive submission, her seeming unresponsiveness while he fondled and kissed her.

You never could tell about women, though. When he mounted her, she had turned suddenly into a wild white horse, heaving and lunging, whinnying as he rode.

Dampness hit his bare skin with a chill as he strode toward the half-open bathroom door. "Chris," he called, "hey, Christina! You in there?"

He knew before he pushed the door open that she wasn't. The luxurious apartment felt empty. For a second, the desolation of the dream from which Nick had awakened him squeezed at his gut. Then he sloshed cold water on his face and went back to check the bedroom.

His watch and the emerald cuff links were on the night table, all right, and his wallet was in his pants pocket. But she had stripped it, the bitch. There wasn't a bill left.

He frowned, trying to remember how much he'd had left after buying the drinks. A hundred bucks, maybe, or a hundred and a quarter.

An expensive lay. He'd had as good or better for a twenty, and the best, of course, was free, the crazy young stuff that threw itself at him—at any halfway successful jock—every day.

He was heading for the shower, still angry, when the phone rang. "Yeah?"

"You get me so mad sometimes . . ."

"All right, Nick, let's not go into the dance again. If you've got something on your mind, spit it out. Because I've got things to do!"

Nick drew a deep breath. "Okay," he agreed happily. "Gabe, we're going to Churchill!"

"To Churchill?" Gabe sat down on the edge of the bed. "Churchill Downs?"

"To Kentucky, Gabe! How does that grab you?"

"The Derby?" Gabe shook his head, trying to clear it. "But, Nick, what horse?"

"You ready for this? Well, hang on to something, Gabe, because we're riding the winner!"

Gabe swallowed. "You don't mean Lucky Jim?"

Nick's answer dripped contempt. "Not Lucky Jim, Gabe, the winner, I said!"

Gabe's knuckles went white as his grip tightened on the

receiver. His voice was harsh with disappointment. "If you're talking about Freeway, Nick, you can skip it. I wouldn't ride for Shelby Todhunter again if it was a guaranteed walkover."

"Goddamn it, are you telling me you'd turn down any Derby mount?" Nick checked himself in midprotest, resignedly. "Don't answer that, I know what you'd say. I'm talking about Magician, Gabe, Magician!"

"But Gordy Cowdin has that mount."

"Not anymore," Nick said. "They just pried him out of a car wreck below Bakersfield. He's dead."

"No!"

"It's true, Gabe. It hasn't even hit the radio yet but you can take it for Gospel. They just called me."

Gabe was silent for a second. "What a rotten thing!"

"Yeah, it's a shame. I never really liked him that much, but he wasn't the worst guy in the world and he was one hell of a rider."

Gabe's silence was longer this time. At last he said, "You just gave me goose bumps, Nick. I could hear you saying the same thing about me, the exact words, the exact expression."

"Well, that's where you're wrong," Nick said. "If it was you, Gabe, I'd be saying you were the worst guy in the world."

It eased the shock a little. "But, anyway, one hell of a rider?"

"Yeah," Nick said, "that you can count on."

"Who called you?"

"The Frenchman. You know, Magician's trainer."

"St. Pierre? He's Canadian."

"That's the one. The owner called him and he called me, the minute they heard."

Gabe's tone flattened into sarcasm. "You'd think they could have waited at least a minute more, wouldn't you? Isn't that how it goes? 'We will now observe two minutes of silence out of respect'?"

"Come on," Nick cut in firmly. "It's a rotten deal for everybody. But that's the way it is, Gabe. A rider gets thrown on the track, you don't stop the race. You keep on riding, trying to win. You may cry your eyes out in the jocks' room afterwards—I've seen you do it yourself—but you don't stop the race."

"You've seen me cry? Never."

"Oh, no? How about when Howie Lochlan went down at Phoenix?"

"Jesus Christ, what a memory. I didn't even know you existed in those days."

"Nobody knew you existed in those days," Nick retorted. "I was there, though. I was still booking rides for Pete Browder that winter."

"Pete Browder! I haven't thought of him in ages, or Howie Lochlan, either, for that matter. Yeah, maybe I did cry that day, but I was just a kid, then, still an apprentice. I'd never seen a jockey trampled before."

"That's not my point, Gabe. I'm reminding you that Howie Lochlan and all, you won that day. By five lengths!"

"Okay, Nick," Gabe said slowly. "It's just that it seems so cold-blooded, arranging for a new rider with Gordy not even . . ."

"Cut it out, I tell you!" Nick's interruption was emphatic. "I don't want you getting hung up on this, you hear?" Gabe could picture Nick's philosophical shrug—a massive heaving of shoulders and paunch which was a Chambley trademark. "Somebody loses, somebody wins and all you can do is accept it, either way. If we don't know anything else in this game, we should know that."

"I suppose."

"So Gordy's out and it's tough, but, Gabe," excitement gathered in the big agent's voice, "I still can't help being glad we're going to Kentucky."

Gabe's pulse began to quicken, too. "And on Magician, Nick, who would ever have believed it?"

20

"On the winner!"

"You really think Magician can take the Derby?"

"Gabe," said Nick Chambley, "there's no way he can lose with us riding him. No way in this world." Then he added, "One thing, though . . ."

"What?"

"The papers will be doing a hatchet job on you as soon as the news is out."

Gabe laughed. "I hadn't thought of that yet, but this will really hit them where they live."

"Will it ever," Nick said. "And Jerry Neal'll be pounding every inch of the way. He was such a close friend of Gordy's and he hates your guts."

"Let him get in line," Gabe said, suddenly bitter. "There are others ahead of him."

"You're going to have to play it cool," Nick warned. "You take another poke at Neal—or any of those reporters—and the stewards will make you sit this one out."

"I know," Gabe said, "I've got a couple of great buddies among them, too. But I'll steer clear of the press, Nick, don't you worry about that."

"It's not going to be easy. They'll be on your tail night and day, crowding you because they know how you hate to be crowded, trying to get a rise out of you."

"Forget it, Nick, will you? I'm not going to talk to them. I'm not going to listen to them. I'm not going to read what they write. As for slugging one of them, I wouldn't give them the satisfaction. Not before the Derby, anyway."

Nick hesitated. "It won't be just the newspaper guys. Shelby Todhunter'll be there and so will Rudy Maldonado. Orv Scott, too."

"Skip it. The last thing I need right now is a quick rundown of the enemies of Gabe Hilliard, okay? I promise you, Nick, I won't do one damn thing I shouldn't. All I'm going to do is win the Kentucky Derby."

"I'll buy that."

"If you really think Magician can do the job?"

"I know it!"

THREE

WESTWARD FROM MIAMI and Fort Lauderdale—but roughly midway between and comparatively close to both—Davie, Florida, did not receive the full benefit of their ocean breezes. The treeless pastureland of Dennis Sullivan's El Rancho Cuyahoga—ten acres owned, ten acres leased with option to buy—was sweltering beneath the brilliant sun.

Mr. Jimpson found himself squinting despite his dark glasses. His gaze, at the moment, was on the whitewashed fence of an extensive paddock where two mares stood head to head like a pair of gossiping women while their foals skittered around behind them.

Earlier in the year, as Mr. Jimpson knew, the four would have been confined to a smaller paddock on the other side of the cinder-block barn and this choice area would have been occupied by the dozen or so boarding thoroughbreds from the north who supported the modest spread. The paying guests were gone now, having returned for the summer to the lesser racetracks of Ohio and West Virginia.

Aside from the two mares and their foals, the horses had dwindled to one colt in the barn, that also belonged to Dennis Sullivan and was recovering from knee surgery, and the saddle pony of a neighbor, being cared for as a favor during his absence.

Mr. Jimpson was oblivious to the pleasant scene before

him, although he turned from it reluctantly to face the couple who had rounded the corner of the small stucco house and were hurrying toward him: Sheila Sullivan, in worn jeans and what was undoubtedly one of Dennis' old shirts with the sleeves cut out, and her son Johnny.

The man shook his head unhappily as they neared. "Wasn't any sense Johnny getting you out here, Mrs. Sullivan. It was Dennis I came to talk to in the first place."

"He's been gone a week."

"So Johnny said."

"But, sure," Sheila went on, her hint of brogue deepening, "we never expected you'd be worrying over what's owing while he's away."

Mr. Jimpson stared down at the papers in his hand. "Well, it's like I told your boy. I want to deliver your order, but Dennis promised to pay me back in February. You heard him yourself, Mrs. Sullivan. And I still haven't seen a penny."

Johnny waved a helpless hand toward the recuperating colt regarding them curiously from his stall. "That was when we thought this horse would be bringing in some more purses. But Davie's Pride is really good, Mr. Jimpson. Everybody says he'd have won the Florida Derby for sure if he hadn't got boxed in on the stretch."

They'd been over this ground already, before Johnny had summoned his mother. "I know, I know," Mr. Jimpson interrupted, "it's always something with thoroughbreds. But the vets get paid. You pay for vanning and horseshoes and silks and I got to get my money like anybody else!"

The boy swallowed. "If you could be patient just a little while longer?" His pleading eyes made Mr. Jimpson uncomfortable, which made him angrier than ever.

"I lost my patience this morning when I picked up my newspaper," he said, turning to leave.

Sheila's work-roughened hand on his arm stopped him. "This isn't the first time we've owed you, Mr. Jimpson, larger amounts than this, if I remember right."

23

"That's true, Mrs. Sullivan, and you've always paid. The thing that gets me," he blurted, "is Dennis owing me for months and then finding out he's spent a fortune to send Davie's Pride to the Kentucky Derby. When even I know he hasn't got a chance to win!"

"Why, Mr. Jimpson," Sheila said, "Davie's Pride wouldn't have to win for us to come out ahead. Second place is worth twenty-five thousand, third's twelve and a half! Even if he came in fourth, we'd get five thousand dollars!"

"Is that so?" Mr. Jimpson was impressed. "I never realized."

"As for spending a fortune to get up there," Sheila said, "Dennis borrowed a trailer and drove Davie's Pride himself. Sure," she added parenthetically, "he'd never trust that colt to anyone but himself."

"Oh?"

"And Johnny and me are getting a lift up tomorrow with a friend that's going to Chicago. The Merritt boys'll be tending things here. The only real expenses are the nomination fee that we paid long since and a hundred and fifty dollars to start in the Derby Trial. But if Davie's Pride can do anything in the Trial, he'll cover his starting fee in the Derby itself."

"Well, now, I didn't understand."

"And if he don't do anything in the Trial, we'll just take him someplace else where he can win," Sheila added. "We're not entirely foolish." Her grip on his arm tightened. "But, oh, Mr. Jimpson, do you have any idea what a feather in our caps it'd be to run a colt in the Kentucky Derby? And if Davie's Pride should win, why, those two foals we've got out there would be worth a fortune. And think what it would do for this area."

"Whoa," Mr. Jimpson said, "slow down."

"But it's the truth, as sure as I'm standing here, Davie could be almost as important to Florida's breeding industry as Ocala is now, Mr. Jimpson, the way it is, so close to the tracks and everything, and . . ."

24

"I believe you, Mrs. Sullivan. You've got me convinced!"

Sheila released his arm and laughed, suddenly embarrassed. "I guess I do get carried away sometimes."

"Well," Mr. Jimpson said, "it don't make bad sense, I mean, if you're not counting on picking up all the marbles." He looked down at the order and bills still in his hand. "Look, if you need this stuff, I'll try to have it here this afternoon, or early tomorrow. And just talk to Dennis when he gets back."

"Oh, thank you, Mr. Jimpson, thank you."

Mother and son stood smiling while Mr. Jimpson walked down to his station wagon, but when he drove away, dust billowing behind him on the rough road, Johnny's expression changed.

"You told him we weren't going to win," he said.

"I did no such thing, Johnny Sullivan. I told him that even if we only took fourth place we'd be ahead. And that's God's own truth."

"Yes, but you let him think . . ."

"Ah, my boy," Sheila interrupted, "let him think what he will, if it makes him happy. It's only ourselves that count."

"Then you do believe Davie's Pride will take the Derby."

She touched his shoulder gently. "We've got the chance, Johnny," she said, "a fighting chance, but you're not to be too disappointed whatever happens. You promised me."

"I won't," Johnny said. "I know what the odds are, Mom. But he will win, I'm sure of it."

Sheila shook her head at him. "You're hopeless. It's a waste of good breath even talking to you, and your father's every bit as bad." She began to grin. "And I'm the worst of the lot of you. Of course Davie's Pride is going to win!"

FOUR

LATER, when he was out of the hospital, Hugh Grundage, junior member of "Sam Grundage & Son, Painters, Azalia, Indiana," could laugh at the fact that he fell off a ladder while he was working on his own house. But at the time, watching his father rush out onto the steep side veranda to see what had made such a dreadful crash, all he could think of was Sam's heart.

"Take it easy, Pop," he called. "Don't you try to come down those steps. I'm perfectly okay."

This was not strictly true. Hugh was feeling no pain as yet but he was pretty sure he'd broken both legs.

Pushing past his grandfather, Hugh's five-year-old son ran down the stairs, scared and almost in tears. "It's not too much to worry about," Hugh reassured the boy. "You just go into the house with grampa and have him call the doctor. I'll be fine till you get back."

He sighed when he was alone. This was a heck of a thing to have happen, with Debbie and the baby coming home from the hospital tomorrow. And he sure wouldn't be able to take Young Hugh to his first Kentucky Derby next week, as planned. They'd both been looking forward to it, but Sam would be more disappointed than either of them. He was always bragging how there'd been a Grundage at every single Kentucky Derby since the race began.

It was too bad, but the old man would just have to accept it. Sam couldn't go because of the heart attack and now Hugh couldn't take Young Hugh. This year, there'd be no Grundages at Churchill Downs.

His last conscious thought was that maybe Debbie'd be up to packing a box lunch on Derby Day, like he remembered taking to the infield at Churchill ever since he was a little kid. And Sam and Young Hugh could spread a blanket on the floor of the sun parlor and eat it in front of the TV.

FIVE

Leaning his six-foot frame against the rail at Laurel Racecourse in Maryland, Morgan Wells held his somewhat angular features in a rigid expression of interest as he forced himself to watch the morning workouts. He evinced the same apparent calm in his greeting when Mack Herman stopped to talk.

Affectionately known as Mister Mack throughout the racing world, the eighty-two-year-old trainer was as straight and spare as the day he first put saddle on a thoroughbred, more than six decades earlier. He was generally acknowledged to be among the shrewdest handlers of horseflesh in the business.

More to the immediate point, it was he who had Lisa Cardigan's Derby entrant in charge and, characteristically, his conversation began with the Canadian bay.

"Were you here when Armada was out on the track?"

"I sure was," Morgan said with genuine enthusiasm. "You've got him in beautiful shape, Mister Mack. If ever a horse looked like a Derby winner, he does."

Morgan regretted the slip even as he made it. Mister Mack was of the deprecatory school, so traditional that its probable superstitious roots had long since been forgotten. He never anticipated victory for any runner in his barn. He never even admitted it until the "official" sign had gone up. And then he expressed surprise at his "luck."

Ordinarily Morgan would not have been guilty of such a breach in tact. He would have to get a better grip on himself.

Mister Mack ignored the blunder. "Your boy handles him just right, Morgan, couldn't ask for better."

"Donnie's a nice little rider," Morgan agreed, "and improving every day."

"Well, it's thanks to you," Mister Mack said. "He was going nowhere at a gallop until you started booking decent mounts for him."

Morgan was pleased. "We've had a few breaks, that's all."

"His break was getting you as an agent." The amenities thus disposed of, the old trainer hesitated. "I've got a problem, Morgan."

"Oh? Anything I can do?"

"I'm not sure," Mister Mack said. "Maybe you can. Have you seen Lisa Cardigan the last few days?"

It was incredible how things spread around a racetrack. Lisa and he had not been deliberately trying to keep their relationship a secret, but all except their most casual meetings had been off-track. Nevertheless, Mister Mack obviously knew all about them. Or, at least, thought he knew. As, undoubtedly, did every stablehand on the Laurel backstretch!

Morgan tried to keep his voice convincingly casual. "Not for almost a week, Mister Mack. Why?"

"Well, I was wondering." The trainer spread his thin, veined hands in a gesture of puzzlement. "I haven't seen her for a week, either. She hasn't come out to the barn to see Armada and you know how she's always been, dropping by to pet him every day."

"Yes, I know."

Mister Mack shook his head. "I swear, it's bothering him

28

not to see her! I've been putting off vanning him to Louis-ville, figuring she'd show up, but I can't wait any longer. We'll have to go tonight."

"No problems about that, are there?"

"Oh, no, everything's been arranged since the day we de-cided to give the colt a chance at the Derby, except that I meant to leave sooner. But he'll have a full week to settle in and he's always been a dandy traveler. Still," Mister Mack said, "she's the owner. Seems funny she hasn't been around all this time. Not even a phone call. I thought, if you had seen her . . ."

"No," Morgan said.

"Or if you were going to see her."

Morgan's impulse was to tell the miserable truth but he merely said, "If I do, I'll have her get in touch."

The old man said, "Thanks, I'd appreciate it," and went away. Morgan turned back to stare once more at the exercis-ing horses.

He wouldn't be seeing her again, of course.

He'd never see Lisa again. At least, not in the sense Mister Mack had meant. Not in a way that would have any meaning at all. And he had been so certain a week ago that she was going to marry him.

She couldn't have realized he meant to propose when he parked on the little side road that night, because she had moved willingly into his arms. It was only when he began to speak that she shook her head.

"Wait, Morgan," she begged. "If you're saying what I think, please don't. Not now."

"It's been so long, Lisa."

"But it's too new to me, Morgan, too soon. I don't really know yet, can't you understand?"

He hadn't understood, naturally. He still didn't understand. How could he, when he had loved her for almost eight years?

He wondered whether things would have been different if he had known who she was when he first saw her sitting alone, looking small and somehow vulnerable in the midst of a noisy, crowded party.

If, that evening, someone had pointed her out to him as the daughter of the fabulous Cardigans, with their shipping fleets and their platinum mines and their strings of fine racehorses, would he have still allowed himself to love her? Probably. He was only twenty-four then and brash. He had abandoned law school in his third year to become a jockey's agent and he had miraculously produced the season's racing wonder, Gabe Hilliard. Perhaps if he had known that she had eloped with Gabe just two days before?

But that wouldn't have altered his feelings either. Morgan had simply looked at Lisa and fallen in love. All these years later in the car, her plea for more time hadn't made sense. He had abandoned his earlier tenderness and her passion had seemed to match his own so unreservedly that he had said triumphantly, "Well, now you know. And now we can get married."

Lisa hadn't moved. Or opened her eyes. "No, Morgan, all this proves is that I want to go to bed with you. And I've known that for weeks. I will. Tonight if you like. Or right now, here in the car."

Perhaps—he had thought this a thousand times in the week since—perhaps that's what he should have done, made love to her that night. But as Lisa had said it wouldn't have proven anything that mattered.

"The point," she had said, "is that I'm not sure I'm ready to remarry."

"It's almost two years since you divorced Gabe, Lisa."

"I know."

"That's a hell of a long time to just lick your wounds." He was trying to keep the bitterness out of his voice.

"I know, Morgan."

"Or maybe you still love him?"

She had opened her eyes then and sat upright. "It isn't that, Morgan. I guess I'm still hurt." She drew a long breath.

"Or my pride is. Maybe that's all it comes down to, Morgan, a bad attack of injured pride. I guess I was spoiled. It was a shock to discover that somebody could just walk out on me."

"Gabe isn't somebody, Lisa. Gabe is just Gabe, a self-centered, miserable son of a bitch, with more hangups than anyone I ever met. I don't know why you married him in the first place."

"You liked him yourself, once."

"I was a lot younger then and so was he and I thought he was the greatest jockey in the world." Morgan touched her hand. "Maybe I was right, Lisa. Maybe with all his faults he's a kind of genius. And God knows he's got reason enough to be a little crazy. But in the end, I only stuck with him because of you. Didn't you realize that I loved you even then?"

"No," she said. "No, I honestly didn't. I loved Gabe and I wasn't thinking of anyone else."

"And you still love Gabe and you're still not thinking of anyone else."

"That's not the way it is. Believe me. Since you came up from Florida with Donnie this time, it's been entirely different between us." She put her hand on his arm. "Oh, Morgan, I've been happier these last few weeks than I've been for years. In some ways, I think happier than I've ever been before in my life."

"Then, for God's sake, Lisa . . ."

She shook her head. "Don't you see, there are too many exciting things happening now, like Armada's turning out to be such a great colt—I never owned a colt like him before—and getting ready to take him to the Derby. I have to wait, Morgan. I have to be sure I'm not just caught up in the general whirl."

He was suddenly furious. He started the car and drove her home in silence. At the door of her apartment he said coldly, "When you are able to decide whether you're excited over me or over a horse, you will let me know, won't you?"

It had been a ridiculous display of temper he thought for

31

the hundredth time as he leaned on the rail. Lisa had asked for understanding and he had walked away in anger. He was paying for it, though, and dearly. Not only had Lisa refused to answer her phone and the notes he'd sent, she wouldn't even come backstretch to pet Armada for fear of meeting him.

SIX

O N THE ·TWENTY-SECOND FLOOR of the imposing new Great Southeastern Insurance Building in Atlanta, Georgia, the Chief of Claims took a call from one of his field men.

"There's nothing to add to my written report," the man said. "I've had him under the closest possible surveillance since he reached Philadelphia. He can't even go to the can without my knowing it. But he hasn't said one interesting thing since Liberty Bell opened. Are you sure there's something worth all this?"

The Chief was a highly irascible man, not noted for his patience. "No, I'm not sure," he snapped. "If I were, you wouldn't be there!"

The field man began to stammer. "I didn't mean that the way it s-sounded, s-sir. But have you ever walked horses or mucked out s-stalls?"

"I've done anything I've had to do," the Chief said uncompromisingly, "whenever I had to do it, for as long as I had to do it. And so will you!"

"Yes, sir."

"And one more thing. Don't you ever again tell me that

someone you're watching can't go to the can without your knowing it. If he goes to the can, you go to the can."

He slammed the receiver down and swiveled to face his secretary, still poised for the dictation she had been taking when the phone rang.

"Young idiot," he said. "I don't care if he is my son, he's an idiot. Expects everything to drop in his lap the first day of an investigation. Why, I remember when I was getting started." He cut himself short, sighing. "Never mind, he'll have to learn," he said and then, with a gesture toward her notebook, "Where was I?"

SEVEN

A T CHURCHILL DOWNS, Lucky Jim's trainer, Buddy Sheffield, had carefully parked in front of the stands instead of at the stables to avoid reporters and now the goddamn car wouldn't budge! And thanks to his own cleverness, there wasn't one soul around to give him a lift back to the hotel.

There were people inside the offices of the track. He had just emerged from chatting with The Colonel and some of the other executives in the Director's Room upstairs. They had been settling down for a companionable pre-dinner drink, which was why Buddy had left in the first place.

Not that being on the wagon ordinarily made him shun such gatherings, but these last few days had been tough. It was the pressure, he supposed, being trainer of Lucky Jim, the favorite—though he certainly shouldn't want to drink now when he had the world by the tail. But he'd never had a reason, they said, even if he hadn't really begun to booze it up until Tad was killed by the hit-and-run on his way home from kindergarten.

"That was why everybody was so patient with you for so long, maybe—your wife, the people you trained for—but that wasn't what made you an alcoholic," the doctors had told him. "What made you an alcoholic was a physical and psychological allergy to liquor as immutable as your being six-two or having gray eyes or brown hair. And if you drink again, you'll be an alcoholic again. It's that simple."

Well, he'd stay away from temptation. He looked around to find a phone. The only spot there might possibly be one was across the street in a building occupied by the Churchill Downs Chapter of the V.F.W. In the bar.

Buddy laughed, the irony suddenly making the whole situation seem ridiculous. After all, he hadn't had a drink for more than four years. He wasn't about to start again. Still when he continued across the street and pushed through the door into the barroom, he was conscious of an unexpected nostalgia. It was a long while since he had shared in this particular atmosphere, in the special camaraderie of such places, but he had been in hundreds of them filled as this one was with an easy mix of locals and backstretchers. Those had been good times.

But then there had been the bad times, he reminded himself sharply. Nights when he took his bottle and fled from that same sociability he was sentimentalizing now, when he holed up in bitter solitude and drank himself right out of everything that mattered to him, wife, work, everything.

Buddy stepped quickly into the nearest phone in a row of booths, ordered a cab and went outside to wait for it on the corner. He was completely unaware that at a side table the columnist Jerry Neal had watched him from the moment he entered, or that at one of the tables he passed Pop Dewey looked after him as he left.

Jerry Neal made a quick notation on the back of an envelope he fished from an incredibly burdened coat pocket. Pop

Dewey grunted and struck a match, but instead of moving it to the tip of his beat-up cigar stump he sat staring at the small flame until it burned his fingers. Then he dropped it into the battered metal ashtray before him and spoke almost idly.

"You know who that was that just went out the door?"

Artie Dobermeyer had been carelessly printing a series of wet rings on the table with the bottom of his beer glass. At Pop's words he raised his heavy, pink-jowled face. "Who?"

"The big tall guy with the tan topcoat."

"I didn't see him," said Artie.

"That was Buddy Sheffield, the trainer of Lucky Jim," Pop said.

Artie turned automatically to examine the door and then, as if its emptiness restored his built-in negativity, he said, "Go on, what would he be doing in a joint like this?"

"I don't know," Pop shrugged, "looked like he was just using the phone. But it was Buddy Sheffield, all right, I know him from the days he wasn't too uppity to even notice you."

Interested in spite of himself, Artie asked, "You really know him?"

Pop took a swig from his glass, wiping his foamy mouth with the back of a weather-beaten hand. "Since he was just a punk kid mucking out stalls for Tom Richardson's old man. I know him from the first day Tom give him a horse to train after old Richardson died. And I know him when he was barred off every track in this country for his boozing."

"They wouldn't do it for that," Artie protested.

"Oh, that's not what they called it. You know how they always put it in the stewards' rulings, 'conduct detrimental to racing,' and that could be anything from sneaking some broad in the tackroom to passing bad checks."

"I know, or hiring unlicensed help."

"But booze is why they slammed Buddy Sheffield, mister, and you better believe it. Because when he got drinking, he got careless with his cigarettes, and he was always drinking.

35

They warned him and they hit him with stiff fines a couple of times and then they give him the ax."

"I still can't see it," Artie said. "Maybe they'd bust a groom or a hot-walker or some other poor bastard like that. But a big trainer? Just for drinking?"

Pop poked a bony finger into Artie's chest. "You don't understand, he's the one burned down Bluegrass Park! And man, oh, man," Pop said, "was that ever a sight to see, like the beginning of Kingdom Come!"

"You were there?"

"I was there," Pop said, turning his palms upward on the table. "I got these scars that night and Tom Richardson lost a real good horse. A couple of others, too, and some fillies, but there was this one special colt." He gestured helplessly. "Dumb, stupid horse. I got him out of there like butter, not a scratch on him, nothing—and then he turns around and runs right back in the burning stall."

After an appropriate silence Artie said reflectively, "So that's what knocked Sheffield out of racing. I never knew. You'd think with all the stuff they write about him and Lucky Jim, Jerry Neal or somebody would put it in the paper."

"That's Jerry Neal over there now against the wall, with the guy from Florida that owns Davie's Pride."

"I saw him, that's what made me think of it. You'd figure a story like that would be right up his alley."

"Knowing's one thing, proving's another. With all the investigations they never pinned it on Buddy officially. Neal put something like that in his column, he'd get the britches sued off him."

"I guess." Artie raised his glass in half salute. "Well, he got himself reinstated, more power to him. I read where he don't take a drink now—or smoke, either, come to think of it —and he's made a hell of a comeback with Lucky Jim."

"Just luck," Pop said. "If the owner wasn't a big lush himself, he'd never even have looked at Buddy Sheffield. The horse is overrated, anyways."

"Lucky Jim overrated? You got to be kidding." Artie broke off. "Oh, sure, that's right. You told me you were with Richardson, so naturally you'd go with his horse."

"That's where you're wrong, mister," Pop said, his eyes narrowing. "I wouldn't work for Tom Richardson if he was to pay me a million dollars. I used to work for that bastard, not now. I'm with Packo's stable. He may not be no aristocrat, but he sure treats his help better."

"Packo? The guy with the trucking fleet that owns Double Seven?"

"That's the one. George Packo. And that's the horse that's going to win, but don't go spreading it around, you hear?"

"You telling me Double Seven's got a chance at the Derby in a field like this?"

"A chance?" Pop snorted. "Double Seven's the best horse I ever been around in my whole life. And I been around a parcel of them. He's going to run and hide."

"The way I figure it, it'll be Lucky Jim on class alone. He's got two Derby winners in his pedigree."

"You're pari-mutuels, ain't you? A cashier? I've seen you in here before."

"I'm a ticket seller," Artie corrected, "but I don't have to work in the backstretch to read the Racing Form."

"Look," Pop said with a shrug, "I give you the tip. You want to stick with the favorite, that's up to you, friend. I wasn't making any cracks. The reason I asked, I was wondering about a union call for Sunday. You think anything's stirring?"

"Just a new president, wanting to gladhand everybody," said Artie. "He doesn't realize how bad the timing is. The week before the Derby he'll get a pretty small turnout, this J. Langdon Mannering."

"Is that his name?"

Artie laughed. "It's pretty fancy, all right. But he'll learn. Give him one Derby under his belt and Mr. J. Langdon Mannering won't make that mistake again!"

EIGHT

THE CALIFORNIA LANDSCAPE was never as green as that of Maryland, Tom Richardson reflected as he stared glumly through the window at it. Not even in the northern part of the state, which had considerably more precipitation than there was down here, thirty miles from the Mexican border.

Nevertheless, his view from the paneled study of the main house at Coronado Hill Farms was insistently spectacular. Behind the gentle roll of fields there was a series of rising slopes and beyond them, touched dramatically now by a sun which had broken through the clouds just in time to set, a stunning backdrop of high mountains.

The house itself was set on a flat-topped hummock which overlooked a cluster of red-tiled buildings and white-fenced paddocks. Thanks to an extravagantly expensive irrigation system, the grass and trees in this area were lush enough to satisfy even Tom.

Actually, if he ignored the determinedly old-Spanish motif of every structure in sight, the pattern of barns, veterinary hospital, thoroughbred swimming pool, training tracks, smaller houses and paddocks was familiar enough. It had, after all, been copied almost exactly from Tom's own Marshfield Farms back home at Glyndon, Maryland. But the 1500-acre gem which was Marshfield Farms had been in the making for almost two hundred years, under the devoted ministrations of Tom's father and grandfather and great-grandfather before him. Kirk and Dinah MacMillan had produced their replica on a scale almost four times as large in less than three years.

Tom turned away from the window restively, shying at the unexpected movement of his carrot-topped reflection in an antique mirror. He liked the MacMillans. He had, in fact, since the day they bought their first thoroughbred from him, five or six years ago, and he had come out here willingly to give them friendly advice on a stallion which had been offered for sale quite unexpectedly. It was only when he learned that one of his colts was ill that he regretted the trip.

Just then Dinah MacMillan bustled in with a tray of drinks. Under her crop of curling white hair strain underlined every one of her sixty-five years.

"Kirk'll be here in a minute," she said. "Have you heard anything yet?"

"Not yet, Dinah." He helped himself to bourbon and branch water at her proffering gesture. "It could be hours on something like this. I just have to sit tight."

"Oh, Tom, I'm so sorry! And Kirk feels terrible that he's responsible for your being so far away."

Tom patted her plump shoulder. "I wish I was home myself, but who could figure anything more was going to happen to Sparky after we shipped him back to the farm? And the honest truth is, I couldn't do a damn thing that isn't being done, anyway. Whalen's one of the best vets in the country, he's known Sparky since the day he was foaled."

The big man clucked sadly. "You wouldn't think that out of all the hundreds of horses I've seen at Marshfield in forty-three years I'd get so bound up in one, would you? I suppose it was because it looked for awhile like he was going to make it all the way."

"At least you've still got Dashing Lad."

"But it was something besides that with Sparky." Tom was so engrossed in pinpointing the phenomenon he hadn't even heard her comforting remark. "We were all crazy about him before we even dreamed of the Kentucky Derby. Maybe it was the way he was born, but I told you about that, didn't I?"

He had, twice, but the present reminiscences made Tom seem more animated than she'd seen him since the first message that Sparky might be dying. "No," Dinah lied kindly.

"I didn't? Thought I'd told that story to everybody in the country. Well, it was the middle of March, storming like Billy-be-damned, with thunder and lightning like you'd never believe. The power went out—we had to start the auxiliary generator—and three mares began foaling at the same time. You wouldn't see a sight to match that in a lifetime, Dinah, the way we were tearing around that foaling barn."

"I can imagine."

"Anyway, just as things are finally calming down, this hand starts laughing fit to be tied. 'Will you take a look over here,' he says. And there's old Pretty Girl standing in her stall as nice as you please, wasn't due to foal for a couple of days yet, never gave a peep the whole night, nobody paying her the slightest mind. And next to her, up on his legs already and trying to nurse, there's Sparky! To top it all off, he was the only colt we had in a solid week, nothing but fillies for seven straight days."

"Was Dashing Lad dropped earlier or later than Sparky?" Dinah asked, but before Tom could reply, Kirk MacMillan hurried in. He was a portly man who looked more like a banker than the adventurer he had actually been, stubbornly prospecting the world for thirty years before he finally struck oil in Alaska.

"Any news?"

"No, Kirk, not a peep."

"I'll still take you to the airport, if you've changed your mind," Kirk offered. "The helicopter's ready to go; I could have you in L.A. in half an hour."

"Like I said before, it wouldn't help. But thanks. Whatever's going to happen, I'll learn it quicker here than anywhere else."

"I know." Kirk busied himself mixing a drink. "It's just that sitting and waiting is so hard."

The telephone made them all jump. Tom paled as Kirk, having answered, held the receiver toward him. After a moment, he began to beam.

"He's going to be all right!" Tom exulted. "He responded to the medicine and he's fine. You hear that? Whalen says he'll be back on the track in no time!"

Dinah threw her arms around him and Tom swung her up off her feet, then set her down with a roar of laughter and collapsed into a chair. "Lord, you'll never know how I was sweating that one out. The way things have gone with that colt, I'd about made up my mind we were going to have to put him down. And that would have broken my heart, I swear it would."

"It's been a rough siege," Kirk agreed. "His coming up lame after the Florida Derby was bad enough. But then to get colic."

They subsided into happy silence, savoring the release from what had been almost unbearable tension. Then Dinah reverted to her earlier theme. "Well," she said, "you've still got Dashing Lad in the Derby."

Tom stirred. "Oh, I got nothing to complain about. Dashing Lad's a doggone nice little colt."

"But you don't think he can win?" Kirk asked.

Tom heaved himself to his feet. "I never said he couldn't win. He's got a good shot at it, Kirk, or I wouldn't enter him. I just thought Sparky was a shade better, that's all. But then, Orv Scott's been insisting all along that Dashing Lad could beat him and Orv's the trainer." He grinned. "Sure I think Dashing Lad can win. I was just being greedy, Kirk. What I really wanted was to take the Kentucky Derby one-two with Sparky and Dashing Lad, and then have Magician come in third! Wouldn't that have set Charlie Talbot back on his heels, if Marshfield-breds had swept it?"

Kirk grinned back. "He'd have cut his throat."

"Him and the rest of the Kentucky Breeders' Association. And Maryland would have declared a state holiday."

"Too bad you sold Magician," Dinah said.

"Oh, no, Dinah." Tom was shocked. "Coronado Hill or Marshfield, if you want to operate a breeding farm, you put them all up for sale, the best first, and don't ever forget it. Because you don't build a reputation palming off the culls."

"You know her," Kirk put in affectionately. "She doesn't want to part with any foal, even the ones we breed for other people."

"I can't help it. I just fall in love with all of them."

"I know," Tom said, "but the fact that I sold Magician is the finest advertising Marshfield Farms can get. Better even than if my own horse wins. And the same with Charlie Talbot, selling Lucky Jim to Jim York." He chuckled. "It's like everything else in this crazy business. Sometimes the ones that don't look so good turn out to be the biggest prizes. I held Sparky out of the sales because in the beginning I thought his legs were a little funny. And the way things have developed, I guess I was right, only he started to look so good."

He sighed, then brightened. "Anyway, he's safe, that's all I care about now. If he never runs another step, he's more than earned his keep, coming as close as he did."

"Whenever you decide to put him to stud, I'll book as many of my mares to him as you'll take," Kirk said. "At whatever price you set for a service."

Tom looked at him reflectively. "You know something, Kirk? I hadn't thought about it, but you might get one hell of a nick—fantastic speed and staying power—if you crossed Sparky's bloodlines with that new Australian mare of yours. We'll talk about it when the time comes. But what I started to say was, it's only a fluke that I have Dashing Lad. Originally, I sold him, to that rancher in New Mexico, remember?"

"Richard Wrayburn, he was in oil, too."

"That's the one. Then his plane crashed two days later and his widow wanted me to take the colt back. I could have made her honor the deal, of course, but I figured what the hell."

"Well," Kirk said, replenishing glasses all around, "it promises to be a humdinger of a Derby. And you've got two cracks at it, Tom, one way or the other. Like to say the same for Coronado Hill some day."

"I'll drink to that," said Tom, lifting his glass.

"It could happen," Kirk said, "and maybe sooner than anybody thinks. California horses have won it before."

"They have," Tom agreed. "Decidedly, Morvich, Swaps."

"And Majestic Prince," said Dinah eagerly. "I was so happy when he won. Kirk and I had just settled here then."

"They always referred to Majestic Prince as 'the California horse,' Dinah, but the truth is, he was from Kentucky, foaled at Spendthrift Farms. And owned by a Canadian, at that," Tom corrected. "Like Freeway this year. He's Kentucky-bred, too, but he's never raced back east, and as far as most people are concerned he's a Californian."

Kirk snorted. "Do you realize the oddsmakers are calling Freeway third choice? Right behind Lucky Jim and Magician?" He shook his head. "Damned if I can figure it. I've been watching that colt since the first day he stepped on a track and give him some real competition, I don't think he's got a prayer."

Tom laughed. "That's what makes horse racing, little differences of opinion like that. But if Dashing Lad can run like Orv Scott swears he can, he's going to surprise a lot of people. Especially Charlie Talbot, I hope, because aside from everything else, I put up fifty thousand against Charlie Talbot's twenty-five that one of my entry would come in ahead of Lucky Jim and now that Sparky's out of it, it's all riding on Dashing Lad!"

He did not add that if he lost the fifty thousand right now he was going to be a little tight at the bank. He didn't have to. Knowledge of that sort always swept through the industry with the same incredible speed of the three fires which had hit Marshfield Farms during the past year, killing twenty-two of the most promising yearlings and necessitating extensive repairs.

The insurance would cover most of the financial damage if the courts upheld Tom's claims. However, Tom had dismissed one of his stablehands after the second conflagration, three after the third—for carelessness or incompetence, not because he considered them guilty—and the insurance company was insisting that the fires had been deliberately set.

If arson could be proven, there was the delicate legal point of whether the "master" could be held responsible for the "man." There was precedence in other fields for such a defense by the insurance company and a court battle might drag on indefinitely.

"To Dashing Lad," Dinah toasted.

"Dashing Lad," Kirk echoed.

"Amen!" said Tom Richardson. "To Dashing Lad!"

NINE

THERE HAD BEEN A PARTY going on at Las Vegas all that day and night, whichever it now was. Inside the velvet-draped casino, where the crystal chandeliers blazed without interruption, it was impossible to distinguish between them.

Not that anyone cared.

Because even in Vegas, where festivity is a way of life, this was a special affair. For openers, it had been going full blast for more than forty-eight hours and the miracle was that any of the participants was still standing. Everyone was, though, with the exception of the host, Bolo Jackson.

Bolo, for Beauregard Logan, was slouched at the roulette table, surrounded by his durable guests and riding the crest of a spectacular streak of luck. He had huge piles of high-priced chips in front of him, confirming what his companions had known to begin with: that the rich get richer. And as the most casual reader of newspaper or magazine was aware Bolo Jackson was very rich indeed.

After inheriting millions—automobile and chemical fortunes, respectively—when his father and mother went down with their yacht during a hurricane off the coast of Cartagena, Bolo had acquired and divorced four blond wives (one ballet aspirant, one folk singer, two models) in somewhat rapid succession. He had since remained single, turning his attention to the doubling and redoubling of his money and—to make him even more eligible, as one cynic commented—he had twice tried to commit suicide within the last year. There was, actually, a third attempt, but Bolo himself did not remember what he had intended when they pulled him out of the car he had smashed into an abutment.

In the group which surrounded him that Friday there were six excited blondes to cheer him on, one of them only seventeen, but Bolo suddenly discovered he was bored. In a sweeping movement, he shoved all his chips onto a single number.

"That's it," he said into the startled silence which followed the gesture. "Last play, win or lose. And if I win," he hesitated, "if I win, what do you say, let's all take off for Louisville and put the whole pot on the longest longshot in the Kentucky Derby."

Bolo did not have the slightest idea of how he was going to finish his announcement when he began it. To save his life, he could not have explained what made him focus on Churchill Downs. He had certainly forgotten the friendly argument he'd overheard earlier between a couple of racing enthusiasts watching a crap game. Now that he thought of it, though, he liked the notion. Somehow or other, despite Bolo's many investments in the state, he'd never been to the Kentucky Derby.

He won.

Ignoring shrieks, Bolo stood up, stretching his cramped muscles, yawning widely. "Okay," he said. "Cash in for me, Glen, will you, I'm going to bed. And see about a plane. Tomorrow, it's off to Louisville."

Glen Logan was Bolo's omnipresent second or third cousin on his mother's side—nobody could ever quite sort out the relationship. He cashed in the chips—twenty-three thousand four hundred dollars. He also chartered a plane.

"But what we'll do when we get there," he confided to one of his cronies, "I'm hanged if I know. You don't just drop into Louisville and pick up a few empty suites during Derby Week. As to getting Derby reservations at this late date for a gang as large as this, forget it. Even Bolo Jackson can't manage that."

Unlike his cousin, Glen had been to the Derby.

The other man, though, had sublime faith in the power of money. "What'll you bet?" he asked. Which reminded him. "Hey, anybody know which horse Bolo's going to play?"

"There's one from Florida that's a longshot," a girl volunteered.

"No, no," another said. "Here it is in the paper, a horse called Sweepstakes, he's a hundred to one."

"The kind of luck Bolo's got, he'll win!"

"You're so right!"

"Well, if it's good enough for Bolo, it's good enough for me. I'm playing him too."

The seventeen year old (who was hoping to make it as a pop singer if she couldn't snare Bolo—or even if she did, after the divorce) snapped her fingers and said, "So am I!" Then she lifted voice into a soul version of "Camptown Races." "Somebody bet on the bobtailed nag, I'm gonna bet on the bay!"

Stephen Foster wouldn't have recognized his song at all.

TEN

T HE COLT under discussion wasn't a bay, anyway. Sweepstakes was brown, a deep, rich brown, with black legs,
mane and tail. Measuring a bare 15 hands at the withers, he
was at least 1 hand—4 inches—smaller and 50 to 100 pounds
lighter than the other three year olds against whom he was
scheduled to run in the Derby. He weighed 985 pounds.

To be entirely accurate, he was not yet three, except officially. Since January 1st is the universal birthday for every
thoroughbred registered by the Jockey Club when each automatically becomes a year older, it is technically possible for a
horse to be born on December 31st and be considered a
yearling the next day, but most thoroughbreds are bred to
arrive in January, February or March. Sweepstakes had been
a late foal, dropped in mid-May, and this was still only April.

Aside from his small size and the fact that he seemed not
quite fully developed—valid reasons to make him a longshot
—there was another psychological strike against Sweepstakes.
To a man, the turf writers and professional handicappers felt
there was something faintly ridiculous about a colt which had
been won in a contest put on annually by a company promot-
ing another of the state's most distinctive products, Kentucky's
fine Burley tobacco.

Not that the prize colt had lacked in breeding. Sweepstakes' sire and dam had both been stakes winners. It was just
that no one could forget those hundreds of thousands of little
pouches of pipe tobacco, requisite to the competition—"SEND
A TAG FROM A BAG AND WIN A RACEHORSE!"

To compound matters, the successful entrant had turned
out to be a skinny little hospital worker with a truly awesome

Adam's apple—who lived in Brooklyn (always good for a laugh). He had submitted three hundred tags from bags, though he didn't smoke. And he hadn't really wanted a racehorse, anyway, he just entered contests for fun.

As always when asked, the sponsoring company had arranged a sale for the colt, and as the little winner had been pointing out ever since, he might have been left with a lot of tobacco on his hands, but $12,000 wasn't hay.

Even worse for Sweepstakes' image, when he came out of the lesser tracks as a serious Derby contender—an impertinence in itself, to many—his owners were Gladys and Brewster Nickel, ex-waitress and ex-counterman, developers of The Nickel Cups, a growing chain of quick-lunch restaurants. Jerry Neal had promptly and contemptuously dubbed their hopeful "The Nickel Nag," and the derisive epithet had stuck.

The object of this ridicule was happily unaware of it. With his companionable black goat Billy curled up in a corner, Sweepstakes was standing blissfully asleep in Stall B of Churchill Downs' new Derby Barn. The impressive structure was an innovation this year. Conforming in appearance to the older barns in the stable area, it had been built to the most modern specifications for comfort, safety and security. It contained two rows of twelve stalls each, divided by a wide passageway. On one side the stalls were numbered 1 through 12, but on the other, to avoid a Stall 13 which might have distressed the superstitious, they were lettered A through L. The Derby Barn also had tack rooms, comfortable living facilities for the grooms of Derby entrants and a guardroom at either end where four men would be on the alert every day until the Derby was over.

The guards were on duty late that afternoon since most of the Derby colts were already on the grounds, and it was outside one of the Derby Barn doors that an argument was in progress.

Sweepstakes' embarrassed trainer Ed Quincy was vainly repeating, "I told you they wouldn't let you in, Mrs. Nickel."

"Well, I don't care, it's ridiculous," Gladys said shrilly. "We own the horse."

"Aw, let's go, Gladys," her husband urged. "We'll come out and see him tomorrow, first thing in the morning."

"No," Gladys insisted, "I want to see him now! It's only because the office girls have left that we don't have the proper pass or button or whatever it is. Look," she added, holding a slip of paper toward the older guard.

They had been over this before, too. He shook his head. "That's a Visitor's Pass into the stable area, ma'am, issued by the gateman as a courtesy to Mr. Quincy till you get your credentials. But like I said, it's not good for this barn."

Gladys tightened scarlet lips, tapping an impatient foot. "That goddamn plane, if it just made connections that got you where you wanted to go at a decent hour."

"Come on, Gladys, will you?"

"We really are sorry, Mr. and Mrs. Nickel," the second guard said. "We know you're who you say you are, we aren't doubting your word for a minute, but there's no way we can let you in here without the proper credentials." He was perhaps twenty years younger than his companion, also a patient man. "Not if you were to argue all night."

Gladys Nickel seemed prepared to do just that. She shook off her husband's restraining hand. "I only want to look at him," she persisted, "and he's my horse. Ed Quincy's told you that over and over and he's got the right . . ."

A soft drawl cut in behind her. "Trouble, Hank? Ollie?"

"No, Mr. Keller." Ollie was respectful. "Everything's under control."

"The hell it is!" Gladys denied, whirling to confront the newcomer. "Who're you?"

He answered mildly, "I'm Fred Keller, ma'am, head of track security. What seems to be the problem?"

"Well, I'm Gladys Nickel, this is my husband, we just flew in and I want to see my horse."

Fred Keller was broad but solid, only a few pounds over the

weight he had maintained during his twenty years on the Louisville Police Force preceding his present job. He had seen all kinds. He smiled. "Sweepstakes, isn't it? Vanned in from Keeneland this morning?"

"That's the one," said Gladys. "We had to be up in Michigan and I want to see if he stood the trip all right."

"Too late to get your credentials, is that it?" Keller asked. She nodded. "Well, let me give you a rundown on the situation, Mrs. Nickel. You see, we have a new setup this year. We've been separating the Derby colts up to now, but this time we've put them all together in one barn so we can give them the tightest security possible. That's what you want for Sweepstakes, isn't it?"

"Yes, but . . ."

"You certainly wouldn't want somebody who shouldn't be in that barn getting close to your colt, would you?"

"Of course not, but . . ."

"Well, nobody can, Mrs. Nickel. Because nobody—under any circumstances—can go in that barn without the proper credentials. It's as simple as that, one absolutely unbreakable rule."

"You could break it!"

"Perhaps so," he admitted. "I'm head of track security, been here a long time and every guard on the grounds knows exactly who I am. I'm their boss. And Lee Ames could, he's my boss and they know him, too. But we set the rules, Mrs. Nickel. It would be pretty senseless to start making exceptions before the meeting's even open, wouldn't it?"

"Lee Ames," Gladys said furiously. "Wait till I get him on the phone, I'll give him a piece of my mind. Let's get out of here," she urged her husband. "I'm dog tired and I'm hungry."

"You're hungry! When I begged you to stop an hour ago and have . . ."

She wheeled on him. "You shut up. Just shut up, you hear, Brewster? The last thing I need right now is your two cents' worth!"

She was still scolding him, with Ed Quincy lagging discreetly behind, as they disappeared around one of the other barns.

"Whew!" Hank was laughing. "Maybe he should have offered her a nickel instead of two cents."

"Man, I wouldn't take that one for free," said Ollie. "Her or her horse."

"I don't know," Hank said, "if she was running, I might just put a bet on her. She don't know when she's beat."

"Sweepstakes isn't that bad a horse, Ollie," Keller said. "I saw him when he was unloading and I've been looking over his record. He's small, but so was Aristides."

It was typical of Churchill Downs—and of almost any backstretch at any other track—that his men understood his point instantly. Aristides had, indeed, been a small colt and winner of the first Derby ever run a generation before any of their fathers had been born. In Ollie's case, fifteen years before his grandfather saw the light of day.

"You comparing this Nickel Nag to Aristides, Mr. Keller?" Ollie asked indignantly. "Why, Sweepstakes couldn't even get on the same track!"

"Maybe not," Fred Keller conceded. "And then, again, he might surprise you."

ELEVEN

T HE LAST TWENTY-FOUR HOURS had been a disaster as far as Shelby Todhunter, Jr., was concerned. First there'd been the fight with Paula lasting until one in the morning, followed by the big family blowup when he got home, then the violent storm.

When he had finally arrived at the stables, exhausted after two hours' sleep, he'd been greeted by the news of Gordy's death. This was gloomy enough, though Shelby hadn't been particularly close to Cowdin. What really bothered him was the subsequent announcement that Gabe Hilliard would be riding in the Derby.

Shelby supposed it was his fury over this which had made him so stubborn about going through with the exhibition breeze he had promised between the second and third races at Hollywood Park that afternoon. But he had shown them. He was Freeway's trainer and when he said Freeway would run, sea of mud or no sea of mud, that was final. Maybe there was some risk to it, but if his mother hadn't backed him, he'd have walked out again. It took them three months to catch up with him the last time, detectives and all. She had to give in when he really set his mind on something, though, no matter what the old man said.

Freeway had worked, all right, the full mile and a quarter, exactly as announced. He'd looked great, too, going through that slop like a bolt of gray lightning. When his fantastic speed was spelled out on the tote board, the crowd had gone wild and Shelby had begun to feel better.

Now at the airport his glance took in the mob of fans being held back by the hard-pressed guards, and his natural twenty-two-year-old exuberance exerted itself. He squeezed Paula's arm. Who would ever have believed a rotten day like this could end so well?

Paula smiled up at him, her short dark curls tousled, her brown eyes sparkling with excitement and pleasure. Thank God she had let him make up. He was never going to fight with her again. He was too crazy about her. He wasn't ever going to drink again, either, though he hadn't had as much as she thought last night. But any liquor acted like dynamite after the other stuff. He would have to lay off that, too.

"Hold it," one of the photographers yelled. "Miss Vance, will you smile up at Todhunter like that again?"

"We'll do better than that for you," Shelby called back. He took Paula into his arms and kissed her, a long, ardent kiss, while flashbulbs popped around them like fireflies.

"Mr. Todhunter, how about one with the two mothers?" This was a latecomer, evidently, since there had been a dozen such shots before.

Shelby groaned amiably but the photographer was already separating him from Paula, urging him into the pose which would appear tomorrow over the caption:

Mrs. William Vance and Mrs. Shelby Todhunter, Sr., co-owners, and Shelby Todhunter, Jr., trainer, shown at L. A. International Airport last night as Freeway, California's Kentucky Derby favorite, planed out for the Big Race.

The pictures of Paula and him would be identified as:

Shelby Todhunter, Jr., and pretty fiancee, Paula Vance, before departing for Louisville last evening with Freeway, trained by young Todhunter for his mother, Mrs. Della Todhunter, and his mother-in-law-to-be, Mrs. Enid Vance, who jointly own California's wonder horse.

"Shelby! Hey, Shelby, just one more picture? With Tucker shaking hands and wishing you luck?" That was the cameraman from one of Kentucky's thoroughbred breeders' magazines. A nice-enough guy. So was Tucker Udell, his publisher, who was particularly vocal in praising Freeway.

"All right," Shelby agreed, "but then that's it, the last one, fellows, because I've got to go."

Tucker's grip was firm as they posed and so warm it startled Shelby. He hadn't realized his own hands were freezing.

"I'll be wishing you luck again at Churchill," Tucker Udell

said, "but in the meantime I'm really rooting for you. And it has nothing to do with personal interest, Shel, because no matter how the Derby turns out, Freeway's already given us a million bucks' worth of publicity."

That was a conservative estimate. Freeway had been a $12,000 find at the annual Keeneland yearling sales, a stroke of luck which was dwelt upon at increasing length every time the roan colt won a race. His earnings to date had already passed 250,000 dollars.

"Thanks a lot, Tucker. We'll have another million's worth for you by the time we come back."

"Got it," the photographer said, waving his hand to release them. "Thanks. And good luck, Shelby."

Shelby waved back. He never really minded the cameramen. At the moment, he didn't even object too much to the reporters who surged around the little family group. Some of them were bastards, of course, who misquoted him or wrote critical pieces about the way he trained the horse, but Freeway kept showing them up, so he wouldn't let them bother him. Not now, anyway.

"How did he take the loading, Shelby?" one of the newsmen asked.

"Great, just great. Went on the plane like a lamb."

"Is he a good traveler?" asked another.

"Freeway? He's a good everything."

"You're going with him, aren't you?"

"You know it."

"How about your parents and fiancée and Mrs. Vance?"

"My father's already on the plane, the others will follow on a commercial flight tomorrow."

"But you're the trainer, Shelby, right, not your old man?" The reporter's voice cut above the rest.

Shelby held his smile. "That's been established a thousand times. My father's a vet, one of the best in the country, but I'm the trainer. Okay?"

"There's a rumor that you and your father had an argument

54

over running Freeway in that exhibition today."

Shelby knew this reporter. "You know how those rumors go, Bill, nothing to it." He hesitated, then his grin broadened. "But if there had been an argument, you saw how it came out, didn't you?"

"How was Freeway after that run?"

Shelby kept smiling. "Perfect. This colt can do anything that's asked of him, anytime, any weather."

"You still don't think it was too long or too fast a workout for him, especially after a rain like that?"

The reporter was a persistent son of a bitch. "Ask Freeway," Shelby said, "after he wins the Derby."

That got a general laugh but his tormentors weren't through. Another asked, "What about Gabe Hilliard?"

"What about him?"

"Well, he was Freeway's regular jockey up until three weeks ago, he'll know your horse's weak points."

"Freeway hasn't got any weak points."

"Can you tell us why you bumped Hilliard off Freeway after he'd ridden the horse to seven straight wins?"

"No comment."

"Is it true that you and he had a fistfight over his attentions to your fiancée?"

Shelby's teeth clenched but he maintained a passable smile as he shook his head. "I've told you, I've got nothing to say about Gabe Hilliard. Matter of fact, fellows, I'm sorry, but that's all I can say about anything now. I've got to take off. Can't keep Freeway waiting."

He kissed Paula again, kissed his mother, kissed Paula's mother, shook a dozen hands and escaped onto the field.

He had managed the scene without losing his temper but inwardly he was seething. And he was shaking so hard he felt as if he would shatter. He'd be okay in a minute, though. One pill when he got on the plane.

It was true he'd decided this morning he'd have to cut the pills entirely, uppers and downers, and he hadn't taken any all day. Which proved he could kick them anytime he wanted to. But he saw now that this wasn't the time to quit. These reporters were tough enough but there would be others in Kentucky, worse bastards, probably, since they'd be eastern press, not predisposed in Freeway's favor.

He would have to stay on the pills at least until the Derby was over, until Freeway had won it.

Then he'd quit.

SATURDAY

ONE

IT WAS WELL BEFORE SUNRISE when Lee pulled up at the
main stable gate. The famous twin spires of Churchill
Downs were still invisible and a dim glow from the windows
of the long press box high atop the grandstand provided the
sole illumination on the office—or frontside—of the track. Here
on the backstretch, however, there was light from every building and the familiar activity was in full swing, having started
in earnest by four o'clock.

The predawn air was heavy with the pervasive aromas of
horse and straw and liniment and freshly perked coffee. From
the barn closest to the entrance Lee could hear the stomping
of hooves and at least two portable radios. He grinned happily at the gateman.

The stable area never ceased to give Lee pleasure. Today he
was conscious of additional savor.

So, too, was the guard. "Yessir, Mr. Ames," he said cheerfully, "they sure didn't let you sleep late this morning, did
they?"

"I am a little early," Lee admitted. "But, then, it's Opening
Day. Listen, did Freeway or Armada arrive yet?"

The gateman nodded. "Mister Mack came in about three
o'clock and the California horse is being unloaded right now.
A beauty, from what I could see of him."

"He is a beauty," Lee said. "I was out on the coast when he

59

won the Santa Anita Derby. Armada's a handsome colt, too, but I want to take a look at the one they brought in yesterday."

"Sweepstakes? I haven't seen him, either, but they say—" He broke off in midsentence.

Lee's lip quirked. "I know. That he's completely out of his class. That he shouldn't be allowed in the Derby. Maybe they're right, though Fred Keller thinks the colt's underrated. Anyway, I'm going over to see him and say hello."

"So if anybody wants you, you'll be at the Derby Barn?"

"Yes, for awhile. After that I'll be on my usual rounds."

To Pop Dewey, leading Double Seven out of Stall H onto the covered dirt walkway which surrounded the Derby Barn, the sights and sounds and smells which so enchanted Lee Ames were simply the air he breathed.

The application he filled in annually for renewal of his groom's license had a space on it for "Last Permanent Address" and Pop invariably printed "Keo, Arkansas." That was, in all truth, the last place where he had been really settled, with his mother and stepfather. But he had run away when he was fifteen. The racing circuits he'd followed ever since hadn't taken him back home for close to half a century.

Tracks and barns, employers and horses could change with every meet, the seasons might be warmer or colder, but the sounds and smells were always the same. Pop no longer even noticed them.

Other contenders were moving about with their handlers on the roofed walkway but Pop ignored them, having already examined them with biased opinion as to conformation and potential. His interest now lay in turning his own charge over to Kenny Perini with the instructions left the afternoon before by trainer Ned Anderson to gallop the big rangy bay for a mile.

Kenny, who was to pilot Double Seven in the Derby, was also handling his daily exercise in order to thoroughly familiarize himself with both mount and course. It was a regimen often followed in preparation for an important race—and by some pretty successful jockeys, too—but Pop wasn't sure he entirely approved. Most regular exercise boys were heavier than the average jockey and the old groom believed that training with the extra weight gave a horse a certain advantage. Well, thought Pop, looking around for Kenny impatiently, he wasn't paid to think, only to do what the trainer told him.

The track would be open for workouts until ten o'clock with a short break around eight for the tractors to put it back into shape after the first hours of hard use. But Anderson had said he wanted Double Seven out on the dirt at six sharp when there wouldn't be too many other horses working.

Pop looked at his watch in annoyance. As always, the gesture gave him a subtle satisfaction since this was a fine and beautiful instrument, both timepiece and stopwatch, and undoubtedly his most valuable possession. That it had come to him as a gift, personally presented by Tom Richardson after an important Marshfield Farms victory some years back, Pop no longer allowed himself to remember.

"Hey, Pop, what time is it?" The question came from a young hot-walker named Tully Borden who'd been drinking beer with him nights over at the V.F.W. bar. A green kid. Pop wasn't sure he had sense enough to keep himself out from under the feet of the horses he walked after exercise to cool them down.

"You got to watch them horses every second," Pop had warned him just last evening. "When you're hot-walking, you got to go round that circle like you was ice-skating, crossing one foot over the other, understand? Because if you ain't careful, them horses'll stomp you quicker than a wink. They like stomping you."

Pop didn't know if the boy had believed him or not, but he'd been real impressed by Pop's racetracking stories, had even sprung for a couple of beers.

"Hi, kid," Pop answered him now. "It's just on six o'clock."

61

"Thanks." The boy gestured toward Double Seven. "Your horse looks great. You working him this morning?"

"Nah, just galloping. If that jockey ever gets here."

Before Pop could really launch into his complaint, Kenny Perini arrived with Ned Anderson and a trailing newsman. It was the latter, evidently, who had delayed both jockey and trainer, probably caught them having coffee at Thompson's Track Kitchen. Mollified, Pop gave Kenny a calloused hand up into the saddle and the horse headed slowly toward the track, Anderson and the reporter walking along behind.

Pop and the kid threaded their way between barns until they got to the fence where they could see Double Seven as he went through the gap and out onto the dirt.

"How is this Perini?" the kid asked. "A good jock?"

"Boy, where've you been?" Pop demanded. "Everybody knows Kenny Perini."

"Well, sure, I've heard his name, but somehow when you're talking about Derby horses, you think of the really big jockeys."

"I get what you mean," Pop conceded. "Kenny's been riding a long time and never made it on a top horse. But he was leading jockey in the country a couple of years ago, rode more winners than anybody else, even if he was on the smaller tracks. He's probably been up on twenty thousand mounts."

The kid laughed. "And like you told me last night, Pop, it's the horse that carries the jockey, not the other way around, right?"

Kenny wheeled Double Seven into his gallop. "Now you watch the way this horse moves," Pop said. "That long stride of his sure covers ground."

By now it was light enough to see the entire oval and the two white spires of the grandstand across from them. Anderson, with the newsman still trailing, had gone into the tower where, on the lower level, observers were beginning to gather. Upstairs, the official clockers recorded all of the morning's workouts.

Double Seven was one of the first on the course, as Anderson had planned, but there were already another dozen horses going around with him, some galloping as he was, some being led by pony boys and the two-year-olds simply learning to adjust to the bustle and distractions of the track.

It was a scene no backstretcher ever found boring, however often he had watched it. The procedure might seem chaotic and confusing to a newcomer like the kid, but it was actually orderly, with set rules followed by all the participants.

A horse that was really "working"—running close to the height of his capabilities—had undisputed right of way, other riders removing themselves from his path around the inner rail, and the sharp rattle of his hooves was entirely different from the slower thuddings of a galloper. The skitter of the two-year-olds gave forth a broken rhythm of clippety-clops which could have been identified without hesitation by a blindfolded horseman.

It was one of these, a sweating, nervy chestnut, which suddenly reared near the gap where Pop and Tully were standing. Its youthful exerciser hit the dirt hard and the colt streaked off on its own, weaving erratically wrong way around the track. The rider, unhurt, scrambled hurriedly out of danger.

There were immediate cries of "Loose horse! Loose horse!" and a pair of outriders who were on duty to cope with such crises set off on their trained mounts to recapture the runaway. It was not an uncommon event, but the colt was extraordinarily speedy and frightened.

When one of the outriders succeeded in circling around ahead of it, the colt stopped, snorted and dodged back past the gap again, reddish tail and mane streaming. Then, evading the other outrider when he made a grab for the dangling reins, it reversed direction once more. For a second it looked as if the colt might emerge through the fence opening and turn docilely toward its own barn. The cluster of men at the gap fell away, hopefully making room.

Instead, the colt wheeled again and headed directly across

the track toward a heavily breathing horse who was pounding along next to the rail, its rider so concentrated on the effort that instant collision seemed inevitable.

Pop who had his eye on Double Seven suddenly shouted, "Our horse is coming right behind. If they go down he'll be on top of them!"

At that instant—the very last possible—the colt avoided disaster by a wild swerve and then stood trembling directly in Double Seven's path. Without hesitating, Pop darted out onto the track and the kid plunged after him.

Grabbing at both the loose reins and the sensitive nostrils, Pop dragged the colt out of Double Seven's way. He managed at the same time to steer clear of the other horses on the track.

The kid didn't.

Intent on Pop and the runaway, he never even saw the colt that knocked him down. He was still unconscious when he was carried off to the hospital.

Double Seven had been bathed and walked around the Derby Barn for half an hour to cool off and Pop had already brushed and rubbed him down before word came that Tully was all right, conscious again, suffering only from mild concussion and a couple of broken ribs.

"Damn fool!" Pop said in relief to Double Seven. "What the hell did he follow me onto the track for?"

Double Seven snorted.

"I swear, it's a crime where they get their help from anymore! In the old days, they wouldn't have let a kid like that loose in the backstretch!"

Pop thought of Tully's wallet, that he had noticed when the boy had been paying for a couple of beers. An expensive one, if Pop knew anything about good leather, and he did after a lifetime around saddles.

"Probably some rich kid," he told Double Seven, "some owner's son, maybe, they're always hanging around." But at least that was better than owners' daughters. The way you fell over girls in the backstretch these days, it could make you sick.

Pop bent to wrap the bandages around Double Seven's legs. This was a process requiring skill and dedicated attention. The wrappings had to be tight enough to give support and thick enough to be protective, but not too tight or too thick, and they had to be pinned with the utmost care. Pop was too preoccupied to think about the kid again.

TWO

THE ASSISTANT DIRECTOR of the FBI usually enjoyed Saturdays. The Bureau never completely shut down, naturally, but in contrast to the regular pulse of Washington activity, weekends in the huge building were remarkably peaceful. Since this was an especially beautiful day, most of his colleagues would head for golf course, road or river and he would be able to catch up on some paperwork.

He barely settled at his desk when Vic, his aide, came in with a memo and announced, "This little bonanza turned up about an hour ago."

The A.D. skimmed the paper, then reread it in astonishment. "Well, that's unexpected," he said. "Are they sure?"

"No question, sir. The two bills are part of the Cardigan ransom."

"Found in the lining of a dead man's coat?"

Vic nodded. "Somebody in Jersey was right on his toes because we just released that list of numbered bills yesterday."

"That makes it definitely interstate, then, since the girl was kidnapped in Baltimore. Anything else on the body, any identification?"

"Not as of half an hour ago. I phoned just before you got here. No head or hands, as you know, but the victim was Caucasian, male, 38 or 40, weight about 185, height about 5-11—before decapitation, that would be—and he'd been dead three or four days. We'll have to wait for the autopsy report to get anything more, but they don't expect too much."

The A.D. tapped the memo on the top of his desk. "Stripped clean, not a tag on his clothing, not another paper in his pockets."

"It seems to be sheer luck we got this much," Vic said. "Apparently the victim had the money in a kind of secret pocket that ripped when the body tumbled down the cliff. Before it was torn, Jersey says, that pocket would have been easy to miss."

"And no way to check fingerprints or dental work."

"Obviously what the murderer intended," Vic agreed. "The doctor reports, by the way, that it looks as if each hand had been chopped off with a stroke of an ax."

"That suggests considerable strength, doesn't it? And the head?"

"Well, it's not official yet, but the doctor believes the murderer tried to chop that off, too, couldn't quite make it and had to finish the job with a saw."

The A.D. grimaced. "That's a dandy picture, isn't it? I don't suppose we have many M.O.'s like that?"

"No," Vic said, "this character's in a class by himself, but the victim was probably dead before the fancy work began."

The A.D. looked down at the memo again. "So all we've got are those two twenty-dollar bills from the ransom payoff, folded around a past-performance chart clipped out of the Daily Racing Form. On Armada, Lisa Cardigan's own horse. Vic, you ever go to the races?"

"No, sir. Truthfully, I'm not sure what that clipping is, though I assume it's some sort of record."

"That's right, it's a listing of a horse's last ten or twelve races, how he finished, what kind of start he got, who the competition was, where he ran, what condition the track was in. An incredible amount of information to help judge what sort of performance he's apt to give the next time out. It's fascinating, Vic, I used to go with the Director when I was assigned to the California office."

He smiled reminiscently. "Now there was a real fan. Scheduled his annual checkup at Scripps Institute in the summertime so he could take his tests in the mornings and go to Del Mar for the races in the afternoons. Tell you one thing, though, Vic. Much as he loved racing, I never knew the Director to carry any past-performance clippings around in his pockets. Have we done anything on the girl's racetrack connections?"

"Not too much," Vic said. "With the Cardigans refusing to let us enter the case officially, we've been pretty limited."

"Well, let's move Inspector Elverson down to Kentucky. Churchill Downs opens today and maybe he can pick up some sort of lead there. The New York office can sit it out with the Cardigans at the hotel, and Elverson can make it back in a hurry if anything should break."

"I'll contact him right away."

"And, Vic, get a list of those ransom twenties to every racetrack now in operation. We covered all the banks, didn't we?"

"Yes, of course."

"Well, send a follow-up to any bank handling racetrack money—any racetrack—and ask them to check those deposits with particular care. If our victim was that involved in racing, perhaps his friends are, too."

Unfortunately, the late Coolie Bascombe's interest in thoroughbreds was not shared by his former partners, Mace Augustine and Rosanna Palmer. The extremely attractive young couple—he so blond and boyish, she so vividly dark—knew nothing at all about racing and couldn't have cared less.

Nevertheless, at that moment, Mace was turning their trailer into a yard on Thornbury Avenue, less than a block from Churchill Downs. With Rosanna slumping on the seat beside him, he drove around to the back of a small clapboard house, drew up under a blossoming magnolia tree near the rear fence and cut the motor with a weary sigh.

"We're here," he announced. "You sure you pulled those curtains good and tight?"

Rosanna's answer was an incomprehensible murmur and he jabbed her with an impatient elbow. "For Christ's sake, don't go to sleep now. We got to talk to this dame, get settled in."

"Well, you don't have to be so rough about it," Rosanna said as she straightened, peering through the windshield at their surroundings. "I can't help it if I'm tired. I wanted you to stop somewhere instead of driving all night."

"I asked you about the curtains, damn it. Can anybody look in?"

"They're fine, fine. And if anybody did get a peek, they wouldn't see . . ." The muscles of his jaw ridged in fury. "But nobody can, I'm telling you," she added hastily.

He climbed out of the cab without replying, and Rosanna scrambled to join him at the side of the trailer.

"Wow, a real fun spot," she said disgustedly. "Why the hell does Coolie want to come to this place?"

Mace's annoyance suddenly dissipated. "You can ask him when he gets here." He put an arm around her shoulders. "You ready, doll?"

They met the old woman as she was coming out of the back door, in such a hurry to check the unexpected arrivals she was still holding her hairbrush.

"Well, well," Mace said, "so you're the famous Good Mary."

"Mercy me," she said, peering up into his face, "I don't know you, do I?"

He gave her his best smile. "Not yet," he said, "but I'm hoping to fix that right away."

Rosanna was just too beat to enjoy the show—all she wanted was to get some sleep. But the old lady bought the whole bit as Rosanna had known she would from the very beginning. Why Mace should have worried about it half the night Rosanna'd never be able to figure, because old ladies always went for him; he reminded them of their grandsons or something. Scraps of conversation floated around her.

"So surprised, couldn't figure who'd be driving in. But whatever made you try here?"

"A buddy of ours told us all about you. Used to go with a girl who roomed here."

"Which one would that be, did he say, Janey or Doris?"

"It was quite awhile back. He didn't mention her name."

Rosanna stopped listening. Suddenly Mace gripped her arm. "Come on, move, will you?"

The old lady was already leading the way into the house. Mace caught up with her in the narrow hallway and Rosanna dragged after them into the cluttered front parlor.

Mace put some money on the table. It looked like a lot to Rosanna, but it was all small bills.

"Sit down, sit down," the old woman urged, "I'll just write out a receipt."

Rosanna shook her head. "If I do, I might never get up again. I didn't sleep all night." She turned to stare disinterestedly at the dozens of snapshots which had been tacked to the wall. There was a yellowed clipping among them, headed "The Good Mary," and involuntarily, Rosanna began to read:

Some people make a hobby of hunting for gold mines or sunken treasure. Some people dig for buried coins or jewelry. One noted author regularly walks city streets with downcast eyes, searching for fallen money.

Good Mary stoops.

A "stoop" or "stooper" in racetrack parlance is a person who seeks lost or discarded pari-mutuel tickets which are still cashable. Since hundreds of thousands of dollars worth of such tickets go unredeemed each year at every track, the effort is sometimes quite profitable.

But yesterday wasn't very good for Good Mary. She

turned over only one "live" ticket all afternoon, worth a mere $2.80 at the window of the Show Cashier—little more than it cost her to get into the Churchill Downs grandstand.

However, on her rounds, she also found a woman's handbag, stuffed with $5,000 in crisp new bills.

There was more. That her real name was Mary Good Gallagher but they called her Good Mary because she *was* always finding things and taking them into the office: wallets, sweaters, eyeglasses, binoculars and once even a full set of false teeth.

Rosanna jumped, startled, as the old lady laughed beside her.

"A grand day that was," Good Mary said, "with the story in the paper and a hundred-dollar reward to boot! But the best was meeting Fred Keller, a fine, dear friend he's been to me ever since, sends me all my roomers. And would you believe, Lee Ames himself come to thank me, right here in this very house, though he wasn't president yet in those days, but he's sent me a season ticket every meeting since, spring and fall."

"Oh, wow," said Rosanna. She hadn't understood a word, but the response seemed to satisfy the old woman.

Good Mary nodded happily. "That's what I was doing when you drove in, getting ready to go. It's miles too early and well I know it," she confided, "but I declare, I just couldn't help myself."

Rosanna nodded.

"Because it's been so long. All the dreary months since November. And now, at last, it's Opening Day!"

"Oh, wow," Rosanna said again.

THREE

B Y 7:45 Dennis Sullivan was exhausted. The morning air which seemed so chilly after the Florida heat, made every muscle in his body ache. It was a blessing that Sheila couldn't see the way he looked leaning on this railing now, watching Davie's Pride circle the track. The reddish stubble was still on his drawn face and she'd be taking the rough side of her tongue to him for not having shaved.

But it had been a bitter long stretch since he'd started north from Davie, with his colt in the borrowed trailer behind. To cover the thousand miles to Churchill Downs would have been a grinding job under any circumstances, as Dennis had known before he set out. There were those who would have driven faster and made fewer halts, but he had stayed under sixty the entire route and stopped every four hours to tend to Davie's Pride.

What he hadn't realized until he was well into Georgia, too late to let Johnny accompany him as the boy had begged, was the strain it had been to go so carefully for so long, as if he had been driving a vanload of eggs with no brakes. Not that a thoroughbred's legs were quite that fragile, but they were thin and delicate and they were holding up more than a thousand pounds. A really sudden, jolting stop could do irreparable damage.

Dennis had barely touched his brake pedal the whole trip, watching ahead for any hint of impending trouble and avoiding it with an agonizing tension which had utterly drained him.

But when he had finally turned in through the stable gate

on Fourth Street a week ago, he had been able to ignore his fatigue. He was so pleased to be at Churchill Downs. Him, Dennis Joseph Sullivan, with a horse he'd be running in the Kentucky Derby!

It was the grueling days since which had taken their toll, keeping up with the careful training schedule, walking Davie's Pride to cool him out after his morning run, bathing him, brushing him, picking the dirt out of his hooves, oiling him, bandaging his legs, mixing his feed and carrying his water and mucking out his stall, not to mention the tack to be soaped and cleaned or the saddle cloths to be laundered.

But Johnny would be here soon to help and somehow he had made it. And so, Heaven be praised, had Davie's Pride, not a whit the worse for wear. He was circling close to the rail of the track now, his long, smooth stride eating up ground.

Dennis smiled and checked his cheap stopwatch, then he froze. Davie's Pride was going too fast. He should have gone on riding the colt himself but he had been so tired. And he had told the exercise boy to work an easy mile at about a minute and forty-six seconds. He had repeated it twice and the boy had nodded a bit impatiently the second time, but at the rate he was pushing the horse, he'd be six or seven seconds under.

Helpless, Dennis kept his eyes on the streaking horse while the exercise boy crouched over him, urging him on. It was small comfort that the fellow at least kept his short whip in his pocket as he'd also been told. It stood straight up above him, the angle making it look like an arrow in his back. Which, Dennis thought grimly, was exactly what he wished it was. And another in the back of the man who had recommended him so highly.

Dennis pushed the little plunger on his watch as Davie's Pride passed the mile pole, then stared at it in dismay. Davie's Pride had covered the distance in 1:36 flat—and had probably left the race he should be running next Tuesday here on this morning's track.

Never before had Davie's Pride been worked this hard so close to a real contest. You couldn't expect a young colt to run his heart out in training and then win races, too. Why, the papers were full of excited comment on Freeway's exhibition at Hollywood Park yesterday, disapproval at its speed being virtually unanimous, and Freeway wasn't scheduled to race again until next Saturday's Derby, a full week away.

Davie's Pride was entered in Tuesday's Derby Trial. Now, if he couldn't race—or couldn't race well enough to earn at least a portion of the Trial Purse—how was Dennis to come up with the additional fees it would take for a start in the Derby itself?

It was a terrible moment for Dennis Sullivan and yet he was conscious of a soaring joy. Davie's Pride was coming around the turn to where Dennis waited at the fence, slowly now, breathing hard, sweat glistening on his trembling flanks. But the ears were pricked up and lively, not lying flat back on his head in utter fatigue as Dennis had expected them to be.

What a horse!

What a wonderful horse!

In the watchtower near the far gap in the fence the clocker for the Daily Racing Form checked the notation he had made and whistled.

"This Sullivan has to be some kind of a nut. You realize he worked his horse faster than a lot of miles are won?"

The track's official clocker shrugged. "It takes all kinds," he said, "men and horses. But you know how these morning glories are. Tear up the track during training and then in the afternoon, when it counts, they don't do a damn thing. This one's never won much."

"I know, but just the same I'll be interested to see how he comes out in the Trial."

"If he makes it to the Trial, after a work like that."

"Right," the Daily Racing Form man qualified. "If he makes it to the Trial."

Just below, in the tower's observation area for less official onlookers, Ed Quincy had also been impressed by Davie's Pride.

"I figured I had enough to worry about with the top four," he told Gladys and Brewster Nickel, "but I wonder now if I've been paying enough attention to that Florida horse. He can go like crazy."

Gladys' disposition had been soothed this morning in a re-union with her colt outside the Derby Barn, but her temper was always hair trigger.

"You think he's better than Sweepstakes?" she demanded.

"Now, Mrs. Nickel, I didn't say that," Quincy replied. "You know I think Sweepstakes has a real chance or we wouldn't be here. He's a game little colt and he's a darn sight better than they think."

"They get me so mad I could spit," Gladys said, her pugnacity diverted. "The whole crew of them, but especially that Jerry Neal."

Brewster Nickel smiled. "The more they knock him, the more we'll collect when he wins, Glad. If they keep the odds where they are, we can collect a hundred grand by betting less than a thousand."

"What for?" she asked. "We'll get more than that in the purse."

"Oh, sure," her husband agreed. "But I enjoy cashing in on longshots. Everybody told us the Nickel Cups wouldn't be successful, either, and if we'd listened to them, I'd still be slinging hash and you'd still be juggling trays."

Ed Quincy cleared his throat. "Remember, I never said Sweepstakes would take the Derby for sure. I only said he's got a chance."

Just then, Sweepstakes was led onto the track for his gallop and if the Nickels heard Quincy they didn't answer.

He shrugged and raised his binoculars. If Sweepstakes didn't win the Derby—whatever the odds—the Nickels would be getting themselves another trainer, anyhow. This was a prospect which, he told himself, wasn't going to make him cry even a little bit. Having a public stable on the minor track circuit and training inferior stock for people with only a horse or two, occasionally three or four, Ed Quincy had lost a great many owners over the years and would again. But he would come up with new ones, as he always had, because, considering what he had to work with, he consistently produced a pretty fair percentage of winners. And even when he couldn't win, he was shrewd enough to drop his charges into slots where they could pick up third or fourth money and just about pay their keep.

The Nickels, though, had been an especially demanding pair. He would have quit them cold, months ago, except for the once-in-a-lifetime shot at saddling a starter in the Kentucky Derby. In Ed Quincy's modest milieu, that fact alone was the ultimate accolade, whatever Sweepstakes did—or didn't do—in the race.

But Quincy was sincere in what he had told the Nickels. He felt that the handicappers weren't paying quite enough attention to Sweepstakes' blazing speed, that they were overlooking the possibility that the small brown colt might get so far in front of the others that they'd never be able to catch him. And there could be a break in the weather. Quincy cast a prayerful look at the sky. Oh, God, if it would rain on Derby Day. Sweepstakes was a tiger on a sloppy track.

It was half an hour before the general offices at Churchill Downs were supposed to open. Even so, as Bunny Ingalls settled into the cushioned chair at her switchboard, there were three simultaneous calls.

Without saying anything beyond a cheerful, "Good morning, Churchill Downs, just a minute, please," she put them on successive holds and tended to her self-imposed first duty of every day. She dialed the Weather Bureau.

Lee Ames came in through the outer door as the forecast concluded and she beamed her satisfaction. "Fair and mild through today and tomorrow," she reported, "probably up to 75 today, no lower than 50 tonight, chance of rain only 10 percent."

Lee smiled at her in obvious good humor. By the big weekend, she would be checking the weather hourly. "Let's pray it stays this way," he said.

"I've been praying," Bunny assured him. She nodded toward her switchboard. "I've got three people on here. If any of them are for you, shall I tell them you're in or out?"

"They're probably all for me and they probably all want tickets to the Derby," he said in mock exasperation, "but you might as well put them through. Give me half a minute to get to my desk." He disappeared through an inner door.

Amusingly, all three were for Lee Ames and if they were all requests for tickets, as he had predicted, it was just too bad, Bunny thought, making the connections in turn. Churchill Downs had been completely sold out for over two months.

Before Lee had finished with the third call there was a fourth for him. "He's busy on another line at the moment," Bunny reported. "Will you wait or would you rather—?"

The man spoke quickly. "I'll hold on."

To Bunny, whose stock-in-trade was voices, this one sounded tense. She frowned slightly, puzzling over a sense of familiarity she couldn't quite place.

She opened the connection. "Mr. Ames is still busy."

"It's all right, I'm holding."

She did know that voice but she still couldn't put a name to it. No matter. Lee's phone was free.

Whoever the caller was, the conversation was remarkably brief, but even as Bunny pulled the cords which ended it Lee signaled her. All his easy geniality was gone.

"Get me The Colonel, Bunny, his wife won't want to disturb him this early but say it's vital. And, Bunny."

"Yes, sir?"

"Don't put anybody through until I tell you. I'm going to be too busy making calls of my own for some time."

FOUR

I N LEXINGTON, KENTUCKY, on such an April morning, it was
virtually impossible to remember that elsewhere there existed worlds of endeavor which did not revolve around the
propagation, training, racing and merchandising of fine horseflesh. As far as Jim York's gaze could reach and, he knew, for
miles beyond any horizon visible from his room in the guest
house at Charlie Talbot's T-Square Stud, this was an area of
white-fenced paddocks, impressive stables and beautiful animals.

T-Square Stud concerned itself only with thoroughbreds,
York's own prime interest, but other breeding farms in the vi-
cinity also produced pedigreed hunters or standardbreds for
harness racing. In this place made famous throughout the
world for the quantity and quality of its champions, a ridiculous jingle—which he didn't have quite right—kept nagging at
the back of York's aching head:

> *Roses are red,*
> *Violets are blue*
> *And some people claim*
> *That their grass is blue, too.*

York had been rejected by the marines in World War II because he was color-blind, so he had no way of judging if the
grass around Lexington really was unique. He cared less. It
was in any event a great advertising gimmick, one he admired
for the subtlety with which it put all rival breeding centers
on the defensive, including those in other parts of the state.
Only three or four counties lay in the limestone-rich basin

which nurtured the famous "blue" grass.

Water filtered through that same limestone was used in the equally notable Kentucky bourbon and the potency of this York was in no mood to question. His pounding head gave all-too-convincing testimony. The truth was, he decided as he turned away from the window, he was sicker than a goddamn hound and this, by an inevitable association of ideas, suggested that what he required immediately was a little hair of the dog. He lifted the receiver of the bedside phone and pressed the button marked DINING ROOM.

"Yes, Mr. York," Reginald said with gentle enthusiasm, "I'm on my way right now."

Amused respect made York smile. The world's finest hotels —even the chain he himself once owned—never gave him better service than Charlie Talbot offered visitors at T-Square Stud. On the other hand, York hadn't picked up any two-hundred-thousand-dollar racehorses at those accommodations.

He thought of the yearling produced by Lucky Jim's own sire and dam that Talbot was proposing to sell him on this trip. Charlie was certainly asking too blasted much for it. A quarter of a million might no longer be an unusual figure for a really fine thoroughbred, but the percentage of colts which ever actually became stakes winners was pretty low. The probability that this one would perform on Lucky Jim's level was even lower. Among horses, as with people, genetic lightning seldom struck full brothers or sisters.

And he, York, already owned Lucky Jim. Still, when Lucky Jim won the Kentucky Derby, the yearling would be valuable for his future stud potential if nothing else.

Reginald was already at the door, his dark face in sharp contrast to his white housecoat. He bore a tray on which there were three tall glasses of tomato juice mixed with beer— York's usual morning-after concoction—and a silver bowl of ice cubes which could go, if so desired, with bourbon or scotch. Antique cut-glass decanters filled with these staples were standard equipment in all guest rooms at T-Square Stud.

78

"You going to be wanting a little breakfast?" asked Reginald.

York shuddered, reaching for the first glass. "You know better than that, Reginald."

"Yes, sir," agreed Reginald, grinning sympathetically, "but I rather ask you than you ever have to ask me. Mr. Talbot went over to the stallion barn but he'll be back soon, he says to tell you, or you can join him there. He has a couple of the visitors with him and some of the other guests is downstairs in the dining room."

York envisioned the damask-walled room below, smaller but no less elegant than the one in T-Square's main house where last night Talbot had hosted a dinner party for sixty. There might be half a dozen fellow guests at the table now, all of them eating. The financier shuddered again and downed the second glass hurriedly.

"I may live, Reginald, but it's going to be awhile before I'm feeling sociable," he said. "When are we supposed to start for Opening Day?"

"The bus will be leaving for Churchill around noon." This was T-Square's own bus, providing luxurious transport for guests, with its own galley and chef and a bar behind which Reginald himself would preside.

"What time is it now?"

"It's coming on ten o'clock."

"All right, Reginald, I guess I'll be able to make it."

Reginald withdrew, smiling, but there followed an almost immediate knock on the door. At York's "Come in," Buddy Sheffield entered.

York glared at the tall trainer who dwarfed his own compact figure. "Jesus," he said, his elaborate disgust only partially humorous, "you look so healthy you make me feel worse than I did before and I wouldn't have thought that was possible." He polished off the final glass and slumped onto the side of the bed.

"I know," Buddy said, "it's a rotten thing to do to a guy

79

with a hangover, show up all bright-eyed and bushy tailed, but you said you wanted me to get here in time for a look at Lucky Jim's brother before we started for Churchill."

"I did," York groaned, "but that was before last night's party."

"You just get up?" Buddy asked.

"About ten minutes ago."

The trainer's practiced eye took in the empty glasses on the tray. "You'll start feeling better in a little while," he promised.

"I hope so, because at the moment I'm ready to turn myself in." York looked up at Buddy as a thought occurred to him. "I suppose, seeing me like this, you're pretty happy to be off the sauce right now?"

Buddy grinned. "I've got to admit I never hanker after the hangovers."

"But you do hanker for a drink sometimes?"

"I don't even think about it anymore. It's been four years you know, Jim."

"Yes, I know. But it seems you'd really want a drink once in awhile, anyway. I'm sure I would if I ever quit."

"If you ever quit, Jim, you could have a drink. You're not an alcoholic, even though you overdo it now and then. As a matter of fact, if I know Kentucky at Derby time, you'll probably wake up with a hangover every morning you're here."

"Boy, that's a great prospect."

"But I'm a different breed of horse." Buddy shrugged. "Even if I wanted a drink, I wouldn't take it. Luckily, I don't want one. In case you were worrying." His tone was suddenly bleak.

York got up from his perch on the bed. "Oh, for the love of God, don't go self-conscious on me, Buddy. You ought to know by now I'm not worrying. It just struck me, that's all, how it would feel to be you, with all the Derby parties and not being able to have even a glass of champagne. None of my business, just curiosity. Don't go off half-cocked."

80

Buddy forced a laugh. "Okay, I won't," he said and then, breaking what threatened to be an uncomfortable silence, added, "Listen, why don't I take a preliminary look at that yearling while you shower?"

"Good idea," York agreed. He went on into the bathroom, then remembered and stepped back through the door. "Hey, wait a minute, you didn't tell me about Lucky Jim himself. How did his training go at Churchill this morning?"

"Right on schedule, couldn't be better. I'll see you later."

Jim York stared at the door which had all but slammed behind the other man. Now he was a little worried. He hadn't been when he first started questioning Buddy. At least, he hadn't been conscious of worrying then. But when he unexpectedly popped back through the bathroom door, Buddy had been standing absolutely still, his eyes fixed on the two decanters on the dresser. And he hadn't been admiring the cut glass, that was for damn sure.

York dropped his pajama coat onto the floor as he started slowly back into the bathroom and shivered, but not from the chill. He was remembering how often before he had picked up warning signs almost telepathically and averted trouble. York's lips tightened. He wasn't sure yet, but nothing—nothing—must jeopardize Lucky Jim's chance to win the Kentucky Derby.

And if that should mean taking the horse away from Buddy Sheffield, he would do it. Jim York hadn't parlayed a builder's license into fifty million dollars on sentiment.

Jerry Neal took the call from Los Angeles at 10:30, which is the busiest time of morning in any racetrack press box, entries for the next day of racing having just been released. In this case, the entries were for Monday, two days away, but the procedure was the same, and each of the local newsmen was industriously typing up the data upon which his readers might base their selections.

In the Churchill Downs press box, on this Opening Day,

there were a score or so of additional reporters from elsewhere, present only for Derby Week. They, too, were hard at work, turning out background stories on the horses, owners, trainers and jockeys who were involved in this year's classic.

Locals and outsiders combined, they were practically lost in the vast reaches of the accommodation, which was one of the finest and assuredly the biggest of any in racing. Still, the comparative handful of reporters, the incessant chattering of the teletype machines and the constant ringing of telephones raised a considerable clatter.

Jerry Neal wasn't even conscious of it. He replaced the phone receiver with a bang, his shoulders characteristically hunched, his black eyebrows drawn into a scowl above his narrow hawklike nose. He was furious with himself for having just agreed to fly out to California for Gordy Cowdin's funeral. Jerry loathed funerals. For that matter, he was on record as absolutely loathing California.

But he had devoted too much copy to the premise that he was Gordy Cowdin's best friend and he had to go. It was his editor who had ordered him to the West Coast rites. A decade ago, he might have used the fact that it was Derby Week as an excuse and it might have availed. The annual excitement in Louisville seemed to inspire Jerry Neal to heights of malice and this had made his celebrated series of "Kolumns from Kentucky" a delight to the rest of the nation, though it usually made the local gentry froth at the mouth. Unhappily, jet-age travel meant that he could attend the funeral and still not miss a single Kolumn.

Even as he bemoaned his fate, however, Jerry's professional mind had turned automatically to the piece he would write now. He had already rushed out a story on Gordy's death—it was in today's papers—and he had not intended to repeat that particular note for awhile, but this new development changed his mind. He began to organize ideas and phrases as he went to get coffee from the press box sandwich bar and took it back to his typewriter.

The sheet he'd been working on was still in the machine and he began to roll it out of his way. It was actually startling to read what he had been writing before the phone call interrupted him:

This year's leading candidate for Good Clean American honors must certainly be Buddy Sheffield, trainer of multimillionaire Jim York's Lucky Jim, who is currently favored overwhelmingly to win next Saturday's Run for the Roses.

Buddy, as I personally have been informed by several hundred admirers, hasn't touched a cigarette or allowed one drop of liquor to pass his lips for more than four years.

So what was Buddy Sheffield doing in the bar across from Churchill Downs?

Jerry smiled, folded the paper and put it in his coat pocket with a wad of other notes. He had more immediate stuff for today's column, but this wasn't a bad little tongue-in-cheek jolt—and strictly libelproof, whatever its implications. He might use it later, if he had space.

After he got back from that damned funeral.

FIVE

THE DREAM WAS always the same. If it was a dream. By now Gabe Hilliard didn't really know, it had come to be so much a part of him. Maybe it was memory, all of it, even what he thought of as the "mountain" sequence, though how he could have really been up in the mountains—and then walk to where they finally found him—nobody could figure.

Maybe it was a dream.

In any case, it invariably began with his stumbling through the shimmering spider webs, feeling them break and wrap themselves clammily around his neck and arms. That made him shudder but it was the best part in the end, with its cold and the blessed dampness.

Mostly he would find himself pushing endlessly through saffron-yellow walls of arid grasses so tall they obscured everything else. They crackled noisily as he thrust them apart with his bleeding hands and rustled pervasively as they closed again behind his small and desperately lonely passage. Toward the end he would be lying in the broiling sun, face downward at the side of a road.

There had been drought in Tennessee the year he was five. Gabe could still taste the dust, so fine and dry it sifted into his parched mouth even when he compressed his cracked lips. Strangely, the wasps or hornets never came into the dream. Unless he was unconscious when they attacked? That would make sense. He had been in a coma when Tillie had stumbled across him.

But if it was a dream, how could he be going over it in his mind this way, analyzing it? And yet, if he was awake, why would he still be choking on a mouthful of powdery hot dust and feeling so utterly, irretrievably alone?

"Would you care for some fruit, sir?"

The voice startled him into wakefulness. He twisted to examine a stewardess who seemed to tower over him, her smile as professionally placed as her jaunty cap.

"What?"

"Some fruit, sir?" She gestured toward the cart she was pushing down the aisle of the plane.

Gabe had an almost overwhelming desire to snarl at her. She deserved to be snarled at. He was damn sure that if there was a manual for stewardesses—and there must be—there'd be something in it about not waking passengers out of a sound sleep to ask stupid questions. But if he did tell her off, he'd probably hit the headlines on every sports page in the country, as he had before and for less. He could see the bold print now:

GABE HILLIARD IN ROW WITH STEWARDESS

Which would be an interesting switch, at that. Ordinarily, it was stewards he fought with.

He grinned up at her, amused by the idea. "I don't want any fruit, but I would like some ginger ale," he said.

When she returned with his drink and he thanked her, her answering smile was less impersonal. Gabe had real charm when he chose to exercise it. Though not much over five feet tall, he was a seasoned athlete, built in perfect proportion. His face was unmistakably adult. Years of exposure to all kinds of weather had marked its strength, but his eyes held a quality of boyish mischief which many women found irresistible.

Sipping the ginger ale, Gabe's glance caught the headlines of a paper being read by a man across the aisle:

GORDY COWDIN KILLED IN CAR WRECK
HILLIARD RIDES MAGICIAN IN DERBY

And just below, to the left, Jerry Neal's black-bordered piece on GORDY'S LAST RIDE.

Gabe's lip curled. Despite telling Nick he wasn't going to look at the papers, he had, of course, and the shameless sentimentality of Neal's column disgusted him. If Neal had written about him like that, he'd be spinning in his grave. Only Gordy, poor devil, wasn't even in his grave yet and Neal would never have written about Gabe Hilliard like that, anyway.

Gabe sighed. He'd never cared much for Cowdin's crowd, but he'd raced against the other jockey a thousand times and there was no way to separate Gordy's death from his own chance to ride in the Derby. They were tied together in Gabe's mind as inevitably as they were bracketed in the headlines. He wasn't going to let it affect his riding, but it did bother him somewhat. Almost superstitiously. Because, to begin with, he'd been supposed to be on Dashing Lad until Orv Scott, Tom Richardson's trainer, assigned Ferdy Garcia instead, an unexpected move Gabe still couldn't understand. But it had left Gabe in a position to accept the mount on Freeway, a deal he much preferred—and that had blown up three weeks ago after his fist fight with Shelby Todhunter.

Now here he was again, on the plane to Louisville to ride Magician. As if he had to be in the Derby, were meant to be in it, even if Gordy Cowdin had to die to make it possible.

The unbidden corollary thought—that after all this he'd have to win—made Gabe feel slightly guilty, because he wanted to win so much. He always did. It made him so furious when he lost that he wasn't fit to talk to until he calmed down. This was what had started his troubles with the press, the fool reporters who used to intercept him as he stalked off the track to ask, "How come your horse didn't make it, Gabe?"

They didn't do that anymore, though. They'd learned better.

Gabe leaned back in his seat, thinking that the Kentucky Derby really shouldn't be different from other races. But it was, and not just to him or the other jockeys. To everybody. It was as if winning the Derby were like winning all the races in the world, wrapped up in one.

That still didn't quite express the way he felt about it, though. Even the losers got something out of taking part in it, as he had in the three he'd already ridden and lost, as he would this time. Because portents and superstitions aside— and despite Nick's assurances—the Derby was going to be tough. He hadn't seen Lucky Jim run yet, but the favorite was undoubtedly the class of the race. Gabe knew Freeway from personal experience and the horse was even better than his partisans realized, he had to be, to accomplish what he did with Shelby Todhunter mismanaging him.

Dashing Lad? Gabe had ridden him too, but not since the previous summer at Saratoga. He looked pretty good so far, but the difference between a two-year-old and a three-year-old in horses was much like that between a boy soprano and an opera star. Some kids improved after their voices changed and some could never again do much more than carry a tune.

Then there were the longshots: Double Seven, Davie's Pride and Sweepstakes. How they would do was anybody's guess.

He had, Gabe realized, omitted Armada. Perhaps because he didn't want to think of Lisa and Morgan Wells. Gabe had heard the scuttlebutt about his ex-wife and his ex-agent. He'd have to see them when he got to Kentucky. But he didn't want to think about them now.

He reached above him and pressed the buzzer to summon the stewardess. He was still thirsty.

Tom Richardson hadn't known Gabe Hilliard was aboard the plane until the jockey went by on the way from the lavatory. Tom's immediate impulse to say hello died instantly as Gabe strode along the aisle without looking either right or left, walking as "chilly" as he rode his races. It was probable that Gabe was deliberately ignoring him since the jockey was reputed to have eyes in the back of his head and Tom, with his red hair and his bulk, was pretty hard to overlook.

There would have been little point in their sharing this trip, anyway. In fact, now that Tom considered the possibility, it would have been downright embarrassing, although he, personally, had the greatest admiration for Gabe Hilliard.

The fact that Gabe had the mount on Magician in the Derby and Tom's horse, Dashing Lad, would be ridden by Ferdinando Garcia would not have affected either man under ordinary circumstances. In a profession where most of its members would eke out a bare subsistence throughout their careers, a top jockey might be offered a choice of several stakes runners and it was accepted practice that he would pick the one he thought had the best chance to win. Or his agent would, which was the same thing.

Naturally, this was no guarantee that the decision was correct. There were stories of jocks wrong-guessing in any number of rich events, including the notable Kentucky Derby of 1964, when the fabulous Bill Shoemaker opted for Hill Rise instead of Northern Dancer—and then was beaten by the colt he had rejected.

It was also understood that an owner was entitled to engage the rider he considered best for his horse. Or his trainer was, which was definitely not the same thing in this instance. Because Tom had wanted Gabe on Dashing Lad and could have had him, since Gabe, unlike some riders, would have honored the tentative agreement made last summer, but Orville Scott had flat out refused to work with him.

Tom wondered for the hundredth time what it was Orv had got into his craw about Gabe Hilliard. It was always difficult to get his head trainer—Marshfield had several—to talk about anything but horses. Orv was so much the stereotype of the tall silent Texan that Tom sometimes found him laughable. However, Orv had been neither closemouthed nor comic that Florida morning some months ago.

They had been watching Dashing Lad on the track at Hialeah, working toward his first race of his three-year-old season, when Tom suggested having Gabe fly in from California to ride the colt.

"Garcia's all right," Orv had said. "Handles the horse as well as anybody."

"Yes, I know," Tom said. "Garcia's one of the best, he was leading boy in Canada for two years." That Ferdy Garcia was also Scott's new son-in-law had no relevance at the moment. The fact did not even occur to Tom. "But if Gabe's going to ride Dashing Lad in the Kentucky Derby, they might as well race together ahead of time."

"Thought we'd put Garcia on him in Louisville, too."

"What?" Tom had turned to face him, startled. "But I thought it was understood Gabe's going to ride him. If the Lad's got what it takes to go all the way, we don't know that yet."

"He'll go all the way. Barring accident."

"Then you think Gabe would be better on Sparky, is that it?"

"No, Rudy Maldonado's still set for Sparky." Orville Scott's slate-gray eyes were not visible through his dark glasses, but Tom could see the muscles tighten along the sunburned jaw. "I've been with you nineteen years this June, Mr. Richardson," he said. "And we always got along. It's your colt, but if you're going to put Hilliard on Dashing Lad, somebody else is going to saddle him for you. Not me. And that would go for any horse we've got in the barn, in any race."

You get to know a man pretty thoroughly after almost two decades, even in the formal relationship the Texan had insisted upon retaining. Tom was aware that his trainer meant exactly what he had said.

"If you feel that strongly about it, Orv," Tom said, relinquishing the jockey. "But I sure can't figure what's got into you. *You* were the one who talked to Gabe about riding Dashing Lad. Don't you remember, at Belmont after he won the Futurity, when it looked like the Lad might turn into a good one?"

"That was last year, Mr. Richardson," Scott had said, and just stood there, leaning on the rail, refusing to discuss the subject any further.

Tom sighed, trying to get comfortable on the plane seat which had never been designed for a man of his size. It was a peculiar Derby for him this year. He didn't have the horse he wanted and he didn't have the jockey he wanted. No Sparky. No Gabe. No Rudy Maldonado, come to think of it, and he'd be riding against them in the Derby, too, on the California horse, Freeway, which Gabe had also been supposed to ride. A peculiar Derby for a lot of people.

Tom was momentarily depressed but then, with the built-in optimism necessary to all horsemen, he brightened. Sparky was okay—he had talked to the farm again before he boarded the plane in L.A.—and Dashing Lad might, after all, be as good as Orv insisted. And Ferdy Garcia was a fine jockey. If Gabe beat them on Magician, well, he'd be beating Lucky Jim too on a Marshfield-bred horse. This wouldn't affect the outcome of the fifty-thousand-dollar bet with Charlie Talbot—Dashing Lad would have to finish somewhere ahead of Lucky Jim for that—but it would be some consolation, anyway. A hell of a lot of consolation.

Tom wondered again at the enmity between Orv and Gabe and told himself again that it was none of his business. But now a dreadful possibility occurred to him. If the two should clash when they came together inevitably at Churchill Downs, Gabe might be suspended for fighting. It had happened before. And if it happened this week, he'd be off Magician, too.

"Oh, no," Tom groaned to himself. "Let him at least ride Magician, please." Then he had to laugh at how amazed Gabe Hilliard would be if he could even imagine that Tom Richardson, the damn fool, was practically praying over him.

SIX

AT HIS DESK in Atlanta—no Saturdays off for him—the Chief of Claims for Great Southeastern Insurance listened impatiently to his son's report of "nothing new" from Liberty Bell Park in Philadelphia.

"All right," he interrupted. "It's 11:15, I have a man who'll be relieving you at noon. The minute he does, you start for the airport."

This time it was the son who broke in. Joyously. "You m-mean I can get out of here? Great! And if I never see another barn again, that'll be too soon."

"Well, you are going to see another barn," the Chief informed him curtly. "Only this one's at Churchill Downs. I want you to get there as fast as you can. I don't have anyone else I can use in Louisville."

"Y-yes, sir." The son's voice was resigned.

"I'll put Miss Ormond on the line in a minute, she'll give you your flight number, who to contact when you arrive, the full details. But, listen, Alan, you take care around there. Tully Borden's in the hospital with a couple of broken ribs and concussion, just lucky he isn't worse."

"You mean he was attacked? That would prove he was getting close to—"

"No!" the Chief roared in disgust. "When are you going to get it through your head that insurance investigation isn't something out of a TV melodrama? Tully wasn't attacked. He'd barely made contact with the subject. The young idiot got himself run over by a horse and you watch out you don't do the same."

In the semigloom of his hotel room in Louisville, Shelby Todhunter, Jr., sat upright on his bed and shouted at his father. "What the hell do you think you're doing?"

Doc Todhunter straightened from his search of the suitcases. The older man's hair was thinner, his face was lined, but the resemblance between the two was remarkable.

"I was looking for these," Doc said sadly, holding out a bottle of varicolored pills. "I realized on the plane last night you must be taking them again. But I hoped I wouldn't find them. All the time I was going through the bags, knowing they had to be there, I still kept hoping."

Shelby leaped off the bed. "Well, you can just put them

back where you found them," he blustered. "And get out of this room. You had no right to come in here."

"If you hadn't been too stoned, you'd have remembered to lock the door."

"Damn it, I said put them down and get out!"

Doc shook his head. "You know I can't leave them."

Shelby started toward his father. "If you try to walk away with that bottle—"

"I wouldn't attempt that again, Shel. You caught me by surprise the last time. I didn't really believe you'd jump me, I thought you were just blowing off steam." His voice broke at the unhappy memory. "But I'm not off guard now, Shel, and we're in Louisville. And there's no Gabe Hilliard to cover for you with the papers."

"He didn't cover for me."

"All right, there's no Gabe to cover for *me* with the papers."

"I'd have killed you if he hadn't butted in."

"Maybe you'll get lucky this time," said Doc bitterly.

Shelby hesitated. At the moment, literally, all he wanted to do was grab his father by the throat, but the old man was watching him too warily. There was no way Shelby could get those pills without raising such hell that half the city would come running. The basic problem, though, was that he didn't know anyone in Louisville who could supply him. At home he would have simply stalked out of the room and bought some more pills, but if his father dumped these, he'd be left without.

He swallowed, letting his hands fall to his sides, deliberately relaxing his fists. Then he took a deep breath and switched on one of the lamps. "Dad, you know I wouldn't do that again. I was out of my head then. I've been sorrier about that than you'll ever believe."

Doc's face looked gray. "I'd like to believe it, Shel, but you certainly haven't acted as if you were sorry."

"I know. But it's true, anyway. I just . . . I guess I'm not very good about saying it." Shel turned away and bowed his head. "I guess I'm not very good at anything, Dad," he said. "You're the one who picked Freeway out at Keeneland and you're the one who's really training him. But I'm claiming the credit. I feel lousy about that, too."

"God, Shel, I don't care."

"Dad, I really did try to quit for awhile, that wasn't a lie. I want to quit, I swear! There's you and Mom and now there's Paula."

His father crossed the room quickly to stand behind him, hopeful and pleading. "If you'll just let us help."

Shelby half faced him. "You really think I could make it?"

"I know it!" Doc said. "Believe me, if you'll—"

Shelby lunged, grabbing the bottle of pills and shoving his father off balance. Before Doc could recover, Shelby was in the bathroom, the door securely locked. He listened tensely for a moment, then heard his father walk slowly away. After awhile Shelby took a chance and checked the bedroom. It was empty and the door to the one adjoining was closed. Shelby tiptoed over and pushed the bolt into place.

Reminding himself that he would have to be more careful from now on, he swallowed a couple of the pills. Paula and the two mothers would be getting into Standiford Field in a few hours and there would undoubtedly be newsmen at the airport, too. He wanted to have himself under complete control before he faced them.

SEVEN

AT 11:45—though it was still a very long wait until today's first "Call to the Post"—the early birds had already started to line up in front of the admission booths when

Artie Dobermeyer checked in through the employees' gate.

The uniformed guard who swung it open had worked the local racing circuit almost as long as Artie had. "Hey," he said, "you're back on the job. I missed you over at Keeneland."

"I'm only working Louisville now," Artie said. "The rest of it's getting to be too much of a grind for me, and my house is here. But I'm sure glad we're open again. I was pretty tired of not working, too."

"Must be nice to be a pari-mutuel man and be rich enough to lay off when you want to," the guard joked. "Me, I got to keep working or the kids don't eat."

"Yeah, well," Artie said. "So you're rich other ways. You got kids."

"I got grandchildren," the other boasted. "Four of them now. You knew my daughter had her second, didn't you?"

The guard still had his wife, too, Artie thought as he went on. But Millie'd been gone almost two years now.

The momentary pang was forgotten as Artie walked toward the pari-mutuel clerks ahead of him. They were standing, waiting for their assignments as sellers or cashiers of the bright betting tickets which would shortly be clicking from their machines, and judging by all the laughter and wisecracks, they were as glad as he was that it was Opening Day.

Most of them were guys Artie had known all his working life at one track or another throughout the country. Since the smaller race meets last only a few weeks or a couple of months at a time, the pari-mutuel clerks—like the horsemen and all but a handful of the higher officials and executives—went through seven or eight moves a year as they followed their individual itineraries. Some of the fellows in this courtyard hadn't seen each other for months, perhaps, but some of them had probably just come from side-by-side windows at Keeneland or Florida.

But wherever they had been or however recently they had met or whatever the number of times they had repeated a similar scene, Opening Day at Churchill Downs in the spring, with the Derby only a week away, was special.

Artie had not quite reached the little groups of men when Lee Ames came up beside him. "Hello, Artie. It's good to see you back."

At Churchill Downs, unlike a lot of tracks where Artie had worked, it was not unusual for the president to know most of the employees. But it had been Artie who was assigned the task of taking Lee on his original tour of the pari-mutuel department years earlier, so there was a particular bond between them.

"It's good to be getting back, Mr. Ames," Artie said. "I missed old Churchill. And it looks like it's going to be a great day."

"Beautiful," Lee agreed. And then added the inevitable, "Let's hope it stays like this for the Derby."

"Amen."

Lee hesitated. "This wasn't an accident, our running into each other, Artie. I was keeping an eye out for you."

"You were?"

Lee nodded. "There's a favor you could do for me, if you will."

"Just name it, Mr. Ames, it's done."

"Are you going to the meeting tomorrow morning?"

For a second, Artie couldn't imagine what Lee was talking about. Then it dawned on him. "You mean that union thing?" He shrugged. "I don't know, I was thinking of skipping it, all it'll be—" He stopped. "Is that what you want? For me to go?"

"I'd appreciate it, Artie. There aren't too many people I'd mention this to, and keep it strictly under your hat, but I've had a phone call that something rough might be coming."

"Trouble with the union you mean?"

Lee frowned slightly. "It doesn't seem possible. We've always gotten along here at the Downs and my tip isn't definite, just something that was overheard. I'll know from other sources the minute this new man makes his speech tomorrow.

But you can give me an angle on the clerks themselves better than anyone else and I may need that."

"Well, sure, I'll go."

"Contact me at home after the meeting breaks up, will you? I'll be anxious to hear."

"I'll call right away."

Lee clapped a hand on Artie's shoulder. "Good," he said. "I knew I could count on you."

Artie was warmed by Ames' confidence but somehow, as he joined the other clerks, the glow of Opening Day had dimmed a little.

EIGHT

MORGAN WELLS had been increasingly uneasy since the conversation with Mister Mack at Laurel the morning before. Engrossed as Morgan was in his unhappy certainty that Lisa was resolutely avoiding him, it had taken considerable time for him to realize the full import of what Mister Mack had said: That he had neither seen Lisa nor heard from her for a week.

It was then, without even formulating his chill sense of foreboding, that Morgan had decided to leave for Kentucky immediately rather than wait until the next afternoon, as he had planned.

The pleasure of sharing the festivities with Lisa, which Morgan had been anticipating before the break between them, had nothing to do with his arrangement to spend Derby Week in Louisville. He would have done this in any case, since his jockey, Donnie Cheevers, was to ride Armada.

If you were a good jockey's agent and your rider were entered in a big feature at an unfamiliar track, you set up at least a couple of other mounts for him in earlier races that afternoon so that he could get the feel of the course.

Since Donnie had never even seen Churchill Downs before, he would also make a morning tour of the oval on foot, to get the gut feel of the surface, to test its resiliency, to check for deeper or firmer areas—for paths, if any—and, above all, to acquaint himself with Churchill Downs' stretch. This was the longest in America, and at least one Derby was supposed to have been lost because the jockey in front misjudged the finish line and relaxed on his horse too soon.

There were only two or three other reinsmen in the country who put out this special effort, but it was one of the things which would eventually make Donnie a really great rider. Walking and riding were two different things, however. Lining up the proper pre-Derby races was still vitally important.

Morgan picked up a couple of speeding tickets on the way, but when he got to Louisville Lisa hadn't checked into the Crown Hotel. Nor had her parents, Mr. and Mrs. Stephen Cardigan, the room clerk added, going through the three reservations which had been made at the same time, nor Mr. Mack Herman.

"Mister Mack will be here in the morning," Morgan said automatically. "He's leaving Maryland with the horse tonight."

"That's Armada, isn't it? The Canadian horse?"

Morgan turned away without answering. Reaction had set in. He hadn't realized how desperately he had convinced himself that Lisa would be at the Crown. The room clerk sniffed and replaced the cards in his file. It didn't matter to him whether the Cardigans showed or not. Every available space had been booked since the middle of February and no reservations for Derby Weekend could be cancelled after April 15th.

Irrationally, considering the week of silence, Morgan

phoned Baltimore to ask if there had been any messages since he left. There had been one. From a man. Morgan hung up before the switchboard girl could give him the name.

Then, clutching at straws, Morgan tried to reach Mister Mack at his trailer court in Laurel. Mrs. Mack, who answered the community phone, said her husband was napping, but that he hadn't heard from Lisa, either.

"Is something wrong, Morgan?" her gentle voice asked, responding to the urgency in his own.

"Oh, well, no, Mrs. Mack, I'm sure not. I just wondered if she'd called, that's all."

Morgan's effort to sound casual failed, though. When Mister Mack was preparing to set out for Churchill, his wife said, "Morgan sounds like he's eating his heart out, poor thing. I wish they'd make up their quarrel, whatever it is, because they're such a perfect couple."

"I'm sure they will, honey. You never saw two people more in love." He nudged her with a reminiscent chuckle. "Unless it was us. And look at the way we used to fight."

And she had replied, "What do you mean, the way we used to fight?"

It had been a hideous night for Morgan. He had finally given up any attempt to sleep and simply waited for the dawn with the growing knowledge that something was terribly wrong. Finally he had gone out to the backstretch and found Nick Chambley talking with Mister Mack. At Nick's mention that Gabe would be in from L.A. on the afternoon plane, Morgan had asked stupidly, "Gabe's on his way—here?"

"I thought the whole world knew that by now," Nick said. "It's in all the headlines."

"But why?" Morgan was utterly confused. "He's not back on Freeway, is he? I thought that was a closed book."

Nick was stunned to discover Morgan hadn't even known of Gordy Cowdin's death. "For the love of Pete, man," he demanded, "where have you been, on the moon?"

Morgan didn't reply. He stared unseeing at Nick, unable to

shake the picture of Lisa in Gabe's arms. Later, he had no recollection of driving back to the hotel or going up in the elevator to his room. All he had been able to feel as he threw himself down on the bed was overpowering relief. She had been avoiding him because she was going back to Gabe, but she was safe. Not lying dead in a ditch somewhere as he had begun to envision.

Now, waking at two o'clock after a solid six hours of sleep, Morgan began to worry again. He couldn't believe that Lisa would return to Gabe. He didn't know how he could ever have believed it, except that he had been sick with fear for her and willing to accept any explanation if only she were all right.

A sharp knock at his door brought Morgan to his feet, startled. He opened it and the taller of the two men in the corridor outside displayed a badge.

"I'm Inspector Elverson, FBI, Mr. Wells," he said, "and this is Special Agent Ted Irving of the local office. May we come in for a minute?"

Everything suddenly clicked. "Oh, my God!" Morgan said. "You're here because of Lisa, aren't you?"

"It would be better to discuss this inside," the inspector said and then, when the door to the hall was closed, "May we ask what makes you assume that?"

"Because I've been going crazy with worry over her. What's happened? Where is she?"

Elverson studied Morgan's face. "Do you mind explaining why you were worried?" His tone made it evident that he would give no information until he had been satisfied on this point.

"All right, let's clear the nonessentials," Morgan said, steadying himself with an effort. "Until I found that she hadn't even phoned her trainer—which was yesterday—I thought she was simply avoiding me. But that put her silence in an entirely different category and I began running down every lead I could think of—some pretty remote ones, I'm afraid—which would prove she was safe. Because what I'd really begun to fear was an accident. Then, when you said you were from the FBI . . ." His voice broke. "Now, for God's sake, will you talk?" The inspector hesitated. "I love her. Please!"

"I'm sorry, Mr. Wells. Miss Cardigan has been kidnapped."

Morgan went white. He stared speechlessly at the two FBI men for a second, then drew a sharp breath. "Tell me," he said. "Everything."

"Unfortunately, there isn't a great deal. We have reason to believe she left her apartment at about 6:30 last Saturday morning with either three men or two men and a woman in slacks."

Morgan swallowed. "We'd been to a concert. I left her at her door no more than five hours earlier."

"No signs of a struggle so—we're guessing—she may have been taken at gunpoint," Elverson continued. "That same morning the Cardigans got a call in Vancouver ordering them to the Waldorf in New York, and on Monday night, following further instructions by telephone, Mr. Cardigan dropped a quarter million in American money on a road outside of Tarrytown. Exactly as specified, nothing but fives, tens and twenties, all old bills, not in sequence, though the Cardigans managed to list most of the twenties."

"And?"

"Nothing, Mr. Wells. That's when we were notified, on Tuesday, when Miss Cardigan hadn't been returned after the ransom payment. And we still haven't been given an official go-ahead, the Cardigans won't permit it."

The telephone interrupted with what proved to be a call for the inspector. Elverson's part of the conversation was a series of noncommittal grunts until he said, at last, "All right, let them know I'm on my way. And make arrangements for me, will you?" He hung up and gestured his companion toward the door. "We're going to have to get back to you later, Mr. Wells. I'm sorry, but we have to leave now."

"You're going to New York," Morgan said rather than asked. "I'm coming with you."

"No, Mr. Wells, you can't do that."

"That was about Lisa, wasn't it?"

"It was connected with the case, yes."

"Then you can't stop me," Morgan said. "I have to go."

Elverson bit his lip. "I understand how you feel, believe me. But you can't do anything to help and you could do irreparable harm."

"I don't see how," Morgan said stubbornly, "they've al-already got the ransom. I have to know what's happening, Inspector, don't you see, I'll go out of my mind otherwise."

"You're a persistent man, Mr. Wells," Elverson said patiently. "I guess I can't blame you for that. But you're still going to have to stay here because anything else could jeopardize Miss Cardigan's life. And she is alive. Or, at least, she was yesterday when the kidnappers had her write a note to her parents."

"They're sure she wrote it?"

"It's unmistakably her handwriting, her father says, and she dated it yesterday morning."

"Thank God," Morgan said.

"Nothing is changed, Mr. Wells." Elverson was grim. "Except that we have even more reason to walk on eggs."

"But what did Lisa say?"

"That she was all right but she'd be killed if her parents called the police. The kidnappers are demanding another quarter million for her return."

SUNDAY

ONE

Gabe hilliard had never felt less like going to bed, despite the day of travel or the fact that his watch, now on eastern time, indicated almost two o'clock.

At The Inn, Louisville's newest and most luxurious hotel-motel, each of the bars, lounges and dining rooms had been given names made famous at Churchill Downs—the Aristides Room for the very first Derby winner, the Regret Room for the only filly ever to earn the blanket of roses and a couple of others Gabe couldn't remember, though he had noticed the waitresses there all seemed to be costumed in skintight versions of jockey pants, bright racing-silk blouses and perky riding caps.

But the Kauai King Room, where Gabe sat, was determinedly Polynesian, and the girl whose legs he was eying wore little more than an artistically law-abiding flower lei and a brief grass skirt made of plastic.

He supposed, by rights, he should have ordered something exotic to carry out the South Seas motif. He supposed, too, that he must be smashed, since the Irish coffee in front of him was his fourth or fifth. He didn't feel loaded, though, just keyed up.

Gene Firestone and Kenny Perini, sitting in the booth with him, seemed equally exhilarated. Not that you could ever tell about Kenny. He was a tight-faced, leathery son of a bitch whose expression was the same drunk or sober. He wouldn't look one bit different in the Derby, urging Double Seven on, than he did right now, steadily downing his bourbon and branch water.

Gene, who'd be up on Lucky Jim next Saturday, was entirely different. In a race, he was the devil himself, grim, tough, foolhardy, sometimes even vicious. He was currently the nation's leading rider, and this in spite of having spent more days on the ground under suspension for his tactics than any other jockey in racing history. Away from the track, he was a pink-cheeked, curly-headed cherub, so baby-faced the waitress had actually demanded proof of his twenty-three years before serving his first Kona Kai. Although tomorrow he would probably regret the number of these flamboyant mixtures he had consumed since Gene, like Gabe, was feeling an excitement which had nothing to do with liquor.

Whether it showed or not, being in Louisville to ride in the Derby carried its own heady tension.

Nick had left the jockeys hours ago, obviously worried, though he had tried to keep his words light. "You young guys may not need any sleep," he had said, "but I'm out on my feet. Remember, though, you're in Kentucky for the Derby. You're in the public eye. Any one of you sneezes in the wrong direction, it'll hit every paper in the country." He had spoken to all of them but his eyes had held Gabe's. "Whatever you do, don't forget that."

Poor Nick. He acted as if he had a stick of dynamite in his hand. With cause, perhaps, Gabe had to admit. The admonition had irritated him at the time, but maybe he ought to call it a day.

Gene's low whistle interrupted the thought. "Well, look what we got here!" he said. "Ferdy Garcia with a couple of chicks."

The others turned toward the entrance and Kenny also whistled. "I'll take either one," he said. "Or both!"

106

"Hey, Ferdy, over here," Gene called hopefully. But the jockey who had just come in, if he heard, pretended not to. He was dark and lithe, with an impassive Spanish face. Skillfully he guided the two girls into a cubicle on the far side of the lounge.

"Fat chance," Gabe told Gene. "He's keeping them to himself."

"That's a cute blonde."

"The other one's more my type," Kenny said. "I go for them Latin babes."

"Don't give us that, Kenny," Gabe jeered. "They're all your type."

"What he ought to do," Gene said wistfully, "is leave them both here for us and go home to his wife. And Gabe could maybe fix it up with that waitress he's been losing his eyes over."

"Ferdy's married?" Gabe asked in surprise.

"Months ago," Gene said, "where've you been?"

"But not enough months ago," Kenny said pointedly. "He and Peggy only got married Thanksgiving and they're expecting the baby any minute."

"I was hunting up in Wisconsin in November," Gabe said, "but you'd think I would have . . . Peggy? You don't mean Peggy Scott?"

"Yeah, that's the one, Orv Scott's kid."

"You're putting me on."

"Nope, that's who he's married to, Gabe."

"Oh, man!" Gabe said. "Orv must have gone through the roof. Did you see the way he kept the reins on her? Why, she couldn't even breathe around the barn without his say-so. As for looking at a jock . . ." He chortled. "So now he's got a jock for a son-in-law."

Kenny grinned. "The way I hear it, she did a lot more than look at the jocks."

"Come on, Kenny," Gabe protested, "that's backstretch bull. Peggy Scott's a real nice kid."

"Did I say she wasn't?" Kenny asked indignantly. "Some of the greatest kids I know got itchy pants. As far as I'm concerned, they're the best kind."

"Goddamn it!"

"Don't tell me you were trying to make her, Gabe?" said Gene delightedly.

"No way," Gabe said. "I took her out a couple of times last summer, that's all. I felt sorry for the poor kid. She had to sneak out just to go to a drive-in." He laughed mirthlessly. "That's how I found out how Scott felt about her and jockeys. He caught me bringing her home. But as to any stuff, I didn't even try. You're riding for a guy, you don't start messing around with his daughter."

"So Ferdy got the girl and Dashing Lad in the Derby, too," Kenny said. "Sometimes it pays to mess around."

Gabe's lip curled. "More power to him." He looked across at Ferdy's booth. "Marriage doesn't seem to be cramping his style any."

"You know Ferdy," Gene said. "Nothing's going to slow him down. Why, I remember once in Detroit that crazy son of a bitch had three girls out at the track, three of them on the same day, stashed away in different sections and every damn one of them was knocked up!"

"I heard that's why he took off and started riding in Canada," Kenny added.

"I heard that, too," Gabe said. "Well, I hope he has ten of them in Louisville. And all ten the night before the Derby."

"Hey, there's a thought," Gene said. "If he does have ten girls, and if each one puts him a tick off in his timing, I can beat him by two full lengths."

"That's about what I figure," Gabe said. "Lucky Jim over Dashing Lad by two lengths and Magician ahead by four."

"Now wait one cotton-picking minute," Kenny said, "you're forgetting Double Seven."

"Double Seven?" Gabe turned to Gene. "What's a Double Seven, Firestone, some kind of soda pop?"

But Gene was too engrossed in his own partisanship to join in needling Kenny. "You think you're going to be ahead of my horse by two lengths, Gabe? Forget it! And I got a hundred bucks that says—"

"So that's how they rob you," a harsh voice interrupted. "The jockeys sit down together and make a deal. Right out in plain sight, too. They don't even pretend they're giving you a fair shake."

He was a red-faced, burly drunk, from one of the several conventions at The Inn, judging by the badge pinned to his lapel. He swayed against the end of their table, regarding them with mean eyes.

"Get lost, mister," Gene said, instantly pugnacious.

"Easy, Gene," Gabe warned. "The guy's loaded, don't pay any attention to him."

The man got louder. "I don't mind losing my money," he said, "but when I drop a bundle like I did this afternoon and then I come in here and see how I was robbed, that gets me sore, you hear?"

"Look, why don't you go home and sleep it off? You'll feel better tomorrow." Kenny's tone sounded mild enough but he was getting angry, too, Gabe realized.

One of the hotel managers and a couple of other conventioneers were bearing down on the drunk.

"Ignore him," Gabe urged Kenny, "they'll have him out of here in a minute."

"Who's gonna get me out of here?" the drunk demanded. "You, you little half-pint freak?" Gabe's jaw tightened but he bit back the impulse to reply. The drunk leaned over to peer into Gabe's face. "I know who you are, you're Gabe Hilliard, the one that's always looking for a fight. Well, any time you think you can take me on, I just dare you to try it."

The manager and the conventioneers began trying to hustle the drunk away. All the way across the room he continued challenging Gabe to "Come outside and fight, you stinking little sideshow bastard."

Gabe drained his cup and slammed it back onto the saucer. He had been called a freak before. He had, in truth, heard every possible insult based upon his diminutive size. He knew he shouldn't let either the epithets or the sorehead drunk get to him. But the pleasure had gone out of the night; he was suddenly tired and dispirited.

He stared glumly across the table at Kenny and Gene, who were working silently on their drinks. The drunk had gotten to them, too. They were even smaller than he was.

Well, this freak had had enough. He was going to bed. But before he could actually move or announce his decision, Gene's irrepressible spirits had bounced back. "Hey, look," he said, "Ferdy's leaving the two chicks."

"He's just going to the john," Kenny said.

"I know, but meanwhile let's get over there and talk to them. Come on."

Kenny hesitated. "Gabe?"

"No, thanks, but don't let me stop you. I'm taking off in a minute, anyway."

The other two jockeys were already sliding into Ferdy's booth when the room's slim hostess arrived at theirs, carrying a round of drinks. She raised a questioning eyebrow on finding Gabe alone.

"They'll be back," he told her, "but we didn't order those."

"They're on the house," the hostess said, smiling, "with the manager's compliments and our deepest apologies." She shrugged charmingly. "You know how some people get when they drink but we're sorry you were bothered like that, anyhow."

She was tall, Gabe thought, pretty close to six feet, and on her the grass skirt looked better than good. His glance took in the long coppery legs, the bare tanned midriff.

And she was completely aware of his attention.

Her experienced glance having sorted glasses, she served Kenny's and Gene's drinks at the proper places. Then, deliberately, she set the Irish coffee on the table before Gabe, her full lips curved into a mischievous smile as she bent unnecessarily low to do so.

"I'm exactly five-ten and three-quarters," she said, "and when you get around to it, I also have brown hair and gray eyes and one crooked tooth in the front that I've always meant to get straightened."

Gabe grinned at her. "Don't change a thing, baby. Truth is, I didn't realize just how insulted I'd been until right this minute. I'm not sure a free drink is enough. If you really wanted to make things up to me, maybe we could go somewhere later and talk about it over another drink."

"Well, we certainly wouldn't want you to go away mad, but that's impossible," she said. Her smile, though, was still mischievous.

"Nothing's impossible."

"Getting a drink after we close is," she said. "Every bar in town shuts down when we do. Now if you'd only suggested a hamburger . . ."

Gabe corrected himself happily. "That's the best idea I've heard all night. I'm suggesting a hamburger."

"And that's the best offer I've had all night. Not the first, you understand, but the only one I've wanted to take. See you at closing time." She turned away.

"Wait a minute."

"Yes, Gabe?"

"Oh. You know who I am?"

"Of course. Your picture's all over the papers, I recognized you the second you walked in."

"That's part of it, then," Gabe said. "I meant to tell you my name and ask yours."

"You're not going to believe this, but it's Varonica, spelled with an 'a' to match the last name. Varonica Varon." She spread her slim hands appealingly. "But don't blame me for that," she said, "my mother pinned it on me. And I do mean 'pinned.' It was in the note they found on my blanket when she ditched me on the nearest doorstep!"

The telephone on the night table roused Lee Ames from a deep, dreamless sleep. He reached for it hastily in the dark before it could ring again, automatically reading the illuminated dial of the bureau clock. Four-twenty A.M.

Daylight Savings, that was. He'd set all the clocks ahead before he went to bed. Realization of the time startled him into complete wakefulness even before he heard the worry in Warren Robbins' voice. Warren was Churchill Downs' publicity director. "We've got trouble, Lee, real trouble. Otherwise you know I'd never call you at this hour."

"What sort of trouble?"

"It's Gabe Hilliard, Lee. He's at The Inn and somebody's beaten him to a bloody pulp. We're holding the lid on it, we haven't even called a doctor yet, but the way he looks, forget about his riding Magician in the Derby next Saturday. He'll be lucky if he ever rides again."

"Oh, God! Who beat him?"

"We don't know, Lee. He couldn't tell us. But I guess we need you down here. The minute we get him to a hospital, it's going to take all the influence you can muster to keep it out of the papers."

"Who's 'we'?"

"Nick Chambley, he's the one who called me, and a girl who works at The Inn. Nobody else knows about it yet."

"All right. I'm on my way. Don't do anything till I get there. I'll bring my own doctor. He can be trusted to hold his tongue. Just sit tight."

"Listen, Lee," Warren said, "Gabe's in this girl's apartment. The Black Gold Building, that's the third one to the right as you drive in, you can't miss it. The name's spelled in lights on the side. She's on the second floor, number 209."

When Warren had referred to a girl who worked at The Inn, Lee had assumed a cleaning woman, someone impersonal. Apparently, he'd been wrong.

"Okay," he said. "I'll be there with the doctor as soon as I can."

His wife stirred on her side of the bed as he hung up. "Lee? What is it?"

"Just something that's come up, honey." He rummaged hastily through the bureau for socks and underwear. "I hoped you wouldn't be disturbed."

"You're going out in the middle of the night?"

"I'll be back soon."

"It must be bad, then."

"I don't know yet, but please don't worry. I'll be dressed and on my way in a minute and then you go right back to sleep, you hear?"

She didn't obey, of course, as he had known she wouldn't even while he urged. When he had finished calling the doctor from the downstairs study, Lee found her backing his car from the garage. She slid over on the seat so that he could climb in behind the wheel.

"You really shouldn't have," he said, kissing the tip of her nose as he leaned across to open the door for her on the other side. "I wanted you to go back to sleep. But if you'll permit the familiarity at such an ungodly hour, may I say I think you're a very nice lady?"

"Well, if it's true, it must be because you're such a very nice . . ." She broke off in mid-sentence, her face twisting.

"Honey, what is it?"

"Oh, Lee, it's beginning to rain!"

TWO

THE RAIN was very slow at first. A few drops, then a few more. Then the sky opened up.

Mace Augustine burst through the door of the trailer in

Good Mary's back yard just ahead of the deluge. "Talk about luck," he said breathlessly, "one second later and I'd have been soaked." He stopped abruptly, his voice chilling. "What in the hell was that door doing unlocked? Anybody could've walked in here!"

Lisa Cardigan did not have to see him to visualize how the pale hazel eyes had darkened in the thin boyish face, nor how swiftly that seeming boyishness had vanished behind a mask of ugly, frightening temper.

Lisa made no reply, of course. None was expected of her, with the heavy tape sealing her mouth. Besides, lying on the hard narrow bunk which protruded over the driver's seat of the van with her head turned toward the carefully draped window, Mace probably thought she was asleep. Angry as he was, he held his words to a low pitch.

The simulation of sleep was a device Lisa had been using to shut out the rest of a world which had become a waking nightmare. Bound as she was, feet lashed tightly, hands cruelly tied together and then fastened to the springs under the bunk, actually sleep was impossible, though she had begun to drift into occasional unconsciousness.

Her wrists and ankles had been rubbed raw. The skin around her mouth burned from the adhesive and she was afraid her jaw had been dislocated when Mace punched her into writing the second ransom note.

Rosanna reacted to the fury of Mace's voice with an intake of breath so loud that Lisa could hear it plainly, but Rosanna also kept her words low. "I had it locked," she said. "I promise you, Mace, I locked it."

"Then what's it doing unlocked?"

"I don't know, but I swear . . ."

"God, what a stupid broad. The stupidest broad in the entire world and that's who I have to get hooked up with."

"But I did lock it." There was the sound of swift movement, then Rosanna's cry, "Mace, let go! You're hurting my arm!"

"You just forgot, admit it."

"I—I forgot. Ow!"

He had apparently given her arm a final twist before releasing her. Lisa could hear him pacing angrily up and down the narrow aisle.

After a second, Rosanna said tentatively, "Mace?"

"Shut up!"

"Mace, please, I'm sorry. I won't forget again. Was everything all right? Did you send the note?"

The opportunity to boast lessened his surliness. "Damn right I did. Put it in the box at the airport when I got off the plane and then went and hung around the entrance to the Waldorf till the mailman brought it. Pretty fast, too, didn't take him more than a couple of hours."

"You're sure? I mean, other people get special deliveries."

"Don't you think I thought of that? After he came out, I called the Cardigans. The old man started asking if she was okay, but I just said, 'Knock it off, did you get the note or didn't you?' and when he said he did, I just hung up and headed for the bus terminal."

Poor Daddy. Oh, poor Daddy!

"But, Christ, Rosanna, is that a lousy trip. We get this next bundle down here safe and I'm never setting foot in one of them crummy buses again."

He hadn't said anything about seeing Coolie Bascombe in New York. Or even talking to him. A strange omission, Lisa suddenly realized, since the man with the impassive face and the slightly slanted eyes which gave him his nickname was supposed to be a partner. The senior partner.

Rosanna hesitated and for a split second, Lisa thought she, too, was wondering about Coolie. But Rosanna only said, "I guess you got reasons, but I still can't figure why you wouldn't just fly back here the same as you flew up. You could have made it hours ago. Or else, why didn't you wait till Monday when you could pick up the money?"

"I got lots of reasons! Like I could fly up because no one's looking for somebody coming into New York, but if they're checking for somebody trying to leave with the money we already got, they'd be watching the airport. Who in their right minds would ride a bus if they had a quarter million?"

"I suppose nobody."

"I'm just playing it extra safe, though, Rosanna. Cardigan's too scared to call the cops, I could tell by his voice."

"But to go up and come back and then go up again for the rest of the money?"

"I don't mind. That bus is a sonofabitch, but what would I do if I stayed in New York? Worry, that's all. This way, I know everything's okay down here."

"Couldn't we take the trailer up there again?"

"No," Mace said firmly. "We always planned to come to Kentucky, so why change it?"

"We did change it, Coolie was the one that wanted to come here."

"Forget it, Rosanna. Day after tomorrow—Christ, this is Sunday already—tomorrow I'll fly up, grab the dough like the last time, one more lousy haul on the bus and then we got it made, baby. You and me will have half a million bucks."

Lisa knew then. Coolie Bascombe was dead. It was he who had initially planned the kidnapping and enlisted the other two to help him carry it out. But Mace must have the entire amount of the first ransom stashed under his bunk as he obviously expected to keep all of the rest. Otherwise, he wouldn't be talking about a half million for him and Rosanna. So Coolie hadn't taken his original cut and Coolie wasn't directing operations from New Jersey as Mace had told Rosanna earlier. Coolie was dead.

And must have been for some time, because he would never have thought of collecting another ransom. That had puzzled Lisa from the moment Mace broached the subject. Even she could see that the odds against a second safe collection had to be more than double those against the first. And for all the years she had known him as a racetrack hanger-on, Coolie Bascombe was a man who played the odds.

The realization sent a chill of horror through her, but the fact that Mace had undoubtedly murdered Coolie for his share of the ransom did not really change her situation. Mace would kill her in the end as inevitably as Coolie had meant to dispose of her from the very beginning. Lisa had never had any false hopes on this point. For her to have survived the abduction would have raised the percentages against Coolie's safety.

If he had lived, she would already be dead. Mace's greed had given her a few extra days, that was all. And considering how miserable these had been and how certain their ending, it seemed to Lisa now to have been a very small boon.

Rosanna had finally reached Lisa's conclusions. "You didn't say anything about Coolie," she gasped. "I really must be as stupid as you're always saying, that I didn't catch on sooner. You got rid of Coolie, didn't you? Before we ever came down here?"

There was a moment of absolute silence. Lisa held her breath.

"Well, what do you know?" Rosanna asked, taking the lack of an answer for the admission it was. Then she said practically, "Did you fix it so they can't pin it on us?"

Relief at her calm acceptance made Mace laugh. "What a dame. Here I figured you were going to give me a hard time, and you take it like I swatted a fly or something."

"You could have told me, at least," Rosanna scolded. "I don't like you lying to me. But Coolie's no skin off my nose, I hardly knew the guy. I just hope you were careful."

"I was careful, all right."

Something in his tone made Lisa shiver. She was afraid her movement might have been seen, but Mace was continuing.

"One of these days I'll tell you just how careful I was, only the hell with that right now, you come over here. All of a sudden, I got other things on my mind."

The silence which followed wasn't silent at all. It was loud with rustling and heavy breathing. Then Mace said hoarsely, "Goddamn, you get me so hot I don't know what I'm doing."

"The same here," Rosanna said shakily. "I'm trembling from head to foot. I don't know why, but it's like you were away a whole year."

She knew why, Lisa thought, trying vainly to shut the provocative sounds from her consciousness.

"For Jesus' sake, Rosanna, come on."

It was because of Coolie's murder.

"Wait, I'm taking them off as fast as I can, don't rip them."

Violent death so often aroused violent passion. Lisa had read that in some college text or other. A century ago, it seemed, in a different life.

"Hold it, baby, put this pillow under you. There, that's the way."

That was why there was so much rape during warfare.

"Oh, Mace, oh, Jesus, I can't stand it, it's so good."

"Slow down, you crazy bitch! Not so fast or it'll be over too soon. Ah, that's it, baby, yeah, baby, that's it."

Sex was the ultimate affirmation of life over death.

That was why she herself wanted Morgan Wells so terribly, why she now abandoned herself so completely to the thought of his possessing her that her wracked body throbbed unbearably. For a moment she could actually feel his hand on her breasts and her mouth beneath the tape strained to open to him.

"Okay, Rosanna, now! Now!"

Lisa knew her own surge of desire had nothing to do with the couple on the nearby bunk. They had made love in the trailer before and she had been utterly unmoved. This was something different. This was because Mace had killed Coolie. Because she herself would soon be dead.

If only Morgan could know how desperately she wanted him. With the trailer quiet at last, Lisa remembered that she had told Morgan her wanting him didn't prove she loved him. She changed her earlier wish. If only Morgan could know how much she loved him.

She did of course, forever and without reservation. She had

realized that even as he strode angrily away from her the last night she had seen him.

How happy she had been. Too happy to get to sleep right away, thinking about how she would go to the backstretch first thing the next morning and tell him. She was actually ready to leave for Laurel when Coolie Bascombe pressed the buzzer at her apartment door.

What a waste, what a sad, useless waste. A hundred years wouldn't have been enough and she wasn't going to have even one day with Morgan. The thought was too desolate. She forced herself to remember instead the good times they had had together. Dancing, the afternoon they had stood for a whole hour in front of the baby giraffe at the zoo, waiting for it to get to its feet, going to the races, visiting Armada.

How strange, she couldn't remember thinking of Armada even once before since she'd been here. Surely she had and then forgotten in this miasma of agony. No matter, she was thinking of him now. Her beautiful Armada, running in the sunlight, with his mane and tail flying, with his brushed coat glistening and those white feet flashing.

There was a superstitious mistrust of horses with four white feet, still kept alive by some horsemen as others still clung to a prejudice against gray horses, though both beliefs had been thoroughly disproven. But it was Armada's dancing feet which had caught Lisa's eye when he was just a skittering foal. What a darling he was, such a pet in spite of all his hard-won triumphs, nickering in delight whenever she approached his stall, nuzzling for a lump of sugar.

Poor Armada, he must be missing her so much. It would be awful if her being gone should send him off his feed or make him lose his edge before the Derby. But would her parents run him in the Derby now? They wouldn't be thinking of racing once they found her body.

THREE

I T WASN'T YET SIX O'CLOCK when the head of Security, Fred
Keller, drove his car in through the Main Stable Gate. The
earlier downpour had settled into a slow, steady drizzle which
sparkled in his lights as he stopped at the open door of the
gatehouse to be identified.

The yellow-slickered gateman looked in the car window.
"I'd say 'Good morning,' Mr. Keller, but with weather like
this . . ."

"Looks like it's going to hang on for awhile, too," Keller
said. "We'll have an off track tomorrow, for sure. Maybe even
for Tuesday's Derby Trial. But that's one thing we can't control. Everything else all right?"

"Oh, sure," the guard answered. "But I hear they had a little
excitement last night before I come on duty. A fire down at
Barn 16."

"Any damage?"

"No, no harm at all. Nothing burned but a bale of hay.
Somebody must've flicked a match or a cigarette on it. Luckily,
one of the stablemen spotted it right away."

Keller shook his head. "You'd think they would learn to be
careful, wouldn't you, the number of fires there've been around
racetracks and all the warning signs and lectures?" He nodded
at the guard and drove on, sighing. You could talk yourself
blue in the face and there'd still be idiots who were careless
with lighted butts and matches, they'd still use defective heat-
ers to warm their quarters or plug in worn electric cords for
their coffee pots.

Trouble was, they were so used to bales of hay, heaped bags of feed, alcohol, horse blankets, oiled leather, and old wood partitions, they forgot how excessively flammable such materials could be. At least they forgot if they'd never been around a really bad stable fire.

There were times Fred Keller could think of Bluegrass Park with the dispassionate calm of long acceptance. Now and then, though, the memory returned in such vivid detail that it blotted everything else from his mind. It was so at this moment. The rain through which he was driving could have been smoke. And once again he could hear the horses.

Bluegrass Park had been an old track, long past its prime, but so much a part of Kentucky's revered racing tradition that fans and horsemen alike had submitted to its obvious shortcomings with affectionate indulgence. Meeting after meeting, its patrons had loyally packed themselves into frontside facilities so decrepit they seemed only to be held up by the always-sparkling coat of fresh white paint. If there had been people in those kindling-wood stands when they literally exploded into flames, the tragedy might have been worse.

As it was, disaster sparked during the night. The exact cause was never established, though there were few who did not consider the hungover Buddy Sheffield's immediate loss of license an answer to the question. The only certainty was that Barn 27—where Buddy had a string of Marshfield Farms horses stabled—went up first.

From there the fire whooshed through one ancient, weathered structure after another with devastating rapidity, the awesome crackle intermingled with the shouts of men singed out of sleep and the shrieks of injured or dying animals.

There had been almost 600 horses on the grounds when the holocaust began, among them some of the country's finest thoroughbreds, and most of those who weren't trapped in their blazing stalls had been turned loose to race senselessly through the burning backstretch. They had rampaged singly or in groups, whinnying in panic, throwing themselves as frantically at fire engines as they did at fences, complicating the hopeless efforts to control the inferno.

Some had run so desperately that they weren't found for days, and some had run back into their flaming barns, which had come to represent their only security. It was a scene Fred Keller would never again entirely erase from his memory. Nor could he ever forget the morning after, when the stricken horsemen wandered about what was left of the backstretch, taking tally of the terrible loss.

Thirty-three horses had perished during the fire. Nineteen others had injured themselves so badly in their frenzied attempts to escape that they had to be humanely put to death. Dozens of grooms and horsemen had sustained greater or lesser burns. And Bluegrass Park was totally destroyed, beyond repair.

Keller forced himself out of the depressing reminiscence and reverted, almost with relief, to his earlier irritation at last night's carelessness. Then he shrugged that away, too. Foolish to get into a lather over it. It wouldn't change a thing. You simply had to accept—and guard against—the fact that the danger of fire was always there and that some of the hands would always ignore it.

But it wasn't only stablemen who were so unbelievably careless. You could drive into any gas station that was open in Louisville this minute, he supposed, and find some fellow or girl lighting up right next to the pumps, no matter how many No Smoking signs were posted. He had caught himself doing the same thing.

Keller headed for Thompson's Track Kitchen. It was too early for breakfast yet—his stomach was still on Standard Time—but some coffee would hit the spot. And maybe a couple of hot biscuits.

Lee Ames was already slumped at one of the tables and, after a swift glance at his drawn face, Keller carried his tray over and asked, "Anything wrong?"

"Do I look that bad?" Lee managed a smile.

"I've seen you looking better."

"I'm just tired, Fred," Lee said. "They rousted me out of bed in the middle of the night."

"Anything I ought to know?"

"It's nothing for your department." Lee grinned. "Your curiosity'll have to wait till later, though, too many ears in here."

Keller grinned back at him. "I do like to know what's going on. But why don't you go back to bed now? We could struggle along without you for one day."

"I suppose I ought to," Lee admitted. "Except that I wouldn't be able to sleep until I've heard what develops at the union hall this morning. I'll grab a couple of hours this afternoon."

The busboy who suddenly materialized at the table cleared his throat. " 'Scuse me, Mr. Ames, the gateman switched a call over for you."

Lee stood, his astonishment erasing all sign of weariness. "Now who the devil would be looking for me here at this hour?" he asked.

By the time he reached the phone, he'd thought of several possible answers, all of which spelled trouble. "Ames speaking," he said with some apprehension.

"Well!" said the Chief of Claims of the Great Southeastern Insurance Company. "I didn't really expect to find you there but I didn't like to call the house. Nice to see you're on the job so bright and early."

"Don't you even sleep on Sunday mornings?"

"Not when I have things on my mind. Listen, there's something you can do for me."

"I could have told you that the minute I heard your voice," Lee said.

"Seriously, Lee, I need some help."

Lee dropped the bantering tone. "Anything I can do, you know that."

"You remember Alan, don't you?" said the Chief.

"Your son? Of course, why?"

"Well, I've got him working on a case for me."

"You're kidding. How old is he now, for heaven's sake?"

"He'll be twenty-two in August."

"Good God!" Lee said. "The last time I saw him, he wasn't out of junior high school." He sighed. "Those years really get away, don't they? I suppose I wouldn't recognize him if I fell over him."

"You didn't," said the Chief, "but he recognized you the minute he saw you yesterday."

"Hold it," Lee said. "You mean he's working on something here?"

"That's why I need your help," said the Chief. "I had it all arranged for him to tie in with one of the regular outfits you've got stabled there, people who insure with us. But it seems you have a brand-new setup for the Derby horses this year and it's almost impossible for him to get close to the man we're checking. I want you to find Alan some kind of job in the Derby Barn."

"You're investigating somebody with one of the Derby horses?"

"That's right, but your new policy—"

"Who?" interrupted Lee. "And for what?"

"Well, now, look."

"Fraud?"

"No."

"Theft?"

"Nothing like that." The Chief hesitated. "I'm not trying to play guessing games with you, Lee, you know that, it's just that we really don't have a thing to go on. It's only a feeling I have that this fellow may know something about a couple of fires."

"An arsonist?"

"I knew you'd overreact if I told you," said the Chief. "We're not even certain there's been any arson. And if there were, I don't suspect this guy. Otherwise, Alan wouldn't be there. He

124

may not have sense enough to pour sand down a rathole, but he's the only son I've got."

The argument was a convincing one. "Well, I can think of something for Alan, all right," Lee said, "no problem about that, but if you're checking somebody in the Derby Barn who has the remotest connection with an arson case, you've got to tell me who he is."

"Lee, do you have any idea how much this company could be sued for if I went around making false accusations?"

"Oh, come on," Lee protested. "Remember me? I'm the guy who worked with you for two solid years in Army Intelligence, I'm not going to spread this. But I have to know."

"I suppose so," the Chief conceded. "But keep this in mind, you hear? We're not even sure the fires weren't accidental. My only interest in this man is that he may give us a hint, a lead."

"You're stalling!"

The Chief sighed. "All right. His name is Clyde Dewey but everybody calls him 'Pop.' He's Double Seven's groom."

"Oh, I know him," Lee said, "he's been around longer than I have, used to be with—" He stopped abruptly. "So that's it. You're investigating the fires at Marshfield Farms."

The Chief chuckled. "I see you haven't lost the old touch, Lee."

"I can't claim any credit for that one; Tom Richardson was telling me something about it the other day. He's got a colt in that barn, too, you know."

"Dashing Lad, yes. As a matter of fact, he's my pick to take the Derby. But whatever you do, don't put Alan in with the Marshfield crew. The little we've learned so far, Pop Dewey hates anything or anyone connected with Tom Richardson."

"So I've heard." Lee laughed. "That seems to be the old man's favorite tune. I suppose it's natural enough, he'd been with the stable for quite awhile. And am I right that he got burned in that last Marshfield fire, just before they let him go?"

"Not if you're talking about those scars on his hands he's always showing, Lee, he got those at Bluegrass Park. Damn near killed himself trying to save a colt of Tom's that he especially liked."

Lee was silent for a second. "Well, that doesn't sound as if I have to worry much about him, but it's rather amazing how things are shaping up. The old man was a Marshfield groom and now here he is with Double Seven in the same barn with Marshfield's Dashing Lad. And Buddy Sheffield used to be Richardson's second-string trainer and he's in the Derby Barn, too, with Lucky Jim."

"I follow your train of thought, Lee, but remember, nobody ever proved Buddy Sheffield was responsible for what happened at Bluegrass."

"A hell of a lot of people think so. Including Buddy."

"True, and I'm not saying I doubt it. But all we really know is that the fire started in Sheffield's tackroom and that he was so stone-damn drunk he still can't remember the fire patrol's hauling him to safety."

"Yes, I've seen the reports."

"Tell you what strikes me funny," said the Chief. "Sheffield was Pop's boss out at the track, but the old man got himself burned trying to save a horse that night and left Buddy Sheffield to take his chances."

"That's not funny around here," Lee said. "We're loaded with people who prefer horses to men. Come to think of it, there are times I feel the same way."

After getting a rundown of Alan's meager backstretch experience and ascertaining where the Chief's son could be found, Lee hung up and examined a rough sketch of the Derby Barn he carried in his pocket. It showed the distribution of the Derby colts and, as Lee had recalled while talking to the Chief, Pop Dewey's Double Seven, in Stall H, was next to Davie's Pride in Stall E, with two empty stalls in between. There were also two empty stalls on Double Seven's other side, separating him from Freeway. Since there were—so far—only eight definite starters in this year's Derby, these had been spaced as widely as possible in the huge twenty-four-stall building.

Lee forgot his cold coffee and his security chief, both waiting for him at the table, and went looking for Dennis Sullivan.

When Lee found him, the redhead from Florida was propped up—that was the only suitable description—against the linked fence along the side of the track. If he had not been so supported, Lee doubted the man could have stood. But despite his haggard appearance and the continuing chill drizzle, Dennis' greeting seemed genuinely cheerful. He nodded to where Davie's Pride was being galloped through the slop.

"That's my son Johnny on the horse," Dennis said. "He finally got here with his mother about an hour ago. They should have been here yesterday, but they had engine trouble along the way."

"Where's your wife now?" Lee asked.

Dennis shook his head. "Poor body, she's all in, it was a rough trip. I took her straight to the motel and made her go to bed." He laughed. "I'd never have got away with it but she was too worn out to argue. And I was too worn out to argue with Johnny. Nothing would do but he'd come right here and exercise Davie's Pride."

"That must be a relief to you."

"Relief, is it?" Dennis exclaimed. "It's the blessing of Heaven, because I'd have let no one else on him after what happened yesterday morning. And tell the truth, I'm not sure I would have made it into the saddle myself."

"You'd have made it," Lee said. He pursed his lips. "There's a favor I'd like to ask you, Mr. Sullivan, if you wouldn't mind?"

"Ask away. But it was me father was 'Mr. Sullivan,' rest his soul. I'm Dennis."

"Well, Dennis, for reasons of security—and this has to be kept absolutely quiet—I've got a boy I want to have working in the Derby Barn. He's a good, willing kid, I understand, doesn't know much about racing but he's been mucking stalls, hot-walking, stuff like that. He'd be a little help, at least, and I'd really consider it a personal accommodation if you'd let him work with you."

To Lee's astonishment Dennis shook his head, a flush rising in his cheeks. "A boy like that would be a big help," he said slowly. "Even with Johnny here, it's going to be hard." He swallowed. "But unless Davie's Pride takes some part of the purse in the Derby Trial, and you know there's no guarantee of that—"

"Oh, I'm not expecting you to pay him. He's on the—uh—association payroll."

Dennis brightened. "Sure, in that case, I couldn't tell you how glad I'll be. It's security, you say?"

Lee nodded. "Sorry I can't tell you more than that."

"No, no," Dennis said quickly, "I wasn't meaning to pry. I was only thinking you'd asked at the perfect time, if you want it kept quiet. With my wife and son just arriving, I can say the boy's my nephew who decided to come with them. How would that be?"

"Dennis," Lee said, "that would be fine!"

A reproachful voice behind them said, "So this is where you got to." It was Fred Keller, his curiosity unassuaged.

Lee began to laugh.

There were, as usual, considerably more than a thousand horses going through their regular training routines in the backstretch. Weather had no effect on accustomed procedure, but on this first morning of Daylight Saving Time the rhythm was definitely off.

It happened every year. Some of the stablemen, grooms, exercise boys, even trainers, had forgotten to set their clocks ahead and were now trying to hustle through their varied chores, many of them on protestingly empty stomachs, a number with hangovers they hadn't yet been able to alleviate.

And, as always, the strain of such unwonted haste had been communicated to their horses.

The hour's change had not affected Orville Scott, however. He had not been to bed at all. He stood at Dashing Lad's stall, watching the groom's labors. Outside the Derby Barn, a growing cluster of damp newsmen and photographers were waiting for Dashing Lad to be led out onto the track for his scheduled seven-o'clock workout. Unfortunately, seven o'clock was long past and there was no sign of Ferdy Garcia.

Ferdy had obviously overslept. But not in his own apartment, as Scott knew only too bitterly. If Ferdy had been home, it was he who would have rushed his wife to the hospital. Instead, Peggy Scott Garcia had had to phone for a cab.

Every time Scott thought of it, he seethed. A cab! She hadn't known where to reach her husband. And she wouldn't call her father.

Scott would never have known Peggy was in the hospital if her doctor—a thoroughbred owner himself—hadn't thought he was doing her a kindness by telling her father she was about to have her baby.

Except that the baby hadn't arrived. It was a false alarm.

"No problem," the doctor had assured Peggy as he released her into Scott's anxious care at daybreak. "Happens all the time. But those pains mean it won't be long now. You be prepared to get back here in a hurry."

Peggy had turned away, docilely allowing Scott to drive her home. She would not embarrass either of them by objecting in front of the doctor, but she hadn't said one word in the car and she had made Scott leave her in the still-empty apartment.

"I see your rider have not show up, either!"

The heavily accented voice startled Scott. He whirled to face Guy St. Pierre, the French Canadian who was Magician's trainer.

"I'm sorry, I didn't quite understand."

"I say your rider have not come and mine have not come,

too." Scott stared at him. "Gabe," St. Pierre explained, "Gabe Hilliard, he was supposed to be here by seven."

"Oh." Scott cleared his throat. "I guess they both overslept."

"It's what I think," St. Pierre said, "but I cannot wait for Gabe. I will find another boy for this morning. The horse must not keep waiting for anyone."

He stalked away, trim and somehow prissy, his narrow back rigid with annoyance. He was almost to the door when Nick Chambley caught his sleeve and urged him into the privacy of one of the guard rooms.

Well, Scott thought, if St. Pierre hadn't known of his feud with Gabe before—and the other trainer obviously hadn't—someone would set him straight in a hurry. Nick Chambley, perhaps, right now. But the fat jockeys' agent did not know Scott's reason. Even Gabe didn't, unless Peggy had told him. And she swore she hadn't, even repeating her vow last night.

How could he believe her, though, when she had also repeated her denial that the baby was Gabe's?

"Still trying to protect him?" Scott had demanded, there in the hospital.

"Oh, Daddy!" There had been another spasm then. After it passed, her voice had changed. It was calmer. "Please, just leave me alone," she said. "I've told you and told you: the baby is Ferdy's. There's never been anybody but Ferdy. I only said it was Gabe's that night because you asked me if he was the father. I was so scared and he was three thousand miles away, where you couldn't do anything."

"I guess I would have killed him then, if I'd been able to get my hands on him."

"You'd have killed Ferdy!"

"But you can tell me the truth now, Peggy, I wouldn't do anything to drag you through a scandal."

She had turned away from him, shaking her head. "I haven't anything more to say to you, you just won't listen," she had said. "Leave me alone."

Scott shied at a touch on his arm.

"Excuse me," Quincy said. "I didn't mean to sneak up on you."

He'd have to take a tighter hold on his nerves, Scott told himself. He was acting like a filly first time in the starting gate.

"You're Ed Quincy, aren't you, Sweepstakes' trainer?"

"That's right," the other said, obviously gratified. "But I didn't expect you to know my name."

"Saw you at Delaware once," Scott said. He broke off as Ferdy Garcia appeared in the doorway of the Derby Barn, forgetting Ed Quincy at his side as he watched his son-in-law approach. His son-in-law, this half-pint, this half-breed who couldn't even speak decent English. Nothing could ever make him believe that Peggy had fallen in love with this—this monkey. The only reason she would ever have let him touch her was because Gabe Hilliard had gotten her pregnant and then abandoned her.

FOUR

THE GRUNDAGE HOUSE—along with most of its neighbors on the pleasant street in Azalia, Indiana—had been put up in an era when people really knew how to build, as Sam Grundage frequently asserted. At the moment, though, standing in his entry hall, he wished for the low ceilings he ordinarily despised, because then there'd be fewer stairs to worry about.

He stared at them, daunted by their number. He couldn't wait, though. He had to climb them now. It might be weeks before he had another chance like this, with Debbie and

Young Hugh visiting Hugh at the hospital and Mrs. Wilcox fortuitously summoned to her own home next door.

Taking a deep breath, Sam began to mount the green-carpeted steps. He had an almost overwhelming urge to hurry, knowing the woman wouldn't be gone more than five or ten minutes at the most, but he forced himself to go slowly, hanging on to the banister. One step and pause. Another step, another pause. When he reached the mirror on the landing he saw that his face was chalky, but the pallor was more from excitement than anything else.

And being so gol-darned scared. He could admit to the fear now. Heck, the way they'd kept him wrapped in cotton wool since the heart attack, he'd almost expected to keel over at the first step. He continued up the rest of the stairs with equal caution but the truth was that even so, having reached the top, he was terribly weak. He wasn't certain he had enough strength left to finish what he had come to do.

He leaned against the wall for several moments before he could walk along the hall and he had to rest again at the door of the front bedroom. Then, heart pounding, he crossed to the big closet which held his son's clothes.

Hugh had been wearing his work coveralls when he fell from the ladder. Wallet and keys, as Sam had hoped, were still in the trousers of Hugh's gray suit, and despite the fear that Debbie might have emptied it, there was money in the wallet. Sam counted it with quivering fingers. A hundred and ninety-three dollars, much more than he needed.

He replaced all but ninety dollars. That should be enough. He'd straighten it out with Hugh when he got home. Now, if he could just make it back downstairs before he got caught.

In some ways, going down was harder than going up. Sam kept thinking he might miss a step and fall. But he didn't. By the time Mrs. Wilcox hurried through the door, he was safely back in his chair.

"Were you able to fix it?" Sam asked her.

"No," she said, "whatever it is this time, I couldn't do a

thing with it. But I didn't phone the plumber, either, no use paying double for Sunday. I just cut the water off until tomorrow."

"That makes sense," Sam said, smiling.

"The baby didn't wake up while I was gone?"

"No, no," Sam reassured her. "Everything was just fine." He bobbed his head. "Perfect."

FIVE

ONE OF THE MEN who'd been keeping vigil stuck his head in the backstretch press building and yelled excitedly, "Hey, Frankie, come on, they're taking Magician, Dashing Lad and Freeway out on the track at the same time!"

There was an immediate scramble of departing reporters and photographers. Within a minute, Jerry Neal had the place to himself. He drew another cup of coffee from the huge urn, shuddering away from the heaped doughnuts and sweet rolls, and began to sip contentedly, listening with a pleasant sense of superiority to the splatter of rain outside.

Not for him that herdlike stampede after the Derby horses, that slogging through mud from barn to track and back again, hanging onto every shopworn tidbit from trainer or exercise boy. He could come up with better stuff elsewhere. Actually, the piece he was idly turning over in his mind wasn't directly related to the race. It was to be his annual snipe at the city of Louisville during the Big Week, a feature which every spring elicited cries of anguish from wounded natives and civic leaders. This year he had a special angle. He had stumbled upon it by the sheerest chance.

At any but the most intimate of gatherings, Neal tried to confine himself to two drinks. A must, he had decided grimly, after the near disaster of his very first venture into society. He had been taken to that party by Moog Arganian, his college roommate, son of a wealthy California lettuce grower, and it had been a shudderingly close thing when Moog found him drunk and shacked up in one of the bedrooms with the guest of honor, a noted golf pro.

Moog had instantly staged a screaming tantrum, but luckily, had turned sick and been forced to flee to a bathroom before his hysterical tirade became comprehensible to the other guests. A half hour later he had emerged in white-lipped, blessedly silent fury. Next day, back at school, he'd tried to stab Neal to death.

Moog still took his love affairs too seriously. He'd been in an accidental gunshot case only a couple of years ago—a muscular young surfer who'd been sharing his San Francisco apartment—but once his passions cooled, he was a loyal friend. In fact, it was Moog who had introduced Neal and Gordy Cowdin on a personal basis.

Neal stirred restlessly. He didn't want to think of Gordy now or the funeral tomorrow. He had to concentrate on the column he was going to write.

Last night, Neal had been forced to exceed his usual cautious limit. Pursued by a drunken widow from an impeccably distinguished family, whose recent unlamented bereavement had brought her into sole possession of a very large fortune, his only escape from her pawing had been to match drinks with her. When he was able to get back to his hotel at last, he'd gone for a walk. To clear his head, he told himself.

That was when he had come across the squad of policemen efficiently clearing the little park on Fourth Street of its youthful occupants. There had been squeals and scuffles, the usual cries and objections, but it had been quite late and the officers had loaded them into the two paddy wagons with no-nonsense dispatch and a minimum of public attention.

Neal had spoken to the driver of the last patrol car as it was preparing to drive off. "What was that all about?"

The policeman had looked at Neal's dinner jacket, the gleaming white shirt. He answered respectfully. "Oh, you know how it is these days, sir. Most of the kids that come in are harmless enough. We only keep an eye out that they don't bother other people."

"But these?"

The policeman shook his head. "This bunch was something else again," he said. "We gave them a routine check and they were all higher than a kite. Don't know on what, yet, but there's a couple could end up in the hospital."

That was going to be Jerry Neal's column on Louisville this year, a double-edged bit which would show at once a city besieged by wandering dope addicts and a police force which brutalized innocent college students who'd come, like everyone else, to enjoy the Kentucky Derby.

That should set young and old on their collective ears. And probably, Neal thought with satisfaction, give the chief of police a galloping case of apoplexy.

It was really a shame, from a purely journalistic point of view, that Neal couldn't see the police chief's face at that moment. Or hear his stricken voice.

"For Pete's sake, get me the mayor. I don't care where he is, find him. And then get ahold of Lee Ames, tell him it's important. One of those kids we picked up on Fourth Street last night was Shelby Todhunter, Jr."

SIX

Bolo Jackson opened his eyes. There were a number of others in the room but it was the 17-year-old would-be pop singer who bent over his bed in insistent solicitude. The Nevada sunlight coming through the window behind her made it obvious that she didn't have a stitch on under her silky dress.

"Go 'way," Bolo told her weakly, closing his eyes. Then, "Glen?"

"I'm here," his cousin answered at once.

There was a long pause before Bolo could frame his question. "Vegas?"

"Yeah, Bolo. Vegas."

Bolo thought. "What day?"

"Sunday."

Bolo's lids flew up. "Sunday? When did I—?"

Glen smiled at him uncertainly. "Friday night, Bolo. You've been out almost forty hours. We were beginning to get a little worried."

Bolo sat up. After a couple of seconds the room stopped spinning and he could see that the blonde had retreated only to the foot of his bed. At his glance, her lips curved into an intimate smile.

He grinned at her. "Worried?" he asked. "I was just getting my second wind, that's all. But now we'll have to make up for lost time, won't we?"

"There, you see?" she demanded triumphantly of the room at large. "I told you Bolo was only tired, that he wouldn't want the party to break up. We are going to the Kentucky Derby, aren't we, Bolo?"

He had forgotten about that. It seemed very remote at the moment. "Sure," he said. "I'd better have some food first, though, I'm suddenly starving. Glen?"

"I just ordered your breakfast, Bolo."

"And a plane?"

"I've been keeping that on standby, I wasn't sure when you'd want to take off."

"Okay, get ready then," Bolo said in dismissal. "I'll be set to go in less than an hour."

Everyone scattered obediently except Glen, who began to pack. "You really want to go to Kentucky, Bolo?" he asked. "I was thinking you should—maybe—go back to Minnesota."

"To the doctor, you mean? What for?"

"Well, I got the bottle out of sight, nobody else spotted it, but . . ."

"What are you talking about, Glen?"

Glen clicked the locks of one suitcase and straightened up. "The number of sleeping pills you took the other night."

"You're crazy!"

"No, I'm not. I should have realized earlier. You had to take too many to sleep so long."

Bolo swung his legs over the side of the bed. "I don't even remember taking pills, Glen. I was out on my feet, but if you found the bottle, I suppose I did. Hell, maybe I did take too many, I don't know. You get groggy with those damn things, that's why they're dangerous."

His cousin hesitated. "You sure, Bolo?"

"As sure as I'm sitting here right now. I'd just won a bundle, I was having a great time, why should I want to check myself out?"

"Well—"

"Forget it, Glen." Bolo was touched by his cousin's obvious concern. He wouldn't have thought that Glen or anybody would have cared. "Hey," he said, "let's talk about more cheerful subjects. Like going to the Kentucky Derby."

"Okay," Glen said. "If you really want to go. But I'll tell you one thing, I think it's crazy to blow that much money on a Nickel Nag like Sweepstakes."

"Is he the longshot?"

"He sure is and for good reasons!"

"Well, that's what I said, didn't I? The whole pot on the longest shot in the Derby if I won?" He shrugged at Glen's nod. "Then that's what I do. How much have I got riding?"

"More than twenty thousand, Bolo. Twenty thousand, four hundred, to be exact."

Just then a waiter rolled in the breakfast Glen had ordered at Bolo's first stirring. Tomato juice, two soft scrambled eggs, crisp bacon, toast, English marmalade and black coffee—Bolo Jackson's invariable breakfast unless he was too hung over to eat. Perfectly prepared. He started on it mechanically, the food like so much sawdust in his mouth.

He hadn't meant to set a trap for Glen. He'd asked the size of the stake to keep Glen's mind off the pills. And the money itself wasn't important. What mattered was that Glen clipped it. Bolo minded most of all being considered such a besotted fool he wouldn't know that he had actually won three thousand dollars more.

Well, it wasn't anything new. He had been accepting Glen's small peculations with ironic disregard for some time. But this reminder of what the score really was came at an unguarded moment, when Glen's solicitude had seemed to be for Bolo himself rather than his money.

It was true he couldn't recall taking the sleeping pills, but if he had taken an overdose, it was too bad they hadn't worked.

He looked up, mask of conviviality carefully in place, as the party began to troop back into his room, laughing, talking animatedly, urging him to hurry because it was all going to be such fun.

SEVEN

J. LANGDON MANNERING teetered on the balls of his plump little feet, his round face smiling welcome from the rostrum. J. Langdon smiled almost incessantly as if to offset the fact that his sallow features, in repose, were somehow threatening. He was wondering if he had made a mistake in calling the union meeting for this time. He had completely overlooked the change to Daylight Saving, and a lot of the pari-mutuel clerks must have forgotten to set their clocks ahead because the hall was less than half full.

But it was possible that the small audience had nothing to do with the date or the weather. Most union members just couldn't care less and that was the way J. Langdon liked it when he was running a local. He had expected a little bigger crowd this first meeting and he had already dragged out his introductory speech, but no sense waiting any longer. Everybody that was going to show must be in the hall by now.

Hold it. Here came a couple more, a short dark kid and an older guy behind him. J. Langdon took a sip from the glass of water in front of him and, bushy black eyebrows lifting, leaned inquiringly toward Jack Phillips, the union secretary at his side.

"The little one's Sal Norvelli, two-dollar seller, still on probation, used to be a jockey," Phillips said sotto voce. "The other's Artie Dobermeyer. He's a two-dollar seller, too, though he's got enough seniority for any other job he wanted. Never a very active member but he's been in the union since it started."

J. Langdon nodded in gratitude to the secretary and dismissed both latecomers with conscious contempt. In his long and frequently stormy career he'd never had much trouble with the two-dollar guys—sellers or cashiers. They were either too new, like the ex-jock, or they were basically cautious. They stayed at the two-dollar windows at the lowest pay rate because they felt safer there, standing little chance of any big money loss.

The ones you had to keep an eye out for were the top-salaried fifty- or hundred-dollar cashiers, the wisenheimers with experience enough and daring enough to run the daily risk of costly overpayments to patrons. Errors could run in the thousands, and the pari-mutuel men had to make up any losses out of their own pockets.

"Well," J. Langdon said, deciding to really begin, "so much for the big load of crap!"

That was a kick in the teeth after the flowery self-introduction. "I've told you who I am. I'm J. Langdon Mannering, duly appointed interim president." He shrugged elaborately. "And we've gone through the routine about what a great guy your old president was and what a shame he had to bow out in the middle of his term on account of his sudden illness."

J. Langdon leaned forward over the lectern and paused dramatically. "Now let's get down to brass tacks. What is your new president going to do for you?" He straightened slowly, enjoying the almost breathless attention he had captured. "What would you say to a fifty-percent increase, straight across the board?"

The men sat in stunned silence.

"You're thinking that's a lot," J. Langdon continued. "Sure it is! It's a hell of a lot, and why not, when they've been throwing nothing but peanuts at you since the year one?"

He waited again, as if he expected someone to answer. No one did. He had known no one would. Not yet.

"If you'd been getting a decent wage to begin with, the kind of dough you were entitled to, well, then, I would have come in like all new presidents. You know how new presidents are, they got to show a little something."

140

There was a small wave of laughter out in front of him. J. Langdon beamed. "So I would have been a good guy, like all the rest, and would have talked about how the cost of living's been going up, maybe gone after a six-percent raise. But I ain't like all the rest, I'm going to tell you the truth. You know who's been cashing in on your sweat? The tracks and the horsemen and the state, that's who.

"They're forgetting one thing, though," J. Langdon crooned. "Without you, they got nothing. You don't handle tickets, they don't operate, that's how simple it is. So they got to pay you your fair share and I say that's fifty percent more than they been paying. What do you say?"

There was silence for several seconds while J. Langdon waited, smiling and confident. And then, to J. Langdon's astonishment, the two-dollar seller who had come in last spoke up from his seat.

"I don't know about anybody else," he said sourly, "but I haven't been doing too bad."

J. Langdon leaned hastily toward Jack Phillips. "What did you say his name was?"

"Artie Dobermeyer," the union secretary whispered.

"Oh," said J. Langdon cheerfully, back behind the lectern. "You don't want more money, Dobermeyer, you got enough?"

"I guess I could always use more," Artie admitted, "but being you're new, you don't know Lee Ames. He's the president of Churchill Downs."

"I'd heard."

"Well, he's not going to sit still for that much of a raise."

"Of course he's not going to sit still," J. Langdon agreed. "He can't afford to, with the Derby less than a week away."

"What's that got to do with it?" Artie shrugged. "The contract don't come up for negotiation till the Derby's over."

"You got a good point," J. Langdon said. "That's the way it's always been, hasn't it? You waited till the big day was past and then you took whatever they threw at you.

"But not this time, fellows," J. Langdon announced happily.

141

"You got yourself a real president now. You got a whole new deal. This year, Mr. Lee Ames is going to have to talk turkey before the Derby."

For the first time the audience began to murmur.

"That's Lee Ames' baby, right? The Kentucky Derby? The race two world wars and a worldwide depression couldn't stop? I don't think Lee Ames will want it to stop now, do you? I think he'll do just about anything to keep it rolling.

"So we're going to get exactly what we ask for, and we're going to ask for it now."

J. Langdon smiled. "Or else," he said, "no Derby!"

MONDAY

ONE

Driving through the mire from backstretch to frontside, Lee Ames' thoughts were not on the news coming over the car radio. If he had been conscious of it, he would have switched it off. But as he pulled into his regular parking spot, he heard the announcement that in Moscow, on this first day of May, the annual parade of Red military might had been staged on one of the most beautiful spring mornings ever experienced in the Russian capital for that date.

Here, where such weather could normally be expected, the cold, miserable drizzle persisted and Lee was still considering this fact as he entered the general office. He expected it to be empty at this hour and was startled when Bunny Ingalls announced from behind her switchboard, "They say now it should clear up by noon."

Lee laughed. "What are you doing here so early? Your husband throw you out of bed?"

"I couldn't sleep," Bunny said, "so I decided I might as well beat the traffic in. I'm always like this Derby Week," she added. "Honest to goodness, you'd think I was going to run!"

"I know," Lee said, "it gets me the same way. But at least I have a better reason than usual. The directors will be coming in at eight and I thought I'd try to get some other stuff out of the way before then. Are you working?"

"Of course."

145

"Good, that's a real help this morning, Bunny. Don't put anybody through on my line, okay?"

"I won't," Bunny said, automatically writing "nobody" and underlining it on her pad. She gestured toward the employees' lounge in the rear. "The coffee must be about ready. Would you like me to bring you a cup?"

"No, thanks, I had some backstretch." Lee pushed through the low gate which separated reception area from inner office, then stopped. "I forgot," he said. "I will speak to Nick Chambley or Artie Dobermeyer. But nobody else."

Bunny stared after him in surprise, wondering what on earth would bring the directors into Churchill Downs at eight o'clock in the morning. Something important, she knew. But she'd find out about it before lunch. You couldn't keep very much quiet around a racetrack.

At his desk, Lee discovered he was too keyed up to deal with routine. He leafed through a stack of memos. His secretary could handle most of it when she got there and he'd cope with the residue after the conference.

Instead, trying to relax, he read the early editions and presently he began to laugh. He hadn't the slightest idea what sort of performance Sweepstakes would give in the Trial or the Derby but the Nickels were certainly running true to form. Yesterday's rain hadn't dampened their enthusiasm for interviews one bit and he had noted, when he was at the Derby Barn earlier, that they were holding forth animatedly to still another cluster of reporters.

Blond hair elaborately coiffed, makeup stark in the unflattering clarity of flashbulb photography, Gladys and the beaming Brewster were pictured in every paper above garrulous accounts of Nickel history and with every ungrammatical quote delightedly left intact.

It had not all been gushing statements on how wonderful it was to be in Louisville and what a thrill they were getting from owning a real Derby contender. Gladys had included some impressively tactless descriptions of the experts who were pegging Sweepstakes at 100-to-1 and Brewster had replied to one of the standard questions with, "No, I won't be satisfied with anything less than the blanket of roses. The last ambition I got in the whole world is to be a good loser."

There would undoubtedly be more of the same in the afternoon papers—and in a few of tomorrow's, too—but then, as Lee knew from experience, the Nickels would mercifully fade into comparative oblivion. Having been so easily approached, having provided such an abundance of material, however colorful, they would be abandoned for other Derby participants less thoroughly exploited. The law of supply and demand was never more strictly enforced than in the allotment of news space.

Lee found himself shuddering at the prospect, however remote, that he might have to cope with those two on the presentation stand next Saturday afternoon. Only the Almighty knew what Gladys Nickel might burst forth with at an emotional moment like that. Lee was instantly ashamed of the thought.

The Derby had always had a sprinkling of unusual figures. There had been Mrs. Rosa M. Hoots, for instance, widow of a penniless horseman so confused he hadn't realized his mare could legitimately be claimed for $1,500 out of a race in which he'd entered her. Lee jeered at himself. He probably wouldn't have wanted Mrs. Hoots to win ahead of time, either. And yet the story of the Indian woman and her dead husband—not to mention her trainer, Three-Finger Webb—was a Kentucky Derby highlight.

The purpose of a claiming race is to bring together horses of equal caliber so that none will have unfair advantage. To insure this in the most practical manner possible, any animal entered in such a race may be subsequently purchased at the specified claiming price. Obviously then no owner will enter a horse worth $10,000 in a contest against $1,500 claimers—despite the certainty of victory—because it would be instantly snapped up by another horseman at the bargain rate.

147

But the Indian, Hoots, evidently had not understood the rules. When his beloved mare was claimed, he simply would not part with her (a loaded shotgun lending considerable emphasis to the stubborn refusal), so Hoots and his mare were barred forever from future thoroughbred competition.

A very minor thread in the tapestry of turfdom, the little incident would quickly have faded into the background except for Hoots' legendary deathbed vision that that same mare would produce a Derby colt.

On the strength of this—and against every law of probability—the Indian widow had persuaded racing's fabulous Colonel Bradley into allowing the insignificant mare a service from his famous stallion, Black Toney. The result was Black Gold, who won the fiftieth Run for the Roses, incidentally beating out two of Colonel Bradley's own more-regally-bred hopefuls in the process.

Black Gold inevitably reminded Lee of Gabe Hilliard, and what had happened to him in the building named after Mrs. Hoots' dramatic winner, but thrusting that worry aside, Lee began to pace his office. It was true that he might not have wanted Mrs. Hoots to capture the cherished trophy. And he'd have been wrong. As he was mistaken now in supposing even briefly that the Nickels' behavior—whatever that might be—could diminish this week's presentation ceremonies. The Kentucky Derby had an existence of its own which gloriously exceeded the sum of its parts.

The fact was his judgment of Gladys Nickel was based on very slight evidence: his own brush with her temper when she couldn't get into the Derby Barn to see Sweepstakes and what he had read about her. He might even like her if he knew her better. He might have liked Mrs. Hoots. And he had always held a secret sympathy with the latter's trainer, who was finally badgered into breaking his stoic silence after Black Gold triumphed.

Three-Finger Webb's victory statement was reported to have been, simply, "I got a stomach ache!"

The ringing phone startled Lee back into the present and he grabbed it eagerly. It was only an apologetic Bunny. "I know you said not to put anybody through, but I thought I'd better check with you on this. It's Mr. Vandermeer—and he says it's practically life or death."

Lee raised an eyebrow. The sedate president of one of Louisville's more important banks was a close personal friend and not ordinarily given to melodramatics. "Okay, Bunny, I'll talk to him," Lee said. And then, "Yes, Paul?"

The deep voice at the other end of the line sounded embarrassed. "Lee, I'm sorry, you know I'd never approach you like this except in a real emergency. I've never asked before."

Lee repressed a sigh, understanding. "You have a VIP client who wants box seats to the Derby, is that it?"

"Not just any garden-variety VIP. This is Bolo Jackson, he's not only a big depositor, he's a major stockholder. I've turned my house over to his party. Grace and I have moved in with the kids for the week. But I just haven't been able to come up with enough tickets."

"How many do you need?" Lee asked.

The banker hesitated. "I know how insane this is going to sound, when people can't even find a pair of box seats."

Warren Robbins, head of publicity, came into the office and Lee grimaced at him. "Come on, Paul, how many? I can't make you any promises, but I'll see what I can do."

"Twelve," Vandermeer said heavily. "Twelve box seats, that's what Bolo Jackson insists I get him. As close to the finish line as possible."

Lee blinked. "Let me call you later, Paul, okay?" He hung up and shook his head. "It's going to be a great day. I can tell already."

Warren's smile was sympathetic. "The Colonel and a couple of the other directors have arrived," he said. "They're waiting for you upstairs."

"Let's go, then."

"Anything from Dobermeyer?"

149

"No," Lee said, "I was hoping to have a little hard information to take into the conference with me, but Artie hasn't
called yet."

TWO

THE MORNING BEFORE Artie had gone directly from the
union meeting to a phone booth and called Lee Ames,
as he had promised. But the track president had already
known about J. Langdon Mannering's proposal.

"We'd been warned that this might be coming," Lee had
said, "though it didn't seem possible. But what I want from
you, Artie, is an honest assessment of the men's reaction. Do
you think they bought it?"

"I'll tell you the truth, Mr. Ames, I don't know how to answer that."

"You talked to the fellows who were there, didn't you?"

"Some of them. I didn't stick around very long."

"All right. How did they take it?"

"Like I said, I don't really know. The whole idea was such
a bombshell, nobody was sure yet how they felt."

"Okay," Lee had said, "let's narrow it down, then. What
about you?"

"Me?" Artie had asked. "I think the guy's lost his marbles."

"Look, I'm not trying to put you on a spot, I simply need
information. My other sources aren't in a position to get close
to the rank and file, and this thing depends on the men, Artie,
so I have to have the truth. Not what you think I want to
hear. But you have my absolute word that however it goes,
even if you're behind Mannering all the way, it won't back-
fire on you."

"You didn't have to tell me that, Mr. Ames."

"If I thought I did, I'd never have asked your help. I just wanted it on the record. Now, why do you say Mannering's lost his marbles?"

"Well, because it's ridiculous," Artie had said. "Anybody who knows anything about racetracks knows he's way out in left field. The biggest track in this country couldn't pay that kind of money and stay in business, let alone Churchill Downs. I told him to his face you wouldn't stand still for a bite like that."

"So I heard, and thanks. You know a strike now, before the contract has expired, would be completely illegal. There's not another union that would honor a picket line in circumstances like these, but if he were willing to strike first and worry about the legalities later, he'd have us by the short hairs."

"That's the whole idea," Artie had said. "And pretty sneaky, too."

"But what about the men? Would they really let this outsider, some character they've never even seen before, ruin a national institution like the Kentucky Derby?"

Artie had thought for a second. "It's hard to say, Mr. Ames. Some guys'll do anything for a big raise."

"They must know they'll never get it."

"They might figure they had a chance with that kind of pressure on management. And it's not just our guys you got to consider, Mr. Ames. It's all the clerks who'll be coming in to work the Derby, the temporaries from other tracks."

"Yes," Lee had said. "Yes, I've been going over just about the same ground myself. But if our fellows would hold, not follow Mannering, I doubt if he could get the temporaries to go along, either."

"Probably not."

"Then find out what the score is for me, Artie, will you? Talk to as many of the regulars as you can reach? I'm not expecting you to make any effort to hold them in line, now, remember that. I just want to see what we've got to work with."

151

Artie had spent the rest of Sunday checking. It had been a relief to find that most of the other clerks shared his own feeling against the strike. He had gone to bed in the happy knowledge that he would have good news to report to Lee Ames in the morning.

Artie had been only half asleep when the phone began to ring. He had been listening to the spout outside his window, gurgling with rain, but it hadn't been noisy, just slow and steady, and he had been thinking of Millie. He often felt a little like guys he knew in the war that had lost an arm or a leg and sometimes they forgot and thought they still had it. He knew very well that she was dead and that if he reached over he would only touch the comforter, bunched up on that side of the bed, but until he did it was as if she were there. It was a good feeling. He hadn't reached.

The first ring had been as unexpected as an explosion in the quiet room. It had rung twice more before he recovered from his shock enough to pick up the receiver.

"Hello?" Artie had said, and then, when there wasn't any answer, "Hello? Hello?"

He knew the line was open because he could hear faint breathing. "Hey, what is this? Somebody being smart?"

When there still hadn't been any answer, Artie had slammed the receiver back on its cradle.

It had rung again almost instantly. "Now, look," Artie had said. "I don't know what kind of gag this is, but if you got something to say, say it."

He had been irritated but he had begun to be nervous, too. The humming line and the soft breathing had started to get to him. "Say something," he had demanded. "I know you're there, I can hear you."

He had waited for what seemed a long time and then he had put the receiver down again. He had not slammed it that time. He had replaced it carefully, with a hand which had begun to tremble.

When the ringing began the third time, Artie had bit his

lip and sat there, listening to it, hoping that if he just didn't answer, whoever it was would get tired and quit. But in the end he had given in.

"Look," he had begged, "I don't know who you are or what you want."

The voice had been muffled and menacing. "We know who you are, though."

"I don't understand. What is this? What do you want?"

"We want you to mind your own business, that's what we want. And to keep your big nose out of ours."

"Wait a minute! What are you talking about? You must have the wrong number."

"Just think about it, Dobermeyer, you'll get the message. You better, if you know what's good for you." There had been a click and that had been it.

Artie had finally understood the threat. J. Langdon Mannering knew what Artie had been doing and was warning him to stop. When the dial tone reminded him he was still clutching the receiver, he had put it down and gone into the kitchen to pour himself a stiff drink. He had needed it. He had been so scared he'd had to finish half the bottle before he could get to sleep.

Now, badly hung over, miserable in body and spirit, he stared through a window at the dripping morning and faced facts.

He had worked at Churchill Downs for a long time. He was shocked to the marrow of his bones at his realization that the Kentucky Derby was in actual danger; he hadn't honestly believed in the possibility before last night's harassment.

And he liked Lee Ames a hell of a lot.

Lee Ames was waiting for Artie's report on the men right this minute. But if it came down to a choice between them and Artie Dobermeyer, then there were no two ways about it. He'd have to tell Ames to get himself a new boy.

Artie felt like a rat but he just couldn't help it.

THREE

GABE EMERGED hazily from the familiar dream, with his usual sense of desolation and the same terrible thirst. He couldn't remember where he was when he opened his eyes.

In the dim light he looked incuriously at the rich pattern of the tightly drawn drapes, the nubby texture of expensive wallpaper, the darkly polished furniture. Then he saw the bureau-desk-and-television-stand and he realized he wasn't home. No matter how luxurious, that combination spelled hotel or motel.

To his left, he heard someone stir. He started to turn his head and the pain hit him. It was awhile before the pills she gave him took effect and he could open his eyes again. By then, the girl had gone back to sit in the chair drawn up beside his bed. She was wearing slacks and a soft yellow shirt, open at the throat, and in the subdued light her thick dark lashes glittered. They were lowered over something she was doing with a ball of thin blue yarn.

"Varonica, Varonica Varon, and your mother pinned it on you." His voice sounded unexpectedly weak.

Varonica looked up from her crocheting and smiled. "You look even worse than yesterday, if that's possible, but you must be better. You didn't remember me then."

"Yesterday?" He considered that for a moment. "But what are you doing here?"

"It's my apartment," she said. "Half mine, anyway. I share it with the girl who manages the gift shop. Luckily, she was spending the weekend with her family in Columbus, so when everything happened, they told her to stay there on a week's vacation with pay. Nick Chambley put up the money and Mr. Ames arranged it with the manager here. He fixed it so that I could stay with you, too."

What she was saying didn't make much sense. Gabe shook his head to clear it and groaned. Involuntarily, he put up his hand and touched heavy white bandages. His arm was bandaged as well. He held it in front of him in amazement.

"What happened?" he asked. "Did I get thrown again?"

"I suppose you could put it that way," Varonica said grimly, "but it wasn't by a horse, Gabe, it was by a damn sight lower breed of animal. A man, or, probably, two men, we're not absolutely sure, but when I found you I'm positive you said something about being 'caught between them.'"

"You found me?"

"Right outside my door!" For some reason he could not imagine, she seemed embarrassed. "I don't know why, I just opened it to see if you were wandering around the hall. I mean, you didn't get here and I wondered if you'd forgotten the apartment number. And there you were, so still, all covered with blood. It was awful."

Gabe closed his eyes. He was silent for so long that Varonica decided he had drifted back into sleep. Actually, he had begun to sort things out.

"It was that drunk," he said at last. "You know, the nasty one? I didn't see him at first, he was standing in back of his buddy, and I got in the elevator with them." He could sense that in the future this was going to be a very bad memory, but right now his growing drowsiness made it seem merely an item of minor interest. "When I came to I was lying on the floor, half in, half out of the elevator."

He tried to draw a deep breath and agony stabbed at him even through the powerful pain killer. "My ribs, too?" he asked, wincing.

"Ribs, back, face," Varonica answered. "We thought at first you must have been hit by a car. It just didn't seem possible that anybody could do that much damage with bare fists."

"They didn't," Gabe said. He produced a lopsided grin. "You've heard about kicking someone when they're down, haven't you?"

Varonica burst into tears. "Oh, Gabe, how can you joke about it? Those horrible beasts, they almost killed you. I thought they had."

After a moment she regained control. "I don't usually fall apart like that," she said. "But every time I think of how you looked . . ."

"Whatever you do," Gabe said, "don't explain it away. There isn't another person in this world who'd cry over me like that. Or that I'd want to."

The drug was making it increasingly hard for him to talk. "If I'd been in my right mind, I'd have had sense enough to go away. I'd have realized what a mess I was, that you wouldn't want me to show up like that."

"Oh, no, I was *so* glad I could help."

"You see?" he pointed out dreamily, after a pause. "That's funny."

He didn't want to go back to sleep. Not yet. "I don't know how I made it to your door. I went up and down in the elevator a couple of times, I'm sure of that. I kept pressing the wrong buttons and I think I passed out once coming down the hall. But I kept thinking I had to get to you. If I could reach you, everything would be all right."

"Thank God you did!"

"That's what I mean, that's funny." His voice was trailing away. Without being aware of it, he held his hand out toward her. "It was like my nightmare when I'm looking and looking and there's nobody. Only this time . . ."

He felt her take his hand. It was all right. She understood. He went to sleep.

When he awakened later Nick Chambley was there, his bulk squeezed into the chair beside the bed, reading his Daily Racing Form. Gabe's earlier confusion had vanished. He knew immediately where he was. He was careful to hold his head very still as he said, "Hi, Nick."

The agent put his paper down in obvious relief. "You really are better, Varonica said you were, but that there was still a lot of pain."

"Only when I breathe," Gabe joked. "And if you say 'I told you so,' you're fired!"

Nick made a face. "If you'd been conscious when I first got here, I'd have quit. God, Gabe, what a terrible thing. But at least you're going to be okay, nothing else matters."

"In time for the Derby, Nick?"

"You really are something, Gabe," Nick said, heaving himself up out of the chair. "The whole time that's all you kept saying—that we shouldn't take you to the hospital, that you would ride next Saturday."

"Quit stalling, Nick. You haven't answered my question. What does the doctor say?"

"The doctor?" Nick's laugh was a derisive bark. "Every time I mention 'Derby' to him, he looks like he's going to faint. He's screaming to high Heaven that you ought to be in the hospital where he could take X-rays."

"But I'm not in the hospital, right? So does that mean you don't agree with him?"

"It means he probably ought to take X-rays of my head, too," Nick said disgustedly. "But aside from the possibility of concussion or some internal injuries, he thinks you just have some busted ribs. If that's all it is, we'll have to see."

"Does St. Pierre know?"

Nick shook his head, ticking off names on his stubby fingers. "The only people with any idea of what's happened are Warren Robbins, Lee Ames, Lee's doctor, the girl, me. And the general manager here at The Inn." He swallowed. "It kills me to let whoever did this get away with it, but I promised the manager we'd hold still if he cooperated. Otherwise I told that bastard we'd sue this place for every dime they ever hope to get."

Gabe shifted position carefully. He was going to need another pill pretty soon. "What else can we do, Nick? If we try to prosecute, the newspapers will have a field day. I'll be out of the Derby lineup so fast I'll set a new track record."

"You may be anyway, Gabe. We don't know if you'll be well enough to ride. And, Gabe," Nick hesitated, "you've got to be well enough to do a real job or we're not riding Magician in the Derby. It wouldn't be fair to the Frenchman or the owner."

"I've raced with broken ribs before."

"I know you have. That's why I'm crazy enough to go along with you now—lie like hell, stall and pray you make it. I want to ride Magician as much as you do. I'm just saying . . ."

"Okay, I know what you're getting at." Gabe raised a hand in concession. "If we can't do it right, we don't try to do it at all. Agreed. But we've got a few days before we have to decide. So just keep the lid on a little longer."

"Until Thursday," Nick said. "We'll have to be sure by then. Thursday morning, when they take final entries for the Derby. That'll give St. Pierre time to get a new jockey."

"Okay," Gabe said. "We'll decide by Thursday."

"What a sight," Nick said, examining Gabe as he stopped for a moment at the end of the bed. "And what a picture you'd make for the front pages if the newspapers ever got hold of this. They'd have to be in color, with all those beautiful purples and blues and yellows."

He began to pace. "I wish I had my hands on those rotten bastards. I wouldn't prosecute them, I'd kill them. But I guess we have to give thanks for small blessings. That you had sense enough to warn Varonica not to call anybody but me and that she was smart enough to follow orders."

"I don't remember even talking to her," Gabe said. "I don't remember a damn thing but trying to reach the door."

Nick snorted. "No wonder. If you'd been any worse off, you'd have been dead. She says when she carried you in she actually thought . . ."

"She carried me in?"

"What did you think, she dragged you by your heels?"

He had completely forgotten, Gabe realized. How tall she was. How little he was.

He moaned.

The big man was at his side instantly, face twisted in concern. "Look, Gabe," he said, "maybe we're out of our minds not to skip the whole thing and take you to the hospital. We don't have to ride Magician, Gabe, there'll be other Derbies."

Gabe closed his eyes. "No way, Nick. Just get me a pill."

He was going to ride in this Derby. No matter what he had agreed earlier, no matter how he felt, he was going to ride Magician if somebody had to tie him into the saddle. What the hell else was he good for? A man his size?

FOUR

SATURDAY EVENING'S SMALL BLAZE of hay outside of Barn 16—as any jackass in the backstretch knew—could hardly have been less of a deal. And yet there it was in this morning's paper, centered toward the top of the main sports page.

FIRE AT CHURCHILL DOWNS
NO THREAT TO DERBY BARN

Suddenly Pop's eye caught a smaller item at the bottom of the next column. "Nine Dead in Chicago Tenement Blaze." The difference between the two made him laugh out loud.

The young fellow on the next cot in the Derby Barn dormitory stopped polishing his boots and looked up. His name was Alan—he had introduced himself when he moved in the day before—and it wasn't quite clear whether he was Dennis Sullivan's son or his nephew. Pop didn't care which he was. Any-one connected with the Sullivans or Davie's Pride was unimportant.

In the course of fifty years on the backstretches of race-tracks from Boston to Baja Pop Dewey had come across thousands of "gyp" horsemen like Dennis Sullivan (so-called because they "gypsied" from place to place). Guys with one or two horses who broke, trained, groomed and mucked out stalls themselves. It was an insecure existence. Though you talked to any one of them and he'd tell you he wouldn't be doing anything else for a million dollars.

They had to really like the life, Pop supposed; otherwise they'd get the hell out of it. Instead, they went on year after year, always scrabbling, always heading for somewhere else in hopes of finding races they could win with their crummy horses. And always believing that someday they'd come up with a "real good one!"

They'd tell you how Man o' War only cost five thousand and Dr. Fager's dam went for thirty-five hundred and Dust Commander, that won the 1970 Derby, was picked up for peanuts at Keeneland—sixty-five hundred, that was all. But their favorite was the 1971 winner, Canonero II, who also came from Keeneland. He had been bought for only twelve hundred dollars.

Like you hadn't heard it a million times. Like you thought they had even that kind of money when they probably didn't have two cents to rub together and were trying to get the van company to give them a little more credit so they could move on again. Pop despised the lot of them. He himself had never worked for any but wealthy stables, with thoroughbreds of the finest breeding.

That Dennis Sullivan was not a regular "gyp," that he had his own small spread and bred horses of his own, these were distinctions beneath Pop's notice. Dennis did his own work. And his colt had been foaled in Davie, Florida, not even in Ocala.

Right now, though, Pop was eager to share the joke about the two news stories. He held his paper up so the kid could see it.

"Ain't this a howl?" Pop asked. "Here they make a federal case out of a little fire that was nothing." Pop pointed to the top of the page. "Honest to God, nothing. I turned in the alarm myself. A bale of hay, that's all it was." His finger moved over the print. "And down here, like they just happened to remember, they mention nine people killed in a tenement fire."

Pop pulled the paper back as Alan tried to read the smaller item. "The rest ain't important," he said. "But don't it kill you? I watched one of them tenements go up once when I was in New York. That's a sight you wouldn't hardly believe if you wasn't there. You can't see nothing but them black walls standing sharp against the red. And the firemen up on the ladders with their hoses. You might just as well spit at a runaway. You know it's hopeless and any minute the whole thing's going to cave in."

The old man laughed again. "Nine people can die and the papers give them a couple of lines. But a little fire that wasn't anywhere near the Derby Barn, and they really go to town."

"It is funny," Alan agreed. "But I guess in a way you have to expect it. The mayor stubs his toe on Main Street and the local paper breaks out in headlines, but the rest of the country could fall into the ocean and they'd stick it on the last page."

"No, it ain't only that," Pop said. "It's because of the horses. People just like to read about them, I guess. They don't have to be Derby horses, either, or even big name horses. Just horses. I don't know why but . . ."

Pop broke off suddenly and stared at Alan's face. "Jesus, can you imagine what kind of headlines there'd be if the Derby Barn burned down? That would make the front page everywhere in the world."

FIVE

In the casual crossing of paths which brought most members of the racing world into occasional contact, Lee Ames and Morgan Wells had met several times. Their last encounter had been during the winter, a season when Churchill Downs officials customarily made a round of the southern and western tracks to personally remind owners of likely three-year-olds that the closing date for nomination to the current Derby was fast approaching. Some years Lee went south while The Colonel or Warren Robbins went west. This year it had been Lee's turn to go out to the coast but he had made a deliberate detour on the way back to see Lisa Cardigan and her colt in Florida.

The Cardigan plans for the Derby were all set, naturally. The Canadians had been established regulars at Churchill Downs even before Lee's own arrival, and Lisa had wanted a Cardigan colt to contend for the roses since she was ten years old. It was a not uncommon paradox that none of her father's expensive and impeccably bred nominees had ever quite made it to the post on that first Saturday in May. But now she had Armada.

Lee remembered meeting Morgan with the Cardigans on the Florida trip but had not particularly linked him with Lisa at the time. The relationship probably was not yet significant then or Lisa would surely have given some indication of it. She'd been confiding in Lee since her first teen-aged crush. The rumors that Lisa and Morgan were in love had not begun until Armada was taken up to Maryland. And, of course, Lee told himself, they might not be true at all. Backstretch gossip was often as erroneous as it was speedy.

Still, Bunny's announcement that Morgan Wells was outside commanded Lee's instant attention. He was on his feet, waiting, when Morgan came into the paneled office.

As they shook hands, Lee was shocked by the agent's appearance. He seemed to have aged ten years.

"I know how busy you must be," Morgan began, sitting on the edge of his chair. "I won't keep you more than a minute, but I need a little information."

"Of course," Lee said, trying not to sound surprised.

Morgan flipped through a small notebook he pulled from his pocket. "I'm trying to locate a fellow named—" he found the page he wanted—"Otto Miller."

"Otto Miller? You mean the trainer who used to handle Steve Cardigan's American string?"

"That's the one. I'm pretty sure I've met the man, but I don't know much about him and nobody around here seems to, either. The racing secretary thought you might be able to put me in touch."

Lee shook his head. "I don't know where Nils got that notion. I haven't seen Miller for a good three years. He's probably in Jersey, though, that's where he usually heads from Florida."

"No," Morgan said, "I phoned up there. He's not on the grounds and nobody has any idea where he is." He rose abruptly.

"Sorry I couldn't help."

Morgan was out of the room before Lee could say another word. Then, with equal suddenness, he was back in the doorway. "You wouldn't know where Gabe Hilliard is, would you?"

Lee swallowed. "You're looking for him, too?"

"He was here," Morgan said grimly. "He was at The Inn Saturday night, but now he seems to have vanished. I just wondered if you'd seen him."

"I can't say where he is, either," Lee said carefully. Which was the truth.

When Morgan had gone again Lee sat back, troubled by the strange interview. There hadn't even been a chance to ask when the Cardigans were arriving. This didn't matter, of course, Steve would call as soon as the family checked into the hotel. And when they did, Lee decided, he was going to have a heart-to-heart with Lisa. The breakup of her marriage to Gabe had all but shattered her. He didn't want to see her hurt again and from what he'd gathered today, Morgan Wells was a man with problems.

In New York, at the monitoring station which had been set up in the Cardigans' Waldorf suite, Inspector Elverson looked thoughtfully at the information Morgan Wells had just given him over the phone.

To one side of the scratch pad Elverson had listed three men whom Wells had been unable to locate: Gabe Hilliard, Lisa's ex-husband; Herbie Kahn, another jockey with whom Lisa had had sharp words over his treatment of one of her horses; and an exercise boy, Jack Whigham, whom she had fired for making drunken advances.

On the other side the inspector had bracketed another missing pair whose descriptions came closer to the estimated measurements of the mutilated corpse which had been found at the foot of the Palisades: a hanger-on named Coolie Bascombe who had tried unsuccessfully to launch Hilliard's career when the jockey was just starting out; and Otto Miller, who had trained for Steve Cardigan sometime earlier and who had expressed bitter disappointment at not having been given charge of Armada.

It was the last who seemed most promising to Elverson now since he had not shown up as usual in New Jersey and that was where the body had been discovered.

"Thanks, Mr. Wells, we'll check these names immediately. But don't stop digging. You never know what may . . ."

Morgan's interruption was furious. "Inspector, I'm staying

down here because you convinced me I could tap sources in the backstretch for you."

"That's true. My men would be as visible as so many zebras there, asking questions."

"Okay, I'm doing what you've suggested. But don't you use that bright pat-on-the-head tone of voice on me again, because if I get the idea you're just trying to keep me out of your hair or that you're not telling me everything that's going on . . ."

"I'm sorry if you thought I sounded patronizing, Mr. Wells," Elverson said. "I certainly didn't mean to and I will keep you posted on all new developments as long as you stay in Louisville. You have my word."

"You're expecting to hear from the kidnapper at eleven?" Morgan asked more mildly.

"That's what he told Mr. Cardigan."

"Well, I'll call back around five after, okay?"

But when he did, Inspector Elverson had nothing to report. Unaccountably, there had been no contact.

The kidnapper hadn't phoned by noon. Nor by one o'clock. Nor by two.

Mace Augustine had been thoroughly soaked but cheerful when he boarded the plane for New York at 6:55 A.M. When he debarked at 9:30, the rain had stopped but he was still at Standiford Field, Kentucky. The captain was making his ninth announcement that the mechanics had finally pinpointed the cause for the long delay and the plane should be taking off within twenty minutes.

Mace was livid with anger at this unexpected hitch in his plans but even as he clattered down the stairway he realized he could retrieve the situation simply enough. He would just make his call at the specified hour from a phone booth in Louisville. If he kept the conversation under three minutes, the Cardigans would never suspect he was calling Long Distance.

And even if the operator should listen in, she wouldn't know what it was all about. Mace was only going to say, "Have you got it?" and when they said, "Yes"—as of course, they would—he'd just say, "Okay, I'll be in touch later." And hang up.

Having reached this decision, he figured he had time enough to go back to the trailer and change out of his uncomfortably damp pants and socks. He could still catch the noon plane and be in New York to pick up the money that night.

Mace got into one of the cabs which was lined up in front of the bustling airport. Instinctively cautious, he did not give Good Mary's address but just told the driver to take him to Churchill Downs. He could walk from there to the trailer.

"Going to the races, huh?" the cabbie asked as he swung toward town.

Mace did not reply but the man was not easily discouraged. "The gates ain't open yet, you know," he said, "not till way after eleven, but I guess you're going through the Derby Museum, huh? We take lots of fares there, whether Churchill's racing or not, they got more than a million signatures in the Visitors' Book."

When Mace didn't answer this time, the driver took the hint. He was silent for the rest of the trip, but after letting Mace out at the entrance to the racetrack, he sat chatting with the guard, his glance turned casually upon his ex-fare.

Mace hesitated, afraid that if he walked away from Churchill Downs it would look suspicious, and the cabbie waved a helpful hand. "Over there," he called. "The museum's on the left."

Mace had no choice. Seething, he followed a party of three men and a little boy into the Kentucky Derby Museum. And there, chatting with a pretty girl behind the souvenir counter, was Good Mary. Standing next to her, and obviously taking part in the friendly conversation, was a man Mace instantly identified as a cop, despite the civilian clothes. He could smell the law a mile away.

166

Before Mace could retreat, Good Mary saw him. Her wrinkled old face became radiant. "Why, here he is, Chief Keller. My young man that I was telling you about, that paid me all that money just to park in my backyard."

Mace could have killed her with pleasure, but with his best boyish grin he took her outstretched hand between his own in apparent pleasure.

"Well, what do you know?" he asked. "I thought this was just a place for us tourists."

"Oh, no, I come in all the time," Good Mary said, "while I'm waiting for them to open the gates. I love it, with the old pictures and programs and all." She remembered her manners. "This is my friend, Chief Keller," she told Mace proudly, "he's in charge of security here at Churchill Downs, and this is . . ."

She groped for the name, evidently annoyed at not being able to think of it.

"August Mason," said Mace, supplying the alias. "Thought I'd just drop over and take a look before the races."

"And how's your pretty little wife?"

"Oh, she's all right, but she's picked up a cold or something. I told her to stay in bed. I never even knew there was a Kentucky Derby Museum till today," he added, changing the subject.

"First trip to Louisville?" Keller asked.

Mace nodded. "But I hear it's great at Derby time." He laughed. "A little expensive but worth it."

Good Mary had just come from putting her three-hundred-dollar windfall into the bank. She said, a bit defensively, "Now, 'twas yourself set the price, Mr. Mason, I never in this world would have asked it."

"Believe me, I wasn't complaining," interrupted Mace hastily. "Of course I offered it, I wanted to make sure you'd let us stay. No, it was hotels and restaurants my friend said were really out of sight."

Without knowing it Mace had answered a question which

had puzzled Keller since Saturday, when Good Mary had shown him the roll of greenbacks. He had, in fact, meant to check up on her new tenants when he got a minute, because it was an excessive amount for a week's parking.

Now he laughed, understanding. The young fellow had obviously been sold the usual bill of goods. "You hear a lot about how people get soaked during Derby Week. Don't you believe it. I'm not saying the rates don't go up then but the raises aren't all that exorbitant and the people you find doing most of the complaining aren't really beefing as much as they are bragging."

Keller glanced at Good Mary. "I don't think she's about to give you any refunds," he said, "but what you paid was far more than most of the better hotels would charge."

Good Mary said quickly, "Shame on us. Here you come to see the museum and we keep you talking. Why don't you sign the Visitors' Book and let us show you around?"

Mace checked his watch. Ten forty-five. Only fifteen minutes until he was supposed to call New York, but there was no way he could get away from this cop in a hurry without arousing his suspicions. Then he noticed the other man was consulting his watch, too.

"I'd like to stay with you," said Keller, "but I really can't right now."

Mace tensed.

"Tell you what I can do, though," Keller said. "I'll drop a word at the pass gate on my way in and after you're through here, you can just take your friend inside." He turned to Mace. "Considering how Good Mary soaked you on the rent, the least we owe you is a free shot at the races."

Mace managed a smile. "That's very nice of you," he said above the old lady's beginning protest.

Keller patted her shoulder. "You know I'm only teasing, Good Mary. But I'll see you later. Both of you."

Ten-fifty. And Mace was stuck not only with a tour of the museum but with a free pass into the racetrack.

There, as the afternoon wore on, Mace Augustine discovered he was having himself a hell of a good time.

"You got to go with me, Rosanna," he said enthusiastically when he finally got back to the trailer. "You wouldn't believe what fun it is. No wonder Coolie wanted to hole up here."

To Lisa, listening, the happy excitement in Mace Augustine's voice seemed incredible, and she couldn't bear to think of her parents, waiting and waiting for the call which hadn't come. But Lisa herself had spent many enjoyable afternoons at the races.

Rosanna had not. She stared at Mace, speechless with incomprehension and shock.

"Of course, Good Mary had to tell me what to do, how to buy tickets and where to cash them. But you get talking to people and there was this one old guy, he let me look at his Racing Form, and you want to hear something? You can really figure what the horses are going to do. Oh, not every time, especially on a sloppy track like they had today, but I had five winners, Rosanna, and I picked out two of them all by myself. I won thirty-two dollars!"

"Let me get this straight," Rosanna said, disbelievingly. "You're pleased over thirty-two measly dollars? You stayed over there all this time and never even called the Cardigans?"

"Come on, Rosanna, I couldn't do anything else. I didn't dare to cut out with the old bat on my tail. Hey, you know what she does, Rosanna? She goes around looking for tickets that . . ."

"Don't tell me," Rosanna interrupted coldly. "I'm trying to find out why you didn't at least make one three-minute phone call."

Mace's tone changed. "You're trying to get a crack in the mouth, that's what you're trying to do," he said. "You *can't* call from a racetrack. They lock up the phones during the races, it's the law. The only phone you can use is in the office in case of an emergency."

"Well, then?"

"Then they monitor the call."

"Oh."

"I would have phoned if I could have. But since I couldn't, what did you want me to do, sit and twiddle my goddamn thumbs? I'll call the Cardigans tomorrow, I told you. They'll still be waiting. After all," Mace asked with a smirk, "what else can they do?"

SIX

At 8:30 on that monday evening the waiters were beginning at last to serve the guests at the Kentucky Breeders' Banquet. This was a customary spring event which simultaneously paid homage to the state's leading breeder of the previous year and welcomed participants to the present running of the Derby.

The invitations had specified cocktails at 6:30, dinner at 7:30, and on the whole, as such celebrations went, things weren't too far behind schedule. Only Buddy Sheffield—and a handful of others who didn't drink—were aware that the fine food had lost some of its flavor while waiting, despite the yeoman efforts of a distraught chef.

Buddy, though, had been over this route before. He had prudently fortified himself with a substantial steak at 5:30 and had made his appearance thirty minutes after the cocktail "hour."

The guest of honor on this occasion was Charles (Charlie) Talbot, of T-Square Stud in Lexington. Sitting at the VIP table to the right of The Colonel, who was tonight's Master of Ceremonies, Charlie was florid faced and beaming with good humor.

The year before, his horses had earned more money than those of any other breeder, not only in the state but in the country, thus taking the coveted title from Tom Richardson, its previous holder. And now, with Lucky Jim already winner of more than a hundred thousand and heavily favored to double that amount by capturing next Saturday's Kentucky Derby, T-Square Stud seemed well on the way toward a second year of victory.

It was to this happy possibility Charlie Talbot referred when, trophy proudly in hand, he began the evening's final speech.

"I know my good friend Jim York here, and his fine trainer Buddy Sheffield, will be pulling for me all the way," he said, "the same as I'm going to be rooting for Lucky Jim all the way, come Saturday!"

The audience applauded.

"And if not Lucky Jim," Talbot went on, "then you know I have to be rooting for one of our other Kentucky-breds: Freeway, even though California's practically made him a native son; or Double Seven, foaled right down the Pike from me in Lexington; or Sweepstakes, from Harrodsburg.

"And if I had to, I might even pull for Florida's Davie's Pride or Canada's Armada. Because my chief rival will always be my good friend Tom Richardson from Maryland and you know I'm going to be rooting for Magician and Dashing Lad least of all!"

There was a good deal of laughter and Tom held up his hand in a victory sign.

"Seriously now," Talbot said, "there's not one of us here who doesn't know how much it means to a breeder to have one of his colts win the Kentucky Derby. We've got a big industry, one that's growing every year, all over the country, and you have to come up with winners. If Lucky Jim can help me lead the nation's breeders in money earned for a second year, I'll be a happy man!"

Talbot paused, took a sip of the water before him, then

leaned slightly forward. "But you know and I know that if there wasn't one penny involved in winning the Kentucky Derby, every person in this room tonight would break his heart to try for it, anyway."

There was prolonged, enthusiastic applause.

"I'm not sure how many three-year-olds there are around right now," Talbot said when he could resume. "Twenty to twenty-five thousand, maybe. Out of them, only a hundred and sixty-nine were even nominated to this year's Derby. And now, unless a couple of you fellows come on in after tomorrow's Derby Trial, looks like we'll be lucky to have eight starters Saturday. Eight, out of all those foals.

"I want to tell you something, I'm proud one of my colts made it this year. And that goes no matter how the Derby turns out. Because in the long run what we all really want is for the best one to win!"

He smiled broadly. "And if that should turn out to be one of Tom's pair, I'll be the first man in line to shake his hand."

Charlie Talbot sat down.

His audience rose, clapping wildly.

SEVEN

Gordy cowdin had entered the world in squalor and poverty, on a worked-out bit of Kansas farmland. His single evidence of foresight insured that he at least left it traveling first class, in the restfully parklike precincts of Glendale's Forest Lawn. Nevertheless, the funeral had depressed and irritated Jerry Neal even more than he had anticipated.

Gordy's mother, an unexpectedly large, raw-boned woman

whom her son had despised and avoided while he was alive, had wept incessantly. Probably, Neal suspected, because she had already discovered that Gordy invariably spent more than he earned—an occupational hazard—and there would be precious little left for her to inherit.

Worse still was the luscious dancer toward whom the jockey had evidently been speeding when he died. Not that Jerry Neal had expected fidelity from Gordy, and not that Gordy had ever denied he sometimes enjoyed girls, too. But this one was such a grossly overwhelming female. And Gordy had never even hinted at her existence.

Well, Neal thought in the limousine which took him directly from the cemetery to the airport, he'd learned a good lesson, anyway. He would never again involve himself with a bisexual. They were just too insincere.

His plane wasn't due to leave for several hours, but even a dreary wait at L.A. International seemed preferable to the funeral-baked meats. It was there, in one of the bars, that Jerry found PeeWee Jones, a radio announcer with whom he'd often shared press boxes, and learned about the possibility of a strike against the Kentucky Derby. PeeWee had heard it some minutes before as he was checking out of his local station.

"That's all they had on the wires," he said when Neal pressed for details. "A rumor that the mutuel clerks might try to hit Churchill for a big raise. But there hasn't been an official confirmation. The Downs isn't talking and so far nobody's been able to catch up with the union head." PeeWee chortled. "There's a handle for you: J. Langdon Mannering."

"J. Langdon, huh?" Neal asked reflectively. "He's moving up in the world."

"You know him, Jerry?"

"He's pulled a couple of stunts like this before, though not quite on this level. I wonder how he got to be head of the union. He certainly didn't make it the legitimate way, he's not the type."

173

"You think he will strike the Derby?"

"Oh, I doubt it, PeeWee," Neal said. "Unless Churchill Downs is stupid. Offer him a quick fifty or a hundred thousand and J. Langdon will ride off into the sunset. A raise for the clerks wouldn't put anything in his pockets."

"Maybe he'd fade, anyway, if they were prepared to fight and let him know it?"

Neal shook his head. "Not J. Langdon. He plays dirty pool just for the fun of it."

By the time Neal boarded his plane, he had decided to give Mannering a ring. It wouldn't be too late when he got to Louisville, only about ten. Keeping Mannering's past out of the column ought to be worth something. And if not, what a juicy piece that could be.

Neal smiled to himself. Sometimes he played dirty pool just for fun, too.

TUESDAY

ONE

"**S**ULTRY PREP WEATHER," the *Louisville Courier-Journal* forecast for the day of the Derby Trial. "Very warm and humid, with a chance of widely scattered thundershowers afternoon and evening, high today in mid 80s, low in mid 60s."

The impending heat could be felt before the sun had fully risen over the backstretch that morning. The mugginess, too. Even Johnny Sullivan, who had been chilly ever since he got to Kentucky, had to remove his jacket. Dennis carried it now over one arm as young Alan Burroughs led Davie's Pride toward the mile gallop which would be his final exercise before this afternoon's race.

Behind them trailed the inevitable crew of newsmen and photographers, swelled by a number of fresh arrivals. The tempo of Derby Week was quickening.

Dennis grunted in surprise as they got to the gap in the fence. The pathways between the barns had been bad enough, but from here the track stretched before him like an ocean of mud, churned into peaks by the hooves of horses who had already been out on it.

"And someone told me the track would be fast for the Trial," Dennis said.

The sportswriter to whom he had spoken said, "It wouldn't surprise me a bit. I've seen it happen."

"When it was as bad as this in the morning?"

"It's better than it looks," another reporter said. "At least, the boys who've been working say the wetness is all on the surface, that it's solid underneath. If it doesn't rain anymore and if the sun comes out hot enough it may be okay."

Dennis looked up at the sky. "It's going to be a scorcher," he said, "but I doubt we'll have anything but a heavy track. Go along, Johnny."

One of the newsmen laughed. "If the track superintendent hears you talking like that, you're in trouble. That little strip of dirt out there is the apple of his eye, built to exact specification for quick drainage and with his own special mix of sand and loam. You watch the equipment he'll have going over it the minute they quit exercising, breaking up clumps, and re-spreading the top."

"How about it, Mr. Sullivan," a newcomer interrupted, "can your horse take an off track?"

"Davie's Pride can take anything," Dennis said, watching his son circling in an easy gallop.

"The Trial?"

Dennis turned to face the questioner, a brash young fellow with three cameras slung around his neck. "Well, now," Dennis said indulgently, "if I didn't think he'd a chance at the Trial—and the Derby as well—we wouldn't be here, lad, would we?"

He returned to his outwardly calm observation of the track. He'd told the truth. But how much of the original chance was left after the other morning he wouldn't really know until this afternoon.

Or whether Davie's Pride would be in the Derby at all.

Double Seven was an unholy mess when Kenny Perini delivered him to Pop Dewey after training. Pop's first chore was to wipe the mud gently from the colt's eyes with a soft cloth dipped in a preparation made for just that purpose. Then,

178

keeping up an unconscious barrage of clucks, croons and complaints, he began to slosh at Double Seven's mired and sweaty hide with spongefuls of water from a big bucket.

Warm as the morning already was, horse and water were warmer still, and as Pop went through this routine, little clouds of vapor rose around them.

The steaming thoroughbred made an unusual picture, and one of the photographers came over, snapping industriously as he approached, circling for angles, checking his light meter.

"Double Seven, right?" he asked from behind Pop. "One of the horses going in the Trial today?"

"Right," said Pop, bending to wipe at a leg.

"You his regular groom?"

"Yep."

"What's your name?"

"Dewey."

"Dewey what?"

"Dewey nothing, that's my last name. First name's Clyde, but everybody calls me 'Pop.' "

"Well, listen, Pop, would you move on the other side for just a second, so I can get a better shot of your face?"

The old man straightened in astonishment. "A shot of me?"

"You and your horse together," the photographer said.

"I guess it's okay," Pop said, "but it can't take too long, I got to get him bathed and covered up. He just come off the track."

A couple of quick clicks and the photographer was gone, leaving Pop in a state of shock. Aside from the regular poses in the winner's circle, where he was just a stablehand holding the horse in position, nobody had ever wanted to take his picture before. But then, of course, he'd never before been groom to a Kentucky Derby colt. He'd come kind of close a couple of times, real close with that one of Tom Richardson's that got burned, but that was all.

If you thought about it, a groom couldn't really go higher

179

than that, having charge of a top horse, taking complete care of him. Pride welled up in Pop Dewey. A picture of him in the newspapers. Never thought a thing like that would happen.

But after Double Seven won the Trial and then the Derby, why, everybody would be wanting to take a picture of Pop Dewey. He'd be famous. He'd be the groom of the Kentucky Derby winner.

Ed Quincy was almost as dismayed by the track as Dennis Sullivan. And like Dennis, Quincy decided it would still be heavy for the Trial.

Such a footing was most difficult of all for a horse. Neither liquid enough nor hard enough, the drying mud sucked at every step, requiring infinitely more effort than any other kind of condition.

"Still," Quincy told the Nickels—who were inevitably on hand to watch the exercise and see any stray reporters who might care to interview them—"Sweepstakes is the smallest colt in the field, so it'll be easier for him to navigate. And Armada will be carrying six pounds more, because he's earned so much more money. Every extra pound can count going a full mile on a track like this. Besides, Armada's got the Number One post position. He'll be on the rail."

"But that's an advantage, isn't it?" Gladys asked.

"On a fast track, sure, the horse has a little less ground to cover. But the way a racetrack drains, the middle always dries out a little quicker than the inside. It will be deeper, stickier going for Armada today than it will be for Sweepstakes, coming out of post position Six."

"Nobody else seems to be figuring it your way," said Brewster. "Armada's even money in the morning line."

"No other way anyone could figure on the basis of past performance," Quincy said. "Don't forget, two of the horses this afternoon aren't even scheduled to start on Saturday. They're eligible, of course, or they couldn't be in the Trial, and I suppose if either Lookaway or Jennifer's Joe looks real good, the owner might run him in the Derby after all. But they're both way out of their class, I've been watching them work.

"Then take Double Seven. He's got the breeding but he's never won at the distance, and though the Florida horse showed a lot of speed the other day—maybe too much for his own good—he's done nothing important.

"Then there's us. And you know what they think of our chances. Armada has to be the favorite, no two ways about it. I'm just saying today's conditions give us a little better edge."

"Even so," Brewster said, "I wish it could've been a fast track. It's safer for the horse."

Quincy squinted at the sky. "Don't waste your time wishing, Mr. Nickel," he said, "start praying. I think we're going to have more rain. And if it comes soon enough, we might give some of these know-it-alls the shock of their lives."

It was a backstretch truism—far more accurate than most—that if twenty trainers were questioned as to the best regimen for conditioning a thoroughbred up to a race there would be twenty different answers. Almost universally, though, they had abandoned the once-standard practice of withholding feed from a horse before he was due to run.

Mister Mack had not. This wasn't because of his age. He had always been—and still was—a great experimenter with modern techniques. As interviewers had been reporting for decades, Mister Mack's credo was a monumentally logical bit of advice which had been given to him by an old "gyp" horseman when he himself had been a mere kid: "Whatever you're doing, if it don't work, do something else."

But it seemed only common sense to him that an animal could move more quickly on an empty stomach than on a full one; and he had also concluded there was a definite psychological benefit to his thoroughbreds in the change of pattern. They understood the second their oats were not forthcoming that they were going to race. They were keyed up, prepared in advance for the contest.

Therefore, when Armada was cooled out and ready to be led back into his stall after exercising, Mister Mack put on his muzzle. This restraint was to prevent the colt from nibbling hungrily at his straw bedding—usually disdained and wholly without nutriment—and buckling it into place was ordinarily a simple chore. But today Armada was stubbornly resistant, and when the struggle was finally over, Mister Mack had to admit to himself that now the muzzle was serving a dual purpose: it also kept Armada from savaging his groom.

The desire to do so was a new and disturbing element in the colt's character. He was naturally mettlesome and lively, and one dared not forget—ever—that the best-tempered horse in the world could kick a man into Kingdom Come without even trying, but lately Armada had turned downright mean.

He missed the girl, Mister Mack thought. And he reminded himself for the hundredth time it was none of his business where Lisa Cardigan was keeping herself or why. Except that it was affecting Armada.

TWO

I T WAS THE ASSISTANT DIRECTOR himself who called Inspector Elverson just before ten o'clock. His controlled voice conveyed only a hint of exultation.

"We may have a break on this case, Jason," he said, "but

first, about that list Wells gave you yesterday, we've located Otto Miller. He's managing a new breeding farm in Illinois."

"And Coolie Bascombe?"

"We're still checking the others. But, Jason, one of the ransom twenties has turned up in Louisville!"

"At the racetrack?"

"Probably, but it was spotted at the bank, so we can't be absolutely sure."

"The one Churchill Downs uses?"

"Yes. As I say, the presumption is that the bill came from their deposit. We'll know definitely if another of them comes in. If it does show up at the track, the pari-mutuel head says he can pinpoint the exact area. They'll be watching for it very closely now."

"That is a break. Your hunch seems to have paid off."

"Maybe," the A.D. said. "What's happening in New York? Last time we talked, you thought Mrs. Cardigan was having a heart attack."

"She was, but a fairly mild one, the doctor says. She refused to go to the hospital, though, so he's keeping her under heavy sedation until something definite happens. As for Mr. Cardigan . . ."

"I can imagine."

"No, surprisingly, he seems to have, well, rallied. If the kidnapper calls today . . ."

"Do you think he will?"

"After yesterday, I wouldn't try to predict, but if he does, Cardigan's come up with a real stunner."

"What do you mean?"

"He's planning to raise the ante. Offer them a million instead of a quarter million, but only for a direct swap, girl for money, right on the spot!"

"Good God," said the A.D.

"My sentiments exactly," Elverson agreed. "But Cardigan figures the kidnappers are unusually greedy. Otherwise they wouldn't be after a second ransom. He believes they won't be able to resist if his daughter is still alive."

Elverson swallowed. "And if they reject the offer of a million dollars, cash in hand, it will prove she's dead and, at least, the waiting will be over."

There was silence for a second, then the A.D. said harshly, "Impossible. We can't allow it."

"I know," Elverson admitted. "But he's absolutely determined."

THREE

HAVING INTRODUCED the newcomer, Lee Ames' pretty secretary withdrew, closing the door gently behind her. There was an awkward pause in the large, comfortable office as the president of Churchill Downs and the union leader frankly appraised each other.

It was J. Langdon Mannering who spoke first. With a gesture which included The Colonel and Kermit Young, director of pari-mutuels, he said smilingly, "Looks like the odds are at least three to one against me."

His sprawl in the big chair facing the desk was almost insolently careless. Lee made a conscious effort to relax his own upright posture. "I suppose the odds depend on what kind of race you're planning to enter. There are some you can win and some you can't."

J. Langdon waved his expensive cigar. "True, but then occasionally you know you have a sure thing. Sort of like the Trial today. Those other horses won't even give Armada a good workout, he's got them so far outclassed."

184

"Perhaps," Lee said. "However, I've been around racetracks too long to consider any horse unbeatable. No matter how much backing he has or how weak his opposition seems."

"You may be right," J. Langdon conceded cheerfully. "Miracles can happen. Still," he said, getting easily to his feet, "I always remember the Damon Runyon saying, something about, 'the race isn't always to the swift, nor the victory always to the strong, but that's the way you better bet it!'"

"You're leaving?" Lee asked, trying to hide his astonishment.

"Oh, I never meant to take up much of your time," J. Langdon said heartily. "I know how busy you must be during Derby Week. I just dropped by for a minute to say 'hello.' After all, since I'm the new head of the pari-mutuel clerks, it seemed like we ought to get to know each other."

"Well, I certainly appreciate your coming in," Lee said. "Sorry you can't stay a little longer."

"I'll be back," J. Langdon assured him.

"I'll be here."

Kermit Young stared at the door Mannering had closed behind him. "Whew, that was short and sweet."

"But not quite to the point."

"Oh, I don't know, Lee," The Colonel said. "I thought you both made yourselves pretty clear. I wasn't expecting him to leave so abruptly, though."

" 'Testing, one, two, three,' " Kermit chanted.

"That's about it," Lee agreed. "An extra Trial at Churchill Downs today. Now all we have to decide is who won it."

FOUR

Varonica was crocheting again, her steel hook flashing
noiselessly as she worked. She was wearing a dress this
morning, a blue one which matched the yarn, and was sitting
beside Gabe's bed as she had been almost every time he
opened his eyes.

Since Nick had told him how she carried him in from the
hall, Gabe hadn't spoken two unnecessary words to her, accepting the intimacies of her efficient care in determined silence. But as his high drug dosage was reduced, his humiliation increased.

Suddenly he struggled into a sitting position, swinging his
legs half over the side of the bed before the pain temporarily
immobilized him.

Varonica was out of the chair in an instant. "Gabe, what's
the matter?"

"Nothing's the matter," he growled, gritting his teeth against
the pain. "I just want to go to the bathroom."

"Oh, no," she protested. "You mustn't. Wait, let me bring
you . . ."

"I don't want a bedpan. I'm going to the bathroom."

"But, Gabe, the doctor." His glare stopped her. "Well, at
least, let me help you."

"Goddamn it, no. I realize it may be hard to understand,
looking at me," he said bitterly, "but I'm a big boy now."

He wrenched free of the bedclothes and stalked toward the
bathroom door.

He was too intent on fighting off his faintness, at first, to be aware that he was wearing only his pajama tops. Behind him, Varonica burst into laughter.

She was back in the chair when he emerged, his sense of the ridiculous unassuaged by the towel he had knotted around his hips. She concentrated tactfully on her crocheting as he climbed achingly into the bed. But her face still held a hint of her earlier amusement. After a second she said, "I suppose you thought I was laughing at how you looked?"

He turned on his side, away from her, and didn't answer.

"I wasn't," Varonica said. "Though, actually, Gabe, you did look pretty funny. I guess a man needs his pants on if he's going to throw a serious tantrum. But the reason I laughed was because it suddenly dawned on me that it bothered you to be short."

For one second Gabe lay absolutely still. Then, wincing at the violence of his movement, he rolled over to stare at her. "Now what in the hell is so funny about that?"

She met his anger with a smile. "Nothing, really, it's just that people worry about such unexpected things. I'm not saying I never noticed you were short. You're a jockey. It's part of what you are. Only, you see, I like what you are. It just never occurred to me that you might not. I've been messed up so much of my life over being too tall."

"You're not too tall," he said involuntarily, "you're beautiful."

"That's what I keep telling myself," she said, "and once in awhile I almost believe it. But it took an awfully good psychiatrist a long time to make me stop feeling like some kind of a freak."

"You're kidding." His anger had disappeared.

"No, I'm not, Gabe. The thing is, I was as tall as I am now when I was twelve. I'd been a skinny little kid, and all at once I turned into a great big beanpole."

She shrugged. "I might have had emotional difficulties anyway, who knows, but in my case there were complications."

She broke off abruptly. "So that's why it struck me so funny for you to mind being short."

Gabe examined her flushed face. "What kind of complications?" he asked.

"Oh, I'll tell you the story of my life another time," Varonica said lightly. "I just didn't want you to think I was laughing at . . ."

"Who raped you?"

She was startled. Her flush deepened. "What makes you think somebody did?"

"I don't know," Gabe said. "The way you stopped so suddenly, and I suppose, if you were so big for your age, people probably thought you were older."

"Anyway, I'm glad you have such a nice, normal imagination, Gabe. But it's a dreary tale. Let's skip it."

"I won't skip it. I want to know."

"Why?"

Gabe hesitated. "I'm not sure why, Ronnie." He interrupted himself. "Is it all right if I call you 'Ronnie'? It just popped out but it seems to fit."

"I don't mind. Varonica Varon isn't my favorite name in this world."

"That's where I came in, isn't it?" Gabe asked. "With you on a doorstep and that name pinned to your blanket? I think it's time you finished the story."

"Well." Varonica surrendered. "The orphanage tried to place as many children as they could in foster homes. Sometimes people would keep us for a few months, sometimes it would be longer. Most of the families had kids of their own, but there were a few couples who didn't.

"When I was older, I was sent to a couple like that. They'd never taken any foster children before. The Institute checked them out, but they had no way of knowing that when the wife picked me, he'd told her the one he wanted.

"He liked them very young and very skinny and very small.

When I suddenly got so tall, he shipped me back. He said I was a 'goddamn freak.'"

Gabe swallowed in shock. "Before you were twelve?" She looked down at her hands. "How old were you?"

"Nine."

"Jesus Christ, Ronnie, he abused you for three years? Wasn't there anybody you could tell, anybody who would help you?"

"The social worker came regularly, but I didn't dare to say anything."

"What about his wife? If you'd told her . . ."

"She knew."

"She knew and she didn't stop him?"

Varonica looked up. "I'm not defending her, Gabe, but she tried to do everything in her power to make it up to me. In one way, I have to be grateful to her, because she taught me to read, to love books. Only she was deathly afraid of him. He was a big strong man and he used to beat her unmercifully. He said he'd kill us both if anyone ever found out."

Gabe closed his eyes. "A big strong man," he murmured. "After he sent you back? Couldn't you have told then?"

"I was still too scared. I never opened my mouth until I was so obviously disturbed that the Institute sent me to a psychiatrist."

"I hope to God somebody did something to him then."

Varonica sighed. "It would have been my word against his and I was seeing a psychiatrist. As for the other kids—"

"They gave him others after you? Girls?"

"Two of them before it all came out, one for almost two years and another who'd been there a little over three months."

"But if you'd all told the same story?"

"After me, he took retarded children. The second girl was also deaf and dumb."

"God!"

"Anyway, the first time the social worker questioned him, they packed up and disappeared."

"So nobody knows where he is? What he's doing?"

"No," Varonica said. "End of story." She managed a small smile. "I don't know what made me tell you this. I've never mentioned it to anyone before except the psychiatrist."

He held his hand toward her and she took it. They sat in silence for several minutes.

Then, when Gabe still didn't speak, Varonica began to worry. "I knew I shouldn't have told you. Now you're upset."

Gabe tightened his grip as she tried to withdraw her hand. "That's what I was thinking about, Ronnie, that I ought to feel terrible. And I do, for you." He painfully propped himself onto his elbow. "But here you've told me such a rotten thing I want to go out and kill somebody and I'm flat on my back with the living daylights kicked out of me. I have to confess, Ronnie, after that little jaunt to the bathroom, I wouldn't bet a plugged nickel I'm going to make it on Magician Saturday."

He couldn't suppress a groan as he let himself fall back against the pillow. "So how come I don't feel terrible?"

The buzzer at the apartment door interrupted them.

"It's the doctor, I guess," said Varonica and went to let him in.

She was mistaken, though. The man she ushered into the room a moment later was Lee Ames. He smiled as she politely withdrew and then turned to Gabe. "I don't suppose you're in much of a mood for visitors," he said. "I've been checking with Nick and the doctor, but I wanted to see how you were myself." He grimaced sympathetically, examining the battered face. "I must say you don't look too well. How do you feel?"

"I've felt better," Gabe said. "I'm glad you came, though. It gives me a chance to thank you for keeping this thing quiet."

"I'm not sure that you should be grateful," Lee said. "I've had some serious qualms about not taking you to the hospital."

"Then we never could have kept it from the press."

"That isn't the most important consideration."

"Maybe not for you," Gabe said, "though I don't suppose it's the kind of publicity you'd like at Derby time. But I would have lost the mount on Magician and God knows how many more in the future after the papers got through with me. 'Gabe Hilliard in new fight.'"

"This one wasn't your fault," Lee protested.

"And all the others were?" Gabe asked sardonically.

"I didn't mean that quite the way it sounded."

"Of course you did," Gabe said. "You believe what you read in the papers the same as everybody else. Anyway, thanks."

He paused, hearing Varonica's voice from the next room. She seemed to be arguing with someone. Then Nick came into the bedroom with a stranger.

"That's some watchdog you've got there, Gabe," Nick said, then noticed Gabe's visitor. "Hi, Lee, I didn't know you were here. This is Ted Irving, from the FBI. Gabe Hilliard and Lee Ames. Mr. Ames can verify everything I've told you."

"The FBI?" Gabe was bewildered.

"Just routine," Irving said soothingly. "Mr. Chambley has explained the reason for your disappearance, but I had to check."

"What for?" Gabe asked. "I mean, why are you investigating me?"

"We're not, Mr. Hilliard. The question of your whereabouts came up in connection with another matter."

"But I don't understand."

Ted Irving smiled. "Sorry I can't explain. However, now that I've seen you, there's no need to take up any more of your time." He nodded to the others. "Thank you, Mr. Chambley. Mr. Ames. I can let myself out."

"For Christ's sake," Gabe said after Irving had gone, "what was that all about?"

"Search me," Nick said. "I had to tell him the truth, but we don't have to worry about his talking to the papers. I couldn't get the time of day out of him myself."

"Yes, but who told them I'd disappeared? You've got St. Pierre squared away, haven't you?" Nick grunted assent. "Then who else would be looking for me? And why?"

The questions echoed in Lee's mind after he'd left the apartment and was walking through the quiet lobby of the Black Gold building.

He couldn't answer the last one, he thought. He had no idea why. But Morgan Wells had been looking for Gabe Hilliard only yesterday.

FIVE

HERE AND THERE among the lesser shed rows there may have been mention of Coolie Bascombe. However, he had no connection with what some stablehands called "the bigfoot horses"—like Armada or Magician, for instance—so his absence was hardly noticed.

In any case, backstretch gossip was more importantly concerned with the broken heart Morgan Wells was supposed to be suffering because Lisa Cardigan had jilted him and run off again with Gabe Hilliard.

There were those who scoffed at this romantic theory. But it did account for the misery Morgan was obviously trying to conceal. And it did provide a reasonable explanation for the otherwise inexplicable nonappearance of Lisa and Gabe during Derby Week. The rumor gained new adherents with every repetition.

The backstretch obviously couldn't be expected to be curious as to where a newspaperman might be, even one as notable as Jerry Neal.

And Shelby Todhunter, Jr., was a Californian. Most of the regulars at Churchill Downs who wheeled among the eastern or midwestern tracks wouldn't have known him if they fell over him.

So they hadn't begun—yet—to realize he wasn't around, either.

SIX

A RTIE DOBERMEYER was at work behind the grille of his Sellers Window, with its WIN $2 sign displayed above. He was in a vile mood. He had heard someone say the temperature was close to 90 degrees and he didn't doubt it for a minute. The bricked area before him was roofed and shady but the way his cubicle felt it could have been the jock's sweatbox.

Actually, Artie had been irritable since he had phoned in yesterday morning and left a message with Bunny that he wouldn't be able to do that extra work Mr. Ames wanted. Irritable and uncomfortably defensive and ashamed, he knew that Lee would not pressure him. For one thing, the president had promised, and he was not a man to go back on his word. Also, Artie had realized, Churchill Downs had a spy inside the union, someone who had already reported J. Langdon Mannering's speech before Artie had called on Sunday morning, so Lee Ames had to know that Artie couldn't help himself. That Artie was scared green.

This made Artie feel worse than ever, but his present, avowed cause for anger had no apparent connection with his low self-esteem. His fury was directed toward the racing fans of Churchill Downs, or, at any rate, toward those who were unexpectedly giving Double Seven such heavy backing. Remembering his conversation with the old groom at the V.F.W. bar, Artie had bet ten dollars on Double Seven the minute his machine unlocked to sell tickets on the Trial. At that time he expected the odds to be 50-to-1 at least. But Double Seven had been played down to 10-to-1.

Hell, Artie told himself, if he liked to bet short odds he'd have taken Armada, who really figured to run away and hide from a field like this. Artie glanced at the big totalizator board where lighted figures showed that Armada was now 1-to-9. He shook his head. If the horse romped, you'd be lucky to get more than ten cents on the dollar. So who in his right mind could put money on any horse at odds like those? As if in answer to Artie's inner question, a blond young man pushed a twenty-dollar bill under the wicket and said confidently, "I'll take ten tickets on the Number One, Armada."

Artie automatically began the multiple punching of the proper key on his pari-mutuel machine and the bright pasteboards began popping through the slot. Then giving vent to his general bad temper, he asked disgustedly, "If you wanted that many tickets, what'd you come to a two-dollar window for?"

The young fellow looked apologetic. "That's right, you do have higher-priced windows, don't you? I forgot. I never bet more than two dollars on a horse before." His face brightened. "But everybody says it's got to be Armada."

Mace Augustine's boyish enthusiasm made no apparent impression on Artie Dobermeyer. He counted the tickets swiftly and shoved them under the grille, his unfriendly eyes questioningly on the next man in line.

"Number Four, two times."

Number Four. Double Seven. Artie jabbed the key twice, angrily.

Christ, thought Artie, if it kept up the way it was going, Double Seven would be down to 5-to-1.

The recorded "Call To The Post" trumpeted over the public address system as the next man stepped in front of Artie. That meant the horses would be moving out onto the track. Only about ten minutes or so now until the Trial began. The betting at Artie's window continued.

"Number Five." That was better, Davie's Pride.

"Number One." Fine, Armada.

"Number Two and Number Three." A real longshot buff. Lookaway at 35-to-1 and Jennifer's Joe at 85-to-1.

"Number One, twice."

"Number One."

"Number One." Good.

"Number Four." Bastard.

"Number Six." Sweepstakes, okay.

"Number One."

"Number One, to show."

"You got the wrong window, lady, this is for Win tickets only," Artie said contemptuously.

The man who took her place at the window was worse. He had to recheck his program hastily to make certain of the number he wanted.

"Come on, mister," Artie demanded. "You're holding up the line."

The man spoke but at that moment there was a roll of thunder and the rain came down as if a water main had burst above Churchill Downs.

"Holy Mother of God!" he exclaimed, wheeling to gape at the unsheltered areas beyond. "Did you ever see anything like that in your life?"

"Let's go," Artie snarled. "You're not the only person wants a ticket, you know!"

The man turned back to the business at hand. "But I told you," he said reproachfully. "I want—" He gave a quick glance at his program again. "That's right. Number Four. Double Seven."

Ed Quincy's seat was completely exposed, but when the deluge began he sat perfectly still, grinning broadly. The Nickels weren't quite so dedicated. They ran for cover, although that didn't save Gladys' expensive new hat. Even in the few seconds it took to reach shelter, the flowers dissolved into a soggy mass.

In the T-Square Stud box the guests also scrambled for protection. On his way up the aisle, Charlie Talbot suddenly found himself jammed against Tom Richardson.

"How do you like this?" Talbot asked. "Crazy, isn't it?"

"It's wild, all right. Sure hope it doesn't do this for the Derby."

"Amen," Talbot said. "Hey, is Scott with you? I missed him at the Banquet last night and I'd like to at least shake his hand."

"You know Scott and dinners, Charlie," Tom said, "but he meant to be here for the Trial. Peggy's having her baby, though, I guess, they called him over to the hospital."

The crowd was thinning in front of them.

"Well, tell him I said 'Hi and good luck,' you hear?" Talbot's eyes twinkled. "Good luck with the new grandchild, that is," he added. "When it comes to Dashing Lad, I'm maintaining a stony silence."

"The same to you and Lucky Jim," Tom grinned. "I got to admit one thing, Charlie, York picked himself a damn good man in Buddy Sheffield. There isn't a better man in the business."

That was the God's truth, Talbot thought to himself as he caught up with his party. There wasn't anybody could top Buddy. As long as he stayed sober.

Talbot sighed. The cardinal rule of his world was that you didn't tell a man how to handle his horse. Talbot supposed that had to extend to how a man handled his trainer, too. And Jim York was a valuable patron whom Talbot couldn't afford to offend. But the way York kept needling Buddy— like at the Banquet last night—was enough to drive anyone to drink.

The stewards were Kentucky Colonels, of course. Their names were Matthew Tyler, Emory Fulton and Philip Appleby, and they were listed at the front of each day's program, although the average fan probably never noticed. Their word on racing matters was absolute.

The three had attained their positions of authority in the traditional manner, rising slowly from levels of lesser responsibility. They all were ex-trainers, each at some point having been successful enough to saddle at least one Kentucky Derby entrant, and Fulton, the smallest, had been a noted jockey as well.

A highly honored official once described the early days of judging American horse races as "three men and a bottle of bourbon in the infield." But the stewards always had to be knowledgeable men, and men, moreover, of unblemished character. That occasionally they had also to be men of great courage was proven, for instance, during the fifteenth Kentucky Derby on May 9, 1889. Then the stewards had to decide on the strength of the naked eye alone that the overwhelming favorite, Proctor Knott, had been beaten a mere nose by the longshot, Spokane. And they had to announce this decision standing, according to that day's newspaper, "in the center of a delirious crowd of spectators, one faction claiming that to Proctor Knott belongs the Derby trophy, while the other shouts for Spokane!"

Today, however, the three stewards occupied their own inviolate domain high above the finish line, in a sealed-off section of the press box, and they had at hand tools of incredible sophistication.

An elaborate communications system kept them in continuous touch with the four patrol judges at their strategic stations around the track; with the three placing judges responsible for setting the official order of finish; with the paddock judge, the track veterinarian, the clerk of scales and a host of others. There were motion picture cameras, highly specialized photo-finish cameras, and several viewing screens. Most valuable of all was the instant-replay equipment which allowed the stewards to examine and reexamine any portion of a race which might affect their final decision.

Such judicial aids were used in every race. It was a point of pride with the three stewards that their procedure would not differ one iota during the Derby, with the country's finest colts participating and millions of spectators, from what it was in the Downs' cheapest claiming race on a rainy autumn afternoon with attendance at its lowest.

Nevertheless, now, the Colonels Tyler, Fulton and Appleby were acutely conscious of the Trial's drama. Where ordinarily only one of them might have kept the necessary official eye on the measured approach to the starting gate, three sets of binoculars concentrated on the horses as they stepped out onto the track. After all, four of these colts—perhaps the entire half dozen—might be taking part in the Derby itself.

The thoroughbreds were mettlesome, prancing, responding to the heightened interest of the crowd. Each had its brightly silk-shirted jockey settling into the saddle, each was accompanied by calming pony and pony boy. The procession had just turned to parade back before the grandstand when the thunder rumbled and the unexpected rain came sheeting down.

"Oh, oh, watch out," the ex-jockey Fulton, murmured.

Davie's Pride, startled by the sudden dousing, reared onto

his hind legs, threatening to unseat his rider. Armada stopped abruptly, those notable white feet planted as stubbornly as any mule's. Behind him the other horses milled about nervously. One of the ponies almost went down on the slickening surface. Lookaway took off on a wild dash up the track, his jockey sawing desperately at the reins in an effort to control him.

The series of minor crises ended almost as quickly as the rain had begun. Lookaway, at the head of the stretch, had been slowed into an ordinary warmup gallop, Armada was ambling along again, the others following as before, and Davie's Pride, though still skittish, had resumed his position as if there had never been any diversion.

"Whew!" Matt Tyler breathed. "For a minute I thought we were going to have real trouble."

"Ummm," Appleby said. He gestured toward the track below. "Is this rain going to change the condition?"

Tyler looked across toward the big "tote" board in the infield, which still officially listed the track as good. "Ordinarily, I wouldn't expect the condition to change," Tyler said. "Not quickly enough to affect the Trial. But this is quite a downpour. And on top of all that rain we had yesterday and Sunday, it might."

"That's what I was thinking."

"It could stop as suddenly as it started," Fulton said.

"If it doesn't within a few minutes," Tyler said, "we'll probably have to make an official change."

Before doing so, the stewards would check with the track superintendent, Churchill Downs' head clocker and the Daily Racing Form Trackman. In the meantime, the three Kentucky Colonels watched the horses warming up around the turn.

The rain continued to pour. Now and then there were rumbles of thunder.

SEVEN

ALTHOUGH THE SLIGHTEST sprinkle of rain drummed noisily on the metal top of the trailer, Rosanna did not hear the torrential downpour begin. She was—at Mace's insistence —giving Lisa a shower. "For Christ's sake," he had said before he left for New York early that morning, "do something about this place. Air it out, clean it up a little. The old lady will be over at the track all day, no one will be nosing around. And while you're at it, give her a bath, she stinks."

How funny, Lisa had thought. She was blushing because the man who intended to kill her said she smelled.

"What for?" Rosanna had protested. "When we're going to dump her and this lousy trailer as soon as you get back?"

"Look, Rosanna," he had said, "instead of just taking off after we get rid of her, let's you and me go to the Kentucky Derby and enjoy ourselves."

"You mean stay in this hole?"

"I promise you, you'll love it. And this guy who showed me how to read the Racing Form has a couple of extra tickets I think I can get."

Rosanna had given up. Just as she had reluctantly agreed to showering Lisa. She had just turned off the water when the thunderclap shook the trailer.

"Oh, my God," she shrieked and threw her arms around Lisa's neck. After a second Rosanna ran to one of the windows and peered out. "That was thunder," she said. "Everything's soaked, but the rain seems to be stopping."

She started rubbing herself with a towel. "I'd have died if

that thunder kept up. I don't know why, but since I was a little kid, it just scares me out of my wits."

Lisa was unmoved by this confession of weakness. She simply stood, her face impassive above the adhesive, while Rosanna finished dressing.

"Now what can I put on you? Nothing of mine," Rosanna said, considering. "And nothing of Mace's, either. It could be traced."

After her body was found, Lisa realized. That was what Rosanna meant.

Eventually she bundled Lisa back into the bunk in her dirty clothes. Then Rosanna settled down to reading a movie magazine, with a thick bologna sandwich and a box of the bourbon chocolates which were a Kentucky specialty beside her.

She was finishing her fourth chocolate when Mace's distinctive knock sounded on the door. He strode by her to glare at Lisa. "You!" he said disgustedly, waving a cluster of parimutuel tickets at her. "You and that goddam horse of yours. He finished dead last."

Rosanna, having closed the door behind Mace, was standing frozen in the tiny vestibule. "Are you telling me you went over to Churchill Downs today?"

Mace turned to face her. "Only for the Trial," he said. "I came home after they decided who won it."

She rushed at him, her voice rising. "Instead of going to New York? Mace Augustine, have you gone out of your mind?"

His punch caught her on the chin. She staggered back and fell on the abandoned bologna sandwich.

"I told you before, Rosanna," he said in an almost conversational tone. "Never yell at me."

She rocked in silence for a second, rubbing her jaw. "But, Mace, how could you stay here?"

"I didn't stay here, stupid. I went to New York, just like I planned." She stared up at him, speechless and confused.

201

"That's right, smart ass, I went to New York and then came back."

Rosanna swallowed in fright. "There was trouble. Oh, Mace, I told you we shouldn't try for more money."

"Will you keep your mouth shut? You told me, you knew, you don't know anything. And you keep talking so much nobody can get a word in edgewise. Her old man's offered me a million bucks."

She examined his face. "What's the catch?"

He sat on the edge of his bunk opposite her. "He says there isn't any and I think he means it. But he'll only give me the money when I hand over his daughter. An on-the-spot exchange. Otherwise, he says, no deal at all."

She mustn't faint now, Lisa told herself, not now.

"It's a lot of money," said Rosanna. "But we can't do it."

"I know," Mace said. "That was my first thought. We let her loose and she'll nail us to the wall."

Lisa grunted frantically.

"Forget it," Mace said, his tone coldly final. "But when I started thinking, Rosanna, you got to hand it to the guy." He laughed. "He's doing the exact thing I did with the old lady here, offering so much she couldn't turn it down."

"You didn't agree!"

"I'll tell you the honest truth, Rosanna, when he sprang it on me, I couldn't say a word. My mind went blank, I swear. Then I asked what he's trying to pull and he says nothing, he just wants a fair trade, seeing that I didn't give her back the last time he paid. He'll meet me anyplace I say. He'll come alone and give me the cash the minute he sees his daughter is okay."

"Oh, Mace."

"I know, Rosanna. Will you listen? So finally I told him I'd have to think it over, I'd call him tomorrow, and then I just grabbed the next plane back. No sense taking a bus, as long as I didn't get the money. I kept going over everything on the plane and then I decided as long as I was here in time for the Trial, I might as well go."

The note of disgust crept back into his voice. "And bet twenty bucks on Armada. Believe me, that's the last time I ever put more than two bucks on a horse again. The big favorite and he's dead last the whole way."

He looked up at Lisa. "Okay, maybe he would have won if he got a chance. But just as they're starting the race, there's this loud crack of thunder."

"Oh, God, I know!" Rosanna said.

"I was thinking how scared you must have been. Well, that noise scared the hell out of a couple of those horses, too, believe me. One horse practically fell sidewise out of the gate. And never mind he dumped his jockey, he kept Armada from taking off until the rest of them were halfway home.

"Then there was this horse named Sweepstakes. He ran like hell even after the slow start. He was three lengths ahead, not another horse near him when he crossed the line. And then the stewards called for an 'Inquiry.'

"I didn't know what that meant when the word lit up on the tote board, but a guy next to me with binoculars said Sweepstakes was bumping everything in sight coming around the turn, the stewards had to look at the pictures and decide how much he interfered with the other horses."

"Mace."

He ignored the attempted interruption. "You should have seen the crowd when the stewards disqualified Sweepstakes and moved him back to fourth place. Everybody was looking for the tickets they threw away when they thought Sweepstakes won. And this other guy next to me—they moved his horse up into first place—he never did find his ticket. You wouldn't believe how crazy he went."

Rosanna had listened to this apparent gibberish with rising impatience. Now she put her hand on his arm. "Okay, Mace, it was a big deal, but I don't care. What are we going to do?

That's what I want to know."

Mace was—for once—contrite. "I guess it seems like I was just wasting time, but I really wasn't. While I was sitting there, waiting for the stewards to decide who won the Trial, I got the answer."

"What answer?"

"How to get the million bucks and be safe at the same time."

"Oh, no, Mace, I'm afraid. We can't."

"Yes, we can, Rosanna. It will be easy. I don't know why it took me so long to figure it out. I'll call him tomorrow and tell him I'll take the deal."

"I won't let you do it," said Rosanna. "You can't turn her loose. And if you meet him, he'll get a good look at you, too."

"That's the whole point," said Mace triumphantly. "All I got to do is kill them both."

Mercifully, Lisa fainted.

EIGHT

AT THE ROWS of typewriters in the long press box at Churchill Downs the newsmen began pounding out their lead stories. Beneath them the crowd still roared in response to the stewards' decision.

Inside the railing which defined the publicity office, one of Warren Robbins' assistants picked up a microphone, tapping it once or twice to attract the reporters' attention. A few concentrated souls went right on typing but most of the sportswriters reached for notepads and pencils.

"Okay, fellows," the young man said, "we'll have this information mimeographed in a couple of minutes for anyone who wants a copy, but in the meantime, these are the official margins of finish: Sweepstakes by three lengths, then Double Seven, a neck, Jennifer's Joe, a nose, and Davie's Pride. Armada was back twenty lengths and Lookaway, as you saw, lost his rider.

"Incidentally, there won't be final word on the jockey's condition until we get the results of the X-rays, but he was able to get up and walk to the ambulance under his own power."

One of the reporters called a question. The amplified reply came back immediately. "Final time of the race was one minute, thirty-five and two-fifths seconds.

"And with the disqualification of Sweepstakes, purse distribution is as follows: Value of the race with six entries was $15,900 . . . of which Double Seven now picks up the winner's sixty-five percent, $10,335. Jennifer's Joe gets twenty percent for second, $3,180. Davie's Pride gets ten percent for third, $1,590. And Sweepstakes, of course, now gets fourth money, five percent, or $795.

"We're rounding up as many statements from the jockeys and trainers as we can for you and we expect to have them mimeographed very shortly."

NINE

THE CHIEF OF CLAIMS was listening to his son's excited voice.

"Right this minute, I don't think Pop could hate anyone. He's so tickled over Double Seven's win you'd think he was the owner instead of the groom. For that matter," Alan added, "you ought to see the Sullivans. Even me.

"But I want to tell you, Dad, I've never been so scared as I was when it looked like Davie's Pride was either going down or through the fence. The track was such a mess to begin with and then Sweepstakes bumped into Double Seven and Double Seven pushed Davie's Pride right up against the fence."

"I take it he's all right?" the Chief inquired drily.

"He's fine, Dad, nobody even cares about his only getting third money. We didn't even care when it looked like all he was getting was fourth, I had a hundred saved and Mrs. Sullivan was going to sell an old family ring to cover the rest of the Derby fee, but now she won't have to."

"You were going to put up your money to enter him?"

"Well, I know you'll think it's dumb, but Dad, the Sullivans are such great people and Davie's Pride . . . oh, maybe he isn't the greatest horse in the world, but he's got a chance, honest he has, it just wasn't his fault today."

The sound the Chief made was more bark than laugh. "You don't have to give me excuses for what you do with your own money, Alan. But for someone who was screaming to high Heaven about this assignment just two days ago, you seem pretty happy."

"Dad, I wouldn't be anyplace else right now for a million dollars!"

"Well," the Chief cleared his throat. "Let's remember you're supposed to be working for Great Southeastern Insurance Company!"

"I am, Dad, believe me. I'm practically living in Pop Dewey's pocket. If you want to know, he loves me like a little brother. But he's so wrapped up in Double Seven right now, he hasn't time to think of anything else."

The Chief was silent for a moment. "You think Double Seven might win the Derby, Alan?"

"I don't know, Dad. He ran a darn good race, even with the bad track and the interference. But Sweepstakes may still have been best, even though the stewards had to take his number down. If Davie's Pride hadn't been bumped, he might have won, and Armada never got a real chance to run. There'll be Lucky Jim and Dashing Lad and Freeway on Saturday, too."

"That's my point," the Chief said. "Double Seven may not win the Derby and if he doesn't, that's when you may hit pay dirt."

"I guess Pop would really come unstrung after the buildup today," said Alan.

"We're still only working a hunch," the Chief said. "But if he has anything to tell, that's when he might tell it."

"I'll stay on it, Dad, don't worry."

The Chief hung up, puzzled by an indefinable sense of satisfaction. Then it came to him.

Not once during this report had Alan called him "sir." Now that the Chief thought about it, Alan hadn't stammered very much, either.

Two hours after the Trial, Ed Quincy was still wet. He sneezed. "With my luck," he told the man on the next bar stool, "I'll probably wind up with pneumonia."

Artie Dobermeyer didn't answer. He stared morosely into his whiskey.

Quincy sneezed again. "Well, anyway, I don't care. He won it, no matter what. By three lengths. And who knows," he added, "maybe it'll rain again Saturday."

Artie didn't hear. He was thinking that it wasn't really the tickets on Double Seven that he'd torn into a thousand pieces when it seemed Sweepstakes had won. It was all the other things. His fear. His shame. J. Langdon Mannering and his goons.

But he should have known better. He'd thrown away a hundred and fourteen bucks.

Others like Artie Dobermeyer tore up their tickets at Churchill Downs that afternoon, but most people simply dropped the bits of cardboard at their feet or into the nearest trash barrel.

The disqualification of Sweepstakes gave Good Mary the most profitable day of her career. Not only did she find two Win tickets on Double Seven worth $22.80 apiece, she also turned up four discarded Place tickets on Jennifer's Joe—and at 85-to-1, Jennifer's Joe had paid $72.40 for his official second-place standing.

Donnie Cheevers was waiting at the airport with Morgan Wells. The young jockey had flown in to ride Armada with such absolute conviction that he would win. And now here he was, about to fly back again with his tail between his legs.

"Upset Loser of the Year," he said bitterly.

Donnie had said the same thing several times since the Trial and Morgan's nerves jangled at the repetition. But competitiveness was what made a good jockey and Donnie Cheevers was one of the best. He hated to be beaten for whatever reason. He blamed rather than excused himself when he lost.

He was frequently referred to as a "young Gabe Hilliard," not only because he, too, had been developed by Morgan but because both riders had surprisingly similar techniques. Fortunately, though, Donnie had a much higher boiling point.

Morgan took a firmer grip on his control, forcing himself to speak soothingly. "Come on," he said. "It's a disappointment, of course, a big disappointment, but that's racing."

"Still, to be cut out of the running like that!"

"There wasn't a damn thing you could do about it, Donnie, stop hitting yourself over the head."

"Coming down the track twenty lengths off the pace!"

"If you'd come any closer, Mister Mack would have bounced you off that colt so fast your head would spin and he'd have been right. What else were you going to do? Push Armada to the limit and use him up in a race already lost?"

"No, of course not."

"Well, that was your only option after a start like that, so forget it. Let's just thank our stars you were able to avoid a bad accident, that neither you nor Armada was hurt. It was a damn close thing."

"I know."

"Then cut it out, Donnie. I mean it. It's over and tearing yourself apart is a sheer waste of energy. We've still got a good shot at the Derby, that's what you have to concentrate on now." He changed the subject firmly. "You sure you've got everything? Your ticket? The reservation for Friday?"

"Got my ticket right in my hand." Donnie gestured with it, then patted his pocket. "And I got Friday's safely tucked away in here."

"Okay. Now, remember, that flight on Friday was the only one I could get you after your last race at Laurel. It's a little tricky, doesn't leave you much time. But whatever you do, Donnie, don't miss that plane. Everybody and his brother will be trying to make it in here on Derby Eve and you'll never get another flight."

"Yes, Daddy, you told me ten times."

"I suppose I am repeating myself," Morgan apologized, "only you've never been here before and you can't imagine what it's like."

The enormous strain which was evident in Morgan's face had been worrying Donnie since his arrival. Mister Mack hadn't known what was wrong and Donnie hadn't dared ask Morgan himself. But whatever the problem was, Donnie certainly didn't want to add to it. He said quickly, "I was just kidding, Morgan. I'll be on the plane, don't give it another thought. And if the card's running late at Laurel for any reason, I'll ask the stewards to excuse me off my last mount. I wouldn't take a chance on missing Derby Day for the world."

"There's nothing like it, Donnie, but it's a long long day for a jock, a tense one. You have to be up in the jockey's room by ten and stay there until after the Derby."

"Right."

"We've got three other mounts that afternoon. We could have taken more but I thought that was just enough to give you a good feel for the course and break up the waiting without tiring you out before the Derby itself."

"I know."

Morgan bit his lip. "I'm repeating myself again. Sorry, Donnie."

They were both relieved when Donnie boarded his plane.

Morgan walked slowly back to his car. Going through the motions of his regular routine, speaking the familiar words required incredible effort, but Elverson had convinced him it might help.

How small the hope of saving Lisa was, Morgan dared not allow himself to think. It was all that kept him from going mad.

WEDNESDAY

ONE

THE MOST BEAUTIFUL TULIPS in the world, thought the head gardener as he examined them anxiously for damage. The reds were Halcro and C. W. Leak. The yellows were Golden Harvest and Mrs. John T. Schleepers. The pinks were Renown and Smiling Queen. And he still had to get them safely through today, tomorrow and Friday.

He had imported them from Holland, kept them in the Churchill Downs greenhouse bins at a meticulously-controlled 60 degrees and planted them in November, exactly 8 inches deep, in his own special blend of soil, bone meal, peat moss and other nutrients.

Now there were 7500 bulbs in the main beds of the clubhouse garden alone, and as he finished checking them the head gardener sighed in relief. His worst enemies in any year were frost, excessive moisture and soaring temperatures. Yesterday he had feared that the months of labor and devotion would be lost. It had happened before.

But so far so good. This morning the sun shone benignly

in a cloudless sky, no rain was predicted for at least twenty-four hours and the temperature wasn't expected to go above 75 degrees. With any luck at all, the tulip display which had become traditional as the blanket of roses for the winner would be in full—but not too full—bloom on Derby Day.

And though most people never even considered the point, this was a triumph of timing almost as difficult to achieve—on a different level—as bringing a colt to his peak for that first Saturday in May.

How formidable a task the latter was, was being demonstrated once again at the Derby Barn. As the head gardener breathed silent thanksgiving on the brick walk, Pop Dewey unwrapped the bandages on Double Seven's legs and discovered that the right front ankle was swollen.

Ned Anderson, who'd been idly watching, cast one stricken glance at the offending hoof and rushed to summon help by way of the nearest guardroom phone. That done, he stepped outside to face the newsmen who had come in full force to interview the trainer of yesterday's upset Derby Trial winner.

His brief announcement brought a barrage of excited questions.

"Look, fellows," he pleaded, his voice strained, "I've given you every bit of information I've got. The horse was all right last night, you saw him yourselves. He cooled out perfectly after the Trial. No limp, no tenderness, not the least hint of trouble. He ate good, he was fine. And now . . ." He cleared his throat. "I haven't any idea how bad it is. I've got to see what the vet says when he gets here."

"But what do you think, Ned? You think this will keep him from running Saturday?"

Anderson spread his hands helplessly. "I tell you, there's no way I can answer that until the veterinarian's gone over him. It could turn out to be nothing." He cleared his throat again in an effort to regain control of his shaking voice. "Or it could be serious enough to put him out of action for weeks."

"But what's *your* opinion? You've seen him."

"I'm not trying to stall you guys," Anderson said. "But right now there's nothing more I can tell you. I just don't know."

Pop Dewey knew, though.

He had wrapped too many legs for too many years.

Inside the Derby Barn, in Stall H, where last night he had been all but incoherent with joy, he buried his face in the sleek neck of the big bay colt, hiding the terrible tears, trying to muffle his harsh, racking sobs.

Pop Dewey hadn't cried since the night his stepfather thrashed him and he ran away from Keo, Arkansas, half a century earlier. But he couldn't help it now. Double Seven was out of the Kentucky Derby.

TWO

ROSANNA WAS READY to climb the walls. Mace's sudden interest in racing was bad enough. He had read her all the reports of yesterday's Trial as if she understood what any of it meant. Disqualifications, stewards' hearings, whether some jockey on some horse was going to be suspended. But now he was making her listen while he read the classified ads, not just to find a secondhand car for the meeting with Cardigan but for his own amusement.

"Hey, Rosanna," he was laughing. "Get a load of this one. 'Kentucky Derby Special.'" He broke off. "Everything's a 'Derby Sale' or a 'Derby Bargain' or a 'Derby Special' or something. Even the ads for department stores and supermarkets.

It cracks me up, honest." He resumed his reading. " 'Fine luxury car be yours at only $2,945, credit rating no problem, previous bankruptcy okay.' "

That did it!

"For God's sake!" Rosanna exploded. "All you want is something cheap, just a set of wheels to pick up the money. Afterwards you'll be leaving it on the street!"

"Relax, Rosanna," Mace said cheerfully from his bunk. "I got nothing else to do for awhile." He looked back at his paper. "Hey, you got to listen to this. 'If you want Hawaiian Vacation and have Derby Box, will trade. Two weeks, all expenses paid, in exchange.' "

"Oh, Mace."

" 'Need good Derby Box, will pay top prices, no questions asked.' " He smirked. "That's because nobody's supposed to sell their tickets over cost. If they're caught doing it, the track won't ever sell to them anymore. 'Derby tickets desperately required for out-of-town guests.' 'Want any Derby Box in Section F-G, any arrangements, Fri.-Sat. combinations or Derby Day only.' "

He dropped the paper and sat up. "I've been meaning to tell you, you know those tickets we're going to get?"

"Ummm?"

"They're for Friday and Saturday, too, so no matter what I pay the old guy for them, it won't be as bad as it sounds. He says Friday's almost as important as the Derby for the breeders and owners. They run some other big race that's been going since Churchill Downs started, the Oaks, that's the name of it. It's just for fillies, but there's always an extra crowd because you can start betting on the Derby then. I better get hold of that old guy today."

Rosanna burst into tears.

Mace scrambled hastily to his feet. "Rosanna, for God's sake, what's the matter?"

"What's the matter?" she said furiously. "You're what's the

matter, Mace Augustine. You make me so goddamn mad I don't know what to do with myself!"

"What the hell are you talking about. You gone crazy?"

"Me crazy!" She wiped angrily at her tears. "You've got to make that call and you've got to get a car and then you're going to try for that million dollars. I know you shouldn't, Mace, but no, you've got to try, and I'm half out of my mind thinking what could happen, and all you can think of is the Kentucky Derby."

He tried to put his arms around her but she pushed him away. "Come on, baby, you shouldn't be worrying like that. I promise you everything's going to be all right. I've picked a perfect place on the map for the meeting and, believe me, I'll check and doublecheck before I go. I know that million's not worth two cents if we don't get to spend it. I been doing all right so far, haven't I?"

She finally let him hold her, nodding reluctantly.

"Well, then, you got to trust me. I'm going to go over that place backwards and forwards, and if—" He stopped, as Lisa suddenly opened blank eyes.

"Mace, what is it?" Rosanna asked in instant alarm.

He thrust her away without answering, strode to the bunk and pulled the adhesive from Lisa's mouth. The resultant agony brought her gaze into focus and she moaned, realizing where she was.

"My father . . . " she said hoarsely.

"That's exactly who I want to talk to you about," Mace said. "Is it true he always stays here at the Crown Hotel, like Jerry Neal says in his column?"

Lisa frowned, trying to understand the unexpected question. Her lips moved but no sound came from them.

"Come on, stupid, yes or no?"

Lisa swallowed. "The Crown Hotel?"

"For Christ's sake," Mace exploded, "I'm talking plain English. Do you or don't you stay there every year like Neal says? If I call your father and tell him to come down here, instead of me going there, is that the place people would expect him to be?"

"You mustn't do anything to my father. Please, please."

"Forget it," Mace said disgustedly. "Stick the tape back on her, Rosanna, I'll find out for myself!" His flash of temper dissipated. "All I got to do is call the hotel, but I'm sure Neal's right." He shook his head. "What a joke. Here I was going back and forth to New York, and they were supposed to be in Louisville the whole time."

THREE

THAT MORNING'S "Kolumn From Kentucky," in addition to speculating about the Cardigans' break with tradition which had inspired Mace's change of plans, had taken note of Gabe Hilliard's strange defection from the jockey colony at Churchill and the fact that Shelby Todhunter, Jr., hadn't been seen at the track. These items, neatly padded with references to Gabe's broken marriage and his fist fight with Freeway's trainer, had not quite filled the allotted space. Neal had finished off with a carefully worded item about Buddy Sheffield's visit to the V.F.W. bar. The implication that he had been drinking, though unstated, was obvious.

A thing of bits and pieces, that column, Jerry Neal decided, finishing his first cup of coffee that morning. But his mood began to lift. The sheer fact of publication somehow invested his words with authority. There was always an amazing difference between scanning his copy when he rolled it out of the typewriter and seeing it in print. The column wasn't bad at all, considering how hastily he had written it to substitute for the one he had planned on J. Langdon Mannering.

Neal poured himself another cup of coffee with a hand which had begun to tremble with fury now more than fear, though it was the latter that had confined him to his bed most of yesterday.

It seemed incredible to think how stupid he had been, making his gleeful notes on the plane trip from L.A. And it wasn't that he hadn't known the sort of man he meant to threaten. He did know, that was the whole point, but he had been certain that his column made him invincible. He was not the only newspaperman who had ever felt that way, of course. Several had died rather spectacularly of the same arrogance, a fact of which Neal was acutely conscious at the moment.

But Monday night when he got back to Louisville he had simply called J. Langdon and made his pitch. J. Langdon hadn't been smiling, for once. Neal couldn't see him, naturally, but he had known.

"Tell you what," the union leader had said, "it's a little late and I have some people here, but your proposition interests me. Maybe we can work out a deal. Let me get back to you first thing in the morning, okay?"

Neal had been pleased with himself when he went to bed. Then, shortly after midnight, he had awakened to find six men in his room, three on each side, shadowy but towering.

They hadn't touched him. They hadn't had to. They had simply stood over him, breathing, and watched him fall apart. He would never forget how cumulatively terrifying their silence had been. Or how, in the end, he had begged, wept, offered anything, if only they would leave him alone.

After awhile—an eternity—the phone had rung and one of the figures had thrust the receiver against Neal's ear.

"I've been thinking it over," J. Langdon had said, with a

smile, Neal was sure. "I know you'll understand but no deal."

Neal stared at the newspaper he had crumpled in his hand at the memory. Now he carefully smoothed it again, drawing reassurance from the familiar by-line. At least he had been able to turn out a passable column, in spite of everything.

And this morning he had thought of someone who would help even the score. Neal reached for the phone, then reconsidered. He'd contact Gil Tobin from a booth outside the motel where there wouldn't be a record of the call.

Gil had no connection with the pari-mutuels, but his own amalgamation of unions placed him miles above the level of a J. Langdon Mannering. And as he had confided to Neal at a party once, "You want to know about labor, Jere? It's like an ocean where the big fishes swallow up the little fishes. But nobody'll ever try for me, because I'm as big as any of them and I'm full of poison besides!"

Gil had been with his most intimate friends at the time and very drunk or he wouldn't have boasted so indiscriminately. And he certainly wouldn't have allowed himself to be photographed in flaming drag. He had realized the danger the second he sobered up but the cameraman had taken the shots for pleasure, not profit. Gil had been able to retrieve them with the negatives just by asking.

He had no idea that Neal had managed to palm one of the prints first. And Neal wasn't about to mention that fact. Not even now. Unless he had to.

FOUR

THE MINUTE THE TRIAL had been decided Tom Richardson had hopped a chartered plane back to Maryland. With the extra hour of Daylight Saving, he had been able to make a quick check on Sparky and even skim through some of the reports on his study desk before dinner. A great deal had happened while he was away. He didn't attempt to evaluate the notes on the numbers of mares in season— Marshfield's own and those shipped in for breeding—or the pregnancy and stallion performance figures.

He had lingered, though, over Doc Whalen's all but indecipherable scrawl on a torn scrap of paper: "31 foals, 20 fillies, 11 colts." The proportion of fillies to colts—almost 2-to-1— might have been disappointing at another stud farm, but Marshfield had been among the first to recognize the mare's significance in the transmission of desirable traits.

Today this was accepted almost universally. In fact, many horsemen had swung to the opposite extreme and insisted the dam was more important than the sire, a far cry from an era —not actually remote—when breeders had considered the mare so negligible for pedigree purposes that few owners had even bothered to bestow distaff names. Still, there remained an ingrained preference for colts, and a prominent stallion in the bloodlines commanded the most attention— and money—at thoroughbred sales pavilions.

Charlie Talbot, at Lexington, for instance (though hundreds of visiting mares shipped into T-Square Stud every year) maintained only 100 broodmares of his own and concentrated on his 44 notable stallions, as against the general ratio of approximately 1 stud to 10 home mares held at most farms. At two covers per day per stallion at the height of the stud season—with fees ranging anywhere from $1,000 to $40,-000 for a live foal as product of the mating—T-Square's income was highest on that phase of its operation. And the comparatively small number of foals actually dropped in Charlie's barns usually brought top bids.

Marshfield went the other way, with 325 broodmares, though there were additional visitors, and only 23 stallions. The result was that Tom always had many more yearlings to sell than T-Square Stud so that their respective total incomes probably were much the same.

Tom was sorry he'd had to be away. But of course he hadn't been able to resist the MacMillan's plea for help. The trip to California had been unavoidable. And he had had to be in Louisville for the Breeders' Banquet and the Trial, just as he would have to return for the Derby. It was lucky he had such a well-trained army of hands, because what breeders had been saying about the Kentucky Derby since its inaugural in 1875 was true: it came at the worst possible time. The busiest of all on a stud farm.

And yet, having admitted that, you also had to admit that the considerable pressure was well worthwhile to the breeders. Each year's Derby evoked so much public interest that stud farm sightseeing always increased appreciably, and though most of those who came would probably never own a horse in their lives, among them, inevitably, were some who subsequently became clients.

Tom had had dinner with his wife and turned in early, in a mood of solid content. Now, on his morning rounds in the warm spring sunshine, his first stop was the paddock where Sparky seemed almost entirely recovered. The colt greeted him ecstatically. Tom clucked and crooned affectionately, stroking the velvety nose, but he couldn't quite repress a pang of regret that the colt was out of the Derby. Tom rubbed his cheek against the sleek neck, amused at the depth of his certitude that Sparky would have won—now that Sparky couldn't be put to the test.

He hadn't been nearly so positive earlier, despite his wager with Charlie Talbot, which now depended solely upon Dashing Lad. About whom Tom was even less certain, no matter what Orv Scott insisted. Because as a great Kentucky breeder had once said, "Records live, opinions die." Every horseman dreams of producing or owning or training a classic thoroughbred. Many think they might have one. But it takes the Kentucky Derby to prove whether they are right or not.

Tom continued on his rounds, thinking of the argument that little statement could provoke among some horsemen— had provoked over the decades. The oldest chestnut of all about the Derby was the one about the first Saturday in May being too early in a colt's third year to stretch him out that full mile and a quarter.

But in Tom's estimation, if the Derby weren't that long, weren't that demanding, it wouldn't be a definitive test over "the distance of ground" that unmistakably identified the true champion, proving stamina as well as speed.

Tom smiled to himself. It had become almost fashionable, he realized, that claim that the Kentucky Derby was too soon and too long. But it was only propounded for 364 days a year. Come the first Saturday in May the only thing any horseman wanted was to have a colt in the running. And he had two, Tom reminded himself gleefully. Dashing Lad and Magician. Al Lester would dispute that figure, obviously. He owned Magician, but both colts had been bred and born on this very ground, so Al could count in his way and Tom would count in his.

In this cheery frame of mind, Tom dismounted from his saddle horse and tethered it to the hitching post in front of the office. This building, with its files, its computerized pedigree sheets, its accountant, timekeeper and clerks, its endless paperwork, was the nerve center of Marshfield Farms.

It was there that Tom Richardson got the shocking news of Orville Scott's death. The trainer had been killed in a car wreck. For a moment Tom was motionless. Then, whitefaced, he picked up the phone again and dialed Churchill Downs.

"I hate to ask you to do this, Lee," the big Marylander said, "but Dashing Lad's groom tells me nobody can find Ferdy Garcia. He's probably catting around somewhere, celebrating the baby. It will take me at least two hours to make it back to Louisville and somebody has got to break the news to Peggy." Tom's voice broke.

"Of course, Tom, she mustn't hear it from strangers," Lee said. "I'll go over to the hospital right away."

It was a task he couldn't very well avoid, Lee thought as he hung up. Nor would he really want to, aside from a natural reluctance to be the bearer of such unhappy news. He had known Peggy since she was a little girl—had met her as he had met Lisa Cardigan when he had arrived at Churchill Downs—and he cared about both in much the same way.

Last night Lee's wife, who always managed to know about such matters, had reported that Peggy's labor had been protracted and somewhat complicated. Considering that she and Ferdy were both small, their son had been unexpectedly large—over eight pounds—and his arrival had ruptured a vein.

But when Lee explained his mission, her doctor said she was strong enough to be told about her father and saw that Lee was instantly ushered into Peggy's room. The nurse had just put her well-bundled son beside her on the bed, and in the manner of all new mothers, she was fussing possessively at the soft blanket, folding it down here, tucking it back there, examining in wonder and pride the exquisitely miniature features.

When Lee walked in she raised a glowing face. "I'm so

224

glad they let you visit while he was here. Look," she said, "isn't he beautiful?"

Lee bent over the baby and made what he hoped were appropriate murmurs of admiration, asking himself how in the name of God he was going to break the news to her.

"I suppose I'll have to learn not to brag like that," Peggy rattled on happily, "but I hardly saw him yesterday on account of the transfusion."

She rearranged the blanket. "He's like a doll, isn't he, Lee? And the image of Ferdy. You wouldn't think you could tell so soon, but I could pick him out anywhere. The same silky black hair, the same straight nose, those high cheekbones . . ." She broke off her catalogue of miracles. "Have you seen my father?" she asked.

"No. No, I haven't."

"I was just wondering. If you did. And what he said. He and Ferdy both saw the baby before I did, you know, isn't that unbelievable? But I was in the delivery room for so long." She stopped suddenly, puzzled at his expression. "Lee, is anything wrong?"

He told her then, as gently as he could.

She stared at him, her arm tightening convulsively around her son. "Dead?" she asked. "My father's dead?"

Lee nodded in desperate sympathy. In spite of what the doctor had said, maybe they should have waited.

"He can't be," Peggy said, shaking her head in childish denial. "He was here all day yesterday, exactly as usual, still trying to make me say the baby was Gabe's. I told him and told him, Gabe never even kissed me, but it was like he didn't want to believe me."

Peggy was completely unconscious of Lee's shock. "I thought I hated him for insisting like that. But I loved him. I just wanted him to know." She looked up at Lee, her eyes pleading. "He must have, Lee, once he saw the baby? He must have known before. . . ?"

225

"I'm sure he did," Lee said huskily. "He couldn't possibly have doubted after seeing that face."

It was only then she began to cry, and mercifully, at that moment, the errant Ferdy came into the room.

Lee left Peggy weeping in her husband's comforting arms and went back to Churchill Downs. He was aware, en route, of a certain sympathy for Gabe Hilliard. Even backstretch rumor hadn't touched on the reason for Scott's hatred of the jockey. Gabe himself hadn't known why he'd lost his chance to ride Dashing Lad in the Derby. And, apparently, he had been totally blameless.

But as he turned into the grounds, he dismissed the matter with a slight shrug. He still didn't like Gabe Hilliard.

FIVE

I N AZALIA, INDIANA, Sam Grundage sat in a wicker rocking chair on his front porch and blamed himself for being a dad-burned fool. He had been trying to build his strength by making secret trips up and down the cellar steps and, for some reason, it had been harder to do it twice today than it had been yesterday. When he got up to the kitchen the second time his heart had been going like blue blazes.

But he had determined he was going to make three trips this morning. Instead of resting, he had made himself go on, stubborn old goat that he was, and had been forced to run the last few steps into the bargain, because Debbie and Young Hugh had been bringing the baby downstairs from her bath and darn near caught him in the act.

Self-castigation had no effect on the terrible weakness still trembling within him, though, and against his will, Sam Grundage began to wonder about Saturday. He supposed he was being mule-headed about that, too. And yet, he couldn't change his plan. There'd been a Grundage at every running of the Kentucky Derby since it began. His grandfather or his father or him. All three of them together on Sam's very first—that had been Old Rosebud's Derby—back in 1914. And his father had been with him when he had taken Hugh to his first Derby; another good one, Whirlaway's, in 1941.

Sam had always meant that someday he and Hugh would take Young Hugh to *his* first. Well maybe they would all go next year when the boy would be six, same age as Sam was when Old Rosebud streaked across the line eight lengths ahead of the nearest rival. Sam sighed. This year was the problem, with Hugh in the hospital. So it *had* to be him, he thought.

SIX

KERMIT YOUNG closed the door of Lee's office behind him as he entered. "I was just leaving to see you when you called."

"Oh? Something on your mind?"

"Nothing that can't wait if you've got something on yours," Kermit said.

Lee slid a folded sheet of yellow paper across the desk to him. "Our friend sent this along, says it's what Mannering will be passing out to the men as they leave work this after-noon, unless we come to terms before then."

The pari-mutuel head was the only person besides Lee who knew that it was the union secretary, Jack Phillips, who was reporting on J. Langdon. But even between themselves they avoided using the name. Jack would be in serious trouble if anyone even suspected what he was doing.

Kermit opened the paper and read the large crude letters. "It certainly catches the eye, doesn't it? A special union call for tomorrow night, huh? Well, he'll have a packed house this time, that's for sure. What kind of terms?"

"Our friend didn't know. Just 'some kind of a deal.' Exact quote."

"Then that means you'll be hearing from Mannering soon."

"I can hardly wait." Lee refolded the yellow announcement and put it carefully out of sight.

"I don't know," Kermit said. "Perhaps it would be worth . . ."

"No, we can't submit to blackmail. And I still don't believe the men will go along with him."

"They're scared, Lee, you heard what's been happening. It isn't as if they were being given a free choice."

"Yes," Lee said regretfully, thinking of Artie Dobermeyer, "I'm aware of that."

"Then there are all these other men coming in, Lee, fellows who don't have any real ties to Churchill. Or even to the Derby, though a lot of them have worked it before."

"How does that situation look, by the way? You going to fill the quota?"

"That's always a good question," Kermit said. "Six hundred and thirty-five extras have agreed to come in which would give us a body in every window, but how many will actually show . . ." He shrugged.

"You sweat that one out every single year," Lee reminded him, "and somehow you always manage."

"Oh, sure, and we will this Saturday unless there's a strike. The first hint of that and they'll stay away in droves. Even the men who show can refuse to work at the last minute if we don't get this thing settled."

"We still can't submit to blackmail," said Lee. "We won't. That's what I have to make Mannering realize. We're pressured by time, God knows, Kermit, but so is he. He has to get what he wants before Saturday or he's drawn a blank. Any fool knows he won't get it after the Derby."

"But why can't we pretend to go along, tape our conversation and then prosecute later?"

"Because it's a shoddy way to do business," Lee said. "The board rejected that suggestion and I agree. In any case, Mannering's too slick to fall into such an obvious trap. He has to be or he'd already be behind bars. You know what the investigators have turned up on him: all kinds of presumptive coercions and not one shred of hard evidence." Lee sighed. "I wish he'd make his move and get it over with!"

"That's why he's dragging it out. To let you stew for awhile."

"Well, don't tell anyone," said Lee, "but the tactic is working. Now, what did you want to see me about?"

"Oh, the FBI called. We notified them earlier that we took in another of those twenties they're looking for. They want permission to send somebody over to set up procedure in case we get any more."

"We did turn up another one, then. Where?"

"In the grandstand. We've pinpointed the section, though we're not sure which window it was. There are about a dozen sellers there, including your friend, Dobermeyer."

"No use being sore at Artie," Lee said. "Considering what we've learned about the way J. Langdon operates."

"I'm not sore at Artie. It's Mannering and his goons I'd like to horsewhip."

"Amen," Lee said. "Any idea what the FBI plans?"

"No, but I told them we'd cooperate, naturally. I suppose they'll explain what it's all about when they get here. You going to be available?"

"I'm not moving out of this office until I've talked to Mannering. Just go ahead, work out whatever it is they want. And maybe Fred Keller should sit in with you. If the FBI's trying to pick someone up at Churchill, that could involve security."

"Right."

"That's all we needed around here," Lee said. "Cops and robbers in Derby Week. We wouldn't want things to get too dull."

The phone rang and both men tensed, but it was only Warren Robbins, reporting from the press box.

"The stewards have decided," he said. "Took them a long time, they ran that film backwards and forwards, but they're setting Mickey Kuzich down. They say he could have controlled Sweepstakes yesterday in spite of all the other factors involved."

"I thought they'd have to," Lee said. "How many days did they give him?"

"Five," Warren said, "starting Friday."

"That means Kuzich can't ride in the Derby."

"No, the Nickels will have to get a new boy."

"Tough on Kuzich," Lee said.

"Happens every day," said Warren. "If the suspension didn't affect the Derby, it would just be another item for the Daily Racing Form. Got something else for you, Lee. It isn't official yet but it's a pretty solid tip: Jim York's supposed to have canned Buddy Sheffield."

"You're kidding."

"No, I think it's true, Lee."

"You mean Sheffield won't be saddling Lucky Jim for the Derby? Why, for God's sake?"

"Did you read Jerry Neal this morning?"

"No," Lee said disgustedly. "After the way he smeared Louisville in yesterday's column, I had enough."

"Well, today he smeared Sheffield, and, Lee, Neal's also beginning to sniff around Gabe Hilliard's absence. Maybe you'd better take a look."

SEVEN

VARONICA DROPPED HER NEWSPAPER on the couch and stood up eagerly as Gabe followed the doctor into the living room. "How is he?" she asked.

The doctor hunched his shoulders. "He's doing as well as can be expected, Miss Varon. But I still think he should be tested more thoroughly at the hospital."

"What about his walking around like this? Shouldn't he stay in bed?"

The doctor glanced at Gabe, fully dressed and determinedly upright, and couldn't suppress a smile. "I suppose if he's mad enough to consider riding in the Derby, he has to start moving around sometime. Just try to keep him from overdoing it."

Varonica grinned at Gabe as the doctor closed the door behind him. "Oh, sure," she mocked, "just try." Then, more seriously, she asked, "Does the new bandage help?"

"Help? It feels like he wrapped me in red-hot cement," Gabe complained. "I can hardly take a deep breath, but I'll make it. Any of that coffee left?"

"Better than that, I put on a fresh pot." She busied herself in the compact kitchenette. "Something to go with it?"

"One of those cinnamon rolls you gave me at breakfast, if you have it," he said, lowering himself gingerly onto a stool at the counter. "But I'd better be careful, if I stick around you very long, I'll have trouble making weight. If the Derby field didn't have to carry 126 pounds, I'd be in trouble already!"

"Is that what you weigh? 126?"

"Good God, woman, watch your language. I'd be out of business if I even came close. I make around 112, if I watch my diet." He picked up the pastry she put before him and gave her an ironic salute. "It isn't easy, though, and at that, I'm pretty lucky. Some jocks practically starve themselves to death and still gain."

"That must be really rough."

"Rough? You wouldn't believe what some of those guys go through. No food, no liquids. Pills, exercise, the sweatbox. Sometimes they end up so damn weak I don't know how they get on their horses, let alone control them. The simplest accident, even a minor spill, sends them straight into shock."

"Oh, no."

"It's true. First thing they do with most jocks is give them a slug of brandy to bring them out of it. But I wouldn't go through that kind of torture. If it was that much of a hassle for me to make the scale—" He stopped abruptly. "Who knows, maybe I would, same as the rest of them. What else could I do?"

Sensing the underlying bitterness Varonica tried to distract him. "Wait a minute," she said, "you've got me all mixed up. You're 112 pounds but you said the Derby horses all carry 126."

"That's with saddle and lead weights in the saddle cloths," said Gabe.

"Oh, I didn't know they counted the saddles." She slid onto a stool opposite him. "But that's stupid. They must be very heavy."

"The saddles aren't heavy, Ronnie, they only weigh about a pound and a half."

"Those big things? Oh, come on, Gabe."

"I'm not kidding you, Ronnie, racing saddles are very light. They have to be." He sipped his coffee. "There are exceptions. A very light jockey might use a ten-pound saddle so he wouldn't have to put too much lead in the saddle cloths. Owners or trainers are always arguing about whether dead weight is harder to carry than live weight, but Bill Shoemaker pretty much settled that one: It's all the same."

"But weight itself makes that much difference, Gabe? It's silly. I love the races and go whenever I can, but I've just never paid attention to things like that."

He laughed. "And you pick your horses by name or number or because you happen to like the jockey's colors?"

"All right," Varonica said, "I know you're laughing at me but I don't care, I have fun, anyway. Of course, from now on, I can just bet on the jockey."

"Oh? Did you have anyone in particular in mind?"

"Well, yes," she said, "I met one the other evening that everybody tells me is very good, maybe the best in the country." She paused, then added mockingly. "His name is Gene Firestone."

"You wait till I get my health back," Gabe said, "I'll fix you for that. But about your question, Ronnie, the way it is figured in racing is that every five pounds will slow a horse down one length going a mile."

"Oh," said Varonica, trying to sound as if she'd understood.

"Let's try it another way. Say you have two horses and each time they race against each other for a mile, one horse always comes in a length in front. He's just that much better. You with me so far?"

Varonica nodded. "Well, it wouldn't be very interesting if you knew ahead of time exactly who was going to win," Gabe said. "That's where the weights come in. In theory, if you put five pounds extra on the better horse—the horse who always wins by one length—those five pounds would slow him down that one length and the other would have an equal chance in the race."

"Like a golfer's handicap," Varonica said.

"Same principle," Gabe said. "And in both cases there are other elements. A golfer may have an easy putt that would give him the game and he's so tense he blows it. One horse has class, heart, guts, whatever you want to call it, he just won't quit . . ." He broke off abruptly. "I've got to be boring you to death."

"You're not."

"Well, one thing more while we're talking about handicaps and that's all, I promise. But to me, this is the most fascinating thing about the whole business. You take a horse that's a pretty good horse and you keep running him out of his class with horses so much better he's always being beaten, you understand?"

"Yes."

"Then, after awhile, you drop him down, where he's racing against a lower class, horses he could beat without half trying —he still won't win. He's got it so firmly stuck in his mind that he's a loser that he *is* a loser!"

Varonica thought for a second. "What if you tried it the other way around?"

"Good girl," said Gabe. "That's exactly what I'm going to find out some day, if I ever go into training. I believe if you built up a horse's confidence . . ." He shrugged.

"Is that what you plan to be, a trainer?"

Gabe slid off the stool carefully and stood up. "I don't know. I might when I can't ride anymore, but a lot of jockeys have fallen flat on their faces trying it." He made a few tentative efforts at exercise, wincing. "Right now, I'm not even sure I'll make it on Magician!"

"There'll be other Derbies," she said easily, beginning to clear the counter.

"Nick thinks Magician can win this one. If I'm on him, that is."

"Well, fine, but not if it's going to be bad for you."

"Wow, you and Nick ought to work up an act together. As if the Kentucky Derby were any old race and nobody cared whether I ride in it or not. Well, I care, damn it, so don't pay any attention if I happen to groan or something, Ronnie, and I won't pay any attention to you. Or Nick. Or the doctor."

His voice rose pugnaciously. "Because when that band starts playing 'My Old Kentucky Home' Saturday afternoon, I have every intention of coming out on the track with Magician."

Tactfully, Varonica concentrated on washing dishes.

"I know you're only thinking of what's best for me, but I'll be all right," Gabe said more calmly.

"Of course you will."

"I didn't mean to yell at you. But it's important to me."

Varonica dried her hands. "Forget it, Gabe," she said, coming out of the kitchenette.

"I'll bring you some of Magician's roses after the Derby to make up."

"I'll take them." She straightened the newspaper she had dropped earlier. "Jerry Neal was writing about you this morning, did you see?"

"That bastard," Gabe said. "Yes, I saw!"

"Gabe, could I ask you a question?"

He ticked off points on his fingers. "The Cardigans didn't tell me their plans, I haven't seen them for over two years. I don't give a damn where Shel Todhunter is. As for Buddy Sheffield, I don't believe a word of it. If he really did fall off the wagon, Neal wouldn't have had to go pussyfooting around like that, I know how he operates. Okay?"

"Okay, but it wasn't Neal's column I wanted to ask you

about." She hesitated. "I've been wondering about Lisa Cardigan. What she's like. I know it's none of my business, but I'm curious. From the little I've heard, she sounds nice. I suppose you wouldn't have picked her if she weren't. But that's what makes me wonder."

Gabe sat on the couch and pulled Varonica down next to him. "I'll tell you about Lisa," he said, "and then I've got a couple of questions of my own, fair enough?"

"What kind of questions?"

"About you."

She raised an eyebrow. "You know about me."

"I'm curious, too," he said. "Is it a deal?"

She nodded. "I've told you the only secret I own already. But ask away."

"No, I'll answer you first. Lisa is nice, Ronnie. Sweet, loving, honest, kind. I'm not very proud of the way I treated her."

"She left because of the way you treated her?"

Gabe's laugh was short. "It was the other way around. I was the one who cut out. But she should have left me. I guess toward the end I was trying to force her to. Only she didn't." He shook his head. "And yet, that's what you would have expected to happen, isn't it?"

"Not necessarily," Varonica said.

"Thanks for the vote of confidence, Ronnie, but let's face it. A wealthy girl from a fine old family married to a poor jock with my background?"

"That's funny," Varonica said. "I don't even know where you were born."

"Tennessee."

"Or about your family or anything."

"Look," Gabe said almost harshly, "do you want to hear about Lisa or don't you?"

"Of course," Varonica said, so startled by his tone that he reached over to pat her hand.

"I suppose I left her for the very reasons that made me marry her in the first place. Just because she was so rich and came from such a distinguished family and was so nice herself."

"Didn't you love her?"

"We're talking about seven, eight years ago, Ronnie. We were babies in the beginning. I thought I loved her. I was— oh, out of my mind that a girl like her would even look at me. It made me feel as if . . ." He shook his head. "I don't know, there's no way to explain how I felt. But I can tell you exactly how being married to Lisa Cardigan turned out. It was like eating in the world's finest restaurants all the time."

Disbelieving, Varonica said, "What?"

"You think that sounds funny but I'm not kidding. It's the best description I can come up with. I've been in hundreds of good restaurants since I started making it, Ronnie. I enjoy them sometimes. The plush atmosphere. The fancy food. I was going to say 'the service' but I never really like that. It's usually too good. I always feel like somebody's watching every bite I take. And I always know I'm mispronouncing the French and I'm not sure about the right fork and when they ask about wines, what vintage, what year . . .

"I'm uncomfortable, that's all. Or maybe not exactly uncomfortable, just not quite at ease. Not the way I'd be in a hamburger joint, say, where nobody gives a damn one way or the other. Can you understand that?"

Varonica studied him for a second. "I think you're saying you were like one of those horses you mentioned before, that couldn't win because he thought he was outclassed."

"Touché!" Gabe said, reaching over to take her hand. "That's one French word I can pronounce, Ronnie, baby, and may I add that I've never been in a nicer hamburger joint in my life?"

"Gee, thanks," Varonica said. "One slice of raw onion coming up."

"Better make that two slices," Gabe said, "you might need

one in self-defense. But first things first, it's my turn, now, right?"

"Your turn?"

"To ask questions."

"Oh, I'd forgotten. Okay, your turn."

"It's about the night we met." He gave her a sidelong glance. "Seems a long time ago, doesn't it? But when I asked you to have a drink with me, what did you think?"

"Why, you must know what I thought, Gabe."

"Tell me."

"Well, obviously, I liked you or I wouldn't have agreed." When that didn't seem to satisfy him, she added, "I particularly liked you or I wouldn't have suggested coming here. If only I hadn't wanted to hurry ahead and straighten things up a little before you saw the place."

"Stop blaming yourself, Ronnie, who could have figured those two maniacs?"

"I know, but I keep thinking if I'd just waited while you said goodnight to your friends and we'd come up together."

"Forget it, it's over. What I'm trying to find out is how you could tell that you liked me. We'd only talked for a couple of minutes."

"There are people you like right away, Gabe, just as there are some you dislike from the start. And I knew quite a bit about you before we even talked. Who you were. What you did. There was something about you . . ."

He hesitated. "Your roommate was away for the night. You must have figured I'd try to make a pass if we came up here?"

Varonica laughed. "No question about it."

"All right. What would have happened then?"

She turned on the couch to face him directly. "I don't know, Gabe."

"You must have some idea."

"It would have depended." She stopped. "Are you asking if I would have let you make love to me? Is that what this is all about?"

"Yes, that's what this is all about."

She smiled faintly. "I might have, if . . ."

"If what?"

"If I'd felt like it after you made that pass." Her smile deepened. "And if you're interested in a wild guess, I think I would have."

"Just like that?" Gabe asked flatly.

"Just like that."

"If you happened to feel like it?"

Her chin lifted, almost imperceptibly. "Would you have had a better reason?"

"Whenever you felt like it?"

"Anytime I felt like it," Varonica said steadily.

Gabe drew a deep breath and got to his feet. "Too bad I missed it."

"What does that mean, Gabe?"

He shrugged. "Nothing. It means what I said. I'm sorry I missed the party."

After a few seconds, Varonica said brightly, "Well, you asked a foolish question."

He glared. "What was so foolish about wanting to know?"

"I wasn't talking about you, I was talking about me." Her voice was cold. "Anything else you'd like to ask?"

"Yes, if you want to know."

"Then go ahead."

"Oh, no," he said emphatically. "The kind of girl you seem to be . . ."

Varonica's eyes were bleak. "Don't stop there," she said. "I can't wait for the end of that one."

"The kind of girl you are, you'd tell me the truth and I don't want to hear it. I've just discovered I'm jealous as hell." Suddenly he grinned. "That's pretty funny, coming from me. I never thought I could be."

He began to pace. "I don't say I'm never going to ask. I probably will. We may even fight over it." He thought briefly and nodded. "I'm sure we're going to fight over it. But nothing that's happened before to either of us makes a damn bit of difference. And whatever might have been between us, it's turned into something else entirely. For me, anyway, Ronnie."

She stood impulsively. "Oh, Gabe, for me, too."

For an instant, facing each other, the disparity in height startled them both. Then Gabe said deliberately, "By God, you are tall, aren't you? But if we sit down on the couch again where I can reach you, maybe we ought to start finding out how you would have felt the other night."

Nick Chambley's distinctive knock sounded on the door.

"This time," Gabe said disgustedly, "he really is fired. But I suppose we can't get away with pretending there's nobody home?"

Varonica giggled and went to let Nick in.

"Hey, you're not supposed to be out of bed, are you?" the agent demanded when he saw Gabe.

"Try and keep him there," Varonica said. "Even the doctor's given up."

"He says it's all right?"

"Relax, Nick," Gabe said. "I've got to start moving or I won't be able to ride a merry-go-round. The Derby's Saturday."

Nick didn't speak until he'd dropped the handful of envelopes he was carrying onto the breakfast bar. "Brought your mail over," he said, then turned for a serious examination of Gabe. "The Derby is Saturday but we have to make our decision now. Final entries tomorrow. Do we cancel or do we go?"

"We go," Gabe told him firmly.

"You sure? You still look like the wrath of God to me. If you have any doubts at all . . ."

"I haven't," Gabe said. He smiled at Varonica. "I couldn't back out now if I wanted to, Nick. I just promised someone I'd bring her some roses."

Nick smiled at Varonica, too. "Well, if it's who I think it is, nobody was ever more entitled." He sank wearily onto one of the stools. "I suppose you've noticed I always talk about how 'we' won a race or 'we' got beat a nose or 'we're' riding Magician?"

"Gabe says all agents do."

Nick sighed. "I don't know why, because in the end, the jockey's the one who really gets out there and puts his life on the line. In any race, not just the Derby." He looked at Gabe. "So, okay. If you say so."

"Coffee, Nick?" Varonica asked. "Before I go inside and do a little housecleaning?"

"I'd like some but don't leave on my account."

"You're not chasing me. I have to do it, you wouldn't believe that room. And we're not letting the maid in these days."

Gabe slid onto a stool opposite Nick and Varonica gave them both coffee. When she'd gone, the big agent lapsed into silence.

"What's the matter, Nick? You look down in the mouth."

Nick stirred a third spoonful of sugar into his cup. "I can't imagine why," he said morosely. "It was a perfectly normal morning at the track. Horses go bad every day, jockeys get suspended, trainers get fired. People get drunk and smash their cars."

Gabe pursed his lips, considering. "All right," he said, "we'll go back and run the rest of the film over again later. First you may as well tell me who's dead."

"Orv Scott."

"He was drunk?"

Nick nodded. "I told you Peggy had the baby, didn't I?"

"Yes, yesterday, a boy. God, this is awful for her."

"I know. But I suppose Scott was celebrating. Anyway, the cops spotted him for drunk on the Expressway. Not much over the speed limit, just weaving a little. But when they tried to pull him over, he took off like a bat out of hell. They say he was going 120 when he lost control."

"Orville Scott," Gabe said. "Christ, that's two of them in

less than a week. Both in cars."

"Please don't tell me there's bound to be a third," Nick groaned. "I've heard that so often today it's coming out of my ears."

Gabe fiddled with the little stack of envelopes Nick had brought. "All right," he said, "let's have the rest of it. What horse went bad?"

In view of all that had happened on that Wednesday morning, it was a considerable time before Nick finished talking and Gabe got back into bed. Perhaps too long a time; he ached all over.

While he waited for the pill to work he went through the mail Nick had brought from the room Gabe was to have shared with him. The note from Orville Scott was in a plain white envelope, stamped but uncanceled. Scott had apparently just handed it in at the desk the night before.

Gabe read the all but incoherent lines with growing horror. "Oh, my God!" he muttered.

Varonica was sitting near him, crocheting as usual. "Is something wrong?"

"No," he said after a minute. "It's nothing."

Then he went into the bathroom, tore the thin paper into shreds and flushed it down the toilet, the words Scott had written swirling through his mind.

". . . wanted it to be you . . . that's why I wouldn't listen to her . . . wanted it to be you, not him . . . only when I saw the baby . . ."

Varonica's puzzled glance met Gabe's as he came back into the bedroom. He forced a smile. "Believe me, it was nothing," he said.

Nobody else—not even she—must ever know that Orville Scott had felt such violent rejection when he looked into the face of his newborn grandson that it had driven him to his death. And whether by accident or design, Gabe himself would never be certain.

EIGHT

THE PEGASUS PARADE, like the Derby itself, began as a fairly unassuming event. Conceived only a few seasons earlier as a pleasant civic addition to the general festivity, it was now a major attraction of Derby Week.

This year's theme—"The Fifteenth State"—celebrated the date Kentucky joined the Union, June 1, 1792, a fine era around which to build a succession of colorful and elaborate floats. These and the bevies of appropriately costumed beauties—including, naturally, Miss Kentucky and a Pegasus Queen—as well as the marching bands and some particularly luminous TV personalities drew between 300,000 and 350,000 viewers to downtown Louisville for the five o'clock step off.

Standing at the window of Morgan Wells' room high in the Crown Hotel Lee Ames could see a substantial segment of the enthusiastic crowd, but his mind was not on the parade. He had known when he arrived to confront Morgan what the answer would be. Morgan's suffering face, the Cardigans' inexplicable absence, the investigation into Gabe Hilliard's whereabouts and, finally, the report late this afternoon that the FBI was seeking ransom money at Churchill Downs had suddenly combined to make Lee understand the truth. Nevertheless, the confirmation he had just forced from Morgan was shocking.

Lee moved away from the window. "It's incredible I didn't see it sooner," he said. "And yet it's so unbelievable. You just don't imagine such a thing could . . ."

"I've covered every mile of that route," Morgan interrupted grimly. "But it's entirely beside the point. The main thing is that if you care for Lisa at all, you've got to walk out of here and act as if everything were fine. Don't come to the hotel again, don't even call Lisa's father when he checks in tonight."

"Morgan, surely . . ."

"No," Morgan said, "that's the only thing you can do to help, Lee. Behave as if nothing were happening. And nobody knows better than I do how difficult that is."

Dusk, when it filtered down on the end of the Pegasus Parade, found Pop Dewey among the spectators, with Alan trailing at a discreet distance. But the old groom had not come to watch the parade. He arrived in the area because he was so miserably unhappy he didn't know where he was.

Ned Anderson could believe in miracles if he wanted to. He had been told by his own vet, the track veterinarian and even Doc Todhunter, in consultation, that the odds against Double Seven's running on Saturday were 100-to-1. But Anderson wouldn't give up. Not him and not George Packo, the owner. They still meant to put up the entry-box fee tomorrow morning to keep Double Seven's name in the Derby lineup.

Pop knew they were just throwing the money away. When his chores for the day were completed with Double Seven's four o'clock feeding, he had headed straight for the V.F.W. bar. The whiskey didn't seem to help, though. The more he drank, the deeper he sank into depression.

Alan had followed Pop into the bar but made no attempt to talk to him. The boy had tried to console Pop earlier at the Derby Barn and the old man had just about snapped his head off. Alan had sat at a table along the wall, unobtrusively nursing a beer, until Pop pushed his way out into the street.

After a second of indecision, Pop had just started walking. One foot in front of the other, one block after another, completely oblivious to distance or surroundings. He had reached downtown and the parade crowds when, suddenly, his terrible absorption was pierced by a harsh voice. "Aww, come on," a man was saying to his companion, "Dashing Lad's got to win. An outfit that sells off hundreds of horses a year, you know if they keep one it's going to be the best. It only stands to reason."

Tom Richardson would have shriveled at the man's cynical —and mistaken—idea of how Marshfield Farms operated. Pop Dewey knew better, too, but at that moment the words hit him with the force of revelation. In the instant they registered, his agony altered irrevocably.

It became something more bitter, more unbearable. Not only was Double Seven out of the Derby after coming so close, but Tom Richardson's horse, Dashing Lad, was still in. All the other horses in the Derby Barn were still in. One of them would stand next Saturday before the world, wearing the blanket of roses which should have belonged to Double Seven.

It was at this point, as Pop Dewey stopped short and then reversed direction, that Alan lost the old man among the milling parade watchers.

THURSDAY

ONE

T<small>HE DAY BEGAN</small> in the backstretch with the familiar quickening of predawn activity, the sounds of alarm clocks, the banging of food pails, the stomping of hooves and conflicting radio programs muted by the same darkness which paradoxically accentuated the odors of frying bacon and coffee.

With the first full light, however, all semblance of normalcy fled, at least from around the Derby Barn.

The younger men accepted the frenzy matter-of-factly. They had been bottle fed in an age of electronic miracles.

Their elders, though, reiterated in awed tones what they had been telling one another on similar Thursdays for some years now: If Plain Ben or Sunny Jim—or whichever equally renowned giant among trainers the speaker might personally invoke—could see the goings-on with them horses, so close to the Derby, he'd be throwing a double-barreled fit.

This was the morning when television took over the backstretch at Churchill Downs. Massive vans of complicated equipment loomed impressively inside the Longfield Avenue entrance and cameras, heavy cables, wires, dollies, and lights were everywhere.

Thank God for the sunshine, despite weather reports predicting rain within twenty-four hours, because aside from the live coverage of the Big Race itself, the material being taped now would make up the bulk of Saturday's program.

There were ironies in the situation. The colts involved were at that moment, undoubtedly, the most tenderly nurtured, the most carefully observed and protected animals in the world. In the building which had been specifically designed and manned to insure against the remotest threat to their well-being, an unfinished meal could be a crisis, a sneeze could verge on tragedy and a misstep could be unqualified catastrophe. Yet, now, at the word of a director or cameraman, each of these treasures was paraded back and forth between surging crowds which were almost as hazardous as the cables strewn along the ground.

But if an air of carnival irrationality prevailed around the Derby Barn, the frontside mood crackled with rising tension. The moment of penultimate decision had arrived. The quality of finality was second only to that of the Derby's own finish, because those colts whose names were not dropped into the entry box for the official ten o'clock drawing of post positions would be automatically eliminated from Saturday's race.

It was not yet time for the drawing but newspaper switchboards from coast to coast were already being besieged by callers eager to check the roster of probable entrants which had been featured in the A.M. sports pages, listed in accordance with current odds.

> Lucky Jim
> Magician
> Freeway
> Dashing Lad
> Armada

Many handicappers guessed that Double Seven would also maintain his options, despite the well-publicized swollen ankle. There was some speculation that Jennifer's Joe might be a further possibility after his surprisingly good showing in the Derby Trial.

But that was the lot. Only nine three-year-olds remaining of the hundred and sixty-nine whose owners had still been optimistic enough to nominate them to eligibility by February 15th. And those hundred and sixty-nine represented less than one percent of the thousands foaled in their year.

No wonder horsemen considered it an honor just to have an entrant in the Kentucky Derby.

Nils Olson was an author whose works appealed to an extremely limited readership. Nevertheless, any of the world's literary masters might have been pardonably envious of the rapt attention devoted to Olson's least word by the owners, trainers and jockey agents who dog-eared his Condition Books in search of proper showcases for their horses and riders.

That no duly licensed horseman or agent at Churchill Downs was to ever be found without the latest edition and that, in fact, these pamphlets also served as handy memo pads and phone directories was simply a fringe benefit.

Though he was titled more formally on letterheads and programs as Director of Racing, Olson was invariably referred to as the racing secretary, as were his counterparts at all other tracks. It was the function of his office to keep close tabs on every thoroughbred at Churchill Downs, noting ownership, registration, certification and records—plus an almost endless amount of pertinent data—and to this end Olson oversaw a large and busy crew of aides.

His own paramount personal task was to devise such a

variety of contests, with so wide a range of requirements, that every horse on the grounds might find reasonable opportunities to run against animals of comparable class and ability. The Condition Books, usually prepared for ten days at a time, listed these upcoming competitions and the specifics for each.

The combinations and possibilities were almost staggering. Olson engineered races of four and a half furlongs, six furlongs, seven furlongs out of the chute, a mile, a mile and a sixteenth. Races for two-year-olds, three-year-olds, threes and fours, fours and up. Races for those who had never won, the maidens; for nonwinners of other than maiden races; for nonwinners of two races since March 15th; for nonwinners of three since January 1st. Races for fillies, or for fillies and mares, or for horses who had never been entered in a claiming race, or for horses who had never started in anything but a claiming race at less than $5,000. Earning limits. Weight allowances. Claiming price ranges. Purses.

Nils Olson tried to provide something for everyone, man or beast, because he had to take into account not only the capabilities of the available thoroughbreds but the personalities and peculiarities of the owners and trainers as well. There were men who would enter their horses if the conditions of a race gave them the slightest chance of winning and there were men who would never participate unless the conditions were virtually custom-made.

Some stables worked their horses into peak form on the training track and sent them to the post ready to go, with no ambition beyond winning a purse. Some used the races themselves as workouts. Mostly this was because actual competition was truer, better training, but sometimes it was because that procedure might achieve eventual long odds and parimutuel rewards. There were occasional mutterings over the latter, but it was a legitimate trick of the trade, the thoroughbred equivalent to the "hole" card in a stud poker game.

Now and then, as in other fields of endeavor, there were

attempts at illegitimate tricks, but, as Nils Olson liked to point out, no medical, bar or banking association—not even the Securities Exchange Commission—made as strong or as consistent efforts to prevent sharp practices as racing generally made to safeguard its patrons. Fortunately, most peccadillos were the responsibility of the Thoroughbred Racing Protective Bureau—often manned by ex-FBI agents—or the stewards, so Olson did not have to worry too much about them.

It was paradoxical that on this Thursday morning, busiest of the year in the racing secretary's office, Nils Olson's interest in the main event was entirely objective. The conditions for the Kentucky Derby had been evolved over the years and set in their present format long before he came to Churchill Downs. Proper nominations having been made, the various entry fees paid as due, any three-year-old was eligible. Colts all carried 126 pounds, fillies—if any—got in at 121 with the standard 5-pound allowance against males, and the winner was assured of at least $100,000. A far cry from that inaugural in 1875, when Aristides carried high weight of 100 pounds and earned $2,850 for his historic victory.

This was not to suggest that Derby Entry Day was an easy one for the racing secretary. On the contrary, filling the other races for that first Saturday in May sometimes presented him with peculiar problems. Many owners—not unreasonably—were loath to run their horses on an afternoon when their own families and friends might not be able to secure seats in the stands. But Olson had learned that such reluctance could usually be overcome by a judicious disbursal of Derby tickets and Lee Ames thoughtfully kept a precious few available for this use each year.

It was to deliver a pair of these powerful persuaders that Lee stopped in to see Olson now. The racing secretary's office was a cubbyhole off the large central room of the weathered building which housed his operation.

"If you come up with one more owner, with one more wife, with one more set of parents coming all the way from Nooksack, Washington. . . ." Lee dropped the envelope on Olson's desk, leaving the humorous threat unfinished. "Where the devil is Nooksack, by the way? I never heard of it before."

Olson grinned. "Nobody else ever did, either. It's somewhere way out west and way up north, that's all I know. But thanks to you, I think we've finally got it made, Lee. We drew Saturday's other races an hour ago and they look pretty good. Now once we get this little riot over."

He jerked his head to indicate the general room, bulging with television equipment and reporters in addition to the participants and other spectators.

"It's a mob scene and a half," Lee agreed. "Any surprises?"

"No. The Derby box isn't officially closed yet but I've talked to everybody. We're going with the expected field of eight."

"So they decided against trying with Jennifer's Joe?"

"The horse just isn't top caliber, Lee."

"Still, after the game way he hung in there Tuesday, a lot of people would have run him simply to be part of the Derby."

"Not the two guys who own that horse. A couple of real old-time hardboots with noses and heads to match. The Trial was a fluke for Jennifer's Joe and they know it."

"And Double Seven?"

"Well, Packo'll never miss the money he's putting up to pass the entry box," Olson said, "and Ned Anderson keeps swearing they'll run." He broke off abruptly. "The big question is whether any of them will be running Saturday. What about the strike?"

Lee's jaw tightened. "We don't know there'll be a strike, Nils. Nothing's certain until the union meeting tonight."

"No word from Mannering?"

"Not a peep since he stalked away from me out on the parking lot yesterday."

"I hear he was madder than a hornet."

"Oh, he was mad, all right," Lee said. "But so was I. Getting me to meet him there to be sure of privacy if my office was bugged. The more he talked in that oily voice of his, the madder I got!"

"Well, two hundred thousand's some bite, I don't blame you for turning him down."

Lee stared in astonishment. "Where'd you get that figure?"

"Why, I'm not sure, several different people."

"Backstretch gossip," Lee said, amused. "You ought to know enough by now to cut any figure from there in half, and then cut it in half again."

"You mean only fifty thousand?"

"So the man said. But what do you mean, 'only'? Fifty thousand's still a good chunk of change."

"Well, sure," Olson agreed. "Still, if that's all he wants, it might be worth it."

"No." Lee's tone was unequivocal.

"But if he stops the Derby?"

Lee leaned forward over Olson's cluttered desk. "That's the first thought everybody has, Nils. That a strike could stop the Derby." He waved a hand. "First thing that popped into my head, too, I'll be honest with you. But we just weren't thinking straight, any of us. It came to me yesterday while I was talking to that crooked little bastard. *Nothing's* going to stop the Derby, Nils, strike or no strike. We'll run if we can't sell one ticket. We'll run if we can't lure a single person into the seats."

He straightened up, slightly embarrassed by his own vehemence. "We can lose our shirts, of course," Lee admitted more quietly. "I'm not claiming for a minute that he can't hurt us. He can. He can damn near massacre us. But no blackmailing son of a bitch is going to keep us from running the Kentucky Derby on schedule. Not while I'm President of Churchill Downs."

The racing secretary fought an unexpected lump in his throat. "Well, in that case," he said, carefully matter-of-fact, "maybe we'd better get the show on the road. The drawing's telecast, you know, and I promised we'd begin at ten sharp."

The two men worked their way through the jammed outer office, smiling and greeting people as they went. Skirting cameras on platforms, stepping over cables, they eventually reached comparative haven behind the counter which ordinarily served to separate Olson's staff from the horsemen. Usually, the area behind the divider held only a handful of his crew. Today, photographers, track officials and other personnel had crowded in to share the excitement.

Against the front of the counter, reporters and cameramen were all but crushing the principals of this morning's ceremony and Olson addressed them good-humoredly. "Come on, now, fellows, you're all going to have to move back just a little if you want us to go ahead. And could we manage to hold the noise down?"

The effort to achieve more space wasn't particularly effective but the decibel count dropped appreciably. Olson smiled at the assembled Derby owners and trainers directly before him and raised his voice. "Ladies and gentlemen, the entry box for the Kentucky Derby is now officially closed. We have a total of eight horses."

He waited a second for the talk to subside before he continued. "This very pretty young lady to my right is Miss Paula Vance. You probably all know exactly who she is, but for the benefit of any strangers among us, she's engaged to Shelby Todhunter, Jr., here, the trainer of Freeway, our unbeaten entrant from California. Miss Vance has kindly consented to draw names out of the entry box for us today."

Olson gestured. "This charming lady on my left is Mrs. Brewster Nickel. She and her husband own Sweepstakes, another of our strong Derby contenders, and she has also been gracious enough to agree to help us this morning. Mrs. Nickel will shake the bottle.

"Now, you two ladies understand how this works, don't you? Inside this box, Miss Vance, we have eight separate entry forms, each bearing the name of one of our eight entries. Inside this bottle, Mrs. Nickel, we have a numbered pellet for each horse, one through eight.

"Now, as you shake the bottle, Mrs. Nickel, and drop out one pellet at a time, you will call out the number on that pellet and then, Miss Vance, you pull one of the entry slips out of the box and read the name of the horse written on it. That horse is then assigned the post position number which Mrs. Nickel has just shaken out of the bottle. Is that clear?"

For once Gladys was speechless. She and Paula both nodded nervously.

"All right then, Mrs. Nickel," said Nils Olson. "If you'll begin?"

With only minor local refinements this was the procedure followed in drawing post positions for all horse races, a lottery conducted in full view of those most concerned, so that every horse in a race was assured impartial assignment. It was ordinarily accomplished with calm dispatch but today each shake of the pellet bottle, each drawing of an entry slip excited comment.

"Number Three," Gladys called, her voice quavering.

"Magician," Paula whispered. There were instant questioning shouts. She swallowed and repeated more loudly, "Magician."

"Number Eight."

"Double Seven."

"Number Four."

"Freeway." Paula squealed and hugged Shelby.

"Number One."

"Dashing Lad."

"Number Seven."

"Sweepstakes."

At this, Gladys Nickel jumped up and down, then threw her arms around Brewster's neck. "Our lucky number," she screamed. "Oh, that's what I was praying for." Finally, she shook out the next pellet. "Number Two."

"Davie's Pride."

257

"Number Six."

"Lucky Jim."

"Number Five."

"Armada."

Armada, Lisa. To Lee, it was an inevitable association. For a moment, the recurrent horror blotted out the continuing tumult around him, the odds and ends of ceremony still being recorded by the whirring TV cameras, the rush of other newsmen and backstretchers out of the big room.

Then, once more, Lee forced himself to concentrate on all the details of the Derby for which he was responsible. He drew a deep, steadying breath and worked his way through the crush. As he emerged from the room, Fred Keller fell into step beside him.

"Might as well walk over to the briefing together," Fred said. "Quite a show, wasn't it?"

Lee halted abruptly on the brick walk. "The briefing!" he exclaimed. He had completely forgotten this morning's scheduled instruction of the pari-mutuel clerks by the FBI. When it was arranged yesterday, he hadn't yet realized that Lisa had been kidnapped.

"Isn't that where you're heading?" Fred asked, puzzled. "It's almost ten-thirty. I assumed . . . "

"No," Lee said, walking on again. "We decided it was better if Kermit handled it. But I do want a word with him first."

Perhaps in spite of what Morgan had said, in spite of what he kept telling himself, there might be a way he could help, if only by facilitating the FBI investigation.

The crowd pouring out of the racing secretary's office had pushed Pop Dewey directly behind Lee and Keller. Because they had stopped so unexpectedly, he had had to check himself sharply to avoid a collision.

He glared after them in acute, though impersonal annoyance as they moved on. Then, muttering, he resumed his own progress. And his interrupted thoughts.

TWO

THE SPOT Kermit Young had chosen for the conference between the FBI men and pari-mutuel clerks served more mundane needs in the normal course of events, as evidenced by the sink and cabinets along one wall, the huge urn announcing available coffee and the table and chairs which occupied the center.

The front-office facility was in the general administrative complex but neatly tucked away from observation. It could be reached only by authorized admission through the reception area. What made it eminently suitable for its present purpose was the fact that it was equally accessible from the nerve center of the pari-mutuel department at the rear. The clerks would be able to enter from there, walking through the computer and manual calculation sections, along the chicken-wired cage of the main money room and past the armed guard who was always stationed at that door without exciting undue speculation.

"We couldn't have asked for a better place," Inspector Elverson told Young and Keller approvingly while they awaited the crew.

"That's what I thought," Ted Irving said. "But I explained yesterday how careful we had to be, that we didn't dare take any chance which might jeopardize a safe return."

Young looked at the FBI men doubtfully. "You really think the boy can still be alive? This long after the payoff?"

Elverson decided the pari-mutuel head had at least one son and slid over the misassumption smoothly. "We have certain information that indicates the victim could be alive," he said.

"Lord, I hope so!" Young exclaimed. "We all do. Mr. Ames has instructed us to give you the fullest cooperation."

"Thank you," the inspector said. "To begin with, Mr. Irving gave me a fairly good idea of what you discussed yesterday before I got to Louisville, but a racetrack is rather unfamiliar territory to me. I could use a few more details."

"Okay," said Young. "The basic proposition is that, for some reason or other, most race fans tend to always play in the same place—their favorite part of the grandstand or their favorite part of the clubhouse. The Turf Club, too, of course, but that's smaller."

"Is this invariable?"

"No, but I'd say it happens better than nine times out of ten," Kermit said. "The percentages are in our favor that the man you're looking for will go back to the same section—maybe even the same window—every time he comes to Churchill."

He pursed his lips suddenly. "We have a problem there, but I'll get back to it in a minute. Right now I'm explaining why I suggested we involve the crew where we pinpointed that second twenty instead of relying entirely on your men. I think our sellers stand a real chance of spotting the passer for you."

"Can your people possibly sell tickets and check serial numbers at the same time, Mr. Young? From what my associate tells me, they work at top speed and handle a great many different transactions."

"They do, Inspector," Kermit said with a laugh. "If you're interested in how many transactions, I've got charts in my office I can show you. That's what makes them experts, they get so used to dealing with money it's almost second nature. I'd back my men against the most experienced bank tellers any day.

"My older men, that is," he added. "But I've already re-arranged our target section, shifted a couple of newer sellers and put in fellows who've been on the job for years."

"There was a problem you mentioned?"

Young grimaced. "We may have two, depending on the

union tonight. But leaving that aside, it suddenly occurred to me that unless we get lucky and grab your man today, the pattern may not apply. All seats are reserved for Friday and Saturday and there's no way of knowing if your man got a ticket in his usual section."

"Then he could be anywhere in Churchill Downs?"

"My guess would be the infield, Inspector, that's almost the only accommodation which isn't reserved on Derby Day, but if he's there, forget it, that would be impossible."

"Frankly, none of it sounds too hopeful," said Elverson, "but we haven't much choice. As we've told you, those two bills are our only solid lead. Now, as I understand it, if a ransom twenty is passed to one of your sellers, the proposal is that he'll call out 'Change!' to alert my men?"

"That's right."

"Is that regular procedure?"

"It's pretty standard, Inspector, that's why I suggested it. We start our sellers off for each race with a minimum amount of cash on hand but there's a roving money man available to any clerk who should need to break a bill. It wouldn't be unusual to call for change of a twenty."

Elverson considered. "Then if one of your sellers calls for change, my men move in on the person at the window, is that it? No fuss, no delay, just hustle him off?"

"Or her."

"Of course. But what if it should be a legitimate request for change?"

"We'll see that the clerks have enough small bills not to need any, and we'll warn them to keep their money out of sight. If they call, it will definitely be a signal."

"Well, you're certainly being helpful," Elverson said. "I wish I thought it would work."

"It could," Kermit said, smiling. "This is a place where long-shots sometimes do pay off."

"So I've heard." Elverson sobered. "There's one slight alteration I think we should make in yesterday's plan, Mr. Young.

If we announce to your men that we're trying to trap a kid-napper, we run a couple of unnecessary risks. One is that word might somehow leak out and scare our prospect off. The other is that the crew themselves may be so nervous they'd put him on the alert."

"What explanation could you give instead?"

"Why don't we tell them that we're on special assignment for the Treasury Department looking for counterfeit bills?"

"I suppose we could do that," Young agreed after a second's thought. "But I can't involve my men without giving them adequate warning. I won't."

"Oh, absolutely!"

Young persisted. "And it has to be clearly understood that all they will do is give the signal. The responsibility for grabbing the passer—if he shows—belongs strictly to your boys, not mine."

"We wouldn't want it any other way," Elverson said. "Because we have to avoid possible danger to your patrons as well."

"Good God!" Young exclaimed. "I'd forgotten all about the people who'll be in line."

A knock at the door cut him short. "Okay, Inspector," Young said, "I'll leave it to you once I've made the introductions." He opened the door to the pari-mutuel clerks. Bringing up the rear with obvious reluctance was Artie Dobermeyer, his red-rimmed eyes darting quickly from face to face. He was searching for Lee Ames, Kermit Young suddenly realized. Artie had assumed—as perhaps the rest had—that this summons was related to the possible strike and he was cringing at the thought of encountering the man he had let down. Kermit had been contemptuous, even bitter over that defection but now, unconsciously, he sighed. Poor Artie, poor scared bastard.

More to the point, though, if the other union members had been equally intimidated, J. Langdon Mannering would get whatever vote he ordered tonight. Poor Churchill Downs.

By the time Elverson and Irving returned to the Crown Hotel, the anticipated contact with the kidnapper had been accomplished. The call had come at eleven on the dot. It was the same person who had called before, the agent monitoring equipment in the Cardigan suite reported. And again, it had been impossible to establish a trace.

The kidnapper asked if Cardigan had brought the money, warned against any attempt to alert the police, announced he would phone again tomorrow and hung up. The tape made of the conversation took less than forty seconds to play.

It was a blow that action had been postponed for another full day—longer, actually, if the exchange were set for after dark as the original ransom drop had been—but there were no real surprises.

What did startle Inspector Elverson was to discover that Morgan Wells was with Steve Cardigan.

"I thought I made it clear, Mr. Wells . . . "

"Forget it," Morgan cut in firmly. "My going up to New York might have endangered Lisa, but we're on my turf now, Inspector. I've been here for days—long before Mr. Cardigan was instructed to come to Louisville. What's more, I arranged for an adjoining suite back in February when I made my reservation. We've unlocked the connecting door, I don't even have to walk through the hall to get in here, so there's no possible way the kidnappers can spot me. And there's no way you can shut me out any longer."

"Just the same," Elverson began.

"If you don't mind, Inspector." Steve Cardigan's voice was steady enough, but his words were heavy with exhaustion. "He has a right to be here. Besides . . . " He turned to stare out of the window, leaving the sentence unfinished.

Besides, as Jason Elverson knew, without Morgan Wells the Canadian would be entirely alone in his agony. His wife was still in New York under sedation to spare further damage to her weakened heart.

"Of course," Elverson said.

He turned and went into the bedroom which had been set up for official use, relieving the two men who loved Lisa Cardigan of his presence. They hardly noticed he had gone.

THREE

TOM RICHARDSON's arrival at the main lobby of The Inn coincided with that of a gala contingent of newcomers about to begin that "once-in-a-lifetime" weekend otherwise known as the Ashland Oil Company's annual Kentucky Derby celebration.

Many of the state's major corporations scheduled yearly festivities around that important first Saturday in May, but this one was noted for being particularly lavish, with an unbroken succession of champagne-cocktail-buffets, dinner dances and horse-country tours which would climax in Saturday night's sumptuous Ashland Derby Ball for the hundreds of guests who had flown in.

Since Louisville boasted no finer facility, the Ashland merriment naturally centered at The Inn this year, and after one look at the crowd, Tom abandoned the idea of reaching the desk. Instead, he sought the information he wanted over one of the house phones along the wall.

"I believe your party is checking out, sir," the operator said. "He may already have left the room but I'll try to connect you."

"No, no," Tom said hastily. "I'll just take a chance and go on up. I want to surprise him."

That he had succeeded beyond his wildest dreams was

abundantly evident when Buddy Sheffield responded to the knocking on his door. He stared at Tom in silent shock.

"Tell you the truth, Buddy, I'm a little surprised to be here," Tom said. "Mind if I come in a minute?"

The trainer pulled himself together. He stepped back to let Tom into the room, gesturing toward the half-packed suitcase on the bed. "I'm just about ready to leave."

"They told me downstairs. Glad I caught you." Tom hesitated. "Going anywhere special?"

Buddy's astonishment had worn off. His face was unfriendly. "Can't say I think that's anybody's business but mine," he snapped.

"Oh, great," Tom said, "you're sore as a bear in a hive of bees and I don't blame you. I'd be, too. But my name isn't Jim York. You ought to know me well enough not to think I'm asking just to hear myself talk."

"I used to know you," Buddy said. "Been a hell of a lot of water under the bridge since then."

"Been a hell of a lot of whiskey."

"I guess I laid myself open for that one," Buddy said grimly. "You, at least, had good reason when you canned me. You couldn't do anything else. But I'm not in much of a mood for wisecracks, Tom. What was it you wanted?"

"Shall I give it to you straight?"

"No use changing now."

"Well, for a start, I came to see if you were drunk."

"You've got your nerve."

"That's a fact," Tom agreed, "but you said I should level with you."

"All right, you son of a bitch," Buddy said furiously, "if that's what you're looking for." He strode to the desk and pulled a wastebasket out from under it. "There. There's the bottle, just like you expected. I bought it yesterday morning after York gave me the shaft. I was planning to get so owl-eyed drunk I'd never come out of it."

He kicked the basket with such violence that it fell over.

The bottle of bourbon slid out onto the carpet at Tom's feet, its seal unbroken.

"Sorry to disappoint you boys," Buddy said. "I wouldn't give you the satisfaction, not you, not Jerry Neal, not York, not anybody. Now you can get the hell out of here and leave me alone. Whether I drink or not is another thing I think is my business."

"Wrong," Tom said, "and you've just proved it. Your business is training horses."

"Not anymore," Buddy said heavily. "Jim York fixed that."

"The truth gets around, Buddy. I talked to four fellows myself who know better."

"Forget it, Tom. After Neal's column there won't be an owner in the country who doesn't believe I fell off the wagon. Why else would a man like Jim York fire me three days before the Derby?" He shook his head. "All because of a couple of lines in a newspaper. Without asking for an explanation, without listening. I tried to tell York I only went into the bar to make a phone call." He broke off, conscious that his voice was shaking. "Look, the hell with it, Tom, it's over and I'm in kind of a hurry."

"Too big a hurry to take over Dashing Lad?" Buddy's jaw went as slack as if Tom had hit him. "You did hear about Orv, didn't you?"

Buddy gulped. "Christ, I'm ashamed to be so wrapped up in myself. I should have thought about it the minute I saw you. I'm really sorry, Tom. About Orv, I mean, and the way you must be feeling."

"We'll talk about that later, Buddy," Tom said. "I don't think it's got through to me yet. I suppose it's going to tear me apart when it really hits, but I know Orv wouldn't want me to pull Dashing Lad out of the Derby."

"God, no! If you even thought of it, he'd . . . " Buddy stopped short.

Tom nodded. "He'd 'come back and haunt me.' Yes. Funny the things we say without thinking. Well, what about it, will

266

you saddle Dashing Lad for the Derby?"

"There's only one answer to that, Tom. But I can't tell you what it means to me, after all that's happened."

"You don't owe me any thanks, Buddy. I need you. Whitey's handling the stable in New York. I can't pull him away from there, he's got thirty head to run."

"I heard."

Tom hesitated. "I have no idea what I'm going to do after the Derby. At the moment, the deal is just Dashing Lad on Saturday."

"Understood, Tom."

"As to terms . . . "

"Later." Buddy put his hand out. "I can't think of anything less important."

Tom grasped Buddy's hand and shook it. Then he asked, "*Now* can I sit down?"

Buddy roared with laughter. "Oh, Tom, I didn't mean to keep you standing. Sit down, sit down. Have a drink if you'd like one. There's a whole bottle of bourbon on the floor."

"You really beat it, didn't you, Buddy?"

"I guess I really did."

"You 'guess'? Why, Buddy, if I'd been you and Jim York pulled the rug out from under me like that, I'd have been drunk for a month. You beat it, Buddy. Now, if we can just beat Lucky Jim."

Buddy grinned. "I'm sorry I'm a teetotaler, I really would like to drink to that."

"Well, I suppose if any man can figure a way to outfox the favorite, you're the one." Tom stared at his new trainer, startled. "I'll take an oath that never occurred to me until right this second, that you'd know Lucky Jim's weaknesses!"

"Maybe you're a strategic genius and don't know it," Buddy said. "I wouldn't want you to count too much on that angle, though. His owner is nothing but a cheap claimer in my book, but Lucky Jim is class every inch of the way."

"What fun would it be to beat him, otherwise?" Tom said.

"If we can. Look, Buddy, I'm not expecting miracles from you when we're practically at the post."

"I realize that."

"Tell you the God's truth, I'm not expecting anything," Tom said. "Or maybe I'm expecting everything, I don't know. Because this has got to be the damnedest race I've ever been in. I started out with a different horse, a different jockey and now, a different trainer."

"Those things happen every day, for one reason or another."

"Oh, sure, but this is the Kentucky Derby. I suppose if I were a superstitious man . . . " Tom got to his feet. "Well, we'll see, won't we? Dashing Lad's up to you now. I've got to get over to the funeral parlor." He sighed. "Orv's being buried in Texas, you know."

"No, I hadn't heard."

"It's how he always wanted it," Tom said, "and Peggy was planning to take him down tomorrow but I've talked her into waiting until Saturday night. It gives her an extra day to get her strength back after the baby. And, then, I was thinking, if Dashing Lad should win, Orv could go home under a blanket of roses."

FOUR

T HRUST UNEXPECTEDLY into camera range that morning during the draw for Derby positions the co-owners of Freeway had resolved to go on really stringent diets. Again. Della Todhunter and Enid Vance, at that moment, were awaiting cottage cheese and lettuce salads in the tearoom of the department store where they'd been doing some pre-race shopping.

It was fortunate they couldn't see the enticingly laden service cart which was being wheeled into Doc Todhunter's hotel room. They could never have maintained their willpower in confrontation with those platters of sizzling country ham steak, the steaming bowls of whipped potatoes smothered with red-eye gravy and the tempting scoops of bourbon ice cream in the fluted silver dessert dishes.

Ironically, Paula and Doc could only nibble at their late luncheon. Shelby couldn't do even that. Shuddering at the sight of the lavish spread, he paced the floor, back and forth, back and forth, like a caged fox.

Paula cast a worried glance at her fiancé's set face. "Honey, you didn't want breakfast, maybe if you could force yourself to eat just a little ham?"

"It's all right, Paula," Doc said quickly, a note of warning in his voice.

Shelby halted beside the table. "It's not all right, Dad," he said. "Last night I thought, maybe it could work. But it isn't going to. You both know that as well as I do. There's no sense kidding ourselves."

"Oh, Shel, please don't be discouraged," Paula begged. "You got through the ceremony this morning beautifully, despite all the reporters and that horrible Jerry Neal. I was so proud of you."

Shelby shook his head sadly. "You don't understand. I can feel it building. I'm going to blow the whole thing!"

Doc pushed his chair back from the table. "No, you're not, Shel. Believe me. It isn't going to be easy, but this time, son, you're going to make it. You're not fighting alone anymore."

Far below the eighteenth-story window the curving Ohio River defined the bustling border between Kentucky and Indiana. Shelby's eyes followed it compulsively as he stared out.

"That's what I'm trying to tell you, Dad. Even with all of you helping me, it's going to be the same."

"It won't be," Doc said quietly. "Not anymore. Not after last night, son."

"It's all different now," said Paula.

Shelby began to pace as before, not answering.

They just didn't know. They couldn't feel the terrible pressure in him. It was like a gigantic black balloon that somebody kept inflating. He couldn't take a full breath on account of it and he couldn't swallow, either, but he kept trying to do both. He hadn't even considered sleeping since he got back to the hotel the evening before. He was too keyed up, he had to continue moving, though every step was an increasing effort.

Yet his father and Paula were right. After last night, nothing would ever be the same. Not just because of his excruciating panic at suddenly finding himself in the middle of the Pegasus Parade without any idea how he had gotten there. He still didn't know where he had gone after he left the two guys from Grosse Point, but that wasn't important. What mattered was the loss of his own identity. He might decide to fly over the moon or drag through the backstretches of Hell, but he wanted to be aware of himself when he did it.

Because if he wasn't Shelby Todhunter, Jr., how could he make Shelby Todhunter, Sr., suffer? And that, he finally understood, had been the whole point.

He had been glad when he was arrested that first night in Louisville. He had been gleeful, waiting in the station house where the paddy wagons had disgorged their haul for leisurely processing, thinking what a jolt his father was going to get. And then, nothing had happened. Early Sunday morning, two detectives had hustled Shelby back to the hotel without creating any stir whatsoever.

"We couldn't do this if the charge against your son was anything more than disturbing the peace, Doctor Todhunter," the older detective had explained carefully. "If he had been in possession of drugs, anything like that, we'd have to charge him."

"No matter who spoke up for him," the other had said.

270

"But he was clean, and you know we try not to interfere with Derby visitors unless they're bothering other people or in danger of hurting themselves."

"I can't tell you how grateful I am," Doc had said. "Just imagining the papers makes me cringe."

"That's why we didn't even book him." The older detective had cast a disapproving eye on Shelby. "It's not to say he wasn't in some pretty bad company. And next time he's told to disperse, he'd better stir his stumps and keep a civil tongue in his head. But being connected with a Derby horse, the publicity would have been all out of proportion to the offense. Like Mr. Ames told the Chief, it would be just as unfair if he was punished more than he deserved. And you would have been hurt, too."

But hurting his father was what it had been all about. That was what had sent Shelby back to the little park the minute the two detectives left, why he had taken whatever it was those guys from Grosse Point had concocted in their college lab.

It was strange now to think of all those years of believing his father didn't care, that he didn't give a damn about anything but horses.

Doc had been stunned the night before when Shelby blurted it out. "Oh, my God, Shel. Was that what you thought when I took you along with me on my rounds as a kid, that I cared more for the animals than I did for you? But how could you possibly have believed that, when I've told you a thousand times what you mean to me? My whole life! Everything in the world!"

Shelby had stared into his father's agonized face. "I don't know, Dad, I don't know what started it."

But it had come back to him even as he was saying the words. He had completely buried the memory and yet, suddenly, it was as if he were standing there in the shaded barn in Chino. That was where it had been, at the old Ursa La Plata Ranch, with the mare thrashing around on the straw, with the acrid sting of medicine in his nostrils and the smell of the sun-baked dustiness outside. And his father, looking so absorbed, so utterly wrapped up in what was happening, had said, "Shel, I know you'll understand this has to come first. I may not be able to save her, anyway, but I can't leave now, son. I'll have to take you to Disneyland another day." It had been his seventh, no, his eighth birthday.

God! All that misery since, because of something so unimportant. Even last night, with the barriers finally down, Shelby had been ashamed to admit to such childishness. Instead, he had said again, "I don't know, Dad. I realize now how wrong I've been. But if you hadn't just said to forget the Derby, to hell with Freeway, let's go home, I guess I'd still think it. Somehow, your saying that has changed everything."

They weren't going back to California, though, not until after the Derby. It was enough that his father was willing. So were his mother and Paula. Paula's mother, mercifully, knew nothing about any of it. But Freeway had to run and, more important, Shelby Todhunter, Jr., must not. Because if he couldn't beat the pills now, he never would.

"Shel?"

His father was still standing beside his chair at the table, with Paula still watching him, twisting at her napkin. Shelby felt as if it had been a long time since any of them had spoken but he supposed it couldn't have been or they'd have moved.

"Yes, Dad?"

"It will get better."

FIVE

"DON'T MENTION MY NAME, Jere, okay?" The harsh timbre of Gil Tobin's voice was unmistakable.

Neal cast a quick glance at the newspapermen talking at adjacent wall phones in the press box. "Don't you mention the name I'm interested in," he warned the union leader in return. "Too many big ears around here. That's why I wanted you to call me back at the hotel last night."

"There wasn't anything to tell you last night," Gil rumbled cheerfully, "or I would have."

"And now?"

"Now I've got even more than you asked for. In fact, I decided to come down for the Derby and give it to you in person."

"You're in town? In Louisville?"

"Yes, but I don't want anyone to know for the moment, Jere, I can't get involved in this officially. I'll tell you about it when you get here. I'm at the old Deerfield Farm, not the main house, the cottage they remodeled round the back."

"I know about that cottage, but there's no way I can come out there today. I'm swamped. It's less than an hour until the National Turf Writers meeting and I'm still working on the column."

"Hey, I heard about your being elected President of the Turf Writers Association. Congratulations."

"It's a lot of baloney," Neal said. "I don't know why I bothered, especially since some of the members didn't even want me nominated."

Gil laughed. "That's why you bothered."

"I suppose," Neal agreed. "To rub their noses in it. Someday I'll have to tell you how I swung it."

"You can tell me this afternoon."

"No, that's what I'm trying to explain. There's this meeting in a little while and then I have to preside over our annual dinner tonight. So, much as I'd like to see you, I don't have an extra minute."

"How about between your meeting and the dinner," Gil murmured, considering. "You could be back in less than an hour."

"I would, except we've managed to snare Wilson Smith as our guest speaker. He's flying his own plane in from Washington and I have to pick him up at the airport."

"*The* Wilson Smith?"

"The Senator himself. He's coming as a favor to me."

Gil whistled. "That is a break. But couldn't somebody else meet him at the airport? I mean, I hate to see you miss the fun. I was planning to make—a certain somebody—just about grovel at your feet."

"You're not saying—is he going to be there?" Neal's hatred for J. Langdon Mannering quivered over the wire.

"That's the whole idea," Gil said. "I figured you'd want to be in on the finish. Look, I really owe you a debt of gratitude for this one, Jere. I only called him to do you a favor, but now that he's told me to take a flying leap . . . "

"Are you saying you told him to back off from that deal he wants to pull and he refused? You're kidding."

"Hell, no, I'm not kidding," Gil said. "As far as he's concerned, it's nuts to me and nuts to anybody else whose toes he's stepping on. He was polite, you know how he is, but that's why I said you did me a favor bringing me in. The kind of stuff he's pulling makes everybody look bad. We can't let him get away with it. Especially when it's for nothing. He's been turned down flat."

"I told you what he was like. He's mean just for kicks. But what can you do if he insists on going ahead?"

274

Gil's heavy voice was amused. "I've got a rather special idea for changing his mind, a very special idea. I'm just sorry you're going to miss the show."

"Wait a minute, let me think." Neal knew it was impossible and yet, he'd do almost anything to see J. Langdon Mannering crawl.

"Say," Gil said, "I just thought of something. If the settlement could be announced in the middle of your big dinner, wouldn't that be a hell of a bombshell?"

Neal laughed. "You know it. Tell you what, I really ought to meet Smith's plane, but if I sent my new vice-president or better yet, a welcoming committee, that would do it."

"Good thinking," Gil said. "And while they're collecting the senator, you can pick up You-know-who and drive him out here. What time shall I tell him to be ready?"

"You want me to bring him?"

"That will really be the clincher, won't it? Unless you don't want him to realize it's all happening because of you?"

"Damn right I want him to."

"Well, then? When he comes out of the lobby let him find you waiting for him in that red car of yours. Or did you fly down this trip, Jere?"

"No, I drove, but what if he refuses to ride with me?"

There was no longer any hint of amusement in Gil's tone. "He may not be too happy about it, but I'm still big enough that when I set up an appointment with somebody his size, he'll come. When I tell him to and the way I tell him to. You just set the time."

"Let's see." Neal was calculating aloud. "The meeting here at Churchill should break up before 5:30. Then I'll have to see about a couple of things. You want to make it, say, 6:15?"

"It's up to you. This is your party."

"Six-fifteen is fine. As long as I can get back in an hour for the dinner."

"Right," Gil agreed. "Oh, wait, Jere, I almost forgot. You will bring what you promised?"

275

Neal smiled. "The picture? I told you I'd give it to you the minute I saw you. I've got it in my pocket now."

"Good boy. See you later, then."

The column was still unfinished, but Neal stood unmoving in front of the phone, thinking.

Well, that was that.

He hadn't been certain until Gil had said, "I almost forgot." But that was bull, Gil hadn't forgotten at all. He wouldn't. Neal frowned. Perhaps he should never have mentioned the picture? But until he had, Gil had been firmly against interfering in the affairs of another union.

Damn J. Langdon Mannering. If he hadn't sent his goons, there wouldn't have been any need to pressure Gil. Neal's jaw set. J. Langdon was about to eat dirt for that night's work and Jerry Neal was going to be right there, watching him. If the deal cost the friendship of Gil Tobin, too bad. Neal shrugged and headed back to his typewriter.

As far as important men went, the labor leader wasn't in the same class with Senator Wilson Smith, for instance. And Smith was coming all the way from Washington to address the National Turf Writers, though Neal had no illusions about the Senator's motives. Aside from a genuine interest in thoroughbreds, Smith had to be aware that the dinner gave him a chance to address a prestigious audience of reporters who had gathered from all over the country. Not an insignificant consideration for a man who could eventually be seeking the Presidency.

Still, his presence did underline the fact that Jerry Neal was pretty prominent in his own right.

SIX

THE SPOT for the proposed exchange with Cardigan, which Mace had scouted very carefully yesterday after buying the used car, was perfect. It lay close to the waterfront on the west side of town, in an industrial area of warehouses and factories which should be practically deserted after nightfall.

It would be hours before anyone checked the ditched car and found the two bodies in it. The original ransom drop up in Tarrytown, New York, had been Coolie Bascombe's idea and everything had gone like clockwork. Except for Coolie, afterward.

This time, the whole plan was Mace's from beginning to end and he was justifiably proud of the way he'd figured to get his hands on a cool million. As he prepared to leave the trailer in the late afternoon for another reconnoitering expedition, his only irritation was Rosanna's lack of enthusiasm.

But, then, if it was left to her, he'd still be in Baltimore, hustling poolrooms as he had been before he got to talking to Coolie that night by accident. And she'd be back in that clip joint where he found her. Unless the cops had busted it by now, the way they should have if they weren't taking a slice under the table.

Every time he remembered his first look at Rosanna, strutting around up on that bar, shaking everything she owned with nothing on her but a couple of beads and any guy that bought a lousy beer grabbing himself a free feel, Mace would get hot. Just thinking of those greedy hands clutching at her nakedness and the things she let them do—especially that greasy bastard with the diamonds and the thick fingers—while she squirmed and giggled made him burn and not only with anger.

Even now, with the million on his mind, he pushed her down on the bunk and gave her something a damn sight better than a stubby finger. She didn't giggle, though, she hollered in pain and pleasure. It was awhile before Mace got back to business.

"Okay, I'm going," he said then. "Make sure you lock the door. I'll be here around nine, nine-thirty."

"Oh, Mace, why so late again?"

"Come on, Rosanna, I told you, I got to see what it's like when it's good and dark and everything's closed. Hell, some of those factories could have guards or patrols or something. I didn't spot any last night but I got to make sure. And now, with Daylight Savings . . ." He stiffened, staring past her at Lisa's unmoving figure. "Hey, is she all right? It just dawned on me, she hasn't twitched a muscle in the last hour, even with all that noise you were making."

Rosanna glanced indifferently at the girl on the bunk. "She just passed out again. Who cares?"

He listened, then relaxed. "Okay, I hear her breathing." He shook his head at Rosanna. "Boy, what a stupid broad. *I* care. Her old man's got to see her alive first thing when I meet him or how will I get him off guard?"

SEVEN

ASIDE FROM Jerry Neal's last-minute decision to have a committee meet and escort Senator Wilson Smith to his honored place at the dinner, with the consequent delays and responsibilities entailed, it had been a most difficult day for the vice-president of the National Turf Writers Association. In some ways, the Professor thought wearily, it had been one of the hardest days of his life.

Simeon Moseby had been known as the Professor for so long that few people would have even recognized his real name, though his fine-boned, aristocratic face and stark-bald head could be instantly identified by legions of racing buffs.

When he had first defected from his ivy-league campus almost half a century earlier the novelty of a Ph.D. becoming a race handicapper and commentator had created a sensation which was no longer possible. Now too many other well-educated men had followed the Professor into his field, but if he had lost his uniqueness, his superb talent transcended the somewhat narrow confines he had imposed upon himself. He had a national following and, as he sometimes pointed out, the distinction of durability.

It was the latter which added tonight to the low spirits he was working hard to conceal as he sat facing his friends and fellow members at their banquet tables. At his age to have been maneuvered into a position like this was galling. The very last ambition he had ever cherished was to be vice-president of the organization he had been instrumental in founding. And to have to chair the dinner in Jerry Neal's unaccountable absence was a humiliation the Professor intended to delay until the last possible second.

The extremely tardy arrival of the Senator had helped postpone the start of the presentations and speeches, but if Neal didn't put in an appearance very shortly, the Professor would have to proceed with the evening's ceremonies.

The truth was, the Professor had never wanted to take any position in the National Turf Writers Association. He had consistently and stubbornly refused to hold office until this year, when he had been persuaded against his will to let an old friend nominate him.

And Jerry Neal had beaten him handily. Jerry Neal, of all unrepresentative turf writers, a member simply by courtesy, not even the specializing type of sportswriter for whom the association had been formed. A cheap, sensational specimen, moreover, who was a mote in the eye of all good newspapermen, whatever their particular beats.

The Professor drew the hateful gavel closer to him and looked doubtfully at Lee Ames, who occupied a front table and was checking his watch. There was an instant hush of expectancy but the old man gave a slight shake of his bald head. Give it just a couple of minutes more.

When the results of the election had been announced the Professor had considered refusing the lesser position with bitter longing, but he had been a practicing turf writer for too many years. In racing, you accepted your losses with grace if you had any class at all.

It had been an even greater temptation not to come to Kentucky this spring. Not to have to hobnob with the triumphant Neal or, worse, have to hear the shocked outrage of his friends. The National Turf Writers, by the very nature of their endeavor, were generally separated from the majority of their fellows in the coverage of their regional racing circuits, which was why it was necessary to hold elections by mail. The annual meeting and dinner—though still mustering only about half the membership—was set in Louisville during Derby Week because that was an event which superseded purely local schedules and brought the greatest number together at any given time.

The installation of officers that afternoon had been every bit as gruesome as the Professor had anticipated. Neal's attitude had been abrasively condescending and the sympathy of his friends had almost betrayed the Professor into admitting his own lacerated pride. Still, their unhappy comments and confessions proved that the members hadn't intentionally rejected him.

As a matter of fact, Neal seemed to have suckered himself into the presidency, using his travels in connection with other sporting events to drop in on turf writers all over the country and ask for their backing. And in his own inimitable way, Neal had persuaded each man that he was the only one being approached. Not, Neal had said, to defeat the Professor—whom everybody knew would win in a well-deserved landslide—but simply so that Neal himself wouldn't be embarrassed by an absolute shutout.

A crude and palpable device, made effective by a promise here and a threat there, it had swept Neal into office.

The Professor sighed, bowing to his fate. He picked up Neal's gavel and rapped for attention. At the same moment, a waiter bowed deferentially over Lee Ames' shoulder with a message. A compelling one, obviously, because Lee cast an apologetic glance toward the Professor and followed the man out of the room.

As he trailed the waiter to a row of telephone booths in the curtained-off anteroom, Lee felt a surge of relief. Whatever the result, the agony of awaiting it was over. For nearly two hours, hosting the party at Churchill Downs' official table, he had been under almost intolerable strain. Forcing himself to eat, smile, make small talk, he had been constantly aware of his watch ticking the minutes away. He hadn't really expected a call from Jack Phillips before 7:30, but the next hour had dragged interminably.

Lee wasn't certain he could have lasted much longer, but now that he was going to find out what the union had decided, he was half reluctant to pick up the phone. It meant so much to Churchill Downs, to the Kentucky Derby, to Lee himself, in a purely personal way. Because no matter how firmly he assured everybody that nothing would be allowed to affect the Derby of which he was Custodian, a strike would at least put a smudge on its proud luster and he would feel that he had somehow failed a great tradition.

He cleared his throat and picked up the receiver, reminding himself not to address the union secretary by name.

"I thought you were never going to call," he said. "What

happened? Why did it take so long?"

There was a gasp, then Kermit Young's voice said, "You can't mean you haven't heard yet?"

Lee swallowed shock and disappointment. "I told you I'd be in touch the minute I got word, Kermit."

"I know, Lee, but it took forever. I thought you must have forgotten. It never occurred to me. My God, this is unbelievable."

"It is. I can't imagine what can be holding things up this way. Unless they're arguing. Our Friend said some of the fellows were going to try for a secret ballot. It could be that."

"I suppose so," Kermit said. "And if they got into a hassle over procedure, Our Friend couldn't leave to phone." His tone lifted. "In which case, I guess we can't complain, because that would mean we still have a chance."

"Listen, Kermit," Lee interrupted. "They've got a call for me on another line. I'll ring you back!"

"No, please, let me hold."

It was awhile before Lee returned to tell Kermit, "Well, that's the one we were expecting, but . . ."

"What did he say? What's the verdict?"

"There isn't any verdict, Kermit. There's been a delay of some sort. Our Friend kept waiting and waiting, thinking something would have to pop, but finally, thank God, he decided he'd better let me know what's happening. Which is nothing at all, not one single thing."

"That's crazy!"

"I know, but the meeting hasn't even started. The clerks are there and so are all of Mannering's goons, but Mannering himself hasn't shown and nobody knows what to do without him."

"What do *we* do now, for Pete's sake?"

Lee sighed. "I can't say for you, Kermit, but I have to get back to the dinner and pretend to listen to the speeches. And go on sweating it out. What else can I do?"

Lee's conclusion was being repeated in essence all over the

big union hall where the pari-mutuel clerks were equally dismayed by the delay. There were no laggards or stay-at-homes among the rank and file this time. The only absentee was a fifty-dollar cashier who had had a heart attack while listening to what his family said was some sort of anonymous phone call. The other clerks had arrived well before the scheduled start of their meeting.

Double doors had been flung wide, an accommodation to the crowd which had gathered outside—voteless, though vitally interested temporaries already arrived to work the Derby. But even so the inside of the hall was hot and reeked unpleasantly of endlessly lighted cigarettes and cigars. The hard benches somehow grew more unyielding with each impatient check of the time.

Sal Norvelli was complaining, again, on this particular aspect of the situation. The ex-jockey exceeded riding weight by a good fifteen pounds or he would never have become a clerk, but he still carried little padding, and whenever he was strung out it seemed that every mended bone in his body—and he had a dozen, most jockeys did—would start aching.

Artie Dobermeyer was too uncomfortable himself to be sympathetic. "You got to sit tight, that's all."

"Yeah, well, I been sitting tight and I'm damn sick of it."

"Yeah, well," Artie mocked him, "who isn't sick of it?"

"I know, but how long do they think we're going on doing it, that's what I'm saying?"

"You planning to get up and walk out?" Artie demanded impatiently. "Old Mannering may not be here but those goons of his are all over the place and they don't miss a trick, I've been watching them."

Artie noted his companion's immediate, darting glance with sour satisfaction. Sal, like him, like every other member in the place, was very much aware of the six men lounging along the walls, three on either side.

They were oversized clowns, the lot of them, Artie thought, with faces set in concrete and looking like they didn't care

283

whether school began or not. But they were getting kind of restless, at that, he decided as he eyed them. They kept changing feet, shifting position a little.

There had been two or three others on the stage earlier, shoving stuff around, putting a pitcher of water and a glass on the speaker's stand, fooling with the lights, getting the mike just so, busy as all get out. Like they expected the Second Coming any minute, Artie sneered to himself. But they had disappeared behind the curtains quite a while back.

Artie made an idle tabulation of Mannering's men. The six in the hall, two or three backstage, another two or three at the entrance, probably a couple with him—thirteen, fourteen men at the most against hundreds of union members!

"That's another thing," Sal suddenly burst forth. "I'm sick of them goons, too, of this whole rotten business that nobody really wants!"

Artie didn't even bother to reply. What was the use of shooting your mouth off for nothing and maybe ending up with a busted head? They were all as bad as he was.

Artie sighed, wishing he had a slug of bourbon, and told himself to cut the crap. Nobody had asked the other guys for their help, their friendship. He was the only one who'd chickened out on Lee Ames.

No matter how many people you were addressing—a dozen, a hundred, a thousand—if you were going to make an effective speech, you had to communicate with each member of that audience on an individual level. Picking one person out of the group and directing your talk toward him seemed to help achieve that end. Lee had employed the device himself on any number of occasions, but it came as a shock to discover that Senator Wilson Smith was funneling the address to the National Turf Writers through him.

Lee was slightly embarrassed, too, because while he had been feigning attention throughout the opening ceremonies, he couldn't have repeated one word that had been said if the

284

Kentucky Derby depended on it. He wasn't certain when Smith had been introduced or how long he'd been talking before that steady, intent gaze penetrated. Smith had evidently made a joke because the audience was laughing. Lee straightened slightly on his chair, forcing himself to concentrate.

"Seriously," Smith continued, "if there's one thing I do know something about it's the pleasures of racing. And on that score, distinguished Members of the Press, I've got a bone to pick with you."

He shook his head slightly at Lee. "Now, we're all friends to racing in this room tonight, but you know the chestnut about 'God protect me from my friends, I'll take care of my enemies myself.' The honest fact is that an awful lot of people who would enjoy racing don't even realize it's available. Oh, they're aware of its existence, naturally. But how they regard it, what they think it is that it isn't—what it is that they don't know about at all—is particularly within your province, gentlemen, and there, if you will forgive me for saying so, is where I feel a great many of you have failed."

He took a sip of water and grinned at Lee. "I was wondering how tactless I dared to be to a roomful of newspapermen while I was flying down from Washington . . ."

Lee stiffened in the sudden recollection that Gil Tobin had been on the Senator's plane when it arrived at Standiford Field.

Gil Tobin! Might his presence explain the delay at the union hall? Could Tobin be discussing the threatened strike with J. Langdon Mannering? Arguing against what was, after all, a patently illegal breach of faith?

The surge of hope died. No, the timing was off, which was why Lee hadn't reacted when he first heard of the union leader's arrival. The plane hadn't landed in Louisville until after 7:30 and the meeting of the clerks was set to begin at 7:00.

Lee forced himself to concentrate on Wilson Smith, who was still talking directly at him.

"I just happen to think," the Senator said, "that horse racing is one of the most colorful and exciting sports in the world. But it's more than that, it's a game in which the spectator also participates, where what he does actually has an effect on the odds. And he's not playing against the track, as so many people tend to feel, he's playing against the other fans. His skill against their skill. His judgment against their judgment."

Smith sipped his water. "That's another thing," he went on. "I'm afraid that some of us—turf writers, for example—tend to concentrate on what I suppose we'll have to call 'championship play,' and it's true that some fans read their Racing Forms with the dedication of mathematical code breakers, but racing can be fun on every level and, again . . ."

Lee furtively consulted his watch. Ten-fifteen. Why didn't Jack call?

"Of course there are people who can't handle racing," the Senator continued, unaware of Lee's tension. "Some people can't handle a lot of things. But why is it that such a large percentage of this country—a country where George Washington and Andrew Jackson and Robert E. Lee, for example, were dedicated fans—has been conditioned to believe that anyone who plays the horses is a go-for-broke gambler? When you know as well as I do that most people who go to the track are ordinary, respectable, middle-class citizens out for an afternoon of fun, either coming home a few dollars ahead or spending no more than they would for any other afternoon's entertainment."

Ten-thirty.

Lee dropped all pretense of listening.

In the union hall an hour or so earlier there had been a curious moment when impatience had come very close to outright defiance. Frustration and resentment had gathered into a gigantic wave of protest. But the sandbag wall of fear had held fast, the swell of rebellion had subsided.

286

Now the big room was oppressively quiet. The clerks merely sat.

It was into this spent, apathetic silence that Jack Phillips, their secretary, walked unsteadily onto the platform, his face lurid in the bright light.

"I guess it's all over, fellows. You might as well break it up and go home." He seemed to be having trouble with his breathing. "Mr. Mannering . . . we just got the news. Mr. Mannering's been killed!"

For a split second, nothing changed. Then a clerk in the front row asked, "Killed? How?"

The secretary struggled to maintain self-control. "It was an explosion, a bomb, they think, under the hood of the car he was riding in. Outside the city limits or we'd have heard sooner, I suppose. It happened around six-thirty." He shook his head. "All these hours we've been sitting here he was dead. But they had a hard time identifying the bodies."

"He wasn't alone?" someone asked.

"No, he was with Jerry Neal," Phillips said, "you know, the columnist. The cops finally identified them through Neal's car. Otherwise there wasn't enough left of either of them . . ." He stopped with a gulp. "Look, you know as much as I do, fellows. I got to get to a phone."

He fled to call Lee Ames.

Artie Dobermeyer did not join the pandemonium of release which erupted around him. As he pointed out to Sal, with a gesture toward the clogged aisles, "No use trying to buck that mob, yet, and we already sat here so long . . ."

"Yeah, who cares?" Sal said happily. "It's over."

But not all over, Artie realized with a pang. Not for him, anyway. Every time he passed Lee Ames he'd remember his failure. They'd both remember.

Well, it couldn't be helped. The worst part of it *was* over. At least, Lee Ames didn't have to worry anymore. The Kentucky Derby was safe.

FRIDAY

ONE

TWO DAYS until the Derby. Those not a part of racing life might have made a different count. Papers elsewhere made reference to the "one day left." But this was horse country. This was Churchill Downs. And as the great trainer Ben Jones had pointed out, it wasn't enough to have your colt ready for the first Saturday in May. You had to have him at his peak exactly at post time late that important afternoon.

So there were still two days.

An incredibly short time. And yet, for some, a very long time as well.

In the backstretch, spirits were soaring. The warm early mist which was beginning to drift away and the silvery clouds hanging low overhead might have been freighted with laughing gas instead of moisture. "Showers and thundershowers ending by midday," the Weather Bureau was predicting. "Partial clearing, mild this afternoon. Fair, slightly cooler tonight; sunny, pleasant Saturday."

There were—as the sports world well knew by now—only eight horses involved in the Big Event; and these, with their

attendant hordes of excited observers, were carefully seques-
tered from the thousand or so other thoroughbreds who still
went about their regular routines in close to fifty less-notable
barns. But Derby Fever had touched everyone on the grounds
with some degree of happy delirium.

And then, of course, there was the additional excitement
produced by last night's terrible explosion on the road outside
of town. The possibility of a strike had been ended and joy on
this score was unalloyed and thoroughly unashamed. To the
horsemen—owners, trainers, hands alike—J. Langdon Mannering was simply a name, and a laughably fancy one at that. He
had represented nothing but a serious threat to their liveli-
hoods and, unthinkably, to the Kentucky Derby as well.

The reaction to his companion's death was different. Jerry
Neal's by-line had been familiar to the racing world for years
and he had visited that very backstretch only the morning before. As one cynic commented disgustedly, "If everyone I seen
today that said he was talking to Jerry Neal yesterday was
telling the truth, he'd be alive right this minute. Hell, he'd
have never had time to go pick up that union guy!"

"You know how they are around here," said his friend,
cheerfully overlooking the fact that he had been making the
same specious claim, "big mouths, every last one of them. It's
just like with Roscoe Goose. He rides the biggest payoff they
ever had in the Derby, that'd be Donerail, back in 1913, paid
$184 . . ."

"$184.90," came the instant correction. "My old man had
him that day."

The other hesitated. "Well, maybe he did, but what I
started to tell you, Roscoe says once that if all the people
that told him later they bet on Donerail that day really did
bet on him, why, the horse would've been lucky if he had
even paid fifty cents on the dollar!"

"Hey, you calling my old man a liar?"

"For Pete's sake, no. I wasn't even talking about your old
man. I was talking about Jerry Neal."

Perhaps the most important aspect of the columnist's death, however, was that it ended the speculation as to whose would be the inevitable third death.

"What'd I tell you?" the superstitious asked. "Gordy Cowdin, Orv Scott and now Jerry Neal! Them things always go in threes!"

The wholesale vindication undoubtedly added a shivery jolt of awe to the current of rising anticipation.

Ned Anderson was oblivious to the general topics of backstretch conversation. He hadn't been worrying about a possible strike, he'd been agonizing over his horse. It was quite likely that he hadn't heard of the bombed car. He certainly hadn't bothered with the newspapers this morning or indulged in any small talk.

Now, in Stall H of the Derby Barn, almost stunned with relief, he was staring down at Double Seven's legs, which Pop Dewey had just unwrapped for inspection.

"There, you see?" Anderson demanded, his voice triumphant. "Nobody wanted to believe me, but there isn't one bit of swelling in that foot. Look for yourself."

Lee Ames and Doc Todhunter were coming in from watching Freeway exercise as Anderson whirled in jubilation to announce his news to the rest of the Derby Barn. "He's okay, you hear me? Mr. Ames, Doc Todhunter, come here a minute. You got to see this."

Pop Dewey couldn't move. He just stayed where he was, kneeling in the straw of the stall with the bandages in his hands, while everybody else came crowding around.

It was true.

Double Seven's front leg was as good as new.

If Pop hadn't been rubbing it and massaging it by the hour, working the oil and liniment into it and the whole time thinking it was no use, just following orders like he had his entire life, he couldn't even have said which leg it had been.

Pop swallowed on a suffocating rush of hope. Was it possible that Double Seven would be in the Derby after all? Could he have been so wrong?

He remembered his despair Wednesday night and the things he had sneaked so carefully into the footlocker under his cot—the ax, the kerosene. For an instant the dark determination comforted him with its heady sense of power. But what was the matter with him, thinking of that? Pop finally got to his feet. Everything was okay now. Double Seven was going to be in the Derby.

Or was he?

Pop tensed, trying to decipher Doc Todhunter's face as the veterinarian told Anderson that Double Seven certainly looked fine. "But we still don't know why he swelled up like that, Ned."

"Nothing showed on the X-rays. It could have been anything," Ned said, "a step he took wrong, some little thing. Or else the swelling wouldn't have gone down, would it?"

Doc shrugged. "There's only one way you're going to be able to tell for sure, Ned, you know that."

"You mean see how he is when he comes back from a workout?" Anderson gnawed nervously on his lip.

"Right," Doc said. "Or wasn't that what you were planning?"

"What did you do with Freeway?" Anderson countered. "You and Mr. Ames were coming back from the track when I called, weren't you?"

"Yes," Doc said. "But all I did—" He corrected himself. "All Shelby wanted Freeway to do this morning was gallop."

"Maybe that's all I'll do with Double Seven, too," Anderson said. "Just give him a nice slow gallop."

"If that's what you'd ordinarily do, Ned." The trainer didn't answer. "But if you think he needs something more than that, after being off schedule. . . ?"

Anderson said, "I don't know, Doc. I'm almost afraid to push."

"I'm not talking as a vet now," Doc said carefully. "You

have your own vet, a good one, too. And God knows I wouldn't tell another man how to handle his horse. But as an old friend."

"Okay, okay," Ned Anderson said. "Of course you're right." He straightened his shoulders and smiled, then he said to Lee, "If Double Seven can't take a blowout today, I guess we have to find out. Because if he can't go three-eighths this morning and come out of it in good shape, he sure as hell can't go a mile and a quarter tomorrow, can he?"

"No," Lee agreed, "I guess not, Ned."

Anderson turned to his groom. "Okay, Pop, get him ready and we'll see. And pray, Pop, pray like you never prayed before. Because that's what I'm doing."

After days of nearly total neglect the Nickels had suddenly come back into favor with the newsmen. Or so it seemed from the number who trailed them to the track to watch Sweepstakes' workout.

And it wasn't because Sweepstakes had been first over the line in the Derby Trial, despite his subsequent disqualification. This accomplishment was duly listed in every analysis of tomorrow's field, but the handicappers invariably added that only a very small percentage of Trial winners went on to capture the Derby. They also pointed out that in this particular Trial there had been a sloppy track and fluke conditions that not only prevented favored Armada from even getting into contention but equally obscured the true abilities of the other colts.

Sweepstakes was still considered The Horse Least Likely to Succeed. His odds held at the dismissive 100-to-1.

Actually, those now besieging the Nickels were not strays returning to the fold but newcomers, the final wave of reporters from publications that were either so small that they sent men to cover only the last two days or so large that assistants had been doing the spade work until today when the stars had arrived. Whatever the paper represented, they found in Brewster Nickel that unfailing accessibility, that uninhibited, eager volubility which, by the law of diminishing returns, had dropped the pair into comparative obscurity earlier.

In Gladys, though, Derby Fever had taken the form of high-strung petulance. Let Brewster talk to the reporters if that was what he wanted. Though why he did, considering what they wrote about Sweepstakes, was beyond her. She ignored the press regally and concentrated on Ed Quincy as they stood at one of the gaps in the fence and watched Mickey Kuzich's replacement drop lightly onto the soft dirt after Sweepstakes' two-mile gallop.

"Are you sure this new boy's going to be as good as Mickey?" she asked for the hundredth time.

"Robbie is at least as good," Quincy answered patiently. "Maybe even better, and he's got the advantage of really knowing this track, he rides here every spring and fall. Mickey had never seen it before and Donnie Cheevers, the boy on Armada, never did before Tuesday, either."

"Robert Roberts," Gladys murmured, as the jockey gathered his gear. "I always wonder why people name their kids that way. You're always coming across them. James James or William Williams or Thomas Thom—"

"Well, I done a lot of things in my time," Quincy interrupted with an unusual hint of asperity, "but so far, Mrs. Nickel, I never picked a jock on account of his name. All I want to know is, can they ride. And Robbie Roberts can."

"I still think all the kidding they must get could affect them," Gladys said. "What really burns me up, though, is that I liked Mickey Kuzich. I just can't understand why they had to suspend him."

"Aw, come on, now," Quincy protested. "The stewards showed you the film. You know they had no choice but to set him down."

"I don't care. Everybody kept saying, 'You see, that's where it happened,' and then running the film again and saying, 'Right there.' You along with the rest of them. But I didn't see one damn thing."

"Well, that's because you're not a trained observer."

"All right, say it was his fault," Gladys conceded. "They could still have waited till after the Derby before beginning his suspension. But, no, they have to do it today. You can stick up for them if you want to, but it isn't fair. That's punishing us, too, and we didn't do anything."

Quincy sighed. "I know, sometimes it can make a difference, though most jockeys can ride any horse well their first time up. But if you look at it the way the stewards have to—"

"The hell with the stewards!"

"If a suspension didn't hurt, Mrs. Nickel, what good would it be? Every jock in the world would figure he could get away with murder on the track. And I do mean murder. One guy out of line can make a mess you'd never want to see. If he could just take a few days on the ground at his convenience, what would he care?"

Gladys was unconvinced. As she had been all the other times Quincy had tried to explain. "I still can't see why they blamed Mickey. How can a hundred-and-ten-pound man really control a thousand-pound horse? It's ridiculous!"

"If he can't, he better look around for some other kind of business. Sure, there are times when a horse is unmanageable, like a racing car when the steering fails, but the stewards know that as well as anybody. If that's the case, they don't give the rider a penalty. It's just one of those things, that's all. But if a jockey could have avoided trouble, as they decided Mickey could . . ."

"But he's so small."

Quincy laughed. "You're letting size fool you, Mrs. Nickel. Jocks may be small, they have to be, but pound for pound, those guys are as strong and as tough as any other athletes in the world. Even tougher. They're laying their lives on the line every time they ride."

He stiffened. "Hey, wait a minute, Mrs. Nickel. They're bringing Double Seven out on the track. I want to see what they're planning to do with him."

Alan, of course, would have followed Pop Dewey over to watch Double Seven in any case but he was slightly surprised when Johnny Sullivan dropped the reins he was soaping to go along.

"You never showed this much interest before," Alan said. "Why now, all of a sudden?"

"It's his first time on the track since he had the trouble with his leg," Johnny said. "I'm kind of curious what Anderson will do. He could just decide to gallop the horse, I suppose."

"Is a blowout the same as galloping?"

Johnny began to laugh then stopped abruptly. "What made you ask that?"

"Pop Dewey said that was what they were going to do, give Double Seven a blowout."

"Oh, the old man's talking to you again?"

"Not what you could call really talking," Alan said wryly, "but it's better than the last couple of days when he snapped my head off every time I opened my mouth."

"Poor old coot. So they're going to give Double Seven a blowout," Johnny said reflectively. "I'll tell you one thing, Alan, I know he beat Davie's Pride the other day—and maybe he can again, though I don't think so, Davie's Pride was bothered in that race—but I sure hope this turns out okay."

"Me, too," Alan said. "All right, I get the idea that a blowout is definitely not the same as a gallop, but you still didn't tell me what it is."

Johnny snorted. "First I better make sure you know what a gallop is!"

"Come on, Johnny, s-so I'm a greenhorn, you don't have to rub it in."

"Just kidding, Alan. But a gallop, even a pretty fast gallop, is strictly for conditioning, to keep a horse in top form without being too much of a strain. A workout is real running, not to the limit but fairly close to what a horse would do in an actual race—and that could be any distance, a mile, even, or more. You understand?"

"Yes."

"A blowout is something entirely different. It's a final tightener, you could call it a 'speed sharpener,' maybe. It's pushing a horse as hard and about as fast as he can go, but not for very long, say three furlongs, more or less, depending on the trainer." He paused. "Three furlongs is three-eighths of a mile, if you're wondering."

"Come on!" Alan protested again. "You know I know that."

"Okay, you straight about a blowout now? Practically every horse will have one sometime close to a race, like the day before or even the same morning."

"Got it," Alan said, "but why a 'blowout'?"

"Search me," Johnny shrugged. "Maybe because it clears the pipes, I don't know. That's just what they call it."

"Hey, there's your father. He came over to watch, too."

Dennis Sullivan was standing by the fence, surrounded by newsmen.

"That mean's my mother's with Davie's Pride or he'd never leave," Johnny said. They didn't join Dennis but found a good vantage point further down the fence and squeezed in. Johnny lowered his voice. "I'm surprised he left anyway, he's been acting so strange."

"Something wrong?"

"I suppose not, but he's got me kind of worried, Alan. He won't eat, he won't sleep."

"He's just excited over the Derby," Alan said comfortingly. "It's so close now I have trouble sleeping myself."

"Yeah, you do," Johnny jeered. "The only trouble you had was keeping your eyes propped up till the end of that program last night."

"I'm not used to getting up so early or working so hard," Alan conceded.

"We'll make a man out of you yet," Johnny teased. "But with my father it's more than being excited. Maybe I ought to be used to him by now, he gets these crazy Irish ideas. Right now he has this terrible feeling that Davie's Pride is in danger and he doesn't want to let the horse out of his sight for two minutes."

"You don't mean he thinks somebody would do something to hurt Davie's Pride?" Alan was shocked.

"Oh, Lord, I don't know. You can't pin him down. It's such a ridiculous idea on the face of it, with the guards on constant duty. But he suddenly comes up with this yesterday morning and I don't think he's had a bit of rest since. You know what he did last night?"

"What?"

"Made himself up a bed on the floor of one of the empty stalls between Davie's Pride and Sweepstakes. And the way he looks, I'll bet he didn't get one wink."

"Well," Alan said, "it'll be over pretty soon."

"Oh, sure," Johnny said, "but it kind of gives me the creeps, too, you know? My father's not the only one, though. He says old Pop Dewey did the same thing, spread a blanket on the other side, between Davie's Pride and Double Seven."

"Pop Dewey?" Alan's voice was sharp. "You're kidding."

"Why would I kid you?" Johnny asked. "I'm only telling you what my father . . . Hold it!" He held his stopwatch poised, eyes narrowed on the track. "Okay, now! Let's see what Double Seven can do."

Alan watched Double Seven's important test with unseeing eyes. He was thinking about Pop.

On Wednesday evening, after he had lost the old man in the parade crowds, Alan had waited nervously at the Derby Barn until Pop had stumbled back into the dormitory, soon after lights out at ten o'clock. The groom had evidently just disappeared into another bar somewhere and no harm done, though Alan still shuddered to imagine the reaction when his report of the incident reached Atlanta.

Last night, the old man had turned in at ten o'clock on the cot next to Alan's and seemed to have fallen asleep immediately, as Alan had done. Could Pop have been trying to fool him? Or had he just awakened and then—like Dennis Sullivan —decided to keep an eye on his horse?

300

These were questions that Alan needed to be able to answer with absolute certainty, though how he would manage to stay awake he wasn't sure. As he had admitted to Johnny, the racetrack regimen really knocked him out.

It was a fact which no longer seemed very amusing.

Up in the tower the official track clocker checked his watch as Double Seven flashed past the brightly painted pole which indicated the finish of his three-furlong blowout.

"I make it 34 seconds," the clocker said, "no fractions."

"Right, and handily," the Daily Racing Form clocker confirmed, but he did not immediately lower his binoculars. He kept them trained on the big bay as Kenny Perini eased him into a canter for the return to where Ned Anderson and Pop Dewey waited at the gap.

"How does he look to you?" the track clocker asked.

"Seems all right. He certainly isn't favoring that leg at the moment." The Daily Racing Form man put his field glasses down and made a notation on the pad in front of him. "But, of course, we'll have to see. It's too soon yet to be sure."

The phone pealed at the track clocker's elbow. "Warren, you couldn't have timed your call better. He just this minute finished. Did three-eighths in 34 flat. No, no signs of trouble, so far he looks okay."

Below the clockers, the usually adequate space reserved for horsemen and reporters was jammed to capacity and still kept out most of the press. In fact, it was the exclusion of so many newsmen which had encouraged Tom Richardson and Buddy Sheffield to observe Double Seven from this spot.

The dramatic succession of events which had seen Buddy fired as trainer of Lucky Jim one day only to become Dashing Lad's the next naturally made them targets for incessant interviews. But at the moment, even the journalists who had managed to squeeze inside were concentrating on Double Seven.

"Thirty-four flat," Buddy said, consulting his stopwatch.

"Pretty good, considering the layoff."

"Very good," Buddy said. "So, now we'll see."

"Yes, I want to take a look when he comes off the track," said Tom, "but then I'm going to have to tear out of here. I promised to show at the Latham's Kentucky Oaks breakfast. That filly they're running this afternoon is one I bred."

"I know. Good luck to all of you." Buddy squinted up at the lowering clouds. "Hope she doesn't mind a little rain?"

Tom laughed. "Hell, Buddy, this filly will probably love it. Her sire was a real mudlark."

"Yeah, but what's that old one? 'Not all fathers have mudders.'"

Tom groaned. "If you're trying to drive me away, that did it. We might as well move outside, anyway."

They edged out of the building and over to the gap where, since both were so tall, they could see above the crowd. Kenny Perini dismounted from Double Seven and uncinched his saddle. Dropping it to the ground with unusual carelessness, he hurried to help Ned Anderson and Pop cover the horse with a gray blanket which was enlivened at each corner by a circular shocking pink patch against which George Packo's black "P" stood out boldly.

"Perini has to be saying a few prayers right now," Buddy said. He and Tom began to move along the fringes of the mob which accompanied Double Seven back toward the barn.

"Seems to be walking normally," Tom said.

"Hope he stays that way but nobody can be certain until he's cooled out. Sometimes it takes awhile."

"I know, but as I said, I can't wait." Tom stopped and gestured. "My car's down this way. Maybe I'll give you a buzz in an hour or so."

"Why don't you? We ought to know by then."

Tom started off. "See you later then."

"This afternoon?"

Tom checked stride and turned. "I can't swear. I'll try to come backstretch before the Oaks, but if not . . ."

"You'll be out in the morning?"

"I will if I possibly can," Tom said. "I sure want to. Only the way it is at Derby time with some of our best clients in town I've got a dozen parties tonight and a whole series of breakfasts tomorrow!"

Buddy chuckled. "And I know I won't see you during the Derby itself. Or have you changed that habit?"

"I considered it this time, Buddy, especially when I thought Sparky was going to be in it. But, no, I'll be watching the Derby from the infield as usual." He spread his hands. "I suppose it's stupid to go on with something I started as a sort of Declaration of Independence from the old man, refusing to sit in the family box. But it wasn't just that."

"I know, you thought they were having more fun out there."

"Anyway, I've been doing it for so many Derbies now that I'm sure not going to break the pattern with Dashing Lad running."

"No, let's not take any chances," Buddy said with a wide grin. "No reason you have to be out front for the race itself, Tom, but what if Dashing Lad takes it? How will you get to the winner's circle?"

"Never you fear, Buddy. If Dashing Lad wins, I'll fly over the infield fence!"

"Seriously."

"I am serious. About coming through the infield fence, I mean. It's got a gate just in back of the Presentation Stand. Naturally, it'll be locked up tighter than a Rocky Mountain tick tomorrow, but I've already arranged with Lee Ames that if I should have to come through, the guards there will open it for me."

"If you can get to the gate, you mean!"

"Leave it to me," Tom said. "You just get Dashing Lad to that winner's circle and I'll be there. What do you think, Buddy? The truth, now that you've really had a chance to study the horse?"

"Dashing Lad's a damn fine animal," Buddy said, "and he's

in top condition, but I don't have to tell you that. Orv was a hell of a trainer."

"Yes."

"For the rest of it, well, it's like every other race in the world. You get your horse to the post, trained the best way you know how and then, if he can go the distance, if the breaks don't go against him . . ."

"I know," Tom said.

"Dashing Lad's got the inside post, that should help at a mile and a quarter." Buddy cast another glance up at the sky. "If it's going to rain, I wish it would hurry up and get it over with, and not too much rain, that could hurt. We've got Ferdy Garcia. He can ride with the best on any man's racetrack, wet or dry, and he knows the horse. So, with any luck, we've got a good shot at it, Tom, as good as anybody."

"Well, here's hoping. If I don't see you until after the Derby." Tom held his hand out.

"Right," Buddy said, his own clasp steady and warm. "Here's hoping."

TWO

THE TRACK AT CHURCHILL DOWNS had echoed regularly over the years to the hoofbeats of the world's finest thoroughbreds, and many of the men who lined its reaches on any morning had seen the very best.

This was a best which differed, almost invariably, with the personal bias of the beholder, and against it—with no exceptions whatsoever—the most impressive modern contender was grudgingly measured.

"Well, sure," the old-timers would concede, "this here seems to be a pretty nice horse, real nice, a long ways better than having an empty stall, but you couldn't rightly put him in the same class as Count Fleet." Or Determine or Assault or Gallant Fox or Citation. The roster was as endless as it was distinguished.

Nevertheless, when Freeway had gone through his gallop that morning, there were involuntary murmurs of awe and appreciation all along the fence. The unbeaten hopeful from California was a truly magnificent creature, with the exquisitely proportioned balance of a "picture" horse and a long, easy stride which was at once graceful and powerful. Under the dull gray of the sky, Freeway's roan coat had seemed even lighter than it was, luminous, almost white.

Doc Todhunter was far too much a horseman to be unmoved by such a spectacle, of course. But even as Lee Ames, at the fence beside him, murmured, "Beautiful!" and Doc nodded, he was thinking how curious it was that this crowning achievement of his career should have so little to do with the elation soaring within him. He supposed he was as religious as the next man, if being religious meant having humble awareness of a force completely beyond one's own control. The practice of medicine, whether it dealt with humans or animals, gave almost daily testament of the miraculous.

But Doc would have been pressed to remember the last time he'd set foot in a church. And yet the only words which seemed to fit his mood sprang, unbidden and unexpected, from some Sunday School lesson out of his childhood: "For this my son was dead, and is alive again; he was lost, and is found!"

Small wonder if Freeway and the Kentucky Derby had suddenly become unimportant to him.

Since this was hardly a subject that he could discuss with the president of Churchill Downs, Doc introduced a different one as the two had walked back to the Derby Barn after Freeway's exercise.

305

"This is the first opportunity I've had to tell you how grateful we are that you found places for Rudy Maldonado's family to stay," he said. "He's never ridden in the Derby before and they really wanted to see him."

"Don't thank me, Doc, thank Warren Robbins."

"Oh, I did, the minute we got here," Doc answered. He grinned. "And you know what he told me?"

"What?"

" 'Don't thank me, thank Lee Ames!' "

"Oh, well," Lee said, laughing, "just glad we could help. It's a little easier for Churchill to come up with last-minute accommodations than it would be for anybody else. We try to keep a few extras stashed away for emergencies."

Doc nodded. "And there are always emergencies during Derby Week. I'm sorry we had to add to them, Lee, but the jockey switch was completely unexpected. You know it was Gabe Hilliard who'd been scheduled to ride Freeway and he doesn't have a wife and parents tagging after him."

"That should be the least of Hilliard's problems," Lee said.

The antagonism in his own voice was vaguely startling. He didn't like Gabe, true, but the jockey's present difficulties weren't his fault and for that matter, from what Peggy Garcia had blurted, his loss of the mount on Dashing Lad wasn't his fault, either.

Doc's hand stopped Lee just as they reached the entrance to the Derby Barn. The older man had also been disturbed by Lee's tone.

"I hate to imagine the rumors that must be going around," Doc said hesitantly, "and I can't really talk about it." He drew a deep breath. "I thanked you for what you did for Maldonado, for instance, and haven't said a word about what you did for us, with the police."

"Forget it."

"You know I never will," Doc said. "But there's one thing I must say, Lee—that I can say to you. No matter what you've heard, Gabe Hilliard is as fine a human being as I've ever

306

met. There's no way I could repay what he's done for me."

It was at this point that the two had been interrupted by Ned Anderson's jubilant announcement of Double Seven's incredible recovery. For the moment, that news had blotted out everything else and Lee, who had intended to get frontside to his office as quickly as possible on this second busiest morning of any year, went instead to watch Double Seven's blowout.

Aside from his personal regard for the people concerned, the colt's fine performance on the track brought Lee a special satisfaction. Because if Double Seven stayed in the Derby, life would certainly be simpler at Churchill Downs.

The Derby inserts for today's program and important pre-Derby wagering—with Double Seven's name included—were already coming off the presses. The printing had started yesterday after the entry box for the Derby was officially closed and post positions drawn and would continue through tomorrow morning. A scratch now would necessitate any number of corrections and announcements.

There was a further consideration in hoping Double Seven would remain in the running, one which could never be ignored in the preparation for any race and that was the possibility of still other late dropouts. Really short fields were not entirely unknown to Churchill Downs, naturally. The Derbies of 1892 and 1905 had each been staged with only three colts and a handful of other Derbies had presented a mere four or five. To modern fans, however, such races weren't as interesting as those with more contenders, nor were they generally as profitable. This year's list was comparatively small to begin with and there was still time for so many things to go wrong.

Lee shook the thought away as Double Seven was being led off the track and back toward the Derby Barn. "What's the verdict?" he asked Doc. "Is he all right?"

Doc's shrug was very slight. "We'll have to see," he said. "You going to be around for awhile?"

Lee decided abruptly that his office would have to wait. "I guess so."

"Might be a good idea," Doc said. "Guess I will, too."

Doc didn't want to stay. He had come to oversee Freeway's routine only because Shel had asked him to and now he wanted to get back to the hotel as quickly as possible.

Late yesterday afternoon, Shelby had finally collapsed into the merciful sleep which was characteristic of post-drug reaction. Doc himself would have induced it sooner but since nobody knew what Shelby had taken, Doc was afraid to give him any medication at all.

Even without this, though, Shelby would now sleep the clock around. It was possible he would not even awaken until tomorrow. And Paula was with him. But Doc was eager to be with him, too. He'd go as soon as Double Seven had cooled out.

Both Lee and Doc had lingered with some vague idea of being helpful if Doc's misgivings should be realized. In the end, though, they might have left as early as they liked. Because even while the hot-walker was leading Double Seven around, it became evident that he was beginning to limp, and all they could do was stand in frozen silence.

There was nothing anybody could say which would have consoled the colt's trainer. Anderson bit his lip and said to the crush of spectators in a shaking voice, "Well, you have to take it the way it comes in this business, I guess. Can't win 'em all, fellows, right?" Then he wheeled blindly and walked away.

They let him go without a word, without a question, and several in that mob of reporters were not ordinarily noted for such tact or sensitivity. But what could he have told them in any case that they did not already know, that they could not see for themselves?

Double Seven was definitely, irrevocably out of the Kentucky Derby. And Ned Anderson's heart was broken.

Alan and Johnny made no attempt to speak to Pop Dewey. As he led the increasingly lame Double Seven past them to

Stall H in the Derby Barn, the old groom's face was stony and forbidding.

The boys gave each other stricken little head shakes and went on with their chores for Davie's Pride as silently as a mother might stand in horror at the scene of an accident to a neighbor's child.

Blessed, beautiful Davie's Pride, who had come back safely to the stall from his own morning's workout and was hungrily nibbling at his oats!

THREE

THE A.D. HAD CALLED Inspector Elverson at seven o'clock that morning. The A.D. himself had been briefed even earlier by an agitated official high in the State Department who had been roused from his sleep in the middle of the night by an equally prestigious member of the Canadian Government. Who, presumably, had been routed from his bed by Stephen Cardigan's telephoned request.

The orders themselves were as simple as they were startling: the FBI was to make no attempt to interfere in the proposed exchange between Cardigan and the kidnappers of his daughter. None.

"But, sir," Elverson had protested, "I explained to him last night that he'd be jeopardizing his own life. And probably with very little real hope of getting the girl back alive."

The A.D.'s tone was dry. "I gather you were quite eloquent in expressing our objections to his plan, Jason. That seems to be precisely what worried him, that we might allow our anxiety over his safety to override our agreement not to intercede without his specific permission."

However, inasmuch as all other aspects of the Cardigan case had been under stringent restriction from the beginning, the FBI was allowed to continue certain of their investigations. Known intimates of Coolie Bascombe—finally identified through the tailor who'd made that jacket with the secret pocket—might go on being discreetly checked.

The stakeout at the racetrack could still be maintained, with one difference. If the man passing ransom bills were spotted—highly unlikely now, since no new twenty had turned up yesterday—he was to be kept under careful surveillance but not picked up for questioning.

The monitoring of Cardigan's calls was permitted as before, so when the kidnapper phoned the Crown Hotel suite as expected at eleven sharp, Inspector Elverson was on duty, listening dejectedly while Cardigan agreed to the suicidal exchange.

The Canadian put down the receiver and nodded to Morgan Wells, hovering at his side. "It'll be tonight," he said.

"I could tell from what you were saying. He wouldn't specify a time?"

Cardigan shook his head. "We didn't expect him to, did we? He's following the pattern he set back in New York."

"And he didn't say when he'll call back with further instructions?"

"No. But in New York there were three calls on the day of the ransom payment." He swallowed involuntarily, remembering. "The one in the morning, much like this. At four to say he was thinking of changing his mind—"

Morgan balled his hands into fists so tight that his fingernails broke the skin of his palms.

"And again at six, with the actual instructions. That was before Daylight Savings. It got dark earlier then. He's apt to make his next call at five today."

"We can't count absolutely on his following precedent," Morgan warned. "There was the Monday he didn't phone at all after saying he would."

"I know." Their eyes met. "So I'll have to stay here, Morgan, just in case. Perhaps you'd better see to the car now."

Morgan hesitated. "If we've miscalculated and he *should* call before I get back, what then?"

"I'll go, of course," Lisa's father said firmly. "In another car. But I'm almost positive he'll stick to the pattern, Morgan. I've had a great deal of time to consider this man, what he's like."

There were undercurrents in the discussion which Jason Elverson found puzzling. He cleared his throat and insinuated himself into the conversation. "Having difficulties with your car, Mr. Cardigan?" he asked.

"Not really," Cardigan said. "A little knock I noticed. I'm sure it isn't anything important, but I certainly can't risk having motor trouble tonight."

"No," Inspector Elverson conceded. "No, you couldn't take a chance on that."

The FBI man withdrew to the next room and pretended to adjust the sophisticated monitoring equipment set up in there. He was wondering why Stephen Cardigan found it necessary to lie about a thing like that. Men like the financier did not send men like Morgan Wells when they wanted a car checked even when, as now, the chauffeur had been left in New York. Men like that picked up telephones and gave orders and hotel employees came scurrying to obey.

Elverson pursed his lips. His orders were not to interfere in Cardigan's attempt to save his daughter. He was not even to follow the Canadian when he set out on that desperate mission. Nothing had been said, though, to prevent surveillance of Morgan Wells.

FOUR

T HE DOCTOR had been poised for departure, just chatting with Varonica and Gabe, when Nick Chambley phoned from the backstretch to announce that Double Seven was definitely scratched from the Derby.

"Poor Kenny Perini!" Gabe said, repeating the news.

It was an obvious thought for another jockey. The doctor's reaction was different. "What a shame," he mourned. "I liked that horse. And I'd have collected very good odds on him, too."

"He'd have had to win first," Gabe reminded him. "But do you mean to tell me you were planning to bet against Magician? My horse? After all we've been through together?"

"It's a long, sad story," the doctor said. "When I was fresh out of medical school I used to put in a couple of days a week as track physician. The first jockey I examined, just a routine physical, was bound and determined I should bet on his mount in the third race that afternoon. So I looked it up in the Form, and nothing. The horse had maybe managed to pick up fourth money once in two years. Then I looked at the tote board and that was showing 99-to-1, as high as it could go. I said to myself, 'The guy's stark raving mad.'"

"Don't tell us, let us guess," Gabe said.

"Of course. I played the favorite, a 3-to-2 shot, if I remember rightly."

"Oh, no!" Varonica said. "And the other horse won?"

The doctor sighed reminiscently. "That I do remember exactly. He paid $248.60."

"How awful."

"Well, for years after that I played any horse that was mentioned by a jockey and didn't cash a single ticket. So now, I never pay the slightest attention to any of them. Besides," the doctor laughed, "I just happen to have inside information that Magician's jockey shouldn't even be riding!"

Varonica's smile vanished instantly. "Is that true? Is it really going to be bad for Gabe?"

"You know how I feel about that," the doctor said. "If I had my way, he'd have been in the hospital. But if there isn't any internal damage that we don't know about, I guess you don't have to worry too much. It's going to hurt, though."

"No, it's not," Gabe contradicted. "You're going to give me something to deaden the pain."

"It'll hurt till all hell won't have it after the race," the doctor said. "I'll guarantee that. We can medicate you and strap you till the cows come home, but you're still going to put a fantastic strain on those ribs."

"I've done it before."

"Then you know I'm right, but you're the one who'll do the suffering, so I suppose it's up to you." The doctor glanced at Gabe's discolored face. "You're not much to look at, but I have to admit you've healed much quicker than I ever expected."

"That's because of radiant health and clean living," Gabe grinned. "All right, now who do you like for the Derby?"

"Well, Double Seven was my upset choice. I suppose I'll have to go with Lucky Jim." The doctor made a resigned gesture. "I hate to go with the favorite, but after all he's got the country's leading rider and Firestone doesn't have any broken ribs." On which jibe, he left with exaggerated haste.

"The doctor and you seem to like the same jock," Gabe said to Varonica. "Isn't that who you said you were going to back, Gene Firestone?"

The green eyes were laughing at her. A few days earlier she would have bantered in return. Now, impulsively, she protested, "Oh, Gabe, you know I wouldn't bet against you, ever."

He slid onto one of the stools at the counter. "You want to hear something funny, Ronnie?"

"I know you'd like some coffee!" She was already in the kitchenette, reaching for cup and saucer.

"If you have it," he agreed absently, "but what I started to say was that I got a shiver right down the middle of my back when you said that."

She looked at him, puzzled. "I can't help it," he shrugged, "that's what happened."

"All I said was . . ."

"I agree," he interrupted. "It doesn't make sense to me, either. It was the tone of your voice, I suppose. Or maybe the whole concept in that one sentence." He gave a slight laugh. "A guy once wrote that he couldn't define poetry, he just recognized it when his skin bristled."

She slopped a little of the coffee she was settling before him, obviously startled. "A. E. Housman."

"There," Gabe complained, "you just did it to me again. Now how the hell would you know his work?"

"If you don't mind my asking," Varonica retorted, "how the hell would you?"

"You did think I could read, didn't you?"

"Come on, Gabe, this isn't the first time you've sprung a tidbit like that."

"So you're not the only one who escaped into books. I didn't have any guide, though," he said grimly. "Or maybe it was because of Tillie."

When he didn't continue she asked, "Who was Tillie?"

Gabe stared into his coffee. "My mother."

"Oh? What was your father's name?"

"Mordecai." He pushed the cup aside and got to his feet. "Let's forget both of them, all right?"

"No, it's not all right," she said, following him to the couch. "You always slide away from talking about your parents.

About anything before you started riding. I'm curious."

"I told you, I don't want to talk about them."

"It seems to me I said that to you once and then ended up telling you my whole history. So you may as well give in. You can't get out of here until tomorrow, anyway." She smiled. "And besides, I'm so much bigger than you are."

He laughed, suddenly realizing how far they had come together. "There's just not that much to tell."

"Then tell me. What did you mean when you said your reading was because of Tillie?"

"Just that she wanted Mordecai to let me go to school. That was the one thing she did try to do something about. But he wouldn't, not a minute more than he had to, so when I finally took off, I read everything I could lay my hands on. Just to spite him."

"What's your mother like?" Varonica prompted.

"She's dead, died when I was twelve." He hesitated. "Tillie was, oh, pretty typical of everybody else around our part of Tennessee. She was a lot like me, at least in looks."

"You called her Tillie?"

"I didn't call her a damned thing," Gabe said bitterly. "I never spoke to her unless she spoke to me and then I just answered. But that's how I think of her."

"Oh, Gabe, you sound as if you hated her."

"I did. Or it seemed as if I did for a long time. Almost more than I did him, because I thought she could have stopped him and she didn't." He sighed. "I suppose, looking back, I made everything worse for her. She probably loved me very much. I heard afterwards that the time I ran away and got lost, she didn't go to bed the whole week, until she found me."

"You were lost an entire week? Gabe, how old were you?"

"Five." He shuddered. "I still have nightmares about it. One nightmare, I mean, that keeps recurring. And I never got up the courage to take off again until after she died. No matter what he did. That was the thing. She was a grown-up

315

who wouldn't have got lost and I felt she should have run away herself and taken me with her."

Gabe picked up Varonica's hand and began twisting a ring she wore on her little finger.

"I can't help it," he said, "I still feel she should have left. Or else killed him!"

Varonica swallowed her shock and just let him turn and turn the ring.

"I haven't any idea why he was the way he was. I've never met anyone who was like him."

"He's dead, too?"

"Yes, he's been dead eight or nine years. Having driven himself like a plow horse, without a dime to his name, still working on somebody else's land and not one soul to be sorry he was gone."

"That's sad."

"I didn't think so when I heard about it. I was glad. I'm still glad that I must have been the worst frustration of his life. You talk about somebody considering you a freak. His son—the runt of the ages."

"Cut it out, Gabe."

He looked up from her ring. "You're right," he said, "it's over. But that was part of the trouble. I used to think he was the way he was because he was so disappointed about my size. I thought it was all my fault."

"You blamed yourself? Because he got drunk and beat you? Oh, how awful!"

He blinked, astounded. "Is that what you've been getting from this?"

"Why, I assumed . . . it sounded . . ."

"My God, Ronnie, I could have stood that. No, Mordecai didn't touch us, he never laid a finger on Tillie or me. As far as I know, he never got drunk in his life."

"But then, I don't understand."

Gabe's face went white. "It was the animals," he said.

"When he got mad he wouldn't open his mouth, but he had this heavy, braided-leather whip . . ."

"No!"

". . . and he'd just start beating and beating and beating, as hard as he could and as long as he could, the horses, the dogs, even the cows or the pigs, whatever was handiest."

"Oh, Gabe, I can't bear it!"

"And the blood would just be . . ."

"Stop, Gabe, please." Varonica burst into tears and threw her arms around him. "Oh, darling, how horrible. I know you should go on talking about it, but the thought of it makes me so sick. And then to think you felt it was your fault."

She hardly knew what she was saying but it really didn't matter. The way she was holding him was agony to his ribs, but that didn't matter, either.

He cleared his throat. "All right," he said, "I never could hold out against a crying woman. I surrender. I'll marry you."

She let him go and stared, the tears still streaming down her cheeks. "What?"

"I said, 'You win, I'll marry you.' That is, if you'll have me?"

"Oh, darling, yes, but I wasn't expecting—I mean, it's the last thing in the world . . ."

"I don't know why you seem surprised," Gabe said. "You never really left me any choice."

"What are you talking about?"

"Well, after all," he said, "you've already carried me over the threshold."

FIVE

Bunny Ingalls checked the Weather Bureau again but the prediction—which had been revised at eight o'clock —was still unchanged. "Showers and thundershowers this afternoon, clearing tonight, fair and slightly cooler tomorrow."

Oh, drat!

On which note of discontent she retired to the employees' lounge for an early lunch in preparation for what would undoubtedly be a hectic afternoon.

She was back at her post in less than twenty minutes. "No sense taking the full time," she told her substitute. "I'd sooner be working than just sitting in there. And I couldn't eat much, I never can this close to the Derby, my stomach gets tied up in knots."

Bunny slid onto her cushioned chair and went to work, glad that the switchboard was so busy.

No sense calling the Weather Bureau again until noon. Probably no sense doing it then, either, though she would, of course. And there could be news. The forecast had already been changed once. It could be a second time. Maybe there wouldn't be any rain at all.

But if it had to rain, she wished it would hurry up and get it over with. Bad enough to spoil Kentucky Oaks Day, but far worse if it held off until tomorrow.

If Derby excitement robbed Bunny of her appetite it had exactly the opposite effect on Lee Ames. He and Warren Robbins were having lunch at the cafeteria closest to the office. Lee often chose to eat there in preference to more formal

318

dining rooms in other areas because it was particularly cheerful. Today it also took the least time.

"Only don't think I'm having lunch this early to clear the decks," Lee said. "The truth is, I'm starving. Tension always makes me eat like a horse." He moved the dishes from his tray to the table. "My wife was telling me this morning she's going to let me stuff myself till Sunday and after that she's putting me on a diet. She says I take off fifteen pounds or else!"

Warren laughed, unloading his own tray. "You both say that every Derby, Lee." After a few minutes, he said, "Got a question."

"Shoot."

"One of those Thoroughbred Protective Bureau men who've come in to work the weekend tells me we've got a section of the grandstand that's beginning to crawl with the FBI. Know anything about that?"

Lee hoped his face did not reveal the sudden pang he felt at thought of Lisa. "Those TRPB boys are fantastic, aren't they? They must all have photographic memories."

"It takes a certain talent to begin with," Warren said, "but look how hard they work at it. They've got a file and a picture for every known racetrack undesirable in the country. In this case, though, so many of them are ex-FBI, they'd be bound to recognize . . ." He suddenly pursed his lips. "Or were you trying to steer me away from that subject?"

"No, I wasn't evading your question, Warren. And yes, I'm aware the FBI's here. Sorry I can't fill you in on it right now."

"That's okay, Lee, I just wanted to be sure you knew."

Lee smiled. "And we're always talking about how fast news travels around the backstretch."

Warren nodded. "Yes, we're not too slow frontside, either." He changed the subject. "Speaking of investigations, I have an idea they're checking Gil Tobin pretty thoroughly about Mannering's death, don't you?"

"Hey, you're pretty sharp! I was talking to the authorities

about that just before I left my office and you're absolutely on target."

"Well, I don't suppose I can claim much credit. His picture's plastered all over the front page and it's almost too obvious, his being in town when something like that happened."

"That's the point, Warren. Those pictures were taken when he and Senator Smith arrived at Standiford Field last night. They've gone over Tobin with a fine-tooth comb, but he was on his way from Washington in the Senator's plane when that car blew up, no question about it."

Warren chewed reflectively. "I suppose he could have had somebody else plant the bomb. He's been suspected of that before."

"He's suspected of it now, though there doesn't seem to be any motive. Neal was a friend of Tobin's—in fact, Tobin talked to him from Washington yesterday afternoon—and Mannering wasn't connected with Amalgamated Unions in any way."

"Well, I guess it would be a terrible thing to say. . . ."

"It certainly would," Lee agreed. "So I'm not saying it." He examined the buttered beans on his fork. "But I'll have to admit I'm enjoying my lunch very much right now. And I can't help thinking how little I might have been enjoying it if we were having a strike."

"I'm with you. And what are fifteen extra pounds as long as the Derby's safe?"

Lee peered past a man who was wearing a broad-brimmed Texas hat. "From what I can see through the window, it isn't raining yet," he said. "That's the one thing we still have to worry about, the weather." He thought of Lisa Cardigan and added quickly, "At least, as far as the Derby is concerned."

The truck from the hothouse had been considerably later than the woman expected. But the roses were here now and she already had the cotton padding stitched into shape as a soft backing under the light, pliant wire.

For a second after the delivery man left she simply stood there, glorying in the mass of deep color. Then, with a final appreciative sniff of the incredible fragrance, she began, with infinite care, to fasten the first rose into a corner.

Tomorrow, when the Kentucky Derby had been run and won, her handiwork would be thrown across the winner's withers. Each blossom must be set just so, turned just so, held securely.

The blanket of roses must be as flawless as the champion it would adorn.

He'd been in a couple of thousand races, had a dozen spills before the one which finally ended his career as a jockey, and he remembered none of them—not even the last—as clearly as he could now recall his fear the first day he got to be the Color Man.

He was up in the jockeys' room, removing from a special Derby rack the glove-satin blouse (gray with shocking pink circle, black "P") which Kenny Perini would have worn if Double Seven hadn't been scratched a little while ago.

He shook his head. The panic of that first day had come back to him as if it were yesterday. And on top of that, he was afraid again, which was just plain silly. Next thing, somebody'd be carting him off to the funny farm and he wouldn't blame them.

Season after season, horsemen put the racing silks for every thoroughbred currently in the barns in the Color Man's care. It was his chief responsibility—and had been for more years than he cared to mention—to assure that from among these hundreds there was a blouse available on any given racing day, in the proper color or combination of colors, for each horse scheduled to run.

The silks, as the blouses worn by the jockeys were traditionally called, were nowadays more likely to be fashioned of nylon or Orlon than they were to be made of their original stuff. Whatever their material, though, their vivid flashing had provided one of the sport's most festive aspects from the very beginning.

But the reason for their use was not esthetic. Nor were the racing colors chosen by each owner—and officially registered for his use upon approval by the New York Jockey Club—meant to be ego boosters, despite the fact that there were few sights more gratifying than watching one's colors come home in front. The primary, entirely practical, purpose of the silks was to allow quick identification of the owners and thus, by extension, of the horses themselves during a race. For a horseman moving his stable into any backstretch, the Color Man was frequently the second stop.

The racing secretary had to come first, for without his certification a thoroughbred wouldn't even be permitted to set hoof on track. Colors were listed almost as carefully, although in an emergency a horse might be allowed to run under makeshift silks. But in that event, the Color Man would scramble to find a blouse as close as possible to the original and any change, however slight, would be carefully brought to public attention.

The Track Announcer, who called every race over the loudspeakers, and the Daily Racing Form Trackman, upon whose observation all official records were based, had to be able to name correctly each horse at every point in a race, but proper identification was important to many fans as well. In action one brown horse was very much like another, and at a distance such distinguishing marks as white feet or stars or blazes might be invisible. The numbers on saddlecloths might be obscured by fences or trees or other horses. Only the silks could be counted upon to personalize the runners.

Even this device had been known to fail now and then because of mud or freak weather but that happened very rarely. In the main, the sport's unfailing effort to inform its fans was extremely effective.

The Color Man knew his responsibility. Enjoyed it, to tell

the truth, so he couldn't understand why he should feel nervous. It wasn't, he was certain, because out of the seven horses still left in the Derby there were only two stables which were really familiar to him. On those silks he didn't know, he had worked out a pretty foolproof system for keeping everything straight.

First he had the general racks jammed with the colors he had no immediate use for. Then he had the racks where he set up the current day's supply of blouses—anything from seventy-five to over a hundred—all hung in order according to race and post position number. And for special races he had a single rack, separate from the others, which now held nothing but the seven sets of silks for tomorrow's Derby. And with only one exception these were real silk. He ran his fingers over them gently, enjoying their luxurious feel.

You never could tell. If anybody was going to skimp on the Derby, you'd think it would be the little Irishman, who everybody knew didn't have a dime. Or the two that owned the coffee shops. But, no, the blouse of which the Color Man was secretly contemptuous—because it was sensibly washable instead of having to be dry-cleaned—belonged to Jim York. And people called him a sportsman.

The Color Man slid the seven hangers along the metal pole. He had checked them several times already this morning but he went through them again, ticking them off one by one as they appeared on his list. Which, of course, was exactly as they were being printed on the Derby programs right that minute.

Number One. Dashing Lad. Marshfield Farms, as if he could possibly mistake that. Blue, white stars on shield, white sleeves with red stripes, red cap. People weren't ashamed to be patriotic in the old days, when Tom Richardson's granddaddy chose his colors. Or would it have been his great-granddaddy?

Number Two. Davie's Pride. No forgetting that this one belonged to a Sullivan. Emerald green, dark-green shamrock over light-green harp, light-green sleeves, emerald-green cap.

Number Three. Magician. Al Lester's familiar combination, yellow and white stripes, orange sunburst, orange cap.

Number Four. Freeway, the California horse. The Color Man thought, as he had before, that Doc Todhunter must have let his wife design those silks. He just picked the horse. Bought it out of the Keeneland sales for peanuts and already it had earned a quarter million. Pink and baby-blue diamonds, pink sash, baby-blue cap.

Number Five. Armada. That was the Canadian girl's horse. She had picked silks almost the same as her father's, just reversing the colors. Black and gold halves, gold sleeves with black chevrons, black cap.

Number Six. Lucky Jim. The silks that weren't silk. Turquoise and sky-blue quarters, white "York," white sleeves, turquoise "Y" on white cap.

Number Seven. Sweepstakes. Scarlet, black coffee pot—with steam rising out of the spout—black cap.

All right, the Color Man told himself. His crazy vision of the colts entering the track for the Derby with the band playing "My Old Kentucky Home" and every horse under the wrong colors could never happen. Even if he made such an incredible error, there'd be the jockeys' valets when he gave them the blouses, the jockeys themselves, the owners, the trainers, all sorts of people who would correct it before it was too late.

But even as he reassured himself, the Color Man's uneasiness returned.

SIX

I T WAS SEVERAL HOURS after Morgan Wells had left the Crown Hotel before the agent trailing him was able to phone his report to Inspector Elverson.

"Subject left about fifteen minutes ago," the agent said, "and in accordance with your instructions, I just let him go."

"Yes, I'm certain he'll get back to Cardigan as quickly as possible. Where are you?"

The agent gave an address. "I'm just down the street from a small repair shop. Subject drove directly to it, waited inside the whole time and then, as I say . . ."

"A 'repair shop'? A garage, you mean?"

"Yes, sir, and more or less a one-man operation, though there are a couple of helpers. Anyway, I talked to the owner after subject left and according to him, all he did was give the car a thorough check and minor tune-up."

" 'According to him?' You think he's lying?"

"Oh, no, sir. He seemed very frank, quite willing to answer everything I asked. It's just that from where I had to wait I wasn't able to see what he actually was doing to the car. But the man seemed to be telling the truth."

"Hmmm. And yet, it took quite awhile, didn't it, if that was all?"

"Yes, I'd say so. Though he apparently has more work than he can handle. He may have been too busy to get to it right away."

"Maybe so," Inspector Elverson said. "Still, I can't quite picture anybody letting Cardigan's car sit around while he finished working on someone else's. Or Wells permitting that kind of delay."

Elverson was thinking aloud. "Another thing. Why would Cardigan send his car to a small garage in that area if all he wanted was a checkup? And how would he even know it existed? It doesn't make sense."

"I imagine he's used this man before," the agent said. "They may even be from the same part of Canada."

"This mechanic is Canadian?"

"Truthfully, I didn't ask, but I think so. He says 'aboot' for 'about'—though I suppose there may be sections of this country where they pronounce it the same way."

"Ummm."

"Should I have questioned him about it, Inspector? Is it important? I can go back very easily."

"No, no, you can come on in. If anything . . ."

If anything, the inspector thought as he hung up, he himself might go and have a talk with the garageman. But then Ted Irving called from Churchill Downs. One of the ransom twenties—against all odds—had been discovered as the first race was being run. And, as Kermit Young had postulated, in the same section where the last one had been passed.

It was only through a lucky circumstance that the bill was noticed so quickly, because it had been accepted by the pari-mutuel clerk without any signal to the FBI men clustered discreetly along that row of sellers. The agent who was substituting for the roving money man had made an automatic double check on all twenties taken in for the race. And there it was.

Elverson was disappointed but resigned. "Well," he told Irving, "it's too bad we missed after coming so close, but it was such a slim chance to begin with. It was just too much to expect that a busy clerk could really spot one of those bills."

"But he did, Inspector. That's the stunner. He did."

"Then I don't understand."

"He says we told them we were after a counterfeit ring. And he says—I'm quoting—that, hell, he knows the difference between good money and bad. This was good, so he didn't give the signal. Figured the number was just a coincidence."

"Oh, Lord!"

"Yes," Irving agreed. "But he says he's sure he can identify the man who gave it to him."

"Hold everything, Ted, I'll be there in ten minutes. I want to talk to that clerk myself."

Artie Dobermeyer displayed a remarkable lack of warmth when Kermit Young brought the inspector into the cage just as the second race began.

He'd had enough of feeling guilty over the strike business and he wasn't about to accept any blame because the FBI hadn't got their man.

"Never mind checking the machine on this race," Kermit told Artie. "The inspector wants to ask you a couple of questions. Jess will take over for you here."

"Look," Artie protested, "I'm responsible for this station and if there's anything wrong with the tally . . ."

"Forget it, Artie," Kermit said. "If Jess makes an error, you won't be charged with it. Come on, you two can talk right back here, it'll only take a few minutes. And I'd like you on duty again for the third race, Artie, I need Jess someplace else."

Artie began to defend himself before Elverson had a chance to speak. "I would have called for change, only you told us you were looking for counterfeit money."

"I understand," Elverson said soothingly. "You had no way of knowing. Believe me, nobody holds you responsible." The inspector hesitated. "I'll be frank with you. I never really expected you men to spot the bill. I'm astounded you could under such pressure."

Artie began to thaw. "I don't know about the rest of the fellows," he said, "but I notice numbers, anyway, it just happens. In a case like this, where I'm specially trying, all I do is check the last three numbers first and then, if they fit, well, I see if the rest match."

"Yes, but there were so many numbers to watch for and none of them in sequence."

Artie gave the inspector a shrewd glance. "I should have known you weren't looking for counterfeiters from that list you gave us. Funny money would be in sequence, not all mixed up like that."

The inspector smiled faintly. "No, it's the real thing we're after. However, Mr. Dobermeyer, there was good reason for the cover story. I'm going to have to ask you not to discuss it."

"Don't worry, I won't. I'll tell you one thing, though, this guy sure don't look like a crook, but I'd know him in a minute. I never forget a face."

"I'm told you took twelve twenties in that first race," Elverson said dubiously. "How can you be certain which person gave you which twenty?"

"It's the same thing as numbers." Artie groped for words to make the inspector understand. "Like this bill you were after. The last three numbers were 731, right? Well, my wife—she's dead now—and me used to live at 731 Helen Place just after we got married. Or take the number 917, that's my birthday, September 17th. Or Millie's birthday was May 11th, that would be 511."

"Yes, I see," Elverson said. And he did. The possibilities for relating numbers personally were apparently endless with the clerk's particular type of mind. "But we're talking about recognizing one face out of hundreds."

Artie shrugged. "Well, it might seem different," he admitted, "but it's really the same. This guy looks kind of like a cashier I once had an argument with at Gulfstream. Anyway, I've seen him before."

"Could he have given you the twenty on Tuesday?"

"What twenty Tuesday?"

"Oh, I thought you'd been told. We set this surveillance because there was an earlier bill."

"I took one of the twenties before?"

"We're not sure. Someone in this section did, but you didn't have the list then, Mr. Dobermeyer, it isn't important. About this man today, do you honestly think you could identify him if you saw him again?"

"As sure as I'm standing in this spot." Which reminded him. "Inspector, I got to get back to my window, the machines will be opening for the third race."

Elverson hesitated briefly, then he said, "Go ahead. Let's see if anything turns up on the next couple of races. After that we might ask you to circulate a little, see if you can spot him."

"What about if I don't get one of the bills but I see the same guy? He won that first race. We don't know, he could've hit the double. He'd buy Daily Double tickets at a special window, so I can't say if he did or not, but I didn't see him before the second race and a lot of people'll hold off on that if they've got a possible double going. He could be playing with the money he collected."

Elverson wasn't entirely certain he knew what Artie was talking about but he had grasped one salient fact and it shook him. "Are you telling me you remember the number of the horse this man played in the first race? Along with everything else?"

"Things stick in my mind," Artie said, almost apologetic in response to such incredulity.

"Well," Elverson said, "if you see this man, whether he passes another twenty or not, yes, give the signal."

He didn't have anything to lose, the inspector told himself, and then—slightly bitter—realized there wasn't a great deal to gain, either. If they did spot the right man, they couldn't touch him. But they could follow him, at least until he set out to meet Cardigan tonight. That wouldn't overstep the boundary of this morning's orders.

Artie was back on duty just before the buzzer sounded and his locked machine released. He started to work immediately, punching tickets for the third race.

Elverson moved around to the front where, from behind the Daily Racing Form one of the local agents had provided, he could watch the lines of people before the various windows.

Observing Artie at his station it seemed impossible that he had time to even look at his clients, let alone recognize them. They came so steadily, so quickly.

A young man in a blue jacket.

Another young man, carrying a light raincoat, with a girl walking at his side.

An older man in a turtleneck.

A woman who waddled.

An elderly fellow with iron-gray hair.

"Change!" Artie Dobermeyer called loudly.

Elverson held his breath, but it was all right. The elderly man did not seem to notice anything unusual in the clerk's voice.

He turned away from the window, still counting the smaller bills and tickets Artie had given him in return for his twenty.

Smoothly, separately, four of the agents from Ted Irving's office began to follow.

SEVEN

ASIDE FROM THE PRACTICAL work Lee Ames' position involved, there were equally important social requirements, and although The Colonel attended to many of the niceties with unstudied graciousness, they occupied much of Lee's time as well.

During the track's spring and fall meetings, he spent most afternoons in the pleasant Directors Room or circulated among the members of the Turf Club and their guests who were often horse owners and frequently friends.

It was on one of these social rounds that he met Charlie Talbot and the house party which had come over from Lexington on the T-Square Stud bus. Among them, naturally, was Jim York, who was beginning to show the amount of liquor he had already imbibed, even though the fifth race was barely over.

Since York had also been drinking heavily the last time Lee and he had met and since that furious confrontation still had the horse world buzzing, it could have been an awkward moment. Obviously, Jim York expected it to be. He stiffened perceptibly. But Lee greeted the group pleasantly and made a subtle point of including York in the general discussion of how things were at "Chitlin' Switch"—the horse people's affectionately derisive term for Lexington.

There was a notable difference in weather between the two cities. Lexington, slightly to the south and less than a hundred miles to the east, often seemed much colder, not quite as springlike as Louisville in late April or early May. Especially this year, everyone agreed.

Jim York relaxed.

And so did Charlie Talbot, whose difficult patron was becoming a considerable social burden. Talbot's patience was particularly strained because York, certain that Lucky Jim would take the Derby, was sounding less and less like a buyer for Lucky Jim's yearling brother. The loss of such a sale would have taxed the indulgence of the least practical of breeders, which Charlie Talbot was not.

York followed when Lee began to move along. "I thought you might be holding hard feelings about the other day," he said.

Lee smiled. "It was a misunderstanding, Mr. York, and it's forgotten. I regretted having to be the middleman. But the ruling isn't Olson's or mine," he pointed out. "It's standard procedure at any recognized track that no thoroughbred may be allowed to run unless he has a licensed trainer."

A recognized track, as York knew, was any track subject to the rules of any state racing commission, or just about every place with pari-mutuels.

"I can see that most of the time," he said, "but I still think they should have made an exception in this case. After all, Lucky Jim had a trainer up until three days before the Derby."

"A fine trainer," Lee agreed.

York gave him a bloodshot glance. "You think I shouldn't have bounced Sheffield, don't you?"

"That is strictly your business," said Lee. "How a man deals with his personnel or his horses is his affair, unless the stewards should be asked to intercede. My only official concern is that the rules of racing be complied with at this track. And since you wouldn't accept Nils Olson's explanation . . ."

"What's he? Just a hireling."

"Perhaps that's how it seems to you, Mr. York," Lee said, his face impassive. "But the racing secretary is a great deal more than that around here. However, as I said before, we didn't set this rule. You had let your trainer go and since you yourself are not a licensed trainer, you had to have a new one."

"For three days? That's what burns me. Buddy Sheffield had him ready. And the balance of his training schedule was pasted up in the stall. All the groom had to do was follow instructions."

"Well," Lee said, "it's unimportant now. You've hired a licensed trainer, he'll saddle Lucky Jim tomorrow, so there's no problem."

"It's the principle of the thing," York persisted. "Making me pay a man for nothing, a man I don't even know."

"Ike Drury? He's been around for years," Lee said. "He knows what he's doing."

York's face flushed with contempt. "The man's a hack, a has-been. I wouldn't let him touch Lucky Jim. And you know what I'll have to give him? Five percent of the purse."

"You'd have had to pay Buddy the standard 10 percent," Lee said quietly.

"Yes, but he earned it, he's the one . . ." He stopped himself abruptly.

Damn, he had to watch that. He'd said it before. And Sheffield might decide to sue, no matter how many people said he wouldn't.

"Well, it's over, Mr. York."

York put his hand on Lee's arm, delaying what he recognized as an attempt to escape. "Don't you think they should have gone along with me?" he demanded. "Tell the truth! They knew I couldn't pick up a decent trainer overnight, that I'd have to grab anyone, anyone at all who'd take the horse at the last second."

The man was an out and out boor. Lee resented being clutched at, not to mention the stale bourbon York was breathing into his face.

Fortunately, Warren Robbins intervened. "Hi, Mr. York. Lee, I hate to break in like this but something important's come up. Could I borrow you for a minute?"

"Of course," Lee said. "If you'll excuse me?"

"Sure," York said, swaying slightly as he released Lee's sleeve. "I didn't mean to hash it over like that, anyway. Just wanted to say I'm sorry I lost my temper the other day. No hard feelings?"

"No hard feelings," Lee said, finally escaping down an aisle with Warren. "What's the problem?" he asked when they had reached a fairly secluded spot.

Warren grinned. "Not a darned thing," he said. "I just happened to be passing and you looked as if you wouldn't mind being rescued."

"You never had a better idea in your life. A little more of that and I'm afraid I'd have really told him off. He had the gall to complain that he couldn't pick up a top trainer overnight. As if a top man would touch him after what he did to Buddy Sheffield."

"I've got news for you. He's lucky he got anybody. From what the backstretch says, he was turned down right and left —and by some guys I wouldn't have expected to be that fastidious. But poor Ike's been having a rough year, he couldn't afford to refuse."

"Speaking of the backstretch," Lee said, "I meant to ask you during lunch. Have you heard anything about why Hilliard lost the mount on Freeway? There's been a lot of nasty innuendo in the papers but nothing definite."

"The story seems to be that Gabe made a pass at Paula Vance and Junior jumped him for it."

Lee frowned. "That can't be it. Not from the way Doc was talking this morning. In fact, he's the one who roused my curiosity." He shook his head. "Well, it doesn't really concern us. But you know something, Warren? I'm beginning to think Hilliard's a much-maligned character. If I didn't detest the little bastard so thoroughly, I'd almost start being sorry for him." He laughed. "That would keep me from worrying about York, anyway."

"What's to worry about York?"

"This afternoon's performance. If Lucky Jim wins tomorrow, I wonder if he'll be sober enough not to fall flat on his face in the middle of the presentation ceremonies."

EIGHT

At five minutes after four, from the privacy of Lee's office, Elverson contacted the Cardigan suite.

"Did the call come?" he asked Ted Irving, who was monitoring.

"Nothing."

"Then Cardigan may have been correct in believing the schedule would be an hour later because of Daylight Savings."

"That's how it looks. But if anything should break, I'll get in touch with you immediately. Anything doing at your end?"

"Nothing new," Elverson said. "It's a holding action, that's all. I did tell you that second twenty was also on the list?"

"Yes, the last time you called," Irving said, "and I've been thinking. That seems to indicate your pari-mutuel clerk was wrong about which horse the subject picked in the first race, doesn't it? Unless he lost his winnings on the second?"

Elverson began to laugh. "I was wrong, Ted. There is something new here. Our subject is now buddy-buddy with one of your men!"

"You're kidding, Inspector."

"No, I'm not. Believe me, there wasn't a thing your man could have done to avoid it. I was watching. The subject struck up the conversation. But no problem, I've already moved another agent onto that detail, told the original man to stick around for a couple of races and then leave. All right?"

"Of course."

"The point is, that clerk was absolutely on target. The subject did win on the first race and he did hold off on the second because he had a chance on the Daily Double. He was bemoaning the fact that he missed by only a nose. Apparently, though, what he does is put his winnings to one side, in a separate pocket, and count them up at the end of the day. He only plays with the money he's brought and he always brings exactly fifty dollars."

"He told my agent all that?"

"Yes, he's a talkative one, isn't he?"

"A little too talkative and a lot too trusting if he were what he seems."

Elverson sighed. "Yes, aside from those two bills, you'd swear he was just a man at the races, having a good time. And then I remember what it's like where you are. How's Cardigan taking the delay?"

"You know. Just waiting."

"And Wells?"

"He went into his own suite about fifteen or twenty minutes ago."

Elverson stiffened. "He wasn't there at four?"

"No." Irving had caught the discrepancy. "But he should have been, shouldn't he? Hang on a second, Inspector, let me check." His voice was dejected when he got back on the line. "He's gone."

"Damn."

"I'm sorry, I guess I should have been more alert. But he didn't say anything special, just walked through the connecting door."

"I know," Elverson said. "I wouldn't have noticed, either, I'd have been so certain he'd be back in time for the call in case it came at four. But I think I'll head in now, anyway. Nothing I can do here, really. Your men have everything under control. Be there as fast as I can."

This was not as fast as it would have been on another afternoon. In all seasons, the main entrance to the Crown

Hotel was thronged with patrons and visitors. It was old but beloved, one of the few reminders of luxurious tradition in the rapidly growing, modern city. Moreover, it was situated at the busy core of that city's downtown. There were always conventions to fill its rooms, dinners or meetings to engage its many party or banquet facilities, clients who returned to it loyally year after year.

On the day before the Derby the area under the proscenium before the great gilt-marble-and-red-plush lobby was a madhouse, despite the hoarse directions of a splendidly uniformed doorman. Red-jacketed bellboys were breathless from their efforts to cope with the steady stream of arriving cars and cabs, but still guests and luggage were left waiting on the sidewalk.

The six-car space allotted as an unloading zone was hopelessly inadequate to the demands being made upon it. Would-be registrants were double parked in increasing numbers, a situation which did nothing to facilitate traffic flow along the comparatively narrow streets already crowded with rush-hour residents.

Elverson, inching his car past the Crown, was relieved when he finally reached the corner and could turn. But when he started to pull into the hotel's adjacent parking lot he was informed by a harried attendant that this, too, was incapable of handling today's needs and was directed apologetically to an auxiliary lot two blocks away. And yet, the inspector had noted as he passed, Stephen Cardigan's black Cadillac was sitting directly in front of the Crown's entrance, despite the fact that its position compelled all other cars to pull out around it, compounding the frenzy.

Men of the Canadian's wealth and importance were exceptional even at the Crown but today the doorman must have required a most convincing argument before permitting such an imposition. And he was probably considerably richer for the marvelous quality of his understanding.

Cardigan could not have given the true explanation, of

course, but there was reason for the arrangement. It had been one of the conditions of the first ransom payoff that Cardigan leave his car in open view for some hours before the time of his departure for Tarrytown to insure that he came alone. Also, the Cadillac's placement avoided possible complications after the instructions came. Cardigan would want no delay in keeping his rendezvous.

An unfortunate turn of phrase, Elverson decided, walking back to the hotel, since it brought to mind, unexpectedly and chillingly, a line of verse: "I have a rendezvous with Death."

The inspector's mood was unrelieved when he got upstairs to discover that, contrary to his expectation, Morgan Wells had not yet returned to the Cardigan suite.

Mace was still over on the west side of town patrolling the section he had chosen as the site for the night's meeting when he pulled up at an outside phone booth to make the call to Cardigan. It wasn't quite time so he sat in the car, waiting for five o'clock.

It hadn't rained, which was something, but it had been a gray, threatening day and the car had been like an oven, even with the windows rolled down. The wig he was wearing was as uncomfortable as a hat and the moustache was driving him nuts. He supposed it was because this was the third day and because he was by himself that he felt depressed. Not excited, keyed up like he'd been when they were collecting the first ransom.

He'd give the girl's old man a couple of good jolts, he promised himself in an unconscious effort to raise his spirits. He'd pretend to be sore about the change in plans. Hint he was about to back out of the deal, the same as he had in New York.

When he finally made the call, though, it wasn't that much of a kick. Cardigan sounded upset, all right, but not as much as the last time. It didn't do a thing for Mace.

"Look, I'll call you back later," he said. "Never mind when, you just be ready to jump the minute I tell you. Jump, you hear? And if you try to pull anything, you got a dead daughter on your hands!"

He hung up and got back into the car but he didn't return to his patrolling immediately. He simply slumped at the wheel. He was sour on the whole thing. Even a million dollars didn't seem as exciting right now as being down to nothing but one thin dime and taking some know-it-all for a fin in the poolroom.

But he'd come out of it once he got the money, he knew. And Rosanna would stop being so edgy, she'd go back to being her old self instead of hassling him all the time. And over the stupidest things. This morning she had been giving him a hard time because he paid the old guy so much for tickets that were good for two days, since they could only go once. When she didn't even want to go on Derby Day!

It was then that the realization hit Mace. He had to get to the trailer. Now, as fast as he could. If it wasn't too late already.

He burned rubber as he pulled away from the curb and headed for Thornbury Avenue and Rosanna. She was going to throw a fit when she saw him driving into the yard in this car, wearing his fake hair in broad daylight. But he had to take the chance that he could make it and get Lisa out of the trailer before Good Mary got home.

The trouble was, he'd been acting as if this was just picking up money like New York and all he had to do was wait until dark. But it wasn't. This was everything, meeting the old man, finishing the two of them off together and then the money.

And Lisa Cardigan had to be in the car before he made the next phone call. Because once he did that—once he gave instructions where the meeting was—Cardigan had to be in plain sight every second.

Mace didn't think the father would try to pull a fast one— he hadn't the last time—but thinking wasn't good enough. Mace intended to be right there watching when Cardigan got into that black Caddy, checking that nobody else got in and hid in the back seat, making sure nobody was trailing behind.

Mace pounded the steering wheel, his fists sweaty in the gloves he'd worn all day as protection against leaving fingerprints. How could be have been so dumb? To make things worse, the journey seemed endless. Early evening traffic was heavy all across the city and he was a stranger, forced to stay on the main arteries with which he had become partially familiar, because he couldn't risk getting lost.

At last he swung into the yard, ran to the trailer and began to pound on the door. There was no answer. It took him a second to realize he hadn't given the usual knock, that Rosanna must be cowering in panic. He rapped the regular way, calling at the same time, and when she finally opened the door a crack he burst in.

"Don't say a word!" he warned her. "Just move. I got to get her in the car and get out of here."

"Oh, Mace!"

"One word and I'll hit you so hard! Help me!"

But Rosanna was incapable of movement. All she could do was stand and stare, her face drained of color.

Mace pulled Lisa off the bunk so roughly that she stirred into consciousness and began, automatically, to struggle against him. He punched her and carried her out to the car.

"A blanket," he called hurriedly to Rosanna as he dumped Lisa onto the floor in the back, but there was no response. He went back into the trailer himself, grabbed a blanket off his bunk, threw it over Lisa, jumped behind the wheel and took off. Leaving Rosanna still motionless with fright.

Mace was disgusted at her helplessness until he was safely caught up in the traffic which had begun to break from Churchill Downs after the Kentucky Oaks. Then he thought of the expression on her face and began to laugh. It was easy to be amused now, to be indulgent. He had made it. And he felt great, as excited as he'd ever been in New York.

He wondered if Rosanna had moved yet. Stupid broad! But they'd have themselves a hell of a time tonight. He laughed again. They'd have to celebrate twice. Once for Lisa Cardigan and once for her old man.

"Subject stayed at Churchill Downs until the end of the last race," Irving told Elverson at 6:30, relaying the report he'd just taken over the phone. He looked at his notes. "Subject engaged in conversation with three men and a woman, on separate occasions. These contacts seem to have been entirely casual."

"Well, he had to have *somebody* to talk to after your agent left!" The hint of humor faded as Elverson glimpsed Cardigan's pacing figure through the open door into the next room. "At least we know he didn't make that five o'clock call."

Irving consulted his notes again. "After that, he drove to a small private house on La Salle, parked in a single garage adjoining, closed the garage door as if he did not intend to leave again soon. And that's it."

He forestalled the obvious question by adding, "Car's a three-year-old Chrysler, fully paid, registered by Eustace and/or Bella Potter of that address. He's sixty-six, a retired accountant, she's sixty-three, they've owned the house for twenty-two years, no police record of any kind. Not even a parking violation."

"Excuse me?"

The voice coming so unexpectedly from behind made the two FBI men whirl. A small, slim young man was staring at them—and their equipment—from the connecting room of Morgan Wells' suite.

"I didn't mean to barge in but the door was half open. I thought Morgan was in here."

"Who are you?" Elverson asked.

"I'm Donnie Cheevers."

"Armada's jockey," Irving explained. "Wells is his agent."

"That's right," Donnie said, "I just got in from the airport.

341

But where is Morgan? He said he was going to meet me."

"Oh, Donnie." Cardigan had stopped in the opposite doorway. "Morgan had to leave for awhile, why don't you just go ahead and settle in? Unpack, have some dinner, take it easy for tomorrow. Morgan should be back pretty soon."

The FBI men exchanged frustrated glances. "Pretty soon" could mean anytime. And even when Wells got back to greet his jockey, they still wouldn't know where he'd been!

NINE

THE WEATHER REPORTS for that part of Indiana had been similar to those in Louisville, but in Azalia, toward evening, it had actually begun to rain. A soft spring rain that made a gentle murmuring outside.

It was a sleepy sort of sound for a mother with a week-old baby and a lively young son to cope with while her husband was in the hospital. Not to mention a father-in-law who was recovering from a heart attack. Sam Grundage's daughter-in-law went to bed an hour earlier than usual that night, almost as soon as it was dark.

Sam himself gratefully turned out the lights in his room downstairs only a few minutes later.

The large living room of Paul Vandermeer's home in Louisville's Seneca Park section had been a serene and gracious one, or so Bolo Jackson had thought, when the banker turned it over to the marathon party so short a time before.

Bolo nursed his scotch-on-the-rocks and assessed it now in deep depression. They had certainly turned it into a mess.

But it wasn't even the obvious things like the overflowing ashtrays, the soiled glasses. It was them, he decided. Just their presence in the room spoiled it. They were all so loud, though it was the youngest blonde who particularly grated on his nerves at this moment. She was screaming with laughter. "Say it once more," she demanded. "I want to get it straight, so I won't forget!"

Glen raised his glass in salute and for the third time repeated obediently,

> *"I can't drink many martinis,*
> *Three or four at the most:*
> *Five, I'm under the table,*
> *And six, I'm under the host!"*

No wonder she considered that hilarious, Bolo told himself sourly. It was so apropos. Not that she had limited herself to him. He drained his glass but the scotch wasn't doing anything for him. The more he had—and the drunker the rest of them got—the soberer he felt. And the more depressed.

He supposed he was irritated at having discovered her with his cousin this morning, pumping away like a couple of dogs on the floor of Glen's room.

But why should he be, Bolo wondered. That was exactly what they were, what he had known they were, a couple of dogs. A bitch who was always in heat—or pretending to be— and a mangy, thieving hound.

"Well, if you like that so much, how about this?" another girl called, raising her martini.

> *"Here's a toast to the lady jockey,*
> *She may be proud but she's never cocky!"*

Bolo walked away from the appreciative shrieks onto the bricked terrace outside. The magnolia trees and the lilac

343

bushes and the cool dampness smelled good. It was supposed to rain, but it hadn't yet. Perhaps it would sometime during the night.

Even at the end of the pleasant terrace, as far from the open living room doors as he could get, the raucous conversation pursued him.

"I always wanted to do that and I kept asking Bolo, but he wouldn't." That was the youngest blonde.

"Go to a breeding farm? There must be a million of them around here. Why wouldn't he?"

"He said he didn't want to watch but wouldn't that be a blast? I have a friend that did once and she told me . . ."

"What do you mean, watch?"

"The horses, stupid, when they're doing it. That would really be something to see, wouldn't it?"

"She wasn't in Kentucky, was she?" one of the men asked.

"No. I don't know. It might have been someplace out west."

"I didn't think it would have been here," he said. "Why, I was at a horse farm in Lexington once, where they had this Austrian or German stud master and, man, he ran that stallion barn like head doctor in a hospital. If you even suggested a thing like that to him, I bet he'd have you shot at sunrise."

"I don't care, I still think it would be fun and someday, you wait."

Bolo walked down into the garden, away from the sound of their voices. He would have liked to walk on out of the little iron gate at the end of the pathway and never come back, never see or hear any of them again. But if he did that tonight, Glen and that little bitch would think it was because of them and he wouldn't give them the satisfaction.

Tomorrow, after the Derby, he'd get rid of all of them. Ship them back out to the coast and forget them. Glen, too. He'd dumped parties before but he'd always hung on to Glen. This time he would make a clean sweep of it.

It was a good thought, there in the garden. But not new, Bolo had to admit. He'd made the same decision on other desperate evenings. The catch was that he inevitably came full circle to the fact that if he did get rid of Glen, who was his only family, he had nobody. Nothing.

And then what?

TEN

A MILLION DOLLARS—even in fives, tens and twenties—were not as bulky as might be supposed. They fit into the suitcase without difficulty. Not a very large suitcase, either, nor very heavy.

Steve Cardigan was aware he was trembling as he carried it along the heavily carpeted corridor, but he was fairly certain no one else could tell. When one of a bank of brass doors opened to admit him into an elevator, none of the other passengers paid him undue attention.

In the lobby, the doorman came hurrying to carry the bag out and open the door of the Cadillac with more than usual flourish.

"I had some lot of trouble talking the police into letting it stay here, Mr. Cardigan," he said as he set the suitcase inside. "They kept asking me about it and I kept telling them you'd be moving it in a little while. They were getting pretty impatient."

Cardigan stared at him so blankly that the doorman added, "You know, sir, you've been here before. They always block this street off on Derby Eve." His gesture drew Cardigan's attention to the fact that there wasn't another car in sight except his own, shining darkly under the lighted canopy.

Derby Eve, when everybody spilled out of hotels and res-

taurants and parties and bars, tooting horns, throwing stream-
ers and waving pennants. In earlier years, cars and people
had mixed companionably but now certain streets were simply closed to all vehicles and this was one of them. Cardigan
had forgotten about that completely. He promptly forgot it
again. Without answering, he slid behind the wheel and
drove away.

Ten minutes later, carefully following the route the kidnapper had outlined in his final call, at the specified twenty-
five-mile-an-hour speed, Steve Cardigan spotted the car behind him. It had one distinctively brighter headlight and
whenever he turned, the other car followed. There was no
possibility of coincidence.

For one furious second, Cardigan thought it was the FBI.
In spite of the diplomatic strings he had pulled. In spite of
the renewed promise he had forced from Elverson just before
he left.

Then, with a jolt, Cardigan knew. The kidnapper was in
that car and so, please God, was Lisa. He tried to see her in
the rear-view mirror, to see how many people were in the
car behind but it was impossible. The glare of mismatched
headlights made an effective curtain.

He himself, though, must be clearly visible. He could almost feel the eyes at his back, probing his lone figure . . .
checking . . . assessing.

Mace Augustine could, indeed, distinguish the man ahead
of him, sharply outlined in the glow of street lamps as he approached them or against the lights of automobiles coming
from the opposite direction. Mace laughed when he saw that
the careful pace evidently annoyed other drivers. They would
slow down meekly for a few minutes behind the two cars
and then, growing impatient, would invariably swing out and
pass.

It was tedious going in an area where, as they got closer
to the street he'd picked, there was little need for care, less
and less traffic. Mace, however, was a hunter with a prize

346

quarry in his sights and his finger tightening on the trigger. The rising anticipation was pleasurable. Besides, he was so pleased with himself and the way he had overcome all the unforeseen complications of the last few hours that he did not mind prolonging the moment.

First, there'd been the heady triumph of snatching the girl out of that trailer just at the last second. And then, having driven her around until it was time to make it downtown, had come the shock of discovering the police blockades put up for Derby Eve.

The papers were loaded with information about what was going to happen tomorrow. They were full of maps and warnings about certain streets that would be temporarily one-way and other streets that only the buses could use. But who knew they made such a big thing about the night before? And how was he going to keep a good watch on Cardigan's car without being allowed to park near the Crown Hotel— or even drive past it, for Christ's sake?

Mace had really touched bottom for awhile, but he'd come up with the answers. Even having to park the car (with the girl carefully covered so nobody could see) four blocks away. He'd waited on the mezzanine of the Crown itself, which had windows directly above the entrance, watching for half an hour before he phoned instructions, and he had stayed right there until Cardigan came downstairs and drove away with that bag he'd seen the doorman put in.

Then, while Cardigan followed the first part of the directions Mace had worked out from the map—making almost a full circle—Mace had had time to get to his own car and pick up the Cadillac's trail. It had worked perfectly. But now the old man was making the final turn into Greenwood Court and Mace Augustine could stop patting himself on the back, because this was it.

Cardigan, his heart beating wildly, slowed to a crawl, trying to locate the alley halfway down the block where he had been ordered to stop. It was a long but narrow street, lined

347

on either side by ancient brick factories and loft buildings, some now boarded up, and the corner lamp posts did little to illumine its center. He wasn't supposed to park right in front of the alley. He was to leave at least twenty-five feet between the Cadillac and the entrance. It was a puzzling specification. Unless it meant that the kidnappers intended to pull to the curb ahead of Cardigan. Perhaps with the thought of using the dark alley as an escape route in case of trouble?

Cardigan reversed until he was at the correct distance. As he did so, the automobile which had been following picked up speed, whizzed past and disappeared around the next corner.

Cardigan cut his ignition and lights and sat waiting. Could I have been mistaken, he wondered. Could that car have just happened to make all those turns? No, it isn't possible. That man had to be the kidnapper. Oh, God, no sign of Lisa! Wait, the car's coming back!

Cardigan tensed, watching the car approach, expecting it to slow, but again it went by him and vanished. The man was evidently circling the block. Checking, toying with his victim for kicks or merely trying to soften him up in a ghastly war of nerves?

On the third time around, convinced that everything was as it should be, Mace drew smoothly to the curb in front of the Cadillac, switched off motor and lights and turned in his seat, expecting Cardigan to rush forward. Cardigan didn't get out of his car, though, and after a few moments, Mace got out of the jalopy and strode back.

"What the hell are you waiting for?" he demanded as Cardigan rolled his window down half an inch. "Get out here where I can see you. Come on, move."

Finally the voice had a face, however shadowed. Cardigan's nerves steadied. "No," he said calmly, "I'm eager to make the exchange, as you know. But I'm not a fool. You will have to bring my daughter to where I can see her."

Mace stared at him in disbelief. Then his gloved hand

whipped out Coolie Bascombe's gun and aimed directly at Cardigan's chest. "I said move or I'll blast you right through the goddamn window."

Cardigan shook his head. "All that will accomplish is noise," he said coolly. "Unless you have a silencer. I had every window in this car—and the windshield—replaced with bullet-proof glass today. There is no way you can get at me—or at the money—unless I choose to unlock these doors. And I have no intention of doing that until you bring my daughter back to this car, where I can see that she is all right."

Mace was livid with fury, speechless.

"You see," said Cardigan. "Your money is here in this suit-case—a million dollars in small bills—if," his voice suddenly failed him. The alternative was one he dared not pursue. But he managed to face, unblinkingly, the malevolent glare he felt rather than actually saw in the dark.

"Why, you son of a bitch!" Mace had recovered from the shock of being defied.

He wheeled and ran toward his car. Then he pulled the rear door open and unceremoniously dragged Lisa out from under the blanket. Whether she had already been conscious or his rough handling roused her, she knew something was happening. Her eyes were open and scared.

She could not walk with the straps around her ankles and Mace had to drag her over to the Cadillac. The minute she saw her father she began to struggle against Mace's hold, to make agonized little sounds, shaking her head warningly as they got close. When they were no more than a foot away from Cardigan Mace put the gun at her temple and said, "Okay, you satisfied? Because if you don't open that door and come out this second, she's dead."

Again Lisa began to shake her head but Cardigan said, "Lisa, it's all right!" At sight of her Steve Cardigan realized, suddenly, how little he had dared to hope, and joy all but undid him.

He fumbled at the latch with fingers which had become utterly nerveless and he was begging. "Please, don't hurt her, I'm coming out, I'm trying."

Once her father had succeeded in releasing the lock and was turning the handle, Lisa sagged in weakness and despair. There was nothing she could do now to save him.

"Hold it!" Mace ordered sharply. "Before you open that door, throw your gun out here!"

Cardigan shook his head. "I don't have one. I came unarmed, as I promised. All I wanted was to know that Lisa was safe."

Mace gaped realizing that Cardigan was telling the absolute truth. He hadn't even brought a gun. And after going to all that crazy bother with the glass, when it didn't help one bit as long as the girl was outside. Mace began to grin as he pulled Lisa with him toward the rear of the car so that Cardigan could open the door. The gun was still at her head.

"Okay," Mace said, "come on out. And bring that suitcase with you. I got a little checking of my own to do."

Cardigan obeyed. "It's all here."

Mace didn't doubt it for an instant. Nevertheless he insisted, "Open it."

"On the pavement?"

"Put it on the hood." Mace shepherded Cardigan around the door, following with Lisa. "And don't forget, all I got to do is squeeze this trigger."

"Please, I'm not going to do anything." Cardigan lifted the suitcase onto the Cadillac and pressed the snaps so that the lid flew up.

And there it was. Mace gulped. A million dollars.

"Do you want to count it?"

Mace shook his head as exultation surged over him. "No," he said. "Close it up again. And now . . ."

His finger tightened on the trigger but it was simply a reflexive response to his thought. He had been over this too many times in his mind to forget at the last minute. The girl had to be second. There was no way she could stop him when it was her turn. And as long as she was alive, her old man couldn't do a damn thing, either. Him and his bullet-proof glass, ha!

"Put the suitcase down and get back in the car."

"My daughter . . ."

"In, I said. Or she gets it."

Cardigan hesitated. "I've kept my share of the bargain."

"Good for you," Mace said contemptuously. "Get going."

There was no alternative. Cardigan set the bag carefully down on the pavement and moved out around the open door —with Mace backing cautiously against the rear of the car again, staying out of reach, just in case, as the father began to slide onto the seat.

This is it, Steve Cardigan was thinking. This is the moment.

It was what Mace was thinking, too. As Cardigan settled under the wheel, Mace sent Lisa crashing to the ground with a little shove and swung the gun.

And in that split second, Morgan Wells leaped from behind the car.

Mace whirled, sensing the movement at his back, but he was too late. Morgan had grabbed his wrist and was trying to wrest the gun away. It went off in the air, thunderous in the quiet street, and then, as Mace fought, both glove and gun began to loosen in his sweaty hand.

He brought his head up full force against Morgan's chin— a staggering blow—just as the gun fell to the pavement where Mace had flung Lisa. He was after it like a cat as Morgan reached for his own gun, but Lisa was even quicker. With her bound feet, she kicked Coolie's gun under the car, out of immediate reach, and Mace fled into the alley.

Morgan went after him but it was a hopeless pursuit from the beginning. This was territory Mace had explored over and over again, he was smaller, more agile, and Morgan had been cramped in the trunk of the car for hours. When Mace disappeared into a narrow space between two buildings, Morgan gave up and went back, back to Lisa.

She was still lying on the street, with her father working ineffectually at the cords which had been so cruelly knotted. Steve Cardigan was sobbing, terrible wracking sobs that shook his entire body.

"Oh, God, Lisa, I'm sorry I'm being so slow. What have they done to you?"

Fortunately, Morgan had a pocket knife. He cut the bonds at her hands and feet swiftly, then reached for the adhesive but, at this, Lisa moaned and shrank away from him.

They understood when she reached up herself, hesitated briefly, then ripped the tape away all at once. Her father's violent exclamation cut through the faintness which threatened to overwhelm her and she saw that his eyes were sick—sick over what the tape had done to her.

Morgan was staring, too.

"I must look so awful," she wailed, the weak tears beginning. "Don't look at me, Morgan, I love you too much, please don't look at me. And, oh, no, don't come near me, either, I need a bath! He said . . . he said I . . . stank . . ."

But Morgan Wells wasn't listening. He was shouting with triumph as he picked her up and cradled her.

She was alive!

And she loved him too much!

SATURDAY

ONE

IT WAS MIDNIGHT in downtown Louisville and the noisy crowds were still happily celebrating Derby Eve. But at Churchill Downs, under the starless sky, both horses and men slept too soundly to note the fact that technically it was now the first Saturday in May. At least, most of them did.

In the Derby Barn—as in the rest of the stable area—the period from 8:00 P.M. to 4:00 A.M. was ordinarily uneventful. Backstretchers might not quite go to bed with the birds but they certainly got up with the horses, which set definite limits on their sleeping hours; only a handful on any evening were still awake after nine.

Occasionally a van might arrive from another track to be unloaded or a groom might be up with an ailing animal, but these were the exceptions. The huge overhead doors at either end of the Derby Barn were rolled down and locked and only two of Fred Keller's crew kept watch—a man in each guardroom—instead of the four who maintained the busier daylight vigils. Entrance could be made, if necessary, through the small regulation doors beside the big ones.

When the work schedule for the Derby had been drawn up, Keller had pointed out to Lee that a single man would suffice in the off hours if they simply locked one end of the barn entirely for that shift.

"There aren't that many people coming or going after eight o'clock," Fred had said, "and even if they belong in the dormitory at the locked end, they can walk down to the other end to get in, how much effort would that take?"

"I considered that for awhile," Lee had answered, "and you're right. We could get by with one guard. But I'll feel better with two on duty, anyway. It's only for a couple of weeks and suppose something did come up that required both big doors to be opened in a hurry?"

Fred had understood the point perfectly.

In case of fire, Lee was saying obliquely. If, somehow, in spite of all the care and planning, there should be a fire and the horses had to be moved out in a hurry, two guards would be needed. Lee did not want to risk the possibility, however remote, that when the big metal doors were down and locked, the only man able to open them might be at the wrong end.

So, now, Ollie was on duty at the desk in his cubicle, unsuccessfully trying to concentrate on the intricacies of a correspondence course on TV repair. After awhile, he stretched, pushing the book aside, and glanced around. The niche in which his desk was set was glassed on three sides so that he could see outdoors as well as in. Not that there was a doggone thing to see. Hank was diagonally across at the other end of the barn, clearly visible at his similar station. In the cone of light from the shaded lamp above his desk Hank, as usual, seemed to be eating.

Otherwise, all there was to look at were the dark shapes of stables outside, with the moths circling the dusty bulbs and the shadowy rows of stalls inside, barely discernible in the glow of low night lights.

Except . . .

356

Ollie tensed at a movement along the left side of the barn, then relaxed. Poor Dennis Sullivan—you couldn't mistake that walk—carrying his pillow and blanket, so that he could bunk in the empty stall next to his horse again.

Ollie pursed his lips reflectively and picked up the special Kentucky Derby Edition of the Racing Form. The sight of the Irishman had reminded Ollie that he wanted to take a closer look at Davie's Pride in the past-performance charts. He wasn't a Kentucky-bred, but he might not be a bad long-shot chance at that.

From his end of the barn, Hank, too, saw Dennis Sullivan. But Hank's reaction was totally different. As he chewed methodically on his liverwurst sandwich, he wondered what Dennis was worrying himself sick for. His horse didn't have a chance. Not against Lucky Jim and Magician, or even Dashing Lad.

TWO

THORNBURY AVENUE was dark and quiet as Mace tiptoed past Good Mary's little house and around to the back yard where the trailer loomed gray under the magnolia tree. It was dark, too. Rosanna was wide awake, however. She opened the door instantly at Mace's signal.

"Don't turn any lights on," he warned quickly.

"Mace! Oh, my God, where have you been? I've been going out of my mind, worrying."

"Keep your voice down," he said, "and just grab whatever you need. We're leaving!"

"What happened?"

"They pulled a fast one on me, is what happened," Mace said furiously. "That old bastard had somebody stashed in his trunk. Now, will you move? Once that bitch starts talking . . ."

Rosanna's voice was horrified. "You mean you left her alive?"

"Her and her old man!"

"Oh, Mace, she knows our names, everything. She can tell them all about us, about Coolie!"

He groped for her arm and found it. "Listen," he said urgently, "I know that, I had plenty of time to think, getting here."

Rosanna began to whimper.

"But it's still not too bad, baby. We got a quarter of a million and knowing who we are don't mean a thing. If we dye our hair, change the way we look, she could never identify us. Anyway, I've got it all figured, Rosanna. There's a hundred thousand people here for the Derby and when they start heading for home afterward . . ."

He paused, thinking. "We can leave then or we can just stay here and lay low, that might be even better. But you hear me, Rosanna? If we just get the hell away from this trailer and don't fall apart, we'll still be all right. They'll never catch us."

He was talking to the wind he realized in dismay. Rosanna had already fallen apart. When he let go of her arm, she went on standing right where she was, in the center of the trailer, moaning and wringing her hands.

"Not catch us, Mace? Are you crazy? Of course they're going to catch us. Oh, God, I begged you not to go through with it. I kept telling you something was going to happen."

Her voice had begun to rise hysterically and now it took on a bitter, accusatory edge. "But you wouldn't listen to me. Oh, no, Mace, I was a dumb, stupid broad and you knew so

358

much, you were so goddamn smart, nobody could tell you anything."

Predictably, he hit her. His fist landed on her jaw with all the force of his own self-condemnation and frustration. She fell with a series of thuds that rocked the trailer, from wall to bunk to floor. Mace stood frozen, listening, very close to panic himself. A racket like that must have been heard all over the neighborhood. After a second, when no lights went on outside, he relaxed. Things sounded so loud simply because they were closed in.

"All right," he said sourly, "you been bugging me for days and I got enough without that. It's over! Now get up and get moving, like I told you to begin with."

Rosanna didn't answer.

He squatted down beside her. "Come on, Rosanna, will you? You're wasting time." He found her shoulder and shook it before he finally understood that he'd knocked her out. He had a momentary pang of remorse, but he hadn't really hit her that hard. She must have banged her head against the bunk. Anyway, he had to bring her to in a hurry and he couldn't even see her.

He sighed at both the delay and the necessity to turn on a light but the latter no longer seemed too important. No matter how fast the Cardigans talked, the daughter didn't know exactly where the trailer was. There was no way the cops could find them this quick. He stumbled over Rosanna's leg as he tried to get around her to reach the lamp. Boy, she was really out cold. But when he was able to see, finally, he knew he was wrong.

Rosanna wasn't unconscious, not lying twisted up so funny, so still, not breathing. Rosanna was dead.

Mace stared at her, shaking his head, denying the truth. But then immediacy grabbed at him. He pulled the case with the first ransom out from under his bunk, switched off the lamp and carefully locked the door behind him as he left.

THREE

THE CONTINUOUS NIGHT WATCH at the Derby Barn had bothered Pop Dewey from the minute he decided what he had to do to even things up. Never before had he had to worry about anything like that. With the other two fires—not counting the one before he ran away from home or any of the little ones—it had been easy to wait until the patrol passed by and everybody else was asleep. Or passed out, like Buddy Sheffield that night at Bluegrass.

In the beginning, Pop had been afraid the Derby Barn itself was going to make things harder for him. It was only once he settled down to really planning that he saw how everything that had been put in for protection could be turned around to work in his favor.

The main objective in building the Derby Barn had been to keep the wrong people out. That was why there was a barred window instead of an outside door for every horse, like there would be in most other stables. That was why the only way in or out of the stalls was through the wide interior corridor. And that was why they put the huge metal doors at either end, the same kind you'd have in a garage only about four times larger.

They had thought about fire, though. Those doors would roll up at the push of a button and the inside was as safe as humanly possible, with nonflammable plastic stalls, with brick and stone and concrete and steel every place you looked instead of wood. And on top of that, they had installed the best sprinkler system they could buy. Pop had heard it cost two hundred dollars for each of the heads in the ceiling. They were supposed to be so sensitive they would go off if a fistful of straw caught fire—before the horse that was in the stall even had a chance to get nervous. That's how quick those sprinklers were.

The architects had even built in protection against arson. The water lines and the electric wires ran straight into the guardrooms and down the walls in plain sight, so nobody could fool around with them, and from there they were buried deep in the ground. You couldn't figure where they were outside the Derby Barn, Pop had looked. But if he could get around the guards, nothing else would matter. How much help would their sprinkler system or their electric doors be once Pop cut the pipes and wires?

Oh, the doors could be operated by hand. Very little in a racetrack ever depended entirely on electricity. There was usually a manual backup that you could turn to if the current failed in a storm, or in an accident like the time a plane crashed into the light poles near Tropical Park. Men worked out the odds on every race with paper and pencil, right along with the computers, in case the machines got out of whack or the power went—and damn near as fast as the computers, too. And men still stood by with stopwatches, in case something happened to the electric timer during a race.

So the doors could also be raised or lowered by hand. Pop had watched them testing. But it sure took a lot longer that way. And you couldn't even budge them manually unless you first unhooked them from the electric arm. Most people wouldn't remember that fact in an emergency, even if they knew about it.

Pop could see the scene in his mind. The horsemen, only half awake, rushing to the stalls to get their horses, and nobody thinking about the big doors at all until they were ready to dash out through them. The horses kicking and

struggling and everybody forgetting the doors had to be unhooked before they'd move.

The only problem was that the guards would see him.
There was no way to carry out his plan without their knowing he had done it. The answer to that, when it came to him
after Double Seven's leg swelled up the second time, was such
a simple one that Pop wondered why he had taken so long to
think of it. It didn't make any difference if the guards knew
who set the fire once it was too late to stop him.

Pop had trembled with excitement at the realization. The
truth was, he wanted them to know. He wanted everybody to
know. Pop Dewey, old dog Pop Dewey, that nobody gave a
second thought to. And he'd be the guy that kept them out of
the Kentucky Derby, the whole rotten bunch of them.

There wouldn't be a Kentucky Derby.

And that picture the photographer took of him the morning of the Trial and then never used—after the fire it would
be on every front page in the country. In the world. And
everybody would be looking at him, really seeing him, not
just barely noticing some guy in work clothes standing next
to a horse.

Double Seven!

That had been Double Seven with him in the picture. If
things worked the way he planned, Double Seven would be
caught in the Derby Barn, too. For a moment, Pop had hesitated. Then bitterness overwhelmed him. Double Seven was
just another horse. There had been so many of them and
maybe he should have known better after fifty years, but
when you came down to it, Double Seven was the worst of
the lot. Raising Pop's hopes, twice, and then going lame on
him. Without further reservation, Pop had returned to considering strategy.

Now, lying on his cot in the dormitory, Pop thought again
of how famous he would be after tonight. They wouldn't
bother with that old picture, he suddenly realized. There'd be

new pictures, hundreds of them, all showing Pop Dewey by himself. Clyde Dewey.

What they did to him afterwards wouldn't matter. He'd be even, once and for all. With everybody. He listened to Alan's breathing in the adjacent cot in the dormitory and then, very carefully, he slid out from under his covers.

FOUR

IN THE BEDROOM of his house on La Salle Street, with his wife sleeping at his side, Eustace Potter wished he could stop thinking of "that nice young fellow" he had met at the track.

Potter sighed and leaned over to peer at the illuminated dial of the nightstand clock. It was past midnight, more than an hour since he'd turned the lights out. If he didn't roll over right this minute and stop worrying, he was going to spend the most exciting afternoon of the year feeling like he'd been drawn through a knothole.

But it was no wonder he was having trouble getting to sleep, after the visit from the FBI. It was still slightly embarrassing to remember that when they had knocked on his door at ten o'clock in the evening, his first thought was that they were after him for having accepted a hundred dollars for those two tickets, even though he hadn't asked for it, the young fellow had forced the five twenties on him. But the FBI didn't care about the money, just the man who had given Eustace Potter those bills.

Potter turned over in bed again. The worst part of the whole terrible thing was that if a nice-looking boy like that could turn out to be what the inspector had said, then who could you trust in this world anymore? It had been hard to believe.

But the inspector had said, "You mustn't have the smallest doubt in your mind, Mr. Potter, for your own protection. I'm assuming that you are planning to go to the Derby yourself tomorrow, that those were extra tickets you sold, not your own?"

"Why, of course I'm going!"

"Then I can't warn you too strongly. I doubt if this man will use those tickets now, but he has no way of knowing we've spotted those bills. He may feel there could be safety in a crowd like that. If he does," the inspector had added grimly, "we'll be ready. But, Mr. Potter, if you should happen to see him—at the Derby or anywhere else—you mustn't let him suspect for a second that you know anything more about him than he himself has told you. This is a killer, Mr. Potter, a vicious, cold-blooded killer."

In the darkness, Eustace Potter swallowed nervously. Would he recognize the boy with the wig and moustache the inspector had mentioned? Potter tried to imagine how they would change the young face. He failed and swallowed again. The fellow could come and sit right down in the seat next to him and he might not even know who it was.

But that wasn't true. The seat next to him was one of the pair he had sold. It was reserved. So no matter how disguised, if somebody sat there . . .

Stop thinking about it, Potter told himself. Think of something else. The Derby. Go over the Derby horses, like counting sheep. Armada, Magician, Lucky Jim, Sweepstakes, Dashing Lad, Davie's Pride, Freeway, Double Seven . . .

No, Double Seven was scratched.

What would you do if a murderer came and sat down right next to you?

FIVE

O LLIE GLANCED UP from the Daily Racing Form to make the visual check which had become almost automatic with him. He did it at regular five-minute intervals when he was on this shift. Nothing outside. Nothing inside.

He couldn't even see Hank. The other guard hadn't been in sight the last time Ollie looked, either. Still in the can, Ollie decided, and went back to his consideration of the Derby entrants' past performances. He decided you'd have to throw out Armada's poor showing in the Trial, that had been a freak.

When he looked up again and Hank still hadn't returned to his desk, Ollie's eyebrows drew together in a little frown. Even though the night shift was dull, Hank was too conscientious to be off post for more than five or ten minutes. Ollie waited, staring at the light over Hank's desk. Finally, he got to his feet. He'd better check, Hank might be sick.

Ollie was halfway the length of the barn when all the lights on one side of the building went out. His first impulse was to go back for the flashlight he had left on his desk, but whatever had happened to the power on Hank's side of the barn, his own didn't seem to be affected. He could see quite well.

Instead, drawing his gun from its holster, he continued along the wide corridor, a gesture which startled him when he realized what he had done. Electricity was always cutting off for some unimportant reason but this was the first time he could remember pulling a weapon on duty or feeling the need to. In fact, as he opened the door to Hank's guardroom, he felt foolish to discover that he had all but shoved the gun into Pop Dewey's stomach. The old man was just about to come out and even in the poor light he looked scared to death.

"Sorry, Pop," Ollie said, reholstering it, "what're you doing here? Where's Hank?"

"I just come in to get a couple of aspirin from him," Pop said, his trembling voice sounding bewildered. "And I can't make out if he had a heart attack or what, he's laying over there by the wall."

It was a sight to startle a man loose from what little wits he had left, Dennis told himself, staring at Pop as the old groom passed the stall next to Davie's Pride. His white face floating like a specter and not a sound from anywhere but the soft shuffling of his feet.

Dennis would have sworn he hadn't slept. He had simply been stretched out on the blanket, and, as he had promised, keeping his ears open for Pop. That had been a bit of a surprise, learning exactly what young Alan was doing in the Derby Barn. Dennis had been curious but he had never asked. He had been glad to do Lee Ames the favor in the beginning and after that he'd taken a liking to the boy for his own sake.

A good lad, Alan was, hard-working and willing. And most endearing, a staunch supporter of Davie's Pride. But the thought that he was an insurance investigator seemed almost as funny to Dennis as the fact that the subject of this surveillance was Pop Dewey. Perhaps some hint of his amusement had shown when the boy told him that afternoon, because Alan had said almost defensively, "You understand, nobody thinks Pop did anything. It's just my f-father has this feeling he might know something about what happened at Marshfield and that maybe I could get it out of him. But it looks like a lost cause. If Pop knows anything, he's never going to tell it to me. Since the trouble started with Double Seven . . ."

"Sure, it's hit him hard, and no wonder."

"I swear, I get sick every time I look at him," Alan had said, "thinking how he must be feeling. But as long as I'm on this assignment, I'm supposed to stick with him. And that's the problem, Mr. Sullivan, because Johnny says he was up wandering around last night, that you saw him. But I never knew a thing after I hit the pillow."

"Yes," Dennis had agreed, permitting himself a small smile, "you do sleep pretty sound, at that."

"Well, I guess even my father can't expect me to be on duty twenty four hours a day." Alan had stopped. "Or maybe he can. But what I was wondering, Mr. Sullivan, do you think you'll be awake again tonight?"

"Wide awake," Dennis assured him firmly. "Your father's not the only one that gets feelings. And to make certain sure, I took me a nice long nap while you and Johnny were working this afternoon. So if you're asking would I keep an eye on the old man for you . . ."

"Oh, no!" Alan had been very earnest. "I don't want you to do my job. Just if he does get up again, could you come in and give me a shake? I'll take it from there."

"I won't be sleeping, anyway, Alan, I'll gladly watch him for you."

"No, it's my responsibility and I'd never have even asked you except for fear of falling asleep."

Dennis had patted the boy's shoulder. "Say no more, Alan. You've my promise. If he sets foot out of the dorm tonight, I'll rouse you."

But he himself must have dozed, Dennis thought. He had heard Ollie go by a little while ago—just when some of the lights went out—and never noticed whether the young guard returned to his station. And now, here was Pop coming from the other end of the barn and Dennis hadn't heard him pass the stall to get there.

Unaccountably, Dennis' heart quickened. Unless Ollie hadn't come back? And unless Pop had circled the barn on the

367

outside? It was then, as Pop reached the guardroom and was clearly outlined by the light above Ollie's desk, that Dennis was able to see what the old groom had in his hands.

A hatchet. And a gun. Which meant that in the darkened guardroom at the other end, Pop must have done something to Hank and Ollie!

The Louisville Fire Department had a station about half a mile from Churchill Downs and it was there, when Pop Dewey cut the utility lines in Hank's guardroom, that the night dispatcher came to instant attention.

"We've got another interruption in the alarm system at the track," he informed the captain.

"Oh, Lord!"

The captain's sigh was not unreasonable under the circumstances. The least faulty connection or short circuit in the backstretch automatically triggered a warning flash on the board at the station house and, with so much wiring involved, this occurred with annoying frequency. Worse, since the signal merely indicated a break somewhere on the grounds without pinpointing exactly where it was, each false alarm meant a laborious check of every barn until the problem had been located. On one memorable day, the short circuit hadn't been found until they reached the very last building.

"Okay, let's roll," the captain said with resignation. "But no sense hitting the sirens anymore than we have to. Just wake the whole neighborhood for nothing."

"Let's hope!" the dispatcher said.

The captain's mood changed instantly. He'd been a lot younger when Bluegrass Park went but that was one fire he'd never forget. "Right," he agreed fervently. "Let's hope and pray."

Dennis shook off the horror which had momentarily immobilized him in the empty stall. Even as Pop disappeared inside Ollie's guardroom, Dennis was running to the cubicle at the other end of the barn. There he found Hank and Ollie on the floor, trussed like turkeys, both unconscious but—glory be—alive.

Their labored breathing seemed louder as the rest of the lights in the Derby Barn went out. Dennis had automatically begun trying to free the two men but now he straightened. They were unconscious, they'd be no use even if he did get them loose and he had to have help.

He groped his way from the guardroom into the cavernous barn, trying not to make a sound, expecting it to be as silent as before, but Pop was dragging things around, his flashlight dancing crazily over the blackness as he moved. Dennis couldn't see what the old man was doing, but as long as Pop was busy, Dennis could get out at this end of the barn.

He didn't even look at the big electric door. Instead, he ran to the small one which ordinarily wasn't locked, since the guard on duty kept it directly under observation. Now it was. And the keys which were always dangling from the inside of the lock were gone.

At the Main Gate to the backstretch, the gateman, the fire captain and the drivers of Churchill Downs' own small fire patrols stared at each other.

"No sign at all?" the captain asked.

The gateman shook his head sympathetically. He had been through this before. "Glad it's a false alarm, Captain, but wish we could give you some idea where the trouble is. You heard yourself, though, the boys on the trucks haven't spotted a thing."

"Well," the captain shrugged, "nothing for it but to check. Might as well get on with it."

"Like the last time?" a patrol driver asked.

"Guess that's as good a procedure as any," the captain said. "If you fellows will start on this side and work toward the middle, we'll work back toward you from the Derby Barn."

In the blackness at the locked door, panic threatened Dennis Sullivan. Then, with an inward groan of relief, he clapped his hand to his forehead. He'd been so dismayed at being cut off from his own dormitory, where Johnny and Alan were sleeping, that he'd forgotten the four grooms in the dormitory at this end of the barn.

The five of them should surely be able to handle one daft old man, in spite of the gun and the hatchet. In his haste to get to the dormitory door Dennis almost fell over something on the floor, though he was only half conscious of the little ping it made or the gurgle of its contents spilling onto the straw underfoot.

But when Dennis reached the dorm, he found it was locked, too. It was then he smelled the kerosene. That was what had been in the can he had kicked over. Kerosene, soaking into the straw at the base of the big door, where there should never have been any straw.

There was no question now what Pop Dewey was up to. Perhaps he had known all along, Dennis realized. Only he hadn't wanted to believe it. The old man meant to set the Derby Barn on fire. That was what he was doing down at the other door, getting the straw ready there, too.

And if he had locked everything at that end as he had at this, then there wasn't a blessed soul in the world to stop him, except Dennis Joseph Sullivan.

The fire captain made surveys at Churchill Downs before every opening, spring and fall, so he had been on the grounds not much more than a week ago. That had been in the daytime, though. The backstretch looked entirely different in the small hours of the morning as he drove along the narrow blacktop road, with the fire truck following. He was actually in front of the Derby Barn before he realized anything was wrong. Then he grinned as he walked back to talk to the men in the truck.

"Looks like we've hit it first crack out of the box, for a change," he said. "The break's got to be here, because there isn't a light showing, inside or out."

"No signs of fire, that's for sure," one of the men agreed, "so it must be just a wire or something."

The captain turned to regard the building with a slight frown. "No sign of a guard, either," he said. "And shouldn't there be? Didn't I hear they were going to keep a twenty-four-hour watch on the Derby horses?"

"That's right, Captain, I read it in the paper."

"Well, then, what's he doing," the captain asked, "sitting around in the dark? No auxiliary lamp, no flashlight? One of you fellows alert track security. Something's fishy here. The rest of you wait a minute. I'm going to take a closer look."

Alan suddenly sat upright on his cot, every nerve alert. The night light from a nearby barn cast a faint glow through the dorm windows but it wasn't enough to show whether Pop was still on his own cot or not. Alan listened. He could hear heavy snoring from the corner where Freeway's groom was sleeping and to his left Johnny turned over with a sigh. But Pop wasn't there.

Alan felt around for his pants and began to pull them on hastily. He had been afraid of this: it was, he supposed, what had wakened him. Dennis Sullivan had obviously decided not to rouse Alan, after all, but simply to maintain his own watch on Pop.

It was well meant. All the Sullivans were kind. This was Alan's job, though. He didn't want somebody else doing it for him.

Pop didn't scatter the straw in front of the second door as hastily as he had at the other. He took his time, spreading it into a neat thick matting. He didn't just dump the kerosene, either. He poured it in a slow trickle, sometimes zagging it up and down, sometimes going around and around with it, while he hummed tunelessly under his breath. It reminded him, all at once, of the endless exercises in penmanship the teacher had made him do so many years ago. Push-pull! Circle! Stay inside the lines!

He still hadn't reached the important part. Even taking care of the guards and the power and the water hadn't been the big thing. All that really mattered were those plain old kitchen matches bulging out his pockets. He had hundreds— he'd emptied out a whole box—but the fact was he needed only sixteen that he'd strike on the bottom of his boot and then toss two into each occupied stall when he was ready to leave. Oh, yes, and another couple for each end of the barn.

Twenty matches and that was the end of the Kentucky Derby!

What he was doing now was just the finishing touch. This was what would scare everybody the most, a wall of flame shooting up in front of them, with the heat and the smoke and the crackling. It would drive the horsemen crazy, just when they found out they couldn't budge the big doors.

Pop stopped humming abruptly, holding the can motionless in momentary confusion, remembering the change in plan. It had come to him only a few minutes ago, the realization that he could lock the men in the dormitories. They weren't going to be able to reach their horses, like he'd been imagining from the beginning. Pop shrugged and dumped the rest of the kerosene.

Then he stiffened, holding his breath. That had sounded like a footstep behind him. Pop yanked the gun out of his belt even as he was whirling to catch Dennis Sullivan in the glare of the flashlight.

"What do you think you're doing?" Pop demanded, his voice shaking at the narrowness of his escape. A minute more, one minute more, and this tricky Irishman would have been right on top of him.

Dennis drew a deep breath. "It's more to the point what you're doing, Pop," he said. "You can't be truly meaning to do a terrible thing like this? Burn the Derby Barn and the horses?"

Pop lowered the light a little to make certain that Dennis could see the gun held ready, aiming straight at him. He saw it, all right, Pop noted with gleeful satisfaction. Scared greener than a shamrock, that's what he was. It made Pop feel good.

"Don't figure nobody can stop me," Pop said. "Not while I got this!"

He chuckled, hefting the gun, enjoying the weight of it and the sense of power. Funny he never thought of carrying one before. And lucky he'd been smart enough to take this from Ollie. Pop chuckled again.

Then he squeezed the trigger . . .

"At least, I think it was then he shot off the gun," Dennis told everyone later, "things were happening so fast I can't be sure the banging didn't come first."

"No," Fred Keller said, "I talked to the fellows while you and Hank and Ollie were being patched up. A couple of my men had just arrived, the fire captain had sent for them. He was explaining why he thought there was something wrong when they heard the gun go off. That was when they began pounding on the door."

Dennis grinned. "Lucky for me. It was the racket they made at his back that made him drop the flashlight. And with that . . ."

The grin widened. "If only I had a picture of what went on then. I couldn't see my hand in front of my face, mind you. The light smashed when he dropped it and everything was blacker than a pail of pitch. I just made a leap for where he'd been standing when I saw him last. But the strength of him. I had trouble just holding my own and all the time I could hear the banging and the people shouting, 'Open up in there, somebody get this door open!' Then the gun went off again."

Fred nodded grimly. "I know. The men outside heard the shots."

Dennis paused, looking at the absorbed faces. "It was the first one nicked my arm, the others didn't matter. But have you got the picture now, the two of us fighting in the dark and the horses stamping and whinnying like they'd gone clean out of their senses?"

There were nods.

"Well, that's when young Alan walks in from our dorm, through the only door Pop hadn't locked. He was still half asleep, with no more idea what was going on than a newborn babe. And he said—I'll never forget it as long as I live—he said, kind of puzzled, 'Mr. Sullivan, is that you? Is there anything wrong?'"

Dennis doubled over at the memory of that uncertain voice in the darkness. Then he wiped his streaming eyes gingerly where the lashes had been singed off and added, "God forgive me, I'm not really laughing at the lad and him still in the hospital.

"He'd absolutely no way of knowing; the dorm is soundproof. All he could tell when he opened the door was that it was pitch black inside the barn and full of noise. And only the mercy of the saints Pop hadn't taken his suitcase out of there and locked that door, too. Because if Alan hadn't been right beside me when the straw went up, there'd be a different ending to the story altogether and I doubt I'd be here to tell it to you, either."

Lee felt sick every time he considered what might have happened and the ugly alternatives had been haunting him since Fred summoned him from his bed.

"That's the point I haven't got quite clear," he said to Dennis. "You and Pop were struggling, he certainly had no opportunity to set the straw on fire?"

" 'Twas all those matches, don't you see? He'd put an entire box of those wooden kitchen matches in his pockets, I'm told."

"That's what Pop said at the hospital," added Fred.

"They must have rubbed together in the fight," Dennis went on. "I'd no thought at all his coat was burning, I doubt he knew it himself. Then, without a bit of warning, whoosh! The whole end of the barn was in flames. We'd been rolling on that straw, you know, we both had kerosene on us, but poor Pop was right on the straw when it caught." Dennis looked at Keller. "Have you any further word from the hospital, Fred?"

Keller hunched his shoulders. "We keep calling and they keep saying he's got a good chance. That's about all we'll know for awhile. But after the confessions he's made tonight— Bluegrass Park, one of the Marshfield Farms fires and a few earlier ones—they'll never turn him loose again."

"Poor old soul," Dennis said pityingly. "Who'd have ever believed it?"

Ollie shook his bandaged head, chagrined at his own stupidity. "I sure didn't, not even when I found him in Hank's room. I swear, it just never dawned on me. He's been around forever and I had it in my mind something was wrong with Hank, anyway. When Pop told me Hank was lying on the floor, I just bent over to look and wham!"

Hank was also suffering from head injuries and lowered self-esteem. "I guess we're lucky he only used the flat side of the ax, but the next time somebody asks me for a couple of aspirins, no matter how long I've known them . . ."

"It's over," Keller said, "not much sense crying over spilled milk. I don't think either of you will make that kind of mistake again."

"I kept having this feeling that something was going to happen," Dennis said wonderingly. "Only I'd never have dreamed of a terrible thing like Pop had in his mind, never. And I couldn't have stopped it without Alan, the two of us together with the fire extinguishers only just managed it." He looked at Lee. "If you hadn't come to me that day and asked if I'd give him a spot . . ."

Lee's expression made it plain how grateful he was for the same lucky circumstance but he said, "Well, Dennis, there just aren't words to tell you how thankful we are to you. Even the check will be very inadequate."

"What check?"

"The one we were deciding on while you were over at the hospital. I spoke to all the owners with horses in the Derby Barn, they all want a chance to chip in, and so does the insurance company, and, of course, Churchill Downs."

"Now, hold on a minute," Dennis said. "I'm surely not expecting a reward for what I did. I'm only thankful myself I could do it. It was Davie's Pride I was saving, too, you know."

"It isn't meant as a reward," Lee said. "It's simply a small evidence of appreciation. And when you think of all we would have lost if it hadn't been for your courage, the ten thousand is hardly more than a token."

"Ten thousand?" Dennis exclaimed. "Why, Mr. Ames, I couldn't take any sum of money like that."

Lee laughed happily. "It was my father who was called 'Mr. Ames,'" he mocked Dennis gently. "Don't you remember, Dennis? My name is Lee."

SIX

MOST OF THE BACKSTRETCH was still asleep when Lee and Fred got outside the immediate area of the Derby Barn. Indefinably, though, it had begun to feel like morning rather than night and as the two paused for a second, someone's alarm clock started to shrill.

"Tired?" Keller asked.

"I suppose I will be. Thank God I went to bed early. I'd had a few solid hours before you called me. Anyway, I couldn't go back to sleep now."

"No, neither could I. I'm wide awake."

"Well, okay, then," Lee said, "the kitchen ought to be open by now. Come on, hop in the car, I'll buy you a cup of coffee."

"The way I feel," said Keller, "I'm willing to spring for the coffee. I might even consider treating you to a couple of hot biscuits. And that's in spite of your being such an awful liar."

Lee laughed, starting the motor. "I knew you'd caught that. But Dennis doesn't know me as well as you do, Fred. He believed it, which is the important thing. And I will talk to the Derby owners later, I'm sure they'll go along when they find out what happened."

"Can you imagine Gladys Nickel if you woke her up in the middle of the night to announce you expected her to kick in with a reward?"

"I couldn't really disturb anybody this early," Lee said. "But I'll make you a little bet right now, Fred, that the Nickels'll kick in a damn sight more willingly than Jim York."

"Are you trying to hustle me?" Fred asked. "I've seen Gladys Nickel when she was worried about her horse."

"Anyway, whoever does or doesn't go along, we'll see that Dennis gets his ten thousand. Every time I think of how close we came to disaster . . ."

Fred shuddered. "I'm trying not to think of that."

They had reached Thompson's Track Kitchen and were working on ham and eggs (to go with the biscuits and coffee) when Fred asked, "What about the boy, Alan? Are you considering a check for him, too?"

"There's no way we could get Alan to accept anything more than our thanks," Lee said. "He's too much like his old man, and the Chief would blow a gasket at the very idea. You know I worked with him for several years in the army, don't you?"

"Yes, so you said."

"Well, the Chief I actually did wake up tonight. Tell you the truth, Fred, that was one of the high spots of my career. He damn near went through the ceiling when I told him what had happened. He had a hunch about Pop, but that kid is the apple of his eye. He'd never have given him this assignment if it had seemed the least bit dangerous. At the same time, he's tickled pink that Alan handled himself so well. Talk about proud fathers."

"That'll please the boy, at any rate."

"It will if Alan's learned to understand his father. And if he hasn't, I'm planning to fill him in, because the Chief will never come flat out and give him a compliment. If I know the old man, he'll come tearing in here in a couple of hours just to see for himself that the kid's all right, that I wasn't lying when I said all Alan did was blister his hands a little. And then the Chief will start grousing about how much money this is going to cost him."

"Why should it cost him, Lee?"

"His company, which he considers the same thing. Now that Pop's confessed to the one fire he did set at Marshfield, the insurance company will have no excuse to hold up payment on the other two claims."

"Hey, that's right, I'd forgotten."

"Well, the lawyers may still quibble over the third, but that was the smallest, least costly of the three. Pop wasn't trying to burn the place down that time, he apparently just wanted to get even with another stableman."

Fred shivered. "From what he says, that's all he meant to do at Bluegrass Park, and we all know how that turned out." He preferred a more cheerful train of thought. "Tell you one thing. I hadn't considered it before, but Pop's confession is going to finally take Buddy Sheffield off the hook. No matter how Dashing Lad performs today, Buddy's a winner."

Lee stared at him. "I'll be damned."

"Surely you knew he thought he was responsible?" Fred said. "A terrible burden that would be for a sane man."

"No!" Lee said. "No, that's not what I was talking about. You said today, Fred. Today, Derby Day. And I haven't even worried about the weather for the last couple of hours."

They were still laughing when one of the security men found them at the obscure table they had chosen in a corner.

"Sorry to bother you while you're eating," the guard apologized, "but could you come over to the gate, Mr. Keller? We knew you were on the grounds and we have a kind of sticky situation there."

"Sure," Fred said, "I'm finished, anyway." He got to his feet. "What's the problem?"

"Well, it's Mr. Cardigan and his daughter, sir."

"They're here? At this hour of the night?"

Lee's chair crashed backward in the violence of his rising. He was already running for the door. "Come on, Fred, hurry."

By the time they reached the gate, Lee had explained and his chief of security was staring at him in disbelief.

"Oh, my God," Fred said. "There's one the backstretch missed completely."

It was an unexpected reaction which surprised Lee into a roar of relieved laughter. But when he got out of his car and walked toward his friend, who was standing with the gateman, Lee was subdued. Steve Cardigan was smiling but his face mirrored every painful hour of the last two weeks.

Beyond words for the moment, they gripped hands and then, as Lee started to speak, Cardigan shook his head. "Another time, Lee, all right? We know how you feel but it's just too soon to talk much about it."

"Right," Lee said and leaned to greet the two in the car almost casually.

Lisa was in the back seat, holding tightly to Morgan's hand,

379

her face thin and drawn, made even more pallid by the heavy makeup which couldn't actually cover the ravages of her ordeal. But her happiness was unmistakable.

"Well," Lee said to Steve as he straightened, "what can we do for you?"

"What is apparently a very great favor," the Canadian said in amusement. "I've got a plane standing by to take us to New York. Alice is expecting us and, of course, Lisa's anxious to see her, otherwise nothing would persuade her to miss the Derby. But she'd like to see the colt before she leaves and somehow or other, we seem to have mislaid our credentials."

Lee began to laugh again. "Under the circumstances, Fred, I think that just this once . . ."

But Fred was already on his way toward Lee's car. "You come right ahead, Mr. Cardigan," he called. "Follow us. We'll take you in ourselves!"

The big stable was already back to normal when they reached it. The floors had been hosed down and cleaned of kerosene and burned straw, power and water had been restored and there were the usual four guards on day duty. Even the telltale odor of smoke had dissipated and only the charred paint on one of the overhead doors remained as visible evidence of what had occurred there such a short time before.

In any case, the Derby Barn was too busy to think about the fire. Armada, alone, seemed entirely untouched by the general excitement. He was wearing his muzzle, so he understood that he was to race today and ordinarily he would have been moving about his stall with the special restlessness which was due more to rising anticipation than it was to hunger. But not this morning. Armada was sulking in a corner, head hanging, long tail dispiritedly motionless, back deliberately turned against the world.

Then, suddenly, the big bay quivered. With a slight tentative snort he brought his head up, nostrils flared, ears pricking. Lisa was still at the end of the barn and Morgan had to support her uncharacteristically slow progress. Even so, Armada had recognized her footsteps. He was straining at the stall door, whinnying joyously over it, long before she could get to him.

And if she slipped him a few forbidden lumps of sugar during that happy reunion, Mister Mack never noticed. He was near one of the guardroom doors with her father and Lee and Fred, speechless with shock as they told him, very briefly, where Lisa had been.

When they were back in the car and headed for the airport, Lisa said, "Poor Armada, I just hate to leave him again so soon."

"We noticed when we had to almost drag you out of there." Morgan gave her a teasing glance. "Wish I thought you hated leaving me half as much."

"Oh, Morgan, darling, if you only knew."

His arm tightened around her. "I do, Lisa. I keep pinching myself to prove I'm not dreaming, but I know. Anyway, you're going to bed the minute you've seen your mother, and I'll be in New York before you wake up. And then, if it's all right with you, sir," he said to her father, "I'm never letting her out of my sight again."

Cardigan's eyes smiled at Morgan in the rear-view mirror. "I doubt if I have any say in the matter, Morgan. And if I did, after last night, how could I refuse?" He shook his head. "I was completely against the idea when Morgan broached it, Lisa. Fixing the trunk so he could come, too, with the speaker and the air vent and the special lock that would open noiselessly from the inside. And the bullet-proof glass. That was a stroke of genius. It did exactly what Morgan intended, infuriated the kidnapper so much he never thought to suspect anything else. But when Morgan first suggested it, all I could see was how many things could go wrong. And if that car had pulled up in back of us instead of in front . . ."

Lisa shivered and Morgan said, "But it didn't, darling, everything's over now."

"Almost," Steve Cardigan said grimly.

"Right," Morgan agreed. "But maybe, with a little more luck, they'll be picked up this afternoon."

"Oh, darling, couldn't you just let the FBI handle it and come to New York with us?"

"I will, if we don't catch them today," Morgan said. "But we didn't allow Elverson to question you for more than five minutes when we got you back to the hotel, honey." He smiled at her. "It seems to me, at that point, your father and I had some ridiculous notion we were going to be able to bundle you straight into a hospital bed."

"I just couldn't!"

"We realize that now, Lisa, and of course you have to get to your mother as quickly as possible. But you've given us all kinds of details since then that I should pass along to the FBI. And if those two should go to the Derby today . . ."

The possibility that Rosanna Palmer and Mace Augustine might actually appear at Churchill Downs was a longshot, Morgan thought, easing the Cadillac out of the airport after Lisa and her father lifted off. But if they did, Morgan wanted to be there.

The strength of his feeling toward the pair astounded him. He had decided years ago against practicing law, but the turn of mind which had made him consider a legal career in the first place hadn't radically changed. He was a rational man, a logical one, with his strong emotions always under control. But his fury against Lisa's captors was so intense that he found within himself an utterly unexpected desire to have a hand in trapping them.

If the kidnappers weren't caught today, he would give it up. He would stay in Louisville only until the Derby was over. This conclusion suddenly jolted him into the realization that he had completely forgotten the Derby's real significance.

The most important race of the year—and his jockey was riding Lisa's horse in it. Why, Donnie Cheevers would be at the track in little more than an hour. Which settled any earlier thought Morgan had had that he might grab a little sleep. He couldn't. He was going to Churchill Downs. The least he ought to do was stay with Donnie until it was time for him to go up to the jocks' room at ten.

Morgan supposed he couldn't get in touch with Elverson much before then, anyway. It had been midnight when the inspector told them about the local man who'd sold Derby tickets to Mace Augustine. And the FBI were, presumably, entitled to a decent night's rest.

Unfortunately for Jason Elverson other people were less accommodating than Morgan. Even as the agent was watching Donnie Cheever pace the track, just before six o'clock, the inspector and his men were deployed around the trailer in Good Mary's yard.

Fred Keller had finally realized why the name Mace Augustine had been bothering him since Cardigan's mention of it at the Derby Barn. He had remembered the obvious alias—August Mason—of the nice young man he'd met at the Derby Museum.

Fred himself had moved the old lady and her roomers safely away from the house before Elverson gave the signal to move in on the trailer. But all their careful precautions were wasted. The only person there was Rosanna and she was no longer a threat to anyone.

Elverson looked down at her. So young, so pretty, she really didn't look like a monster. But from what Lisa Cardigan had told them, Rosanna Palmer was as bad as Mace Augustine. Or had been.

The inspector sighed and turned to Irving. "Well, that's two out of three, Ted. Better get word to your men they're looking for a man alone now."

"You think he'll try to leave town?"

"I don't know," Elverson said, "but the alternative presents a rather interesting question: If you were he, and presumably carrying a suitcase full of money, you wouldn't want to wander around the streets all night, would you?"

"That would be asking for attention."

"Right. And, yet, where the devil would you find a place to stay in Louisville on Derby Eve?"

That was the problem Mace had faced when he fled the trailer hours earlier. But after a few panicky moments, the solution had been easy. He was now comfortably asleep in a pleasant room on the tenth floor of the Crown Hotel.

Mace had followed the man to whom it was rented when he made his staggering way upstairs from the bar. He was under the bed, no longer even bleeding from the knife wounds which had dispatched him without unnecessary noise. Mace had placed the DO NOT DISTURB sign on the outside of the door. He was completely safe until it was time to leave for the Derby. If he went to the Derby. He might not, he might just stay in the room.

"Kidnappers, right in my own backyard, Chief Keller? Those nice young people?" Good Mary shook the fluff of hair she had been brushing when Fred came to hustle her outside.

"It is hard to believe," he said. "But I suppose I should have been suspicious. I was curious at their paying you so much, until you introduced him."

"I know," the old lady said, "such a good-looking, honest face. Sure, it feels like a goose walking over my grave, the thought of him now. And her lying dead under my very windows."

Fred patted her thin shoulder. "I don't want it to upset you too much, Good Mary, you hear? It's a terrible thing but it's finished. They'll be moving the trailer out of your yard in a little while and they may want to ask you a few questions, but after that, you're to put it out of your mind."

The face before him blanched in alarm. "I'll gladly help in any way I can, Chief Keller, but they'll not be holding me up too long, will they? Because I'd never want to miss the Derby and there's a line over there already."

He smiled, relieved. However upsetting the experience had been, Good Mary's spirit was beautifully intact. "You'll be in time, I promise."

"I can't feel all bad, to be blessed with a friend like yourself," Good Mary said. "It's been a dreadful beginning to Derby Day, Chief Keller, but, sure, it looks now like it'll be a fine one!"

She was absolutely right. There wasn't a cloud in sight, even the normal haze had disappeared and the Morning Star was fading into a dawn that was pink with promise. It was going to be a perfect Derby Day.

Naturally, that was what the backstretch was saying happily, over and over. In between the excited discussions of what had almost happened at the Derby Barn and the startled rumors that were just beginning to circulate about the kidnapping.

"Tell you one thing," Warren told Lee when they were both frontside, "the FBI's damn lucky Pop Dewey went off his rocker last night. Otherwise the Cardigan story would be all over the place before this afternoon and if the kidnapper were mad enough to consider coming to the Derby he'd be scared off."

The astonished lift of Lee's right eyebrow was because "lucky" was hardly the word which would have occurred to him in connection with the arson attempt. "Inspector Elverson informs me the Derby may be their only quick lead to this Mace Augustine. His connection with Coolie hasn't produced anything and if he lays low, doesn't spend any more twenties for awhile, he could be pretty hard to find."

He sighed unconsciously. "It's not exactly what I'd wish for Derby Day, Warren, but I'd sure like Churchill Downs to be of help in nabbing him. I saw Steve Cardigan's face this morning. I just can't believe this man will come to the track, though, he has to know they're looking for him."

"Oh, obviously," Warren agreed. "I'm just saying that screaming headlines would probably erase whatever chance there is."

From that point of view it was also fortunate that this was the first Saturday in May. On the morning of the Big Day itself the backstretch was virtually deserted by the newsmen who had swarmed through it with such constancy during the preceding week. Everything which could be written about the Derby—except for the actual running—was already in print.

And if, as Warren said, Pop Dewey had been a blessing in disguise for the FBI, he represented an absolute godsend for the afternoon papers. Derby Day inevitably presented them with the dilemma of featuring in advance an event which would be over before their ink was even dry. This year they had a very different, highly dramatic Derby story, one which had broken too late for the morning editions, and in return they had given Pop Dewey coverage which exceeded his wildest imaginings. Pictures had been ingeniously enlarged from the regulation shots automatically taken by the official track photographer in the winner's circle after every race, big or small.

Pop had held hundreds of horses for hundreds of such photographs over the years, his insignificant figure lost among the widely beaming owners and trainers. But now everything else had been neatly blocked out. It was Clyde (Pop) Dewey alone who dominated the front pages.

He wouldn't know this until later, of course, when he had

fully recovered. But the enormous scrapbook of clippings would be very impressive at the institution in which he would spend what remained of his life. Nobody there would ever doubt that Clyde (Pop) Dewey was a very famous man.

Since the newspapers couldn't possibly break the Cardigan story until it would no longer matter, the only danger of immediate publicity lay in radio or TV bulletins. Ted Irving took care of that by explaining the situation to the local stations. They agreed willingly to withhold any reference until after the Derby.

It was such a straw they were grasping at. They all knew that. But they had so little else.

The first thing, naturally, was to clear the area immediately surrounding the two seats Mace was known to have bought, not only to protect innocent ticket holders but in order to plant agents in their places. Lee coped so effectively with this aspect of the preparation that only his secretary knew what prodigious effort it entailed. The first six substitutions were simple enough, since the Cardigan box was available. From there on, each seat was an increasing problem. Somehow, though, Lee managed six more changes.

Then he had to find a seat for Morgan Wells. And still another—at a safe distance—for the used-car salesman who had been traced from Mace's abandoned vehicle. He would watch for the wanted man through binoculars.

The Potters were left to the last, pending the outcome of Elverson's appeal to the man who had sold Mace the tickets. "You see, sir," the inspector said, "if Augustine comes, he'll be expecting to find you there. In fact, it may arouse his suspicions if you're not. So if you felt that you could stay, it might be of tremendous assistance to us."

"Well," said Eustace Potter nervously, "if you say there'll be agents all around . . ."

"Front and back and both sides, Mr. Potter, including Mr.

Irving and me. I can promise you'll be safer in that seat than you would be in your own home."

"I guess I wouldn't mind," Potter decided at last. "Only what about my wife?"

"Oh, we'll find her another seat," Elverson said.

Mrs. Potter had other ideas. "If he stays, I stay," she announced firmly. "And that will throw this kidnapper off his guard even more. After all," she pointed out when the inspector hesitated, "when he comes and sees man and wife together, what could be more normal?"

"What, indeed?" Elverson asked, smiling at her appreciatively. "*If* he comes, Mrs. Potter; it seems highly unlikely, but we're very grateful."

Hours of concentrated work went into these arrangements but when they were finally completed, Ted Irving sighed. "Wish there was more we could do, Inspector, but I'm afraid that's about it."

"Yes," Elverson said. "We've got everybody in this section who can positively identify Augustine, except for Keller, who might scare him off. The only thing we can do now is sit and wait. See if he shows up."

SEVEN

COMING OFF THE TRACK at seven o'clock that morning, Lucky Jim lost a shoe. A horse in frequent competition usually had all his shoes replaced every three or four weeks— and since the horses who raced weekly, sometimes twice a week, were generally cheaper stock, that could be a problem to the small owner who was wondering how to come up with the necessary twenty or twenty-five dollars. The shoes were changed so often because the toe grabs at the front of the aluminum plates wore down under the heavy usage. They didn't ordinarily come loose, but it wasn't uncommon.

Not even when, as now, Lucky Jim had been sparingly raced on his way to the Kentucky Derby and despite the fact that Buddy Sheffield had had him re-shod only a couple of weeks ago. And it wasn't important. Although, it could have been vital if it had occurred during his blowout. Or worse, the backstretch pointed out, if the shoe had held on a little longer and then come off in the middle of the Derby.

As it was Ike Drury simply summoned one of the licensed farriers working on the backstretch and watched with an experienced eye as the colt's hoof was trimmed of an infinitesimal bit of horn and measured. It was a process most thoroughbreds accepted placidly enough, since it entailed no pain whatsoever, but Lucky Jim had always reacted nervously to it. Both the trainer and the groom were required to hold him still. Fortunately, the young fellow who had come was exceedingly competent, knew exactly what to do and how to do it.

Still, thought Ike as he murmured automatically to soothe Lucky Jim, he probably never would get used to the modern farriers, no matter how good they were. There was such a difference between these fellows, carting their neat little boxes with the neat little labels all over the place in station wagons, and the blacksmiths around the racetracks when Ike got started. The new way was better, no doubt of that. The aluminum shoes were better, too, so much lighter and, in spite of a seemingly endless variety, pretty standardized, requiring only minor adjustment.

"Whoa, boy, take it easy, now, nobody's going to hurt you," the trainer said.

But the truth was, Ike decided, he missed those big old

forges and the way the sparks used to fly while the iron shoes were being pounded into proper fit. You took the horse to the blacksmith in those days, he didn't come to you.

"Steady, boy, that's all right!"

Everything was changed, though. Who would ever have dreamed in those days of the automatic hot-walkers that had taken over most backstretches now? Looking like enormous wagon wheels going around above your head and all you did was just hook your horse on to be walked by a motor till he'd cooled out. The new hot-walkers could handle three or four horses at a clip, actually, and you never had to wonder if they'd had a few too many to drink, maybe, or jerked too impatiently on the shank. But Ike didn't like the machines, either.

"Guess I'm going to have to put a couple of new nail holes in this hoof," the farrier said, looking up in a tacit request for approval. "I always try to use the old ones when I can but these may have loosened up a little, it's probably why he dropped the shoe."

"If you have to, you have to," Drury agreed.

The groom nodded. "That's the truth," he said. "This horse sure can't win no Derby on three feet."

Buddy Sheffield had gone out of his way to speak to Ike Drury pleasantly the first time they'd met in the Derby Barn under what might have been somewhat embarrassing circumstances for the older man. It wasn't poor Ike's fault that Jim York was such a bastard. After that, though, Buddy stayed as far away from Lucky Jim and his new trainer as possible.

Now, bringing Dashing Lad back from the morning's exercise, Buddy took the long way around to avoid the little group working on Lucky Jim's hoof. He frowned speculatively. The same thing had happened to Lucky Jim in Florida the morning of the Flamingo Stakes. And Dashing Lad had won the race that afternoon.

Buddy hadn't thought at the time there was any connection, but who knew? History might repeat itself. Except that Orv Scott had been handling Dashing Lad then and he himself had saddled Lucky Jim. A strange world it was sometimes. But very beautiful to Buddy Sheffield today.

EIGHT

T HE DINING ROOM at the Professor's motel was almost entirely filled with people who were evidently intent on getting an early start for Churchill Downs. Nevertheless, when he entered from the lobby at 7:15, later than usual for him since he didn't go backstretch on Derby Day, neither hostess nor cashier was on duty inside the arched doorway and there wasn't a waitress to be seen.

You could hear them, though, the Professor noted in amusement as he chose a table for himself and sat down. The excited shrieks from behind the decorative screen shielding the kitchen door were self-explanatory.

"Magician!"

"I've got Lucky Jim, he's the favorite!"

"Dashing Lad!" That was a male voice, one of the kitchen help, probably.

"Oh, blast, just my luck. Sweepstakes."

"Armada."

"Freeway. I've got Freeway. And my boyfriend's from California, too."

"Davie's Pride. Well, I guess he's got some chance."

The girls were obviously taking part in a pool they'd set up

391

on the Kentucky Derby. And how many similar pools were centered around this race all over the country was anybody's guess. Thousands and thousands, undoubtedly, everywhere seven people could be gotten together, and most of the participants would never have seen a track, except on television. From his waitress's glum face when she finally approached, the Professor decided she must have drawn Sweepstakes. She remembered to put the extra pat of butter on his "bacon, two scrambled and grits," however, and when she served them, she'd regained her smile.

The check for his usual breakfast was a dollar more than usual. He grinned, left the girl a little extra to make up for Sweepstakes, and cast an appreciative glance at the sign which offered a Kentucky Derby Box Lunch at $3.75—a couple of pieces of chicken, a ham sandwich, a bit of cole slaw, a dab of salad, a smell of honey and a biscuit. The cab fare had been upped two dollars for the occasion, too, but when the Professor got to Churchill Downs, he paid it cheerfully. He expected it, he had been to the Derby before. He had also been to the Mardi Gras and the Indianapolis 500 and the World Series.

Inside, the Professor found two guards instead of the usual one in the little cubicle from which the press elevator rose. They were already deep in Derby Day problems, with additional complications in this particular instance because the three Chilean journalists whose right to enter seemed to be in question spoke only halting English.

Canonero II, Venezuelan-owned winner of the 1971 Derby, had excited feverish intercontinental interest in the race in spite of his having actually been a Kentucky product—or, perhaps, partially because of that fact, since he'd been bought at the regular Keeneland sales for an incredible $1,200. In any case, more and more fine thoroughbreds were being imported from South America and, inevitably, there were growing numbers of Latin-American correspondents now joining those who had been attending the Derby in force for many years.

With the Professor's good offices it was quickly established that these were, indeed, the legitimate carriers of what proved to be substitute cards, issued when their original credentials were stolen. The numbers of the stolen cards, along with perhaps a dozen others, were chalked on a wall blackboard, and if the thieves presently tried to get upstairs to the press box with them, they were in for a rude awakening.

These elaborate precautions probably seemed excessive to the trio of foreigners but they would understand presently. Even now, as they all reached the top and got out of the elevator, the press box was beginning to fill. By the first post— 11:30 on Derby Day—the area which seemed so enormous all the rest of the year would be quite crowded. By the time of the Big Race itself, there would be a fantastic crush. And not everyone present would actually be working press.

The staff of Warren Robbins' department strove with remarkable success to keep the reporters who should be there from being elbowed aside by those whose claims were tenuous at best, but it took dedicated effort. Tickets were sought for this event by "sports editors" from every two-page weekly within striking distance, whether it carried racing news or not, and there were always surprising droves of julep-carrying television "technicians" or radio "announcers." There were even, now and then, important personages without the slightest connection with any of the media, for whom Lee Ames was forced to find last-minute space.

The Professor turned the grateful Chileans over to one of Warren's assistants, dropped his paraphernalia next to the typewriter at his assigned space and, binoculars in hand, pushed a sliding glass door aside to stand on the outer balcony. He had made it with only minutes to spare. Three, to be exact, until it was eight o'clock and the first happy rush of spectators would begin to fill the infield.

This was a spectacle the Professor enjoyed no matter how

393

many times he watched it. Every available inch of space around the fence vanished immediately, like a magnet in a box of metal filings. And, yet, many of those who had waited outside the gates for hours, some of them racing through the long, echoing tunnels under the racetrack the second they were admitted, didn't seem to really care about grabbing off the strategic viewing places. They quickly dotted the entire grassy enclosure with blankets and lunch baskets, cushions and chairs, an occasional folding cot or beach umbrella, countless radios, even a few portable TVs.

Some of the people undoubtedly chose their spots with an eye to the food and liquor stands, the mutuel windows or even the restrooms, but most seemed content just to be there on Derby Day.

Unbelievable, thought the Professor. But as Tom Richardson had said once in an interview, he joined them every year because they seemed to be having such a doggone lot of fun that he couldn't resist. Neither, in his own way, could the Professor.

His attention was caught by the flashing hands in a party of four couples who were chatting animatedly in sign language and then, amusingly, by five boys who were settled next to five pretty girls. The Professor wasn't sure which group had deliberately decided to spread beach blankets next to which, but they were obviously about to get together.

There were numerous other such groups of young people as well as many older couples, but the infield was most notably crowded with the families who invariably shared that day together on the grass. Two or three generations, sometimes four, many of them, as the Professor knew, coming from out of state for this gala gathering.

Not all of those below were carefree participants in the pleasant spring ritual. The Professor could see the uniforms of the National Guardsmen and he was aware that there were dozens of plainclothes security forces scattered among the crowd—TRPB men, detectives, even a few policewomen. Their purpose—beyond the obvious one of crowd control, if that should become necessary—was to protect the lambs from any roving predators.

There were always some wolves in so large a congregation, and it struck the Professor that his matter-of-fact acceptance of this premise was slightly depressing, but then he smiled. His glance had settled on the grass to the side of the presentation stand, outside the infield fence, where a spit-and-polish corps of youthful color bearers was going through an elaborate routine.

This couldn't be the same corps which had held this honor last year or the year before but they always seemed identical. And every Derby morning brought this panicky rehearsal of steps and turns and maneuvers from boys who were already drilled to perfection but scared silly by the fact that it was Derby Day at last.

At a hail from behind, the Professor turned to face a handicapper from another newspaper, one who was apparently too shocked to engage in any such nicety as formal greeting.

"Hey, Professor, I've just been reading your column and I can't believe it! You're picking Freeway to take the Derby? Freeway?"

The Professor laughed outright. "I can't remember when I've heard a better expression of outraged eastern establishmentarianism."

"That isn't it. He was bred in these parts, anyway. But who's he ever beaten?"

"Everybody he's been asked to beat," the Professor pointed out mildly.

"Well, yes, I grant that, but that was on the coast."

"True. It could make a difference. It has before."

"And you still went out on a limb? I'll tell you, Professor, I think this is one prediction you'll have to eat!"

"I probably will," the Professor agreed, "and wear sackcloth and ashes to boot." He shrugged. "That's happened before, too. In last year's Derby, as a matter of cold, uncomfortable fact. But, meanwhile, I happen to think Freeway can win this one. Who did you pick?"

"Oh, Lucky Jim, who else? Magician scares me a little, though. He's got the best chance to edge the favorite, I guess, and I'd hate like hell to see Gabe Hilliard take it. He doesn't even talk to me."

The Professor slid tactfully over the point that Gabe did talk to him. "Yes," he said, "I like Magician, too. He's my second choice."

An hour later, Shelby Todhunter, Jr., exclaimed joyously, "Well, I don't believe it. Finally, somebody who's picking Freeway to win."

"The Professor, you mean?" Doc asked. Shelby nodded. "I saw it earlier, when I was backstretch. It's quite a rave, Shel, read the whole thing."

But Doc's mind wasn't really on the Professor. He was enjoying Shelby. The boy had only been awake a little while, he was still in pajamas, papers strewn around him on the bed, but the long sleep and the huge breakfast he had just packed away seemed to have worked a miracle.

Now here he was, happily discussing Freeway and the Derby as if he'd never taken—or needed—a pill in his life. They weren't out of the woods yet, Doc reminded himself. There had been good periods before, when Shel had said he wanted to conquer the pills, when he had actually seemed to be kicking the habit. And then gone back.

But there had never been this closeness between them—not for years, anyway—nor this complete absence of underlying animosity. It really was different this time.

Shelby looked up from the Professor's piece with a pleased smile. "That is a rave, isn't it?"

Doc grinned. "But don't forget, Shel, the Professor admits

that his selecting Freeway could well be the kiss of death!"

"Uh-uh, not today, Dad," Shelby said. "The Professor will come out of this smelling like the roses Freeway will be wearing in the winner's circle this afternoon. You realize there isn't another handicapper picking Freeway? Half of them don't even think he'll be in the money!"

"That's just here in the east," Doc reminded him.

"I know," Shelby said, "I wish we had this morning's California papers." He threw the covers back and swung his feet onto the floor. "We'll see those when we get home but what do you say, Dad, you want to start getting ready?"

Doc hesitated briefly. "The first race doesn't even go off until eleven-thirty."

"But it's Derby Day. Mom and Mrs. Vance are chomping at the bit. Paula told me on the phone they've all been ready for an hour and you know they serve a special breakfast out at the track Derby morning. Lots of people get there early."

"Now, don't tell me you're thinking of eating again."

"I'm making up for lost time, Dad," Shelby said. "Don't forget, you're the one who taught me a hungry horse is a healthy horse. So how about it?"

"Sure, if you want to, son. If you feel like it?"

"Never felt better in my life, I swear."

"Okay," Doc agreed, "up and at 'em. I'll go get ready."

He really did feel good, Shelby told himself under the shower. Too bad his father couldn't relax. He tried to hide it but he was worrying over what the long tense day might do.

Shelby himself had no doubts. He had known when he opened his eyes this morning that he'd never touch another pill. Just as surely as Freeway was going to win the Kentucky Derby.

NINE

At NINE-THIRTY, the telephone rang in Room 1032 at the Crown Hotel. Mace sprang out of bed, startled wide awake by the unexpected noise. It went on and on, two loud peals and a pause, until Mace was ready to smash something.

When it finally stopped, it took a couple of seconds for his bunched muscles to relax. The call meant the guy under the bed had friends in Louisville, Mace realized. And that meant he didn't dare to stay, there was too much risk of possible visitors.

No hurry, though. The guy wasn't in his room, that was all. He could be anywhere. Nobody'd come looking for him yet. Still, Mace didn't try to go back to sleep. He began to prowl the room, wondering about the cops.

A dark suit hung neatly from a pole in the dressing room off the bath. There were also a couple of pieces of luggage. Mace opened the first bag out of sheer curiosity. As he had imagined, it contained more clothing, none of which was any use to Mace. The guy under the bed was roughly his own height, but a good fifty pounds heavier, with a beer-barrel pot.

Mace pawed through the garments until he came across the folded underwear at the bottom. Long johns. He couldn't believe it. He flung them aside and opened the other suitcase. This proved to be loaded with samples of bandage, of all crazy things. There were also several kinds of adhesive tape, arm slings and knee supports, but mostly rolls and rolls of different bandages. The guy under the bed must have been a salesman.

Mace was about to abandon the second case, too, when the idea came to him. Gaze narrowed speculatively, he reassessed the dead man's luggage, then got his own bag, opened its lid and eyed the money inside. The night before, this bag had been his most worrisome problem after he left the trailer—one he was going to have to face again when he left this room. Carrying it around town would attract attention, but where could he check it, even if he were willing? The cops would be keeping an eye on every possible public locker.

He looked at the money doubtfully. All those packets of bills. Still, if he taped them to his body, good and tight, with some of this guy's bandages wrapped around, and then pulled a pair of those long johns over the whole thing, the suit in the closet should fit him perfectly. It would be a partial disguise, too, because they would be searching for a thinner man.

He froze. And what if he bandaged his head? Maybe put his arm in one of the slings, like he'd been in a car accident or something? Exultation swept over Mace. That would really do it. He could walk up to anybody and they'd never know it was him. No phony moustache or wig that the police might be expecting, after last night. Just the bandages and some dark glasses.

The phone shrilled, as persistently as before. Son of a bitch, it wasn't ten minutes since the last time. Mace gulped and went to work. Ten minutes later, the phone rang again. But by then, it didn't matter to Mace anymore. He was already on his way to the Kentucky Derby. Along with at least a hundred thousand other people.

TEN

A S IN THE THEATER, in racing too the show must go on.
Its human performers are equally bound by tradition
and contract; and a jockey who is to appear in any race at
any track is normally expected to check in, ready to "suit
up," about an hour or an hour and a half before he is due to
ride, the precise margin of leeway depending upon local reg-
ulations. Failure to show or tardiness can draw a fine or even
a suspension.

There are other refinements dedicated to the proposition
that the fans are entitled to the program which has been
promised. A jockey may be punished for failing to make his
riding weight after he has implicitly committed himself to it
by acceptance of a mount. By the same token barring last
minute illness or injury an owner or trainer is subject to
penalty if he does not produce the horse to be saddled at the
scheduled hour, with all specifications as to entry properly
met.

Inevitably, there is some flexibility in such rules, but they
can be stretched only for good reason and only with the stewards' permission. Allowance would be made, for instance, if a
rider were flying in from out of town for a particular race and
plane schedules made it impossible for him to check in with
the others.

Today, Ferdy Garcia had been granted an extra hour in
which to take his wife and new baby out of the hospital. The
stewards might ordinarily have required the jockey to wait
until after the Derby or to send a friend, but in this case, they

agreed, there could be no delay or substitution. The train on which Ferdy and Peggy would carry her father's coffin home to Texas for tomorrow's burial was leaving at eight that night.

Each of the stewards had known Orv Scott well. It was a small enough thing to do for him, however indirectly. It was the last thing they would ever be able to do for him.

All other riders at Churchill Downs on this momentous Saturday—including those whose mounts were in the so-called "Midnight Matinee," the ultimate race on the long program and not due until almost eight hours later—were supposed to be in the second-floor jockeys' room by 10:00 A.M. This rule imposed a certain hardship but it had evolved of necessity: a jockey who got caught up in the Derby Day crowds might never make it to the post on time.

It was five minutes before ten when Morgan put Donnie on the escalator with a few final words of advice and encouragement. As he turned away, he almost collided with Gabe Hilliard, who was also preparing to check in. The two had met on a number of other occasions since their old association broke up. The proscribed circles of the racing world made such contacts unavoidable. But since Gabe had been confining himself pretty steadily to the west coast and Morgan's territory was mainly in the east, it had been quite a while.

Morgan hadn't the faintest idea how Gabe would respond to a greeting. He had undoubtedly heard of the relationship between his ex-wife and his ex-agent. He might be resentful of it. Nevertheless, Morgan said affably, "Gabe, I was wondering when we'd run into each other. Glad to have a chance to say 'good luck' in the Derby."

What in the name of God had happened to Gabe's face? Equally astonishing were Gabe's grin and handshake. "Thanks, the same to you and your rider," he said. "As for the way I look, Morg, pick your eyes up off the floor. I got jumped by a couple of sorehead drunks I never saw before, that's all."

"But are you well enough to ride?"

"Oh, sure," Gabe said lightly. "You know me, just a couple of bruised ribs. The big thing is, how's Lisa? If what Nick heard on the backstretch this morning is true . . ."

Morgan said grimly, "It's true. But Lisa's going to be fine."

"It must have been a hideous experience all around," Gabe said, appraising Morgan's ravaged face. "You know, the FBI tracked me down to ask questions. Maybe I should have guessed then." He shook his head apologetically. "I'm afraid I was pretty self-engrossed at the time. Besides, it's almost impossible to think of something like that happening to anyone you know."

"Well," said Morgan, "it's over now."

"Thank God she's all right," Gabe said, then hesitated. "I've got to beat it upstairs, Morg, but is the rest of it true, that you two are planning to be married?"

"Yes, Gabe, as soon as possible."

Gabe paused again. "I don't suppose it matters, Morg, but for what it's worth, I'm glad. I mean that from the bottom of my heart, I'm really glad. Will you tell Lisa that I wish you both every happiness?"

Morgan said, "Thank you, Gabe," and "Yes, I'll tell her," evenly enough but he couldn't quite conceal his surprise.

Gabe laughed. "Yes," he agreed, "I do seem to be mellowing." He stopped. There wasn't time to fill Morgan in about Ronnie now and no real reason for his impulse to do so. He had made his point. "Look, I've really got to go or I'll be late. Don't forget, now, the very best to you and Lisa, you're both great people." He disappeared, taking the escalator steps two at a time, as Morgan stared after him.

It wasn't a meeting Morgan had anticipated with relish but he discovered now, as he finally turned and began to walk along the red brick pathway, that it had left him feeling pleased. As if whatever bitterness there might have been between them was gone at last. Lisa would be pleased, too, Morgan thought, when he told her.

He supposed that in some ways a dissolved alliance of any kind—especially one as close as that between jockey and agent —was a little like a broken marriage. There were always the bad things which caused the split and who could ever say whose fault those were? Or even if they were anybody's fault? But there were good things too in such a relationship, if only at the very beginning. It was a loss when these were entirely wiped out by what came later.

Morgan smiled to himself. Who could ever have believed this encounter would end with such satisfaction? Then Morgan remembered Mace Augustine and his smile faded. He did not notice the beds of perfect tulips beside the walkway as he strode off in search of Inspector Elverson.

The jockeys' room at Churchill Downs was comparatively new, a spacious and luxurious accommodation on a par with the best at much larger tracks. Gabe had to run a long obstacle course of catcalls and comment from the riders he knew before he reached the far corner where, by tacit agreement, those entered in the Derby were gathered separately.

Since Ferdy Garcia had not yet arrived, there were only five men watching Gabe's approach and two were complete strangers. One of them had to be Donnie Cheevers, Armada's rider; the other, Billy Hendricks, who had the mount on Davie's Pride. Gabe would sort them out in a minute.

Gene Firestone and Robbie Roberts were jockeys Gabe had met rather frequently and liked. Today Gene would be on Lucky Jim, the favorite, and Robbie, taking over for the suspended Mickey Kuzich, would ride Sweepstakes, the longshot.

Of them all, Gabe had undoubtedly seen Rudy Maldonado most often, since they were both California based. However, they had never been close and then, last summer, the Del Mar Futurity had triggered a fist fight between them as they left the track.

It was perhaps ironic that Rudy was riding Freeway this afternoon. The day of the fight Gabe had been Freeway's jockey and Freeway had won by three lengths going away. The trouble had started when Rudy accused Gabe of deliberate crowding on the turn into the stretch and the resultant melee had cost them each a hundred-dollar fine.

Accusations of this sort were common enough, and Gabe had made his own furious charges of foul as often as they were claimed against him. Usually, such arguments ended as quickly as they began, but Rudy had never spoken to Gabe since. He didn't reply now to Gabe's general greeting, though his stony black eyes regarded the newcomer with the same shock as the others.

Gene Firestone whistled. "So that's where you've been all week," he said, "hiding that face. What hit you, an atom bomb?"

"Remember the drunk in the Kauai King Room, Gene?"

"You're kidding! He did that to you?"

"Not alone, he had an even nastier friend. They jumped me without any warning."

"Any damage we can't see?" asked Gene.

Gabe laughed. "Nothing much," he lied. He turned to the two strangers. "Which one of you is Donnie Cheevers?"

"I am."

"I was just talking to Morg downstairs," Gabe said. "You're a lucky kid to have him for an agent, they don't come any better." To the other boy, Gabe said, "Then you must be Billy Hendricks?"

"Yes, sir."

Gabe blinked at the youngster and Robbie Roberts laughed. "Kind of gets you the first time he pulls that, doesn't it? But Billie's not been around long enough to forget his manners."

"After all, Gabe," Gene said, "you are old enough to be his father!"

"In a pig's eye I am," Gabe retorted. "I'm only thirty-two."

At that moment, The Colonel cleared his throat behind them and they turned. "I suppose you know why I'm here," he said. "It isn't a long tradition as such things go at Churchill Downs, but I always like to come up and say a few words to you boys in the Derby, to wish every one of you good luck in the greatest race of them all and to remind you that each of you, today, is a representative of our fine sport."

Gabe had heard The Colonel's little speech three times before and it had hardly varied. It was much the same today, a cross between what Gabe imagined might be a football coach's pep talk and a referee's admonition before a prizefight.

What caught Gabe's interest this morning was the expression on the two kids' faces, the way they kept their eyes glued on The Colonel's earnest face. For that matter, Robbie and Rudy were giving the handsome old man equally rapt attention. They'd never had mounts in the Kentucky Derby before, either.

There was nothing like it for a jockey that first time, Gabe thought. Or, really, any time. He himself might not be hanging on The Colonel's familiar words, but he certainly felt deeply what The Colonel was trying to convey. To be in the Derby *was* a special achievement for everyone concerned and it *did* call for heights of dedication and good sportsmanship.

Even the irrepressible Gene Firestone was touched. He gave a self-conscious laugh when The Colonel finally left after shaking hands all around. "I felt like I ought to stand at attention and put my hand over my heart."

"Yes, it is pretty effective," Gabe agreed. On impulse, he turned to Maldonado. "How about it, Rudy?" Gabe asked. "It's too big a day to hold grudges. Shall we let bygones be bygones?"

Rudy stared in astonishment at the hand Gabe was proffering. Then he spat through his teeth. "Go to hell. I'm riding Freeway this time," Rudy said.

405

ELEVEN

THE TREE-SHADED CAMPUS of the University of Louisville lay only a few blocks from Churchill Downs, and at Derby time a considerable portion of its student body found temporary employment at the racetrack.

Some of the boys—particularly the business and economics majors—worked for Churchill Downs itself, in Kermit Young's department as mutuels clerks or accountants. Others were attached to general maintenance.

The largest contingent, however, was hired by the nationally known concessionaire which fed the crowds and provided sundry additional goodies as well. Along with the overnight mushrooming of booths which dedicated themselves entirely to the speedy dispensation of the traditional mint juleps in special glasses that were prized souvenirs in themselves, there were numbers of stands where all manner of bright hats, pennants, scarves, pins and novelties might be purchased.

The remainder of the students were employed by the professional ushering service which, with these local recruits and its own highly skilled personnel imported for the occasion from such cities as Chicago and Indianapolis, were responsible for escorting Derby ticket holders to their reserved seats or boxes.

In most sports, showing arrivals to their proper places completes the job. At racetracks, however, the fans are always on the move from seat to pari-mutuel windows or down to the paddock to watch the horses being saddled. On Derby Day, the hardest task is keeping patrons out of sections they aren't supposed to enter. Each year, varying techniques for its more efficient accomplishment were propounded and tested. Today, the ushering service had fallen back on one of the most basic of all such devices—distinctively colored pasteboards for each section.

The area of the grandstand where Mace had bought his two tickets was identified by an unmistakable electric purple. Elverson had originally given some consideration to the desirability of alerting all ticket takers and ushers to a check of seat numbers in the target section. However, he had been convinced that the sheer size of the crowd coupled with the inexperience of so many of the attendants would make this highly impractical.

He had been forced to rely on the fact that if Mace came to the Derby at all, the only probability of catching him was at one of the seats he was known to have bought, now surrounded by FBI agents. It was fortunate that Elverson had bowed to the inevitable, because when Mace arrived at eleven o'clock, he was keyed to pick up the slightest hint of danger. If anyone even looked sidewise at him . . .

The harried young student didn't. Color was all that interested him and having seen the bright purple ticket, he waved Mace along without so much as a glance. Mace began to relax.

Boys were stationed inside the section to lead newcomers to the correct aisle and seat but Mace avoided them. Instead, he stood for a second where he could observe the man who'd sold him the tickets. And the woman next to him, who must be his wife.

Mace smiled in satisfaction. He had figured it right. Nobody had a clue about the tickets he'd bought. If the old goat had heard the first whisper, he'd never be sitting there like that, checking the program with his wife and then, as Mace watched, turning to make some crack to the two guys sitting behind him.

407

Mace was almost tempted to go and sit down, knowing he couldn't be recognized with the bandages and dark glasses, but he knew he didn't dare. The old man talked to anybody and everybody. That was how Mace got to know him in the first place. If Mace sat next to him today, he would certainly try to strike up a conversation—to ask why Mace had sold the tickets to someone else, for starters—and he wasn't sure he could successfully disguise his voice even if he came up with a good answer.

Instead, Mace decided to circulate. From time to time, the bandages drew smiles and comments but these were, as Mace had foreseen, entirely unsuspicious. In fact, most people who noticed him evinced a kind of camaraderie. They would not have let a mere automobile accident keep them away from the Kentucky Derby, either!

Artie Dobermeyer noticed the man with the bandages, too. He asked for the Number Six horse in the first race, a real long shot.

Now why should that have been such a surprise, Artie wondered. In the split second it took to push change for a five under the grille, Artie made one of his automatic appraisals. There was something familiar about the mouth and chin, but if he'd seen this man, it must have been before his accident. The bandages and dark glasses threw Artie off. He just couldn't place the face.

The long shot ran out of the money but the man with the bandages was back at Artie's window for the second, smiling cheerfully. That smile rang a bell, all right, Artie must have sold the guy tickets before. He wanted Number Seven this trip. That was more like it. Practically an even-money favorite, with Donnie Cheevers in the saddle, getting himself a little practice on the track ahead of his Derby ride on Armada.

Artie frowned. Armada. Somehow, there'd been a click in

his mind about the man with the bandages and Armada. Only Artie couldn't quite put his finger on what it was.

In the grandstand Eustace Potter settled back into his seat, sorting money and tickets. "Here's what I collected for you to show, $2.80," he said to his wife. "If you had listened to me, Bella, it would be $5.80. I told you that horse was going to win. And here's your ticket for the next race."

He turned to the man sitting in back of him. "I know you're on duty, Inspector, but I brought you a ticket, too. Number Four, he's 9-to-1, I don't think he'll do anything."

"Number Four?" Bella Potter exclaimed. "You said you liked Number Eight."

"I do like Number Eight, that's what I got." He shrugged apologetically. "But there was this fellow near the window, telling this other fellow the Four horse could be a sleeper, just came up from Florida. So I got that, too, and a ticket for the inspector as well. As long as he's here, he ought to have a horse in one race, at least."

"Why, that was very nice of you," said Elverson. "But let me pay for it."

The old man waved his hand. "I just won the last couple, it's my pleasure." After a moment, he added, "It's getting pretty late. Looks to me like your man isn't going to come."

"I'm afraid you're right, Mr. Potter. However . . ."

Potter nodded in understanding. The inspector's incompleted sentence meant the FBI wasn't giving up yet. No matter what, they'd stay until the Derby. Too bad for the inspector, Potter thought, so much work down the drain.

For himself, Potter was both relieved and a little disappointed. It would have been pretty exciting if that young fellow had come and sat next to him. But, then, there was more than enough excitement to satisfy him when Number Four came home a full length ahead.

"That fellow at the window was right! At least, you had

some luck this afternoon," he said, turning to Inspector Elverson. But the seat behind Eustace Potter was empty. So was the one next to it, where Ted Irving had been sitting.

TWELVE

IT HAD BEEN sometime earlier, as the horses were moving onto the track for the sixth race, when Tom Richardson worked his slow way through the crowded tunnel which ran directly beneath their hooves. Emerging at last into the infield, he surveyed the masses of people and drew a long breath.

He had been at a prerace breakfast, followed by a prerace brunch and from there to a protracted prerace luncheon which had engaged him until only a short while ago. Each of these affairs had been Derby oriented, but until this moment, he hadn't felt that it was really Derby Day. Now, finally, it was!

This was undoubtedly a childish reaction, as he had admitted to Buddy Sheffield yesterday, but there was the cumulative effect of the years as well, so that each Derby Day came to include some emotional content from all the First Saturdays which preceded it and, Tom supposed, a little of every picnic, carnival, fair or ball game he'd ever attended.

He was ambling along aimlessly, simply enjoying the sights and sounds, when the man fell almost directly in front of him. Tom had to sidestep with considerable agility to avoid stumbling over the old fellow.

Tom bent down in concern. "What happened? Did you hurt yourself? Are you all right?"

Sam Grundage nodded to the last question. "I just . . . it's the sun," he said faintly.

Tom assessed the pallor of the man's face, the bloodless lips. "Here," he said, "let me give you a hand. There's a first-aid mobile unit over this way."

"No!"

The vehemence in the weak voice was unexpected. Tom said, "You don't seem very well, sir. I think you ought to have some medical attention."

"No, please!" The man was pleading. "If I just rest a little bit."

Tom hesitated. "Well, at least, let's get back out of the way."

"I can't move," Sam Grundage whispered. "In one minute, one minute." He closed his eyes.

Already the flow of people was shifting subtly, cutting a new course away from them, through different openings. Tom grabbed at the leg of a man who was passing and gestured toward the paper cup in his hand. "Say, have you got any ice in that?"

Bolo Jackson stopped to stare down, startled. "Why, yes."

"Would you mind fishing out a couple of chunks?"

"What?"

"I think this man's about to faint," Tom explained. "I thought a little ice on his forehead might help."

"Oh, sure," Bolo said. "I didn't realize what you were talking about." He dumped the liquor out of the cup, then turned the ice into a handkerchief. "There isn't very much, I'm afraid, most of it's melted. But I imagine they'd have a doctor someplace around."

"No," Sam Grundage said again. "I don't want anybody like that." He opened his eyes, already refreshed by the cold pack Tom was applying. "You don't understand," he said. "They'd try to make me go to the hospital and I've come too far to leave now. I've got to stay for the Derby."

411

"But good Lord," Tom said, "if you're taking that much of a risk being here . . ."

Sam said, "I knew that before I came and it's my life."

The eyes of the other two men met above him, then Bolo Jackson drew a deep breath. "Fellow's got a point," he said. "It is his life. And he knows what he wants to do with it, I guess. Which is more than a lot of other people can say."

The note of bitterness did not escape Tom Richardson. He glanced curiously at the other's face, realizing as he did so that it seemed familiar. "Well, yes," Tom admitted, "but he still needs help."

"I'll stay with him," Bolo said. "I've got nothing else to do if you want to keep going."

Tom shrugged. "I wasn't headed anywhere in particular. Not for awhile, anyway. Tell you what, though, if you will stay with him for a minute, I might go dig up some more ice. Even that little bit did some good."

With close to fifty thousand people in the infield—and despite all their hampers and baskets and box lunches and thermos bottles—it was a considerable time before Tom got back, but when he did, Sam Grundage had recovered pretty well on his own.

"I wasn't sure what you'd like," Tom said, "but while I was over there, it dawned on me you might not have wanted to fight that mob to get yourself something to eat, so I brought some sandwiches and soda." He grinned at Bolo. "And a drink for you, too, since you poured yours out. Scotch and water it smelled like. Was it?"

Bolo looked surprised. "You didn't have to bother about that." His tone showed his pleasure, however.

The old man was frankly delighted. "I'm hungry enough to chew grass," he confessed, "probably the whole trouble. When I got here I was just too darned excited to think about food and then, well, you saw the crowd. You're right, I didn't feel like bucking those lines. But I was telling Mr. Jackson here—

my name's Grundage, by the way, Sam Grundage—that I'm doggone grateful to the both of you, going out of your way to help me like this."

"I'm Tom Richardson," Tom said, "and I'm sure Mr. Jackson was as glad to lend a hand as I was." He dropped onto the grass, facing the other two, and set the cardboard tray between them. "Come on," he said, "dig in, there's plenty for everybody. I swear, I never thought I'd eat again myself, considering all I had before I got here, but I reckon I can stand a little something. Anyway, people are supposed to have a picnic on Derby Day and I just realized it's been awhile since I had anybody to have a picnic with."

They began to eat companionably, in silence, at first, as they devoted themselves to the food. It had been awhile, Tom thought, several years, since his youngest boy went off to prep school. From here on, though, Tom meant to make a few changes. Let the kids fly back for Derby Day, like they'd been begging, even if the trip did mean a few missed classes. He had been wrong to overrule them, he saw now. He'd been cheating them out of something important.

Cheating himself into the bargain, because it made a whale of a difference, having somebody to share the infield with. He hadn't realized how much until right now. It was too bad Lu's spill made her back a bit tricky to cope in such a crowd; though he supposed she'd have to stay in the box, anyway, with the guests they invariably entertained at the classic.

As he ate hungrily, Sam Grundage was also reminiscing. He had known from the second he walked through the gate this morning how lonesome he was. He'd never been to the Derby by himself before. There'd always been somebody in the family. This year he hadn't even dared ask his friends. They'd have been as bad as anybody, trying to keep him home. And every doggone one of them wrong—him along with the rest, worrying ahead of time about the trip. Except for not eating and feeling a bit lightheaded, he'd been fine.

Sitting on the infield grass, Sam Grundage had a real good feeling. So many strangers had helped him. Those boys last night, giving him a hitch out of Azalia, he didn't know what he'd have done without them. It was darn near midnight before they came along. It showed how mistaken you could be about youngsters these days, because they'd gone clean out of their way to take him into Columbia, right to the bus depot. He'd never have asked them, they had just done it themselves when they found out where he wanted to go.

And now there were these two. Doggone, Sam Grundage thought, they didn't even look like strangers. He felt as if he'd seen them before, the both of them.

Bolo Jackson was thinking back, too, not so much remembering as trying to find some point of reference for this experience which was so unlike anything which had ever happened to him before. The unexpected, undemanding friendliness, the impromptu picnic. Had he ever been at a picnic as a child? He couldn't recall it, if he had. And certainly, it wouldn't have been anything like this. He supposed it was because his parents had been interested in such different things, sailing mostly. They had enjoyed racing cars in Europe and South America, but above all else they had loved the challenge of the sea, that in the end had defeated them. He had been so young when they died. He had had too little of them and they had left him too much money.

After awhile, Sam and Tom began to talk. About past Derbies, about the family tradition which had made it so important for Sam Grundage to get to this one, why he had had such trouble arranging to come.

It was an entirely different world, Bolo thought, with a twinge of something much like envy. And he'd entered it through the merest accident. He had come to Churchill Downs with his party, meaning to stick the dreary day out with them. Then, suddenly, he just couldn't stand them a moment longer. He had walked away and simply been swept

414

up by the crowd rushing into the tunnel.

It was a world that Sam Grundage had no desire to leave, very obviously. And yet, in a paradox which Bolo found somehow touching, the old man had risked dying in order to go on living in it.

"You're very quiet, Mr. Jackson," Tom said presently.

Bolo smiled. "I know almost nothing about horses," he said, "but I enjoy listening to you two."

"I keep feeling I know you from somewhere," Tom said. "I was wondering if you'd ever been to Marshfield. We get a lot of visitors."

"Marshfield?" Sam asked. "Marshfield Farms! Then you are that Tom Richardson. I recognized the name the second you mentioned it, but I just couldn't believe it. Why, you've got Dashing Lad in the Derby today."

"That's right," Tom said, with a grin at the old man's excitement.

"That's my horse, the one I've picked. You see? I've got it marked right here on my program."

"I sure hope you win, Mr. Grundage."

"Well, what do you think?"

Tom shrugged. "There's no way you can ever tell. He's a nice colt, they don't come bred any better, if I say it myself. I've got high hopes, believe me, but then, I've had high hopes before."

"I read about Sparky," Sam said sympathetically.

"Yes, Sparky," Tom agreed. "He didn't make it at all, but I've had others before him that did and still lost."

"I don't rightly know if I could take that," said Sam. "I mean, to come so close and then lose."

"That's racing, Mr. Grundage," Tom pointed out. "It's no contest unless you've got a chance to win, like the rules say. But it's no contest if there isn't a chance you'll lose, either. No horseman can figure it any other way. Or a fan, you know that."

415

"It's different, though, if you're just betting a little money. Owning one of the horses, that must be hard."

"Oh, you hate to lose, sure, but all you can do is start looking forward to the next race. Or, if you're talking about the Kentucky Derby, next May!" Tom laughed. "Hope springs eternal in racing, Mr. Grundage. Like my Daddy always used to say, 'No man ever committed suicide with a two-year-old in his barn.'"

Bolo Jackson stiffened. Had he been mistaken? Did Tom Richardson know who he was, after all, to make that crack about suicide? But a sharp glance at his companions reassured him. Richardson had undoubtedly seen Bolo's picture in some newspaper but such photos were seldom up-to-date and Jackson was a very ordinary name. Neither of them had placed him, Bolo was positive.

"Your Daddy sounds like a smart man," Sam was saying. "I guess you'll be all right no matter how things turn out today. From what I read, you've got enough two-year-olds to fill a stack of barns."

Tom heaved himself upright. "I'll start thinking about them when the Derby's over. Right now, if you two are finished, I think I'll just concentrate on Dashing Lad. You realize post time isn't much more than an hour away?"

The other two also got to their feet. "Well, I really can't thank you enough, Mr. Richardson," Grundage began.

"It'll take us awhile to get through to the fence," Tom said, "that's why I think we'd better get going. But I've got a note from Lee Ames that I'm supposed to give to the guard over at that gate by the presentation stand, so we ought to be able to scrounge a pretty good spot to see from."

Sam Grundage gasped. "You mean you want us to go with you?"

"Why, of course," Tom said. "Come on, I'll go ahead, Mr. Grundage, to clear the way a little, and Mr. Jackson will stay behind, so you don't get pushed around too much. Right?"

"Right," said Bolo Jackson.

Slightly dazed, but with growing pleasure and excitement, Tom Richardson's two companions trailed him through the increasing jam toward the fence.

THIRTEEN

TEN MINUTES BEFORE POST TIME for the seventh race, Artie Dobermeyer finally nailed down the errant memory which had begun to nag at him from the moment he saw the man with the bandages. When it came, it was as if his mind were going with the speed of one of those movies they showed you on television sometimes, trick photography, where you could watch a plant poke up out of the ground and put out leaves and buds and then burst into full bloom. You knew it had taken months for all that to happen, but it looked like it was only a second.

The whole thing clicked while the man was pushing the twenty-dollar bill at him and saying, "Number Eight."

Number Eight, the favorite. This same man had given him a twenty before, for ten tickets on Armada, the day of the Derby Trial. Armada, a 1-to-9, with Donnie Cheevers riding. And he'd been annoyed about it, Artie remembered, and then the guy had given him this big smile.

Damn, Artie thought. In spite of the bandages and the dark glasses, he should have placed that smile sooner. It showed a tooth on each side that stuck out a little, not real bad, you'd hardly notice it, but the first clerk who taught Artie how to operate a pari-mutuel machine had teeth exactly like that.

Artie's flash of triumph died as he realized that the twenty he had just taken was one of those on the FBI list. Artie punched the ticket in outward calm, but his mind was in a turmoil. What did he do now? There wasn't an FBI man in sight, he hadn't seen one all day.

Artie gritted his teeth and counted out change. There wasn't anything he could do until the man with the bandages left the window and disappeared into the crowd. After that, Artie lost no time. Despite cries of anguish from those waiting on line, he stuck the "Closed" sign on his grille and picked up the phone.

The FBI was pretty quick, too. Although it took Artie a good five minutes to catch up with Kermit Young—and lucky it didn't take longer on Derby Day—Young was able to reach the inspector right away. Elverson and Irving were at Artie's station by the time that race went off.

Suddenly, reaction set in and Artie began to shake like a jalopy with its motor being gunned.

Elverson pretended not to notice. "This could be a fantastic break, Mr. Dobermeyer," he said, "but we'll save the thanks for later. As I understand it, this man's been at your window before every race today?" Artie nodded. "Then we can assume he'll come back to you for the next one?"

"Could be," Artie said, "but it don't make any difference. The way he's decked out with bandages and dark glasses, you'll be able to spot him even in this mob."

"I'm certain we can, with the description you've given us," Elverson said, "but we have to be very careful. There are just too many innocent people around." He paused, considering.

"Those bills are from the Cardigan ransom, aren't they?" Artie asked.

"Yes."

"That's what I figured when I heard about the kidnapping this morning," Artie said. He swallowed. "And this guy's the kidnapper?"

"We think so," the inspector said, "and if we're right, he's both dangerous and ruthless. So, you see, it would be a real help if we had an idea of where he's going to be in order to prepare. How long until the next race, Mr. Dobermeyer?"

"About three quarters of an hour, they space them further apart on Derby Day."

Elverson turned to Irving. "That should give us plenty of time?"

"I can have my men positioned within fifteen minutes."

"Good. Better get started then, Ted."

"Right."

Irving darted off instantly but as Elverson started to follow, Artie plucked at his sleeve. "Hold it," he said, "the windows will open for the eighth race any second, Inspector. This bird could be here for a ticket right away."

"Is he apt to do that?" Elverson asked. "Come early, I mean? He waited until fairly close to the last race before he came to get his ticket, didn't he?"

"It depends," Artie pointed out. "If he's trying to make up his mind which horse to play, he could take awhile. But if he already knows the one he wants . . ."

Elverson gave Artie a searching glance. The clerk's shakes had eased but he still seemed nervous and upset. "You'll be back on duty, won't you? We wouldn't want to scare him off with any last-minute changes."

"Sure, I'll be working this race."

"Well, the problem may not arise, but if he should come up to you before we're ready to move, just act naturally. I know this has been a shock, but do you think you can manage that?"

Artie gulped noticeably at the prospect. But he said, "I'll be okay."

The inspector gave him an encouraging pat on the shoulder. "I don't doubt it, Mr. Dobermeyer," he said. "You've been fine already, a tremendous help."

The praise made Artie feel pretty good, but he wished he had a slug of bourbon. He didn't know what he'd do if the guy with the bandages got back before the FBI.

When Jason Elverson left the row of mutuel windows it was with the intention of promptly rejoining Irving and organizing procedure.

Unfortunately, his physical progress was agonizingly slow. Attendance was at its peak and as the Derby neared there was increasing tension. People seemed more active, noisier. Voices were definitely higher, keyed-up.

And coming toward him was a man whose heavily bandaged head stood out from the crowd like a pearl displayed against black velvet. Mace Augustine! The logical, the sensible course was for the inspector to continue exactly as planned. He didn't dare take the risk that Augustine might break away from a single-handed capture. But Elverson's every instinct, all the years of training and experience, made it impossible for him to just let this man walk away on the assumption he'd be picked up later. The inspector did the only thing he could do, which was to turn and follow, to keep the quarry in sight until the local agents should arrive.

Because of the crush, he had to stay a great deal closer than would have been desirable or feasible under any other conditions. So close, in fact, that when Morgan Wells suddenly approached, Elverson couldn't attempt any sort of explanation. With a warning shake of his head and a gesture not to speak at all, he simply grabbed Morgan's arm and drew him along. If Irving's estimate of how long it would take to get things set up was accurate, there were only about ten minutes to go.

To the FBI man's dismay, however, even as he had this comforting thought, he saw that Mace had led them toward the row of mutuels windows and was stepping onto the end of the line in front of Artie Dobermeyer.

Elverson immediately fell into place behind, with the puzzled but alert Morgan at his side. Again the inspector gestured warningly against any discussion.

A young fellow and his girl moved in behind them and began animatedly discussing the horses listed on their programs. Casually, Elverson did the same, though what he was saying was probably utter nonsense. After a second, Morgan joined in.

It was a considerable queue, as, inevitably, they all were on Derby Day. To Elverson, it seemed quite slow, but he realized they were covering ground steadily. Mace would reach the window and be gone before Irving could possibly get his men into position. Nevertheless, as Mace neared Artie, Elverson looked around hopefully. Some of Irving's agents must already have arrived. If they had, though, Elverson couldn't identify them. He had met only a handful of the locals and he didn't see any of those now.

But in the line next to his, the inspector did spot a familiar face: Eustace Potter, no more than three feet away, his own stop-and-go progress keeping pace with Elverson's. The FBI man moved hastily to Morgan's other side, using him as a shield, shaken by the narrowness of his escape. Only luck had kept the old man so absorbed in a last-minute check of his Racing Form that he was unconscious of anything else.

Mace stepped up to Artie's window. Potter had reached the adjoining window at the same time and he, too, having finally made up his mind, ordered his ticket. Then he, like Mace, turned away, but not to the right, as did Mace Augustine. Mr. Potter moved to the left and the two collided heavily.

Mace stepped back quickly—perhaps not certain in this ultimate test that his disguise was really safe. Morgan instinctively fell back to give the old man passage.

And Eustace Potter said happily, "There you are, Inspector! You didn't have much luck about the seats, maybe, but I sure picked you a winner on that last race, didn't I?"

What happened next was so sudden, so unexpected, Artie couldn't figure it out. One minute, he was heaving a sigh of relief as the kidnapper turned away. The next, the kidnapper was backed up against the grille, hanging on to some scared old man, holding a knife at his throat and yelling for everybody to get out of his way if they didn't want to see the old guy dead.

Artie didn't have time to think. He just grabbed his pencil, stuck it through the bars against the kidnapper, and hollered the first thing that came into his head, from one of his favorite TV shows. "FBI. Drop it or I'll shoot!"

If Artie had thought, he'd have been too scared to pull an idiotic stunt like that. And too smart, because a pencil couldn't fool anybody for more than a couple of seconds. But that was just long enough. The inspector and Morgan Wells jumped the kidnapper before he could recover, a couple of other FBI agents popped up out of nowhere to help, the lines opened up to let them cart him off, and one minute later you'd never have known anything had happened at all. The lines formed again and everybody was buying tickets exactly as they'd been before. And Artie Dobermeyer was selling them.

Once that race started and the machine locked, though, realization swept over him and he collapsed. He couldn't even walk into First Aid, they had to carry him.

The nurse was still holding the smelling salts under his nose when Lee Ames hurried in, with Kermit Young at his heels. Artie straightened, his face reddening at this first meeting with the president since the day before the union meeting. But when Lee left moments later, Artie's shame over the Mannering affair had been erased by praise and admiration for what he had done this afternoon.

Kermit Young said, "Believe me, Artie, the whole department's as proud of you as Mr. Ames, but I'll have to hurry off now, too. You just stay here and take it easy."

Artie stared at him in astonishment. "You mean, not go back to my window?"

"Don't worry, I'll find somebody to cover. Nobody expects you to work after an experience like that."

"But I've got to! The next race is the Derby. You know I'd never miss that, Mr. Young." Artie was on his feet. "And I feel fine now, just fine."

FOURTEEN

As EACH PLATEAU of intensity on the Richter scale of earthquake measurement is not a single step upward from the level below but, rather, has a force ten times stronger than the one preceding, so excitement had begun to rise geometrically with the imminence of the Kentucky Derby. Now there was a great shout. Through a gap in the fence at the backstretch side of the oval, a colt was being led onto the outer rim of the track. Behind him came another, and another, and another, until there were seven.

The seven.

On their way at last from the Derby Barn, and from all those days and months and years of preparation, to be saddled in the frontside paddock. Comment ranged in degree of expertise from neighbor to neighbor, from infield to Turf Club, from owner's box to press box, from grandstand to stewards' stand, but no one who could see that little string of thoroughbreds watched in silence. Or was unmoved at the sight.

Yet, except for the hubbub that caused an occasional nervous skitter, these might have been any seven horses en route to any race, each obeying his groom's slight forward pull on the leather shank more or less placidly, plodding slowly along the edge of the track.

It took several moments for the procession to reach the frontside at that leisurely pace but when, finally, the seven colts disappeared into the passageway under the stands which led to the paddock, the tumult did not subside. If anything, the pitch was higher. The Derby was so close.

Twenty-five minute . . . twenty minutes . . . fifteen . . . and it would begin.

FIFTEEN

O F ALL THOSE INVOLVED in the actual mechanics of day-to-day racing at Churchill Downs, the track veterinarian was one of the very few whose ordinary routine was disrupted by the fact that this was an extraordinary occasion. His mornings were generally spent in the backstretch, going from barn to barn and looking into the physical condition of the horses, with particular regard to those scheduled to race that day and those whom, for some reason or other, he had placed on the "Vet's List." This catalogue went daily to the racing secretary's staff and automatically barred any animal on it from racing until the medical ban had been officially lifted, by him, in writing. The track veterinarian had proceeded as usual this morning.

On any regular afternoon, he shuttled from stable area to frontside in order to observe the entrants in each race as they stepped onto the track, in the paddock while they were being saddled, at the starting gate and, again, as they crossed under the wire at the finish.

He was able to accomplish this remarkably conscientious chore only by dint of driving back and forth through the infield tunnels. On Derby Day, obviously, that was quite impossible.

Instead, on this afternoon, his duties on the far side had been delegated to an assistant and he himself confined his attention to the paddock, finishing line and only those starting-gate activities which took place on the grandstand side, as did the Kentucky Derby.

The vet was waiting next to the official identifier when the seven Derby colts emerged from under the stands and were led toward the saddling paddock. The identifier, as his title implied, bore the responsibility for ascertaining that any given horse was that horse, not some other which might resemble it, and his efforts, like those of the track vet, were fairly evenly distributed between backstretch and frontside.

During the early hours of training, the identifier was invariably stationed at the gap near the observation tower so that he could correctly name for the clockers those horses who were going through workouts. This was to protect the basic tenet in racing—the fans' "right to know"—and it was a task which required that the identifier familiarize himself with the physical characteristics of every thoroughbred on the grounds.

The job entailed not only personal inspection but a careful attention to the descriptions on the registration slips on file in the racing secretary's office, and on the basis of these, the identifier maintained his own book of pertinent data, added to daily. It was against this he methodically checked the 150 to 160 horses which went by him onto the track for workouts each morning.

A simpler method of identification, of course, would have been to ask each rider the name of his mount, and the identifier did do that, naturally. But his years of experience had shown him this was too simple.

Some trainers preferred that no one realize exactly how good their horses might be, in order not to scare off lesser opponents in a race or, perhaps, to get higher odds, and would make every possible attempt at camouflage, with changes of tack or personnel or other sometimes quite imaginative devices.

So the identifier always double checked, beginning with the readily apparent "white spots" like stockings, stars, stripes or blazes, and, lacking these, such other markings as the scablike "night eyes," scars, particularly large knees or idiosyncrasies of gait.

The afternoon identifications, though perhaps even more important, were considerably easier. As each horse entered the frontside paddock to be saddled for a race, all the identifier had to do was have the groom turn back its upper lip and check the large, legible numbers which were obligatorily and painlessly tattooed on the pallid pink inside.

This was what he did now, though by this time he was as familiar with each of the seven as he was with the palm of his hand. One by one, he ticked off the numbers against his list and then, responsibility temporarily at an end, he turned to the vet, smiling. "Who do you like for the Derby, Doc?"

The vet shook his head. "Damned if I know. All I'm sure of is that every one of them is in fine condition. Lucky Jim has a powerful pair of hindquarters and an unbelievable stride. He must cover a good twenty-five or twenty-six feet when he's going full speed." He grinned a little sheepishly. "I told my wife to take a flyer on Sweepstakes, though. He's a lot smaller, but he's quick. And you have to admit the price is right."

"She can go on a real shopping spree if he wins," the identifier said. "If she'd asked me, I'd have told her Davie's Pride or Armada, if she likes price horses." He laughed. "And I suppose if that mob out there could hear us now, they'd never believe their ears."

The vet looked at the hundreds of people who had squeezed against the paddock fence to watch the Derby horses being saddled. "You're probably right," he agreed. "I'll bet every last one of them figures we have inside information. Well," he said, "maybe they've got something there. If anybody could get it from the horse's mouth, it would have to be you!"

If, in comparison to the bedlam outside the fence, the inside of the paddock seemed a center of calm as the horses were led to their separate stalls for saddling, there was nevertheless a sizable company gathered there.

Every colt had its exhilarated contingent of bystanders, including groom, trainer, owner or owners and guests. In addition, there were the ubiquitous photographers and an assortment of track officials: The Colonel, the racing secretary, the publicity director and one or two others, moving from group to group with the traditional last-minute handshakes and impartial good wishes.

Upstairs in the jockeys' room, resolute face contrasting with his cheerful silks, each rider went through the weighing-out ritual with full gear in hand and under the sharp eye of the clerk of scales. Seven times the needle hit the 126-pound mark squarely and then, at a signal from the paddock judge below, the jockeys took the escalator down to join the others inside the fence while their mounts were made ready.

At this point, Lee Ames and his wife, the governor and his lady and an escort of other state or local dignitaries made their way between ranks of uniformed honor guards to the Presentation Stand and in a moment or two the University of Kentucky band struck up "The Star-spangled Banner."

As the final notes of the anthem released everyone from attention, a roar went up from the packed stands and infield and, involuntarily, all eyes turned to the opening through which the Derby field would emerge.

Now! Now! Now!

The crowd wasn't entirely accurate. Ninety seconds, the paddock judge was deciding. That was all that was left for final instructions to the jockeys, no more. He tried to get the horses moving from paddock to track at about twelve minutes before post time for any race, and normally a little leeway wasn't particularly significant. But for this one, with television commitments to millions of viewers, he had to be exact.

His main responsibility of checking carefully that each horse was carrying the proper equipment, that weighted pommel pads and saddles were in place, was over. He stood, watch in hand, the seconds ticking away, while around him, in the seven groups, conversation grew more excited, more hurried.

Fans were often curious as to what was said to the jockeys just before mount-up. There were, undoubtedly, instances where special instructions were required, where a trainer might call attention to some horse's peculiarity or suggest an effective strategy against a specific field. Today, however, there was little need for much beyond pleasantries and expressions of mutual encouragement.

The one exception was Guy St. Pierre. His first glimpse of Gabe's battered face had answered his week-long questioning. "If Nick Chambley had told me about this," he began angrily.

Gabe grinned. "That's exactly why he didn't," he said, and thought of his taped ribs that St. Pierre still didn't know about.

"You're sure you're all right, Gabe?" Al Lester asked.

"Look, I give you my word, I wouldn't have held the mount if I thought my riding Magician would hurt his chances, Al!"

"That's good enough for me," Lester said. "The only thing Guy worried about was your unfamiliarity with the horse. Nobody but Gordy ever rode him in a race before."

"I know," Gabe nodded, "that's why I came to Louisville early, to make you feel better about that aspect, but I've ridden hundreds of horses I'd never seen before a race. It won't make any difference this time, believe me. If Magician can run far enough and fast enough, we'll win."

The paddock judge's raised voice cut all conversation short, in the time-honored order: "To your horses, gentlemen!"

Obediently, the jockeys moved to where the colts were being held in a ring, in post-position sequence.

From the track, the trumpeted "Call To The Post" blared out, with a resultant thunder of noise from the crowd.

"Riders . . . *up!*"

Gracefully, almost as one, as precisely as practiced dancers in a ballet, the seven jockeys mounted their horses and then, again according to post position, fell into line behind the red-shirted lead outrider and followed him slowly along the dirt passageway under the stands. At the end of this tunnel, the outrider paused briefly, raised an arm in signal, and from across the track, the band began to play "My Old Kentucky Home."

This moment, repeated annually, was generally conceded to be the most thrilling and emotional of any sports year. More than a hundred thousand people surged to their feet in singing the hauntingly plaintive melody—the words were printed in the programs—and it was a safer bet than any other made on that sunny afternoon that practically all the women and a large number of the men were moved by it to the verge of tears.

No one who has never experienced that mass response can really understand it, and yet many television viewers found themselves experiencing the same emotional reaction. As everyone is a courtesy Irishman on March seventeenth, so, on the first Saturday in May each viewer is at least a temporary Kentuckian.

At Churchill Downs, however, there were a handful of men who dared accord only the briefest acknowledgment to the appeal of the moment. While the sentimental singing was still going on, as the Derby colts moved slowly out onto the track to be joined by the accompanying ponies and make the customary right, then left turns, three men, at least, were engrossed in committing the colors of the silks to memory and rechecking their mental bracketing of those colors with the proper horses.

These three were the Daily Racing Form's Trackman, Churchill Downs' own official announcer and the man who would call the race for television. Upon each, thoroughly experienced and practiced as he was, the Derby exerted extraordinary pressure.

Undoubtedly, in the larger scheme of things, it was the racing paper's reporter whose accuracy was most important. His correct placing of the horses and their positions throughout the classic would become not a part of the record but the record itself. His view of the event, with the commentary he would add immediately after the finish, would be carried in every newspaper or magazine which published the chart of this race and later bound into the permanent chart books of racing history, there to be endlessly referred to by handicappers and horsemen alike.

To the average fan, perhaps the only salient notation was which colt had won which Kentucky Derby in which year. To a breeder or prospective owner, it could be vital to know how the losers had run, why they had lost, if they had been in contention at any part of the race and for how long.

The track announcer's tension was more immediately personal. He would call the Derby over the public address system at Churchill Downs during its running, and on a day when many of those present couldn't even see the horses, or could see them only part of the time, he filled a considerable need. He similarly announced every race at this track, and others, and often when there was a bigger field than the comparatively easy seven in today's Derby. Nevertheless, his concentration was far more intense than usual. This was one he'd hate to miscall.

As for the television announcer, an error on his part would be heard by millions.

So the three men stood with their binoculars fixed upon the parade to the post, mumbling somewhat grimly to themselves, and thanked their stars that today, at any rate, it was a short field and the silks were so different they could concentrate on the colors alone. There had been Derbies with double or even triple this number of horses and some with silks so similar they were not sufficient identification in themselves.

As the horses began to warm up, galloping around the stretch turn where they would shortly reverse direction and come back to enter the starting gate, cameramen at every station were rechecking their equipment. Movie patrol, photo finish service, news and television photographers, one and all.

They knew better.

They had each done this before, more than once, and most of them within the last ten minutes. Still, it cost nothing to make doubly certain—and wouldn't the Kentucky Derby be a hell of a time to forget the film?

SIXTEEN

P EOPLE WERE ALWAYS TALKING about a jockey's hands, and it was quite true that his touch, his control on the reins and his manipulation of the whip made a considerable difference between winning and losing. Sometimes all the difference. In the final analysis, though, the way a rider used his hands was the reaction to subtle mental processes, no matter how apparently instinctive it might seem to others or even to him.

It was actually through physical contact that man and mount were welded into one of the world's most awesome propulsion mechanisms, that a jockey "knew" his horse on the visceral level and could instantaneously convey commands.

From the moment Guy St. Pierre had given Gabe his lift into the saddle, he had been getting the feel of Magician with his knees, testing, sensing; and as he had turned into position behind Dashing Lad and Davie's Pride to follow the outrider to the passageway under the stands, he had relaxed almost without knowing it.

Everything was all right. Magician was a fine, strong colt and a responsive one. They could work together.

The pills Gabe had taken half an hour before seemed to be doing the job, too. The tight wrapping around his broken ribs was anything but comfortable and would probably be even more binding when he went into his racing crouch, but so far he was feeling no pain.

Not until the procession was going through the tunnel had it occurred to Gabe that the last time he had been in a saddle was ten days ago, at Hollywood Park. Such an unbelievably short, unimportant segment of time, and yet it seemed as if the man who had ridden out onto the "Track of the Lakes and Flowers" had been another person.

The string of horses and jockeys halted for a second as the outrider's hand went up in signal.

Gabe revised his thought. No. He had been himself then, too, he supposed, but somehow incomplete. Now he had Ronnie. A line of verse popped into his mind, "And, oh, the difference to me!"

It was then that the band had begun to play "My Old Kentucky Home" and they had moved out into the core of fantastic sound.

Ahead of him, on Davie's Pride, Gabe saw young Billy Hendricks stiffen as abruptly as if a pin had been jabbed into him; then Billy turned and laughed.

No, Gabe warned the kid mentally, this isn't it. This isn't anything like the noise I was telling you about. Wait until the roar that comes when they've finished singing. Wait till you hear the sound when the Derby starts. Or when you come around the stretch turn and head down that long run to the wire—that's the most unbelievable of all!

But Billy had already faced forward again.

Those who had been in previous Derbies or who had had earlier races today knew what Gabe was talking about. Billy had done neither and Gabe had tried to prepare him ahead of time, the way some of the training centers used recordings of crowd noises to accustom their two-year-olds to actual racing conditions.

The crescendo of screaming excitement at any track as the horses rounded into their final drive was a physical thing, like running into an avalanche of stone. Billy knew about that. But it had been hopeless, seeking words to prepare him for Churchill Downs on Derby Day, with the mountains of sound crashing down upon you from both sides.

The parade having made its turns and passed beyond the point where the starting gate was being angled into position, Gabe bent forward over Magician's neck to urge him into a warm-up gallop. And that drove everything else completely from his mind.

The pain! Oh, my God, the pain!

It was the changed position he realized when he could think again, gritting his teeth against the searing agony. He had been taped standing upright and now his forward crouch was exerting more pressure than had been expected on the binding, on the broken ribs. Or else the doctor's warnings had been right all along and there was internal damage which couldn't be diagnosed without X-rays.

In those first few seconds, Gabe didn't think he was going to be able to bear it. Every thud of Magician's hooves on the solid under surface of the track was torture. Then, as the bandages gave a fraction under the strain, the suffering eased a little. A very little.

He wasn't positive until the horses were coming back to enter at the rear of the starting gate whether it would be enough or not. It was—just barely.

With an assistant starter at each colt's head, Dashing Lad was led into his stall, then Davie's Pride, Magician, Freeway, Armada, Lucky Jim, Sweepstakes.

Gabe sneaked a lungful of air past the pain and bent even further forward, waiting for the ring which would indicate the official starter's squeeze on the automatic release he held in his poised hand and the simultaneous opening of the seven gates.

That dramatic clanging was actually more significant as a signal to the animals than it was to the men. A good jockey "began to ride" long before it sounded, one hand holding his whip down close to his mount's withers in the standard precaution against hitting another horse or rider at the break, the other keeping a firm but light grip on the crossed reins and the horse's mane so as not to either pull too hard or be left behind in the rush. At the same time, the jockey tried to have all four of his horse's feet on the ground in order not to lose that fraction of a second required to put a lifted hoof down.

The bell shrilled, the gates opened, the Derby crowd gave that resounding mass yell which was like no other in the world, but Gabe did not hear it. He had shut out everything except what he had to do.

Magician had broken from the gate smoothly, cleanly, powerfully, and so this time had all the others. For the space of an eye blink the seven were off down the track in an almost perfect row, head and head, matching stride with stride.

Then, as Gabe had projected from his study of the past performances, Sweepstakes pulled in front of the pack, with Freeway two lengths back in second place and Lucky Jim only a head behind.

Gabe settled himself contentedly into fourth position, moving toward the rail to save ground as the field went around the first turn. A quick glance spotted Dashing Lad on his outside, half a length back, with Davie's Pride another half length behind in sixth place. Armada was bringing up the rear with a full three lengths of daylight showing between him and the others.

Armada's position was no surprise—he was a natural late runner—but Gabe would have figured Davie's Pride to be a little closer to the leaders. Apparently they were going to try running him late today, too.

No matter where any of them was at this stage, a mile and a quarter was a long race.

The way Robbie Roberts was riding Sweepstakes, nobody would have thought so, though. Unless Gabe Hilliard's well-authenticated sense of time was completely out of whack, the little long shot had gone the first quarter in something under twenty-three seconds, a blistering pace, and was maintaining about the same in this one.

It was obvious strategy, of course, perhaps the only feasible one. Robbie was trying to "steal" the Derby by getting far enough ahead to be able to hold off the inevitable later challenges. Sweepstakes was now four full lengths in front of Lucky Jim, who had moved up to take the second spot, with Freeway a neck behind, half a length ahead of Gabe and Magician.

That was disappointing. Gabe had hoped Maldonado would push the speedy Freeway into contesting the lead

435

from the beginning, which would wear both front runners down, but Rudy wasn't even fighting for second place at this point. He had Freeway laying third, in good position, biding his time.

Over his right shoulder, Gabe saw that Ferdy Garcia was bringing Dashing Lad up on the outside, which meant that Davie's Pride and Armada were still behind, but that wasn't any immediate problem. Magician was running easily beneath him, under no stress, and Gabe hadn't yet called for any of the latent power he knew was there. He, too, was awaiting the proper moment.

Already, as they swept past the six-furlong pole the speed was beginning to tell on Sweepstakes. He was still in front but now only by two lengths and he wasn't going to hold those for very much longer. Lucky Jim had begun to close ground, with Freeway still running just off the favorite's pace. Ferdy had taken Dashing Lad out toward the middle of the track, making a definite bid now, pulling slightly ahead of Magician and taking aim on the leaders.

Even as Gabe was assessing this new factor, the situation altered drastically before him. The exhausted Sweepstakes, his energies used up in the hopeful early effort, was dropping back steadily.

Lucky Jim had taken over first place at the mile, still holding that meager neck edge on Freeway. Dashing Lad was third now, half a length before Magician. Gabe caught a glimpse of bright green out of the corner of his eye. So Davie's Pride had passed the fading Sweepstakes, too, and was beginning to run hard. But a glance behind showed Armada still in last place.

Donnie Cheevers would be making his move soon, though. It was high time for him to roll, if he was ever going to.

And the same for him and Magician, Gabe decided. He clucked persuasively, releasing his snug hold on the reins and beginning to impel his mount forward with the subtle but unmistakable acceleration of his own rhythmic movements.

"Okay, boy, now! Let's get 'em!"

The words didn't matter. Gabe was hardly aware of what he was saying, what he ever said in the low stream of chatter he kept up throughout all his rides. It was the tone of his voice which was significant and to the urgency in this, as well as to the physical commands, Magician began immediately to respond, his stride lengthening into purpose.

The gathering speed, the steadily quickening output of energy beneath Gabe were both an agony and an exhilarating gratification. His ribs were killing him but this was a horse!

"Yeah, boy," Gabe crooned, "good boy, that's it, atta baby, that's showing them!"

Hugging the curving rail, they drew parallel with Dashing Lad and pulled ahead and now, as Armada came pounding close behind (Armada?!), they had drawn even with Lucky Jim. They were getting by him, as well. They were a nose in front . . . a neck . . .

Gene Firestone glared through his dark goggles and crouched even more pressingly over the favorite, his arm flailing. For a few seconds, Lucky Jim held Magician to that slight margin, refusing to give up another inch, and then, almost imperceptibly, Gabe began to pick up ground again.

Not much ground. Not much ground on any of them. The horses at his rear were bunched too close for comfort as the field straightened out of the last turn. But ahead of Magician now there was nothing except that long, long stretch at Churchill Downs and the streaking roan. Gabe stopped feeling his ribs.

"Just Freeway, boy," he coaxed, "come on, come on, you're going to get him, you can do it, one horse, baby, that's all!"

They hooked their quarry at the sixteenth pole and in that instant, as Magician and Freeway raced in unison, nose and nose, Gabe realized he was going to win.

Because they were gaining . . . they were gaining . . .

They were going to take the Kentucky Derby!

Even as the exultation of triumph surged through him, even as they got a stride in front and Rudy Maldonado gave him one look of utter despair, Gabe sensed that he was wrong.

He could not have put into words exactly how or in the midst of which hoof beat he understood that Magician had already given his best, was still giving his best, and that it wasn't going to be quite enough. The horse was running at the limit of his strength, there was no change that anyone else could have observed.

But Gabe knew.

Perhaps Magician knew, too. If he did, though, he was all heart, game as game could be. He never quit trying, as Gabe never stopped helping him to try.

No matter.

Under the sting of Maldonado's stubborn whip, the roan came on again, inexorably, until the two were head and head as before, flaring nostril to flaring nostril, and then, as Magician's tiring rush still carried him toward the wire, Freeway swept under it to victory.

In Lee's office in the deserted Administration Building, the splash of bourbon against the glass was astonishingly loud. So was Lee's sigh as he lifted the drink to his lips.

He had sat like this in the same comfortable leather chair before, not very long ago and for pretty much the same reason: Because he was just too beat to pick himself up and go on home where he belonged.

He took another sip of his bourbon and began to unwind. He'd get going in a few minutes, he thought, and sighed again.

He felt good, though. How could it be otherwise, after one of the closest, most exciting races he had ever seen?

Lee shook his head in the wonder which still hadn't quite

dissipated in the hours since that incredible finish: Freeway a nose ahead of Armada. Armada a neck in front of Davie's Pride. Davie's Pride only a half length ahead of Magician. Less than a full length separating those first four!

Not quite two lengths separating the first six horses in that seven-horse field, actually, with Lucky Jim a bare half length behind Magician and Dashing Lad a scant half length behind him!

A tremendous Derby, he thought, a great Derby after all. The victory party which had ended only a short while ago had been particularly satisfying, too. Perhaps because even the losers had had a sense of achievement in that finish. Oh, they'd been disappointed, naturally, no blinking that. Still, they had all come so very close.

Except Sweepstakes, thought Lee. He'd faded badly at the end. But even he had played an important part in this Kentucky Derby. That sizzling early pace had helped make it one of the swiftest on the books, only three fifths of a second off the record.

And in a way, the Nickels were responsible for much of Lee's present gratification. They had been such unexpectedly good sports. Which showed how little one could, or should, judge other people's reactions in advance. He would never have dreamed ahead of time that Gladys could be as gracious in defeat as any sportswoman he had ever met. Or that Brewster and Jim York would jovially band together to buy Lucky Jim's little brother because York's colt had lost, on the theory that since the favorite hadn't turned out to be a world-beater, his brother might be better!

A reasonable enough premise, Lee had to concede, but there was a partnership for you. Maybe that was equally logical, though. They were both cut from the same cloth and, at any rate, the deal had pleased Charlie Talbot.

Almost as much as Freeway's victory had pleased the Kentucky Breeders and the Keeneland officials, the "California" horse having immediately become the Pride of the Blue Grass, naturally.

Tom Richardson had suffered two losses—the Derby itself and the fifty thousand to Charlie Talbot, since Lucky Jim had beaten Dashing Lad to the wire. Tom would have accepted these with his usual ease even if the insurance settlement hadn't finally been forthcoming, Lee knew. But in a very funny way, the big Marylander had seemed, well, if not glad, at least not really sorry that Dashing Lad hadn't won. Tom's emotions this year had been all bound up in the unfortunate Sparky. It was as if a triumph for Dashing Lad would have somehow made Tom feel Sparky's exclusion even more poignantly.

Lee had gathered only a hint of that undercurrent at the party, however, because otherwise Tom had been riding high on some wave of secret hilarity. He had lingered only a moment and even now Lee didn't really understand Tom's hasty departure. Something about two friends he'd met in the infield that afternoon and how he had to drive one of them up to Indiana so his family wouldn't worry.

"You'll have to meet this fellow, Lee, when he's a little stronger, you won't believe the wonderful Derby stories he tells. His name's Sam Grundage and there's been a Grundage at every Derby since they started. Then this other fellow's coming home to Maryland with me, says he wants to go into racing."

For some reason, Tom had choked with laughter at that. "This one will really surprise you, Lee. I can't give you his name yet, I promised to keep it quiet for awhile. But he'll be here for next year's Derby with a Marshfield horse, you can make book on that. And with Buddy Sheffield as his trainer, he asked me to suggest a good man."

Mister Mack had put in a congratulatory appearance at the victory celebration, of course, as Lisa's ambassador. Lee smiled. Armada had run a fine race. He'd darn near made it.

But Lee didn't suppose Lisa could be too disappointed about anything, right now. She had come too close to losing her life. And Morgan Wells, Lee reminded himself, thinking of how she had looked at her fiancé so early that morning.

This automatically evoked the thought of Gabe Hilliard and Lee shook his head incredulously. Gabe Hilliard, whom he, Lee Ames, had thoroughly detested for so long and for whom, to his utter astonishment, he had caught himself secretly rooting during that exciting run toward the wire.

Not for Magician, not for any horse, but for Gabe. It seemed unbelievable. Lee supposed, trying to analyze it, that the past week had forced him to realize how much of what was said and written about Hilliard was either erroneous or malicious and that it was small damn wonder if the jockey sometimes fought back bitterly.

Still, this afternoon's switch of feeling remained inexplicable, because Lee had retreated from his misconceptions only as he had to, one step at a time, and having finally acknowledged the truth, had nevertheless clung doggedly to his dislike.

Unless, perhaps, the original animosity toward Gabe had sprung from Lisa's unhappiness in their marriage, and seeing her with Morgan had somehow wiped out the past?

Lee drained his bourbon. Curious, how being tired set him to soul searching. He really ought to cut all this and get going. He didn't, though. He didn't even pour himself a refill. He simply went on sitting.

He was still amazed by Gabe's cheerfulness at the party, by the fact that he had even appeared. He wasn't noted for good humor after any loss and this one which had brought him so close to triumph for a moment must have been more galling than most. He'd been beaten by a man who hated his guts, on a horse Gabe himself should rightfully have been riding, and above all, a Derby winner.

Yet Gabe had seemed almost happy when he appealed to

Lee to get him a rose from the blanket which had adorned Freeway during the ceremonies.

"Rudy's holding it right now and he'd probably spit in my eye if *I* asked," Gabe had said, amused, "but I promised somebody some victory roses and I ought to take her one, at least, don't you think?"

Strange.

Still, when you came down to it, the strangest thing of all had been a scrap of conversation he'd inadvertently overheard between Doc and Shelby Todhunter.

Lee had come up behind them, meaning to offer his congratulations again, personally, in a moment when the two were alone, as Shelby was saying, "I know it was stupid, Dad, but if Freeway had lost, I'd never have made it. I just know it, that's all. But he won, Dad, it's going to be okay!"

Doc had gone white, staring at his son. "Oh, my God!" he had said. "I never realized. I kept thinking it didn't matter to me, one way or the other."

Lee had made a hasty retreat. Obviously, Freeway's winning held meaning for the Todhunters beyond anything he would allow himself to imagine. With the same sense of skirting an unforgivable intrusion, he thrust away his thought that the scene was somehow connected with Shelby's arrest. The important thing was that the boy had said it was going to be all right.

As for the Sullivans . . .

The telephone rang startlingly. Lee answered, "Yes?"

"Phil Appleby up in the stewards' stand, Lee. I wasn't sure you'd still be there."

"I'm just leaving."

"Well, I figured you'd like to hear. We've got the chemist's report on the Derby colts. All tests completed. All clear."

"I was sure of that but thanks, anyway, Phil."

Lee replaced the receiver and, at last, got to his feet.

It was over. This year's Kentucky Derby was officially over.

He frowned slightly, trying to recapture some point he'd been considering when the phone interrupted. Oh, yes, the Sullivans.

Lee smiled and started for home.

Dennis Sullivan had been too happy over Davie's Pride to be capable of any other feeling. Third place in the Kentucky Derby, less than a length behind the winner, that was a triumph beyond anything he'd really hoped for against such competition, whatever he'd said. And Johnny . . . "Well," Dennis had admitted, "you know how boys are, he'd his heart set on winning! But, sure," he had added, grinning, "you can't keep 'em down for long. He's already beginning to plan for next year's Derby."

Lee laughed.

So could he now.

ACKNOWLEDGMENTS

To make individual mention of all those who have so unstintingly contributed their aid to the authors in the writing of this book would require another volume of at least equal length and even then we would run the risk of unhappy omission. This is a blanket attempt to express the inexpressible, our gratitude to each and every one of them.

We would be utterly remiss, however, if we did not here acknowledge our special debt to Lynn Stone and the late Wathen Knebelkamp for their boundless friendship and cooperation and to their staff at Churchill Downs, which has been invariably generous with warm interest as well as time.

This abbreviated list of particular credits would likewise be incomplete if it did not include our heartfelt appreciation of the efforts of Hollywood's Mervyn LeRoy, without whose wonderful enthusiasm and unflagging support we might never have lasted the course, and of Michael Sandler, National General Manager of the Daily Racing Form, and Saul Rosen, retired editor of that publication, without whom *The Race* most certainly would never even have been begun.

Some note must be made here, too, of the few liberties we have taken for story purposes with the procedures and physical realities

445

of Churchill Downs: The Derby Barn described in this novel is entirely fictitious, for example. Entrants in the Kentucky Derby are not all stabled together as of this writing, though they have been on previous occasions and may be again at some future date. We have also taken poetic license with parts of the security setup, the fire-alarm system and one or two other details which do not maintain insofar as Churchill Downs is presently concerned but are or have been true at other tracks.

In the interest of manageable length, we have additionally—and regretfully—been forced to eliminate or compress some of racing's most charming minutiae. Sweepstakes' little black goat, for instance, is only a token representative of the many stallmates and stable pets who would inevitably have been ensconced in the Derby Barn, if it existed.

Racetracks generally have a full complement of backstretch ponies, cats, dogs, birds, chickens and ducks, as well as the nannies and billies which are particularly soothing to high-strung thoroughbred nerves. As a matter of fact, the common phrase, "getting one's goat," springs from early turf terminology and refers to long ago attempts to upset a horse on the eve of contest by removing his favorite companion!

Otherwise, the background of *The Race* is as authentic in both spirit and fact as we could make it, since our aim from the beginning has been to present through the Kentucky Derby, most revered of thoroughbred events in America, the whole world of racing, with all the complexity, vitality, drama, excitement and sheer fun which lie behind the charts, too frequently unseen or unrecognized.

Although some reference has been made to existing publications, organizations, previous Kentucky Derby winners, noted owners, trainers and jockeys for the sake of verisimilitude, any other use of real names or combinations of racing-silk colors or any resemblance to actual persons or equines, living or dead, is purely coincidental.

E.W. and O.O.

446

SWEEPSTAKES

Owners:
 Mr. & Mrs. Brewster Nickel
Trainer:
 Ed Quincy
Jockey:
 Robert Roberts

DASHING LAD

Owner:
 Tom Richardson
Trainer:
 Buddy Sheffield
Jockey:
 Ferdy Garcia

LUCKY JIM

Owner:
 Jim York
Trainer:
 Ike Drury
Jockey:
 Gene Firestone

Owner:
 Al Lester
Trainer:
 Guy St. Pierre
Jockey:
 Gabe Hilliard

The